William Blackstone

Commentaries on the Laws of England

William Blackstone

Commentaries on the Laws of England

Commentaries on the Laws of England
By William Blackstone

Contents

INTRODUCTION.

SECTION THE FIRST.

ON THE STUDY OF THE LAW

MR VICE-CHANCELLOR, AND GENTLEMEN OF THE UNIVERSITY,

THE general expectation of so numerous and respectable an audience, the novelty, and (I may add) the importance of the duty required from this chair, must unavoidably be productive of great diffidence and apprehensions in him who has the honour to be placed in it. He must be sensible how much will depend upon his conduct in the infancy of a study, which is now first adopted by public academical authority; which has generally been reputed (however unjustly) of a dry and unfruitful nature; and of which the theoretical, elementary parts have hitherto received a very moderate share of cultivation. He cannot but reflect that, if either his plan of instruction be crude and injudicious, or the execution of it lame and superficial, it will cast a damp upon the farther progress of this most useful and most rational branch of learning; and may defeat for a time the public-spirited design of our wise and munificent benefactor. And this he must more especially dread, when he feels by experience how unequal his abilities are (unassisted by preceding examples) to complete, in the manner he could wish, so extensive and arduous a task; since he freely confesses, that his former more private attempts have fallen very short of his own ideas of perfection. And yet the candour he has already experienced, and this last transcendent mark of regard, his present nomination by the free and unanimous suffrage of a great and learned university, (an honour to be ever remembered with the deepest and most affectionate gratitude) these testimonies of your public judgment must entirely supersede his own, and forbid him to believe himself totally insufficient for the labour at least of this employment. One thing he will venture to hope for, and it certainly shall be his constant aim, by diligence and attention to atone for his other defects; esteeming, that the best return, which he can possibly make for your favourable opinion of his capacity, will be his unwearied endeavours in some little degree to deserve it.

THE science thus committed to his charge, to be cultivated, methodized, and explained in a course of academical lectures, is that of the laws and constitution of our own country: a species of knowlege, in which the gentlemen of England have been more remarkably deficient than those of all Europe besides. In most of the nations on the continent, where the civil or imperial law under different modifications is closely interwoven with the municipal laws of the land, no gentleman, or at least no scholar, thinks his education is completed, till he has attended a course or two of lectures, both upon the institutes of Justinian and the local constitutions of his native soil, under the very eminent professors that abound in their several universities. And in the northern parts of our own island, where also the municipal laws are frequently connected with the civil, it is difficult to meet with a person of liberal education, who is destitute of a competent knowlege in that science, which is to be the guardian of his natural rights and the rule of his civil conduct.

N O R have the imperial laws been totally neglected even in the English nation. A general acquaintance with their decisions has ever been deservedly considered as no small accomplishment of a gentleman; and a fashion has prevailed, especially of late, to transport the growing hopes of this island to foreign universities, in Switzerland, Germany, and Holland; which, though infinitely inferior to our own in every other consideration, have been looked upon as better nurseries of the civil, or (which is nearly the same) of their own municipal law. In the mean time it has been the peculiar lot of our admirable system of laws, to be neglected, and even unknown, by all but one practical profession; though built upon the soundest foundations, and approved by the experience of ages.

F A R be it from me to derogate from the study of the civil law, considered (apart from any binding authority) as a collection of written reason. No man is more thoroughly persuaded of the general excellence of it's rules, and the usual equity of it's decisions; nor is better convinced of it's use as well as ornament to the scholar, the divine, the statesman, and even the common lawyer. But we must not carry our veneration so far as to sacrifice our Alfred and Edward to the manes of Theodosius and Justinian: we must not prefer the edict of the praetor, or the rescript of the Roman emperor, to our own immemorial customs, or the sanctions of an English parliament; unless we can also prefer the despotic monarchy of Rome and Byzantium, for whose meridians the former were calculated, to the free constitution of Britain, which the latter are adapted to perpetuate.

W I T H O U T detracting therefore from the real merit which abounds in the imperial law, I hope I may have leave to assert, that if an Englishman must be ignorant of either the one or the other, he had better be a stranger to the Roman than the English institutions. For I think it an undeniable position, that a competent knowlege of the laws of that society, in which we live, is the proper accomplishment of every gentleman and scholar; an highly useful, I had almost said essential, part of liberal and polite education. And in this I am warranted by the example of antient Rome; where, as Cicero informs us, the very boys were obliged to learn the twelve tables by heart, as a *carmen necessarium* or indispensable lesson, to imprint on their tender minds an early knowlege of the laws and constitutions of their country.B U T as the long and universal neglect of this study, with us in England, seems in some degree to call in question the truth of this evident position, it shall therefore be the business of this introductory discourse, in the first place to demonstrate the utility of some general acquaintance with the municipal law of the land, by pointing out its particular uses in all considerable situations of life. Some conjectures will then be offered with regard to the causes of neglecting this useful study: to which will be subjoined a few reflexions on the peculiar propriety of reviving it in our own universities.

A N D , first, to demonstrate the utility of some acquaintance with the laws of the land, let us only reflect a moment on the singular frame and polity of that land, which is governed by this system of laws. A land, perhaps the only one in the universe, in which political or civil liberty is the very end and scope of the constitution. This liberty, rightly understood, consists in the power of doing whatever the laws permit; which is only to be effected by a general conformity of all orders and degrees to those equitable rules of action, by which the meanest individual is protected from the insults and oppression of the greatest. As therefore every subject is interested in the preservation of the laws, it is incumbent upon every man to be acquainted with those at least, with which he is immediately concerned; lest he incur the censure, as well as inconvenience, of living in society without knowing the obligations which it lays him under. And thus much may suffice for persons of inferior condition, who have neither time nor capacity to enlarge their views beyond that contracted sphere in which they are appointed to move. But those, on whom nature and fortune have bestowed more abilities and greater leisure, cannot be so easily excused. These advantages are given them, not for the benefit of themselves only, but also of the public: and yet they cannot, in any scene of life, discharge properly their duty either to the public or themselves, without some degree of knowlege in the laws. To evince this the more clearly, it may not be amiss to descend to a few particulars.L E T us therefore begin with our gentlemen of independent estates and fortune, the most useful as well as considerable body of men in the nation; whom even to suppose ignorant in this branch of learning is treated by Mr Locke as a strange absurdity. It is their landed property, with it's long and voluminous train of descents and conveyances, settlements, entails, and incumbrances, that forms the most intricate and most extensive object of legal knowlege. The thorough comprehension of these, in all their minute distinctions, is perhaps too laborious a task for any but a lawyer by profession: yet still the understanding of a few leading principles, relating to estates and conveyancing, may form some check and guard upon a gentleman's inferior agents, and preserve him at least from very gross and notorious imposition.

A G A I N , the policy of all laws has made some forms necessary in the wording of last wills and testaments, and more with regard to their attestation. An ignorance in these must always be of dangerous consequence, to such as by choice or necessity compile their own testaments without any technical assistance. Those who have attended the courts of justice are the best witnesses of the confusion and distresses that are hereby occasioned in families; and of the difficulties that arise in discerning the true meaning of the testator, or sometimes in discovering any meaning at all: so that in the end his estate may often be vested quite contrary to these his enigmatical intentions, because perhaps he has omitted one or two formal words, which are necessary to ascertain the sense with indisputable legal precision, or has executed his will in the presence of fewer witnesses than the law requires.

B U T to proceed from private concerns to those of a more public consideration. All gentlemen of fortune are, in consequence of their property, liable to be called upon to establish the rights, to estimate the injuries, to weigh the accusations, and sometimes to dispose of the lives of their fellow-subjects, by serving upon juries. In this situation they are frequently to decide, and that upon their oaths, questions of nice importance, in the solution of which some legal skill is requisite; especially where the law and the fact, as it often happens, are intimately blended together. And the general incapacity, even of our best juries, to do this with any tolerable propriety has greatly debased their authority; and has unavoidably thrown more power into the hands of the judges, to direct, control, and even reverse their verdicts, than perhaps the constitution intended.

B U T it is not as a juror only that the English gentleman is called upon to determine questions of right, and distribute justice to his fellow-subjects: it is principally with this order of men that the commission of the peace is filled. And here a very ample field is opened for a gentleman to exert his talents, by maintaining good order in his neighbourhood; by punishing the dissolute and idle; by protecting the peaceable and industrious; and, above all, by healing petty differences and preventing vexatious prosecutions. But, in order to attain these desirable ends, it is necessary that the magistrate should understand his business; and have not only the will, but the power also, (under which must be included the knowlege) of administring legal and effectual justice. Else, when he has mistaken his authority, through passion, through ignorance, or absurdity, he will be the object of contempt from his inferiors, and of censure from those to whom he is accountable for his conduct.

Y E T farther; most gentlemen of considerable property, at some period or other in their lives, are ambitious of representing their country in parliament: and those, who are ambitious of receiving so high a trust, would also do well to remember it's nature and importance. They are not thus honourably distinguished from the rest of their fellow-subjects, merely that they may privilege their persons, their estates, or their domestics; that they may list under party banners; may grant or with-hold supplies; may vote with or vote against a popular or unpopular administration; but upon considerations far more interesting and important. They are the guardians of the English constitution; the makers, repealers, and interpreters of the English laws; delegated to watch, to check, and to avert every dangerous innovation, to propose, to adopt, and to cherish any solid and well-weighed improvement; bound by every tie of nature, of honour, and of religion, to transmit that constitution and those laws to their posterity, amended if possible, at least without any derogation. And how unbecoming must it appear in a member of the legislature to vote for a new law, who is utterly ignorant of the old! what kind of interpretation can he be enabled to give, who is a stranger to the text upon which he comments!

I N D E E D it is really amazing, that there should be no other state of life, no other occupation, art, or science, in which some method of instruction is not looked upon as requisite, except only the science of legislation, the noblest and most difficult of any. Apprenticeships are held necessary to almost every art, commercial or mechanical: a long course of reading and study must form the divine, the physician, and the practical professor of the laws: but every man of superior fortune thinks himself *born* a legislator. Yet Tully was of a different opinion: "It is necessary, says he, for a senator to be thoroughly acquainted with the constitution; and this, he declares, is a knowlege of the most extensive nature; a matter of science, of diligence, of reflexion; without which no senator can possibly be fit for his office."T H E mischiefs that have arisen to the public from inconsiderate alterations in our laws, are too obvious to be called in question; and how far they have been owing to the defective education of our senators, is a point well worthy the public attention. The common law of England has fared like other venerable edifices of antiquity, which rash and unexperienced workmen have ventured to new-dress and refine, with all the rage of modern improvement. Hence frequently it's symmetry has been destroyed, it's proportions distorted, and it's majestic simplicity exchanged for specious embellishments and fantastic novelties. For, to say the truth, almost all the perplexed questions, almost all the niceties, intricacies, and delays (which have sometimes disgraced the English, as well as other, courts of justice) owe their original not to the common law itself, but to innovations that have been made in it by acts of parliament; "overladen (as sir Edward Coke expresses it) with provisoes and additions, and many times on a sudden penned or corrected by men of none or very little judgment in law." This great and well-experienced judge declares, that in all his time he never knew two questions made upon rights merely depending upon the common law; and warmly laments the confusion introduced by ill-judging and unlearned legislators. "But if, he subjoins, acts of parliament were after the old fashion penned, by such only as perfectly knew what the common law was before the making of any act of parliament concerning that matter, as also how far forth former statutes had provided remedy for former mischiefs, and defects discovered by experience; then should very few questions in law arise, and the learned should not so often and so much perplex their heads to make atonement and peace, by construction of law, between insensible and disagreeing words, sentences, and provisoes, as they now do." And if this inconvenience was so heavily felt in the reign of queen Elizabeth, you may judge how the evil is increased in later times, when the statute book is swelled to ten times a larger bulk; unless it should be found, that the penners of our modern statutes have proportionably better informed themselves in the knowlege of the common law.W H A T is said of our gentlemen in general, and the propriety of their application to the study of the laws of their country, will hold equally strong or still stronger with regard to the nobility of this realm, except only in the article of serving upon juries. But, instead of this, they have several peculiar provinces of far greater consequence and concern; being not only by birth hereditary counsellors of the crown, and judges upon their honour of the lives of their brother-peers, but also arbiters of the property of all their fellow-subjects, and that in the last resort. In this their judicial capacity they are bound to decide the nicest and most critical points of the law; to examine and correct such errors as have escaped the most experienced sages of the profession, the lord keeper and the judges of the courts at Westminster. Their sentence is final, decisive, irrevocable: no appeal, no correction, not even a review can be had: and to their determination, whatever it be, the inferior courts of justice must conform; otherwise the rule of property would no longer be uniform and steady.

S H O U L D a judge in the most subordinate jurisdiction be deficient in the knowlege of the law, it would reflect infinite contempt upon himself and disgrace upon those who employ him. And yet the consequence of his ignorance is comparatively very trifling and small: his judgment may be examined, and his errors rectified, by other courts. But how much more serious and affecting is the case of a superior judge, if without any skill in the laws he will boldly venture to decide a question, upon which the welfare and subsistence of whole families may depend! where the chance of his judging right, or wrong, is barely equal; and where, if he chances to judge wrong, he does an injury of the most alarming nature, an injury without possibility of redress!

Y E T , vast as this trust is, it can no where be so properly reposed as in the noble hands where our excellent constitution has placed it: and therefore placed it, because, from the independence of their fortune and the dignity of their station, they are presumed to employ that leisure which is the consequence of both, in attaining a more extensive knowlege of the laws than persons of inferior rank: and because the founders of our polity relied upon that delicacy of sentiment, so peculiar to noble birth; which, as on the one hand it will prevent either interest or affection from interfering in questions of right, so on the other it will bind a peer in honour, an obligation which the law esteems equal to another's oath, to be master of those points upon which it is his birthright to decide.

T H E Roman pandects will furnish us with a piece of history not unapplicable to our present purpose. Servius Sulpicius, a gentleman of the patrician order, and a celebrated orator, had occasion to take the opinion of Quintus Mutius Scaevola, the oracle of the Roman law; but for want of some knowlege in that science, could not so much as understand even the technical terms, which his friend was obliged to make use of. Upon which Mutius Scaevola could not forbear to upbraid him with this memorable reproof, "that it was a shame for a patrician, a nobleman, and an orator of causes, to be ignorant of that law in which he was so peculiarly concerned." This reproach made so deep an impression on Sulpicius, that he immediately applied himself to the study of the law; wherein he arrived to that proficiency, that he left behind him about a hundred and fourscore volumes of his own compiling upon the subject; and became, in the opinion of Cicero, a much more complete lawyer than even Mutius Scaevola himself.

I W O U L D not be thought to recommend to our English nobility and gentry to become as great lawyers as Sulpicius; though he, together with this character, sustained likewise that of an excellent orator, a firm patriot, and a wise indefatigable senator; but the inference which arises from the story is this, that ignorance of the laws of the land hath ever been esteemed dishonourable, in those who are entrusted by their country to maintain, to administer, and to amend them.

B U T surely there is little occasion to enforce this argument any farther to persons of rank and distinction, if we of this place may be allowed to form a general judgment from those who are under our inspection: happy, that while we lay down the rule, we can also produce the example. You will therefore permit your professor to indulge both a public and private satisfaction, by bearing this open testimony; that in the infancy of these studies among us, they were favoured with the most diligent attendance, and pursued with the most unwearied application, by those of the noblest birth and most ample patrimony: some of whom are still the ornaments of this seat of learning; and others at a greater distance continue doing honour to it's institutions, by comparing our polity and laws with those of other kingdoms abroad, or exerting their senatorial abilities in the councils of the nation at home.

N O R will some degree of legal knowlege be found in the least superfluous to persons of inferior rank; especially those of the learned professions. The clergy in particular, besides the common obligations they are under in proportion to their rank and fortune, have also abundant reason, considered merely as clergymen, to be acquainted with many branches of the law, which are almost peculiar and appropriated to themselves alone. Such are the laws relating to advowsons, institutions, and inductions; to simony, and simoniacal contracts; to uniformity, residence, and pluralities; to tithes and other ecclesiastical dues; to marriages (more especially of late) and to a variety of other subjects, which are consigned to the care of their order by the provisions of particular statutes. To understand these aright, to discern what is warranted or enjoined, and what is forbidden by law, demands a sort of legal apprehension; which is no otherwise to be acquired than by use and a familiar acquaintance with legal writers.

F O R the gentlemen of the faculty of physic, I must frankly own that I see no special reason, why they in particular should apply themselves to the study of the law; unless in common with other gentlemen, and to complete the character of general and extensive knowlege; a character which their profession, beyond others, has remarkably deserved. They will give me leave however to suggest, and that not ludicrously, that it might frequently be of use to families upon sudden emergencies, if the physician were acquainted with the doctrine of last wills and testaments, at least so far as relates to the formal part of their execution.

B U T those gentlemen who intend to profess the civil and ecclesiastical laws in the spiritual and maritime courts of this kingdom, are of all men (next to common lawyers) the most indispensably obliged to apply themselves seriously to the study of our municipal laws. For the civil and canon laws, considered with respect to any intrinsic obligation, have no force or authority in this kingdom; they are no more binding in England than our laws are binding at Rome. But as far as these foreign laws, on account of some peculiar propriety, have in some particular cases, and in some particular courts, been introduced and allowed by our laws, so far they oblige, and no farther; their authority being wholly founded upon that permission and adoption. In which we are not singular in our notions; for even in Holland, where the imperial law is much cultivated and it's decisions pretty generally followed, we are informed by Van Leeuwen, that, "it receives it's force from custom and the consent of the people, either tacitly or expressly given: for otherwise, he adds, we should no more be bound by this law, than by that of the Almains, the Franks, the Saxons, the Goths, the Vandals, and other of the antient nations." Wherefore, in all points in which the different systems depart from each other, the law of the land takes place of the law of Rome, whether antient or modern, imperial or pontifical. And in those of our English courts wherein a reception has been allowed to the civil and canon laws, if either they exceed the bounds of that reception, by extending themselves to other matters, than are permitted to them; or if such courts proceed according to the decisions of those laws, in cases wherein it is controlled by the law of the land, the common law in either instance both may, and frequently does, prohibit and annul their proceedings: and it will not be a sufficient excuse for them to tell the king's courts at Westminster, that their practice is warranted by the laws of Justinian or Gregory, or is conformable to the decrees of the Rota or imperial chamber. For which reason it becomes highly necessary for every civilian and canonist that would act with safety as a judge, or with prudence and reputation as an advocate, to know in what cases and how far the English laws have given sanction to the Roman; in what points the latter are rejected; and where they are both so intermixed and blended together, as to form certain supplemental parts of the common law of England, distinguished by the titles of the king's maritime, the king's military, and the king's ecclesiastical law. The propriety of which enquiry the university of Oxford has for more than a century so thoroughly seen, that in her statutes she appoints, that one of the three questions to be annually discussed at the act by the jurist-inceptors shall relate to the common law; subjoining this reason, "*quia juris civilis studiosos decet haud imperitos esse juris municipalis, & differentias exteri patriique juris notas habere.*" And the statutes of the university of Cambridge speak expressly to the same effect.

F R O M the general use and necessity of some acquaintance with the common law, the inference were extremely easy, with regard to the propriety of the present institution, in a place to which gentlemen of all ranks and degrees resort, as the fountain of all useful knowlege. But how it has come to pass that a design of this sort has never before taken place in the university, and the reason why the study of our laws has in general fallen into disuse, I shall previously proceed to enquire.

S I R John Fortescue, in his panegyric on the laws of England, (which was written in the reign of Henry the sixth) puts a very obvious question in the mouth of the young prince, whom he is exhorting to apply himself to that branch of learning; "why the laws of England, being so good, so fruitful, and so commodious, are not taught in the universities, as the civil and canon laws are?" In answer to which he gives what seems, with due deference be it spoken, a very jejune and unsatisfactory reason; being in short, that "as the proceedings at common law were in his time carried on in three different tongues, the English, the Latin, and the French, that science must be necessarily taught in those three several languages; but that in the universities all sciences were taught in the Latin tongue only; and therefore he concludes, that they could not be conveniently taught or studied in our universities." But without attempting to examine seriously the validity of this reason, (the very shadow of which by the wisdom of your late constitutions is entirely taken away) we perhaps may find out a better, or at least a more plausible account, why the study of the municipal laws has been banished from these seats of science, than what the learned chancellor thought it prudent to give to his royal pupil.

T H A T antient collection of unwritten maxims and customs, which is called the common law, however compounded or from whatever fountains derived, had subsisted immemorially in this kingdom; and, though somewhat altered and impaired by the violence of the times, had in great measure weathered the rude shock of the Norman conquest. This had endeared it to the people in general, as well because it's decisions were universally known, as because it was found to be excellently adapted to the genius of the English nation. In the knowlege of this law consisted great part of the learning of those dark ages; it was then taught, says Mr Selden, in the monasteries, *in the universities*, and in the families of the principal nobility. The clergy in particular, as they then engrossed almost every other branch of learning, so (like their predecessors the British druids) they were peculiarly remarkable for their proficiency in the study of the law. *Nullus clericus nisi causidicus*, is the character given of them soon after the conquest by William of Malmsbury. The judges therefore were usually created out of the sacred order, as was likewise the case among the Normans; and all the inferior offices were supplied by the lower clergy, which has occasioned their successors to be denominated *clerks* to this day.

BUT the common law of England, being not committed to writing, but only handed down by tradition, use, and experience, was not so heartily relished by the foreign clergy; who came over hither in shoals during the reign of the conqueror and his two sons, and were utter strangers to our constitution as well as our language. And an accident, which soon after happened, had nearly completed it's ruin. A copy of Justinian's pandects, being newly discovered at Amalfi, soon brought the civil law into vogue all over the west of Europe, where before it was quite laid aside and in a manner forgotten; though some traces of it's authority remained in Italy and the eastern provinces of the empire. This now became in a particular manner the favourite of the popish clergy, who borrowed the method and many of the maxims of their canon law from this original. The study of it was introduced into several universities abroad, particularly that of Bologna; where exercises were performed, lectures read, and degrees conferred in this faculty, as in other branches of science: and many nations on the continent, just then beginning to recover from the convulsions consequent upon the overthrow of the Roman empire, and settling by degrees into peaceable forms of government, adopted the civil law, (being the best written system then extant) as the basis of their several constitutions; blending and interweaving it among their own feodal customs, in some places with a more extensive, in others a more confined authority. NOR was it long before the prevailing mode of the times reached England. For Theobald, a Norman abbot, being elected to the see of Canterbury, and extremely addicted to this new study, brought over with him in his retinue many learned proficients therein; and among the rest Roger sirnamed Vacarius, whom he placed in the university of Oxford, to teach it to the people of this country. But it did not meet with the same easy reception in England, where a mild and rational system of laws had been long established, as it did upon the continent; and, though the monkish clergy (devoted to the will of a foreign primate) received it with eagerness and zeal, yet the laity who were more interested to preserve the old constitution, and had already severely felt the effect of many Norman innovations, continued wedded to the use of the common law. King Stephen immediately published a proclamation, forbidding the study of the laws, then newly imported from Italy; which was treated by the monks as a piece of impiety, and, though it might prevent the introduction of the civil law process into our courts of justice, yet did not hinder the clergy from reading and teaching it in their own schools and monasteries.

F R O M this time the nation seems to have been divided into two parties; the bishops and clergy, many of them foreigners, who applied themselves wholly to the study of the civil and canon laws, which now came to be inseparably interwoven with each other; and the nobility and laity, who adhered with equal pertinacity to the old common law; both of them reciprocally jealous of what they were unacquainted with, and neither of them perhaps allowing the opposite system that real merit which is abundantly to be found in each. This appears on the one hand from the spleen with which the monastic writers speak of our municipal laws upon all occasions; and, on the other, from the firm temper which the nobility shewed at the famous parliament of Merton; when the prelates endeavoured to procure an act, to declare all bastards legitimate in case the parents intermarried at any time afterwards; alleging this only reason, because holy church (that is, the canon law) declared such children legitimate: but "all the earls and barons (says the parliament roll) with one voice answered, that they would not change the laws of England, which had hitherto been used and approved." And we find the same jealousy prevailing above a century afterwards, when the nobility declared with a kind of prophetic spirit, "that the realm of England hath never been unto this hour, neither by the consent of our lord the king and the lords of parliament shall it ever be, ruled or governed by the civillaw." And of this temper between the clergy and laity many more instances might be given.

W H I L E things were in this situation, the clergy, finding it impossible to root out the municipal law, began to withdraw themselves by degrees from the temporal courts; and to that end, very early in the reign of king Henry the third, episcopal constitutions were published, forbidding all ecclesiastics to appear as advocates *in foro saeculari*; nor did they long continue to act as judges there, nor caring to take the oath of office which was then found necessary to be administred, that they should in all things determine according to the law and custom of this realm; though they still kept possession of the high office of chancellor, an office then of little juridical power; and afterwards, as it's business increased by degrees, they modelled the process of the court at their own discretion.

B U T wherever they retired, and wherever their authority extended, they carried with them the same zeal to introduce the rules of the civil, in exclusion of the municipal law. This appears in a particular manner from the spiritual courts of all denominations, from the chancellor's courts in both our universities, and from the high court of chancery before-mentioned; in all of which the proceedings are to this day in a course much conformed to the civil law: for which no tolerable reason can be assigned, unless that these courts were all under the immediate direction of the popish ecclesiastics, among whom it was a point of religion to exclude the municipal law; pope Innocent the fourth having forbidden the very reading of it by the clergy, because it's decisions were not founded on the imperial constitutions, but merely on the customs of the laity. And if it be considered, that our universities began about that period to receive their present form of scholastic discipline; that they were then, and continued to be till the time of the reformation, entirely under the influence of the popish clergy; (sir John Mason the first protestant, being also the first lay, chancellor of Oxford) this will lead us to perceive the reason, why the study of the Roman laws was in those days of bigotry pursued with such alacrity in these seats of learning; and why the common law was entirely despised, and esteemed little better than heretical.

[A N D , since the reformation, many causes have conspired to prevent it's becoming a part of academical education. As, first, long usage and established custom; which, as in every thing else, so especially in the forms of scholastic exercise, have justly great weight and authority. Secondly, the real intrinsic merit of the civil law, considered upon the footing of reason and not of obligation, which was well known to the instructors of our youth; and their total ignorance of the merit of the common law, though it's equal at least, and perhaps an improvement on the other. But the principal reason of all, that has hindered the introduction of this branch of learning, is, that the study of the common law, being banished from hence in the times of popery, has fallen into a quite different chanel, and has hitherto been wholly cultivated in another place. But as this long usage and established custom, of ignorance in the laws of the land, begin now to be thought unreasonable; and as by this means the merit of those laws will probably be more generally known; we may hope that the method of studying them will soon revert to it's antient course, and the foundations at least of that science will be laid in the two universities; without being exclusively confined to the chanel which it fell into at the times I have been just describing.

F O R , being then entirely abandoned by the clergy, a few stragglers excepted, the study and practice of it devolved of course into the hands of laymen; who entertained upon their parts a most hearty aversion to the civil law, and made no scruple to profess their contempt, nay even their ignorance of it, in the most public manner. But still, as the ballance of learning was greatly on the side of the clergy, and as the common law was no longer *taught*, as formerly, in any part of the kingdom, it must have been subjected to many inconveniences, and perhaps would have been gradually lost and overrun by the civil, (a suspicion well justified from the frequent transcripts of Justinian to be met with in Bracton and Fleta) had it not been for a peculiar incident, which happened at a very critical time, and contributed greatly to it's support.T H E incident I mean was the fixing the court of common pleas, the grand tribunal for disputes of property, to be held in one certain spot; that the seat of ordinary justice might be permanent and notorious to all the nation. Formerly that, in conjunction with all the other superior courts, was held before the king's capital justiciary of England, in the *aula regis*, or such of his palaces wherein his royal person resided; and removed with his houshold from one end of the kingdom to the other. This was found to occasion great inconvenience to the suitors; to remedy which it was made an article of the great charter of liberties, both that of king John and king Henry the third, that "common pleas should no longer follow the king's court, but be held in some certain place:" in consequence of which they have ever since been held (a few necessary removals in times of the plague excepted) in the palace of Westminster only. This brought together the professors of the municipal law, who before were dispersed about the kingdom, and formed them into an aggregate body; whereby a society was established of persons, who (as Spelman observes) addicting themselves wholly to the study of the laws of the land, and no longer considering it as a mere subordinate science for the amusement of leisure hours, soon raised those laws to that pitch of perfection, which they suddenly attained under the auspices of our English Justinian, king Edward the first. I N consequence of this lucky assemblage, they naturally fell into a kind of collegiate order, and, being excluded from Oxford and Cambridge, found it necessary to establish a new university of their own. This they did by purchasing at various times certain houses (now called the inns of court and of chancery) between the city of Westminster, the place of holding the king's courts, and the city of London; for advantage of ready access to the one, and plenty of provisions in the other. Here exercises were performed, lectures read, and degrees were at length conferred in the common law, as at other universities in the canon and civil. The degrees were those of barristers (first stiled apprentices from *apprendre*, to learn) who answered to our bachelors; as the state and degree of a serjeant, *servientis ad legem*, did to that of doctor.

T H E crown seems to have soon taken under it's protection this infant seminary of common law; and, the more effectually to foster and cherish it, king Henry the third in the nineteenth year of his reign issued out an order directed to the mayor and sheriffs of London, commanding that no regent of any law schools *within* that city should for the future teach law therein. The word, law, or *leges*, being a general term, may create some doubt at this distance of time whether the teaching of the civil law, or the common, or both, is hereby restrained. But in either case it tends to the same end. If the civil law only is prohibited, (which is Mr Selden's opinion) it is then a retaliation upon the clergy, who had excluded the common law from *their* seats of learning. If the municipal law be also included in the restriction, (as sir Edward Coke understands it, and which the words seem to import) then the intention is evidently this; by preventing private teachers within the walls of the city, to collect all the common lawyers into the one public university, which was newly instituted in the suburbs.

I N this juridical university (for such it is insisted to have been by Fortescue and sir Edward Coke) there are two sorts of collegiate houses; one called inns of chancery, in which the younger students of the law were usually placed, "learning and studying, says Fortescue, the originals and as it were the elements of the law; who, profiting therein, as they grow to ripeness so are they admitted into the greater inns of the same study, called the inns of court." And in these inns of both kinds, he goes on to tell us, the knights and barons, with other grandees and noblemen of the realm, did use to place their children, though they did not desire to have them thoroughly learned in the law, or to get their living by it's practice: and that in his time there were about two thousand students at these several inns, all of whom he informs us were *filii nobilium*, or gentlemen born.

HENCE it is evident, that (though under the influence of the monks our universities neglected this study, yet) in the time of Henry the sixth it was thought highly necessary and was the universal practice, for the young nobility and gentry to be instructed in the originals and elements of the laws. But by degres this custom has fallen into disuse; so that in the reign of queen Elizabeth sir Edward Coke does not reckon above a thousand students, and the number at present is very considerably less. Which seems principally owing to these reasons: first, because the inns of chancery being now almost totally filled by the inferior branch of the profession, they are neither commodious nor proper for the resort of gentlemen of any rank or figure; so that there are now very rarely any young students entered at the inns of chancery: secondly, because in the inns of court all sorts of regimen and academical superintendance, either with regard to morals or studies, are found impracticable and therefore entirely neglected: lastly, because persons of birth and fortune, after having finished their usual courses at the universities, have seldom leisure or resolution sufficient to enter upon a new scheme of study at a new place of instruction. Wherefore few gentlemen now resort to the inns of court, but such for whom the knowlege of practice is absolutely necessary; such, I mean, as are intended for the profession: the rest of our gentry, (not to say our nobility also) having usually retired to their estates, or visited foreign kingdoms, or entered upon public life, without any instruction in the laws of the land; and indeed with hardly any opportunity of gaining instruction, unless it can be afforded them in these seats of learning.

AND that these are the proper places, for affording assistances of this kind to gentlemen of all stations and degrees, cannot (I think) with any colour of reason be denied. For not one of the objections, which are made to the inns of court and chancery, and which I have just enumerated, will hold with regard to the universities. Gentlemen may here associate with gentlemen of their own rank and degree. Nor are their conduct and studies left entirely to their own discretion; but regulated by a discipline so wise and exact, yet so liberal, so sensible and manly, that their conformity to it's rules (which does at present so much honour to our youth) is not more the effect of constraint, than of their own inclinations and choice. Neither need they apprehend too long an avocation hereby from their private concerns and amusements, or (what is a more noble object) the service of their friends and their country. This study will go hand in hand with their other pursuits: it will obstruct none of them; it will ornament and assist them all.

BUT if, upon the whole, there are any still wedded to monastic prejudice, that can entertain a doubt how far this study is properly and regularly *academical*, such persons I am afraid either have not considered the constitution and design of an university, or else think very meanly of it. It must be a deplorable narrowness of mind, that would confine these seats of instruction to the limited views of one or two learned professions. To the praise of this age be it spoken, a more open and generous way of thinking begins now universally to prevail. The attainment of liberal and genteel accomplishments, though not of the intellectual sort, has been thought by our wisest and most affectionate patrons, and very lately by the whole university, no small improvement of our antient plan of education; and therefore I may safely affirm that nothing (how *unusual* soever) is, under due regulations, improper to be *taught* in this place, which is proper for a gentleman to *learn*. But that a science, which distinguishes the criterions of right and wrong; which teaches to establish the one, and prevent, punish, or redress the other; which employs in it's theory the noblest faculties of the soul, and exerts in it's practice the cardinal virtues of the heart; a science, which is universal in it's use and extent, accommodated to each individual, yet comprehending the whole community; that a science like this should have ever been deemed unnecessary to be studied in an university, is matter of astonishment and concern. Surely, if it were not before an object of academical knowlege, it was high time to make it one; and to those who can doubt the propriety of it's reception among us (if any such there be) we may return an answer in their own way; that ethics are confessedly a branch of academical learning, and Aristotle *himself has said*, speaking of the laws of his own country, that jurisprudence or the knowlege of those laws is the principal and most perfect branch of ethics.

F R O M a thorough conviction of this truth, our munificent benefactor Mr V I N E R , having employed above half a century in amassing materials for new modelling and rendering more commodious the rude study of the laws of the land, consigned both the plan and execution of these his public-spirited designs to the wisdom of his parent university. Resolving to dedicate his learned labours "to the benefit of posterity and the perpetual service of his country," he was sensible he could not perform his resolutions in a better and more effectual manner, than by extending to the youth of this place those assistances, of which he so well remembered and so heartily regretted the want. And the sense, which the university has entertained of this ample and most useful benefaction, must appear beyond a doubt from their gratitude in receiving it with all possible marks of esteem; from their alacrity and unexampled dispatch in carrying it into execution; and, above all, from the laws and constitutions by which they have effectually guarded it from the neglect and abuse to which such institutions are liable. We have seen an universal emulation, who best should understand, or most faithfully pursue, the designs of our generous patron: and with pleasure we recollect, that those who are most distinguished by their quality, their fortune, their station, their learning, or their experience, have appeared the most zealous to promote the success of Mr Viner's establishment.

1. T H A T the accounts of this benefaction be separately kept, and annually audited by the delegates of accounts and professor, and afterwards reported to convocation.

2. T H A T a professorship of the laws of England be established, with a salary of two hundred pounds *per annum*; the professor to be elected by convocation, and to be at the time of his election at least a master of arts or bachelor of civil law in the university of Oxford, of ten years standing from his matriculation; and also a barrister at law of four years standing at the bar.

3. T H A T such professor (by himself, or by deputy to be previously approved by convocation) do read one solemn public lecture on the laws of England, and in the English language, in every academical term, at certain stated times previous to the commencement of the common law term; or forfeit twenty pounds for every omission to Mr Viner's general fund: and also (by himself, or by deputy to be approved, if occasional, by the vice-chancellor and proctors; or, if permanent, both the cause and the deputy to be annually approved by convocation) do yearly read one complete course of lectures on the laws of England, and in the English language, consisting of sixty lectures at the least, to be read during the university term time, with such proper intervals that not more than four lectures may fall within any single week: that the professor do give a month's notice of the time when the course is to begin, and do read *gratis* to the scholars of Mr Viner's foundation; but may demand of other auditors such gratuity as shall be settled from time to time by decree of convocation: and that, for every of the said sixty lectures omitted, the professor, on complaint made to the vice-chancellor within the year, do forfeit forty shillings to Mr Viner's general fund; the proof of having performed his duty to lie upon the said professor.

4. T H A T every professor do continue in his office during life, unless in case of such misbehaviour as shall amount to bannition by the university statutes; or unless he deserts the profession of the law by betaking himself to another profession; or unless, after one admonition by the vice-chancellor and proctors for notorious neglect, he is guilty of another flagrant omission: in any of which cases he be deprived by the vice-chancellor, with consent of the house of convocation.

5. T H A T such a number of fellowships with a stipend of fifty pounds *per annum*, and scholarships with a stipend of thirty pounds be established, as the convocation shall from time to time ordain, according to the state of Mr Viner's revenues.

6. T H A T every fellow be elected by convocation, and at the time of election be unmarried, and at least a master of arts or bachelor of civil law, and a member of some college or hall in the university of Oxford; the scholars of this foundation or such as have been scholars (if qualified and approved of by convocation) to have the preference: that, if not a barrister when chosen, he be called to the bar within one year after his election; but do reside in the university two months in every year, or in case of non-residence do forfeit the stipend of that year to Mr Viner's general fund.

7. T H A T every scholar be elected by convocation, and at the time of election be unmarried, and a member of some college or hall in the university of Oxford, who shall have been matriculated twenty four calendar months at the least: that he do take the degree of bachelor of civil law with all convenient speed; (either proceeding in arts or otherwise) and previous to his taking the same, between the second and eighth year from his matriculation, be bound to attend two courses of the professor's lectures, to be certified under the professor's hand; and within one year after taking the same be called to the bar: that he do annually reside six months till he is of four years standing, and four months from that time till he is master of

arts or bachelor of civil law; after which he be bound to reside two months in every year; or, in case of non-residence, do forfeit the stipend of that year to Mr Viner's general fund.

8. T H A T the scholarships do become void in case of non-attendance on the professor, or not taking the degree of bachelor of civil law, being duly admonished so to do by the vice-chancellor and proctors: and that both fellowships and scholarships do expire at the end of ten years after each respective election; and become void in case of gross misbehaviour, non-residence for two years together, marriage, not being called to the bar within the time before limited, (being duly admonished so to be by the vice-chancellor and proctors) or deserting the profession of the law by following any other profession: and that in any of these cases the vice-chancellor, with consent of convocation, do declare the place actually void.

9. T H A T in case of any vacancy of the professorship, fellowships, or scholarships, the profits of the current year be ratably divided between the predecessor or his representatives, and the successor; and that a new election be had within one month afterwards, unless by that means the time of election shall fall within any vacation, in which case it be deferred to the first week in the next full term. And that before any convocation shall be held for such election, or for any other matter relating to Mr Viner's benefaction, ten days public notice be given to each college and hall of the convocation, and the cause of convoking it.

T H E advantages that might result to the science of the law itself, when a little more attended to in these seats of knowlege, perhaps would be very considerable. The leisure and abilities of the learned in these retirements might either suggest expedients, or execute those dictated by wiser heads, for improving it's method, retrenching it's superfluities, and reconciling the little contrarieties, which the practice of many centuries will necessarily create in any human system: a task, which those who are deeply employed in business, and the more active scenes of the profession, can hardly condescend to engage in. And as to the interest, or (which is the same) the reputation of the universities themselves, I may venture to pronounce, that if ever this study should arrive to any tolerable perfection either here or at Cambridge, the nobility and gentry of this kingdom would not shorten their residence upon this account, nor perhaps entertain a worse opinion of the benefits of academical education. Neither should it be considered as a matter of light importance, that while we thus extend the *pomoeria* of university learning, and adopt a new tribe of citizens within these philosophical walls, we interest a very numerous and very powerful profession in the preservation of our rights and revenues.

F O R I think it is past dispute that those gentlemen, who resort to the inns of court with a view to pursue the profession, will find it expedient (whenever it is practicable) to lay the previous foundations of this, as well as every other science, in one of our learned universities. We may appeal to the experience of every sensible lawyer, whether any thing can be more hazardous or discouraging than the usual entrance on the study of the law. A raw and unexperienced youth, in the most dangerous season of life, is transpanted on a sudden into the midst of allurements to pleasure, without any restraint or check but what his own prudence can suggest; with no public direction in what course to pursue his enquiries; no private assistance to remove the distresses and difficulties, which will always embarass a beginner. In this situation he is expected to sequester himself from the world, and by a tedious lonely process to extract the theory of law from a mass of undigested learning; or else by an assiduous attendance on the courts to pick up theory and practice together, sufficient to qualify him for the ordinary run of business. How little therefore is it to be wondered at, that we hear of so frequent miscarriages; that so many gentlemen of bright imaginations grow weary of so unpromising a search, and addict themselves wholly to amusements, or other less innocent pursuits; and that so many persons of moderate capacity confuse themselves at first setting out, and continue ever dark and puzzled during the remainder of their lives!

T H E evident want of some assistance in the rudiments of legal knowlege, has given birth to a practice, which, if ever it had grown to be general, must have proved of extremely pernicious consequence: I mean the custom, by some so very warmly recommended, to drop all liberal education, as of no use to lawyers; and to place them, in it's stead, as the desk of some skilful attorney; in order to initiate them early in all the depths of practice, and render them more dextrous in the mechanical part of business. A few instances of particular persons, (men of excellent learning, and unblemished integrity) who, in spight of this method of education, have shone in the foremost ranks of the bar, have afforded some kind of sanction to this illiberal path to the profession, and biassed many parents, of shortsighted judgment, in it's favour: not considering, that there are some geniuses, formed to overcome all disadvantages, and that from such particular instances no general rules can be formed; nor observing, that those very persons have frequently recommended by the most forcible of all examples, the disposal of their own offspring, a very different foundation of legal studies, a regular academical education. Perhaps too, in return, I could now direct their eyes to our principal seats of justice, and suggest a few hints, in favour of university learning:—but in these all who hear me, I know, have already prevented me.\

M A K I N G therefore due allowance for one or two shining exceptions, experience may teach us to foretell that a lawyer thus educated to the bar, in subservience to attorneys and solicitors, will find he has begun at the wrong end. If practice be the whole he is taught, practice must also be the whole he will ever know: if he be uninstructed in the elements and first principles upon which the rule of practice is founded, the least variation from established precedents will totally distract and bewilder him: *ita lex scripta est* is the utmost his knowlege will arrive at; he must never aspire to form, and seldom expect to comprehend, any arguments drawn *a priori*, from the spirit of the laws and the natural foundations of justice.

N O R is this all; for (as few persons of birth, or fortune, or even of scholastic education, will submit to the drudgery of servitude and the manual labour of copying the trash of an office) should this infatuation prevail to any considerable degree, we must rarely expect to see a gentleman of distinction or learning at the bar. And what the consequence may be, to have the interpretation and enforcement of the laws (which include the entire disposal of our properties, liberties, and lives) fall wholly into the hands of obscure or illiterate men, is matter of very public concern.

T H E inconveniences here pointed out can never be effectually prevented, but by making academical education a previous step to the profession of the common law, and at the same time making the rudiments of the law a part of academical education. For sciences are of a sociable disposition, and flourish best in the neighbourhood of each other: nor is there any branch of learning, but may be helped and improved by assistances drawn from other arts. If therefore the student in our laws hath formed both his sentiments and style, by perusal and imitation of the purest classical writers, among whom the historians and orators will best deserve his regard; if he can reason with precision, and separate argument from fallacy, by the clear simple rules of pure unsophisticated logic; if he can fix his attention, and steadily pursue truth through any the most intricate deduction, by the use of mathematical demonstrations; if he has enlarged his conceptions of nature and art, by a view of the several branches of genuine, experimental, philosophy; if he has impressed on his mind the sound maxims of the law of nature, the best and most authentic foundation of human laws; if, lastly, he has contemplated those maxims reduced to a practical system in the laws of imperial Rome; if he has done this or any part of it, (though all may be easily done under as able instructors as ever graced any seats of learning) a student thus qualified may enter upon the study of the law with incredible advantage and reputation. And if, at the conclusion, or during the acquisition of these accomplishments, he will afford himself here a year or two's farther leisure, to lay the foundation of his future labours in a solid scientifical method, without thirsting too early to attend that practice which it is impossible he should rightly comprehend, he will afterwards proceed with the greatest ease, and will unfold the most intricate points with an intuitive rapidity and clearness.

I S H A L L not insist upon such motives as might be drawn from principles of oeconomy, and are applicable to particulars only: I reason upon more general topics. And therefore to the qualities of the head, which I have just enumerated, I cannot but add those of the heart; affectionate loyalty to the king, a zeal for liberty and the constitution, a sense of real honour, and well grounded principles of religion; as necessary to form a truly valuable English lawyer, a Hyde, a Hale, or a Talbot. And, whatever the ignorance of some, or unkindness of others, may have heretofore untruly suggested, experience will warrant us to affirm, that these endowments of loyalty and public spirit, of honour and religion, are no where to be found in more high perfection than in the two universities of this kingdom.

B E F O R E I conclude, it may perhaps be expected, that I lay before you a short and general account of the method I propose to follow, in endeavouring to execute the trust you have been pleased to repose in my hands. And in these solemn lectures, which are ordained to be read at the entrance of every term, (more perhaps to do public honour to this laudable institution, than for the private instruction of individuals) I presume it will best answer the intent of our benefactor and the expectation of this learned body, if I attempt to illustrate at times such detached titles of the law, as are the most easy to be understood, and most capable of historical or critical ornament. But in reading the complete course, which is annually consigned to my care, a more regular method will be necessary; and, till a better is proposed, I shall take the liberty to follow the same that I have already submitted to the public. To fill up and finish that outline with propriety and correctness, and to render the whole intelligible to the uninformed minds of beginners, (whom we are too apt to suppose acquainted with terms and ideas, which they never had opportunity to learn) this must be my ardent endeavour, though by no means my promise to accomplish. You will permit me however very briefly to describe, rather what I conceive an academical expounder of the laws should do, than what I have ever known to be done.

H E should consider his course as a general map of the law, marking out the shape of the country, it's connexions and boundaries, it's greater divisions and principal cities: it is not his business to describe minutely the subordinate limits, or to fix the longitude and latitude of every inconsiderable hamlet. His attention should be engaged, like that of the readers in Fortescue's inns of chancery, "in tracing out the originals and as it were the elements of the law." For if, as Justinian has observed, the tender understanding of the student be loaded at the first with a multitude and variety of matter, it will either occasion him to desert his studies, or will carry him heavily through them, with much labour, delay, and despondence. These originals should be traced to their fountains, as well as our distance will permit; to the customs of the Britons and Germans, as recorded by Caesar and Tacitus; to the codes of the northern nations on the continent, and more especially to those of our own Saxon princes; to the rules of the Roman law, either left here in the days of Papinian, or imported by Vacarius and his followers; but, above all, to that inexhaustible reservoir of legal antiquities and learning, the feodal law, or, as Spelmanhas entitled it, the law of nations in our western orb. These primary rules and fundamental principles should be weighed and compared with the precepts of the law of nature, and the practice of other countries; should be explained by reasons, illustrated by examples, and confirmed by undoubted authorities; their history should be deduced, their changes and revolutions observed, and it should be shewn how far they are connected with, or have at any time been affected by, the civil transactions of the kingdom.

A P L A N of this nature, if executed with care and ability, cannot fail of administring a most useful and rational entertainment to students of all ranks and professions; and yet it must be confessed that the study of the laws is not merely a matter of amusement: for as a very judicious writer has observed upon a similar occasion, the learner "will be considerably disappointed if he looks for entertainment without the expence of attention." An attention, however, not greater than is usually bestowed in mastering the rudiments of other sciences, or sometimes in pursuing a favorite recreation or exercise. And this attention is not equally necessary to be exerted by every student upon every occasion. Some branches of the law, as the formal process of civil suits, and the subtile distinctions incident to landed property, which are the most difficult to be thoroughly understood, are the least worth the pains of understanding, except to such gentlemen as intend to pursue the profession. To others I may venture to apply, with a slight alteration, the words of sir John Fortescue, when first his royal pupil determines to engage in this study. "It will not be necessary for a gentleman, as such, to examine with a close application the critical niceties of the law. It will fully be sufficient, and he may well enough be denominated a lawyer, if under the instruction of a master he traces up the principles and grounds of the law, even to their original elements. Therefore in a very short period, and with very little labour, he may be sufficiently informed in the laws of his country, if he will but apply his mind in good earnest to receive and apprehend them. For, though such knowlege as is necessary for a judge is hardly to be acquired by the lucubrations of twenty years, yet with a genius of tolerable perspicacity, that knowlege which is fit for a person of birth or condition may be learned in a single year, without neglecting his other improvements."

TO the few therefore (the very few, I am persuaded,) that entertain such unworthy notions of an university, as to suppose it intended for mere dissipation of thought; to such as mean only to while away the aukward interval from childhood to twenty one, between the restraints of the school and the licentiousness of politer life, in a calm middle state of mental and of moral inactivity; to these Mr Viner gives no invitation to an entertainment which they never can relish. But to the long and illustrious train of noble and ingenuous youth, who are not more distinguished among us by their birth and possessions, than by the regularity of their conduct and their thirst after useful knowlege, to these our benefactor has consecrated the fruits of a long and laborious life, worn out in the duties of his calling; and will joyfully reflect (if such reflexions can be now the employment of his thoughts) that he could not more effectually have benefited posterity, or contributed to the service of the public, than by founding an institution which may instruct the rising generation in the wisdom of our civil polity, and inform them with a desire to be still better acquainted with the laws and constitution of their country.

SECTION THE SECOND.

OF THE NATURE OF LAWS IN GENERAL.

LAW, in it's most general and comprehensive sense, signifies a rule of action; and is applied indiscriminately to all kinds of action, whether animate, or inanimate, rational or irrational. Thus we say, the laws of motion, of gravitation, of optics, or mechanics, as well as the laws of nature and of nations. And it is that rule of action, which is prescribed by some superior, and which the inferior is bound to obey.

THUS when the supreme being formed the universe, and created matter out of nothing, he impressed certain principles upon that matter, from which it can never depart, and without which it would cease to be. When he put that matter into motion, he established certain laws of motion, to which all moveable bodies must conform. And, to descend from the greatest operations to the smallest, when a workman forms a clock, or other piece of mechanism, he establishes at his own pleasure certain arbitrary laws for it's direction; as that the hand shall describe a given space in a given time; to which law as long as the work conforms, so long it continues in perfection, and answers the end of it's formation.

IF we farther advance, from mere inactive matter to vegetable and animal life, we shall find them still governed by laws; more numerous indeed, but equally fixed and invariable. The whole progres of plants, from the seed to the root, and from thence to the seed again;—the method of animal nutrition, digestion, secretion, and all other branches of vital oeconomy;— are not left to chance, or the will of the creature itself, but are performed in a wondrous involuntary manner, and guided by unerring rules laid down by the great creator.

THIS then is the general signification of law, a rule of action dictated by some superior being; and in those creatures that have neither the power to think, nor to will, such laws must be invariably obeyed, so long as the creature itself subsists, for it's existence depends on that obedience. But laws, in their more confined sense, and in which it is our present business to consider them, denote the rules, not of action in general, but of *human* action or conduct: that is, the precepts by which man, the noblest of all sublunary beings, a creature endowed with both reason and freewill, is commanded to make use of those faculties in the general regulation of his behaviour.

MAN, considered as a creature, must necessarily be subject to the laws of his creator, for he is entirely a dependent being. A being, independent of any other, has no rule to pursue, but such as he prescribes to himself; but a state of dependance will inevitably oblige the inferior to take the will of him, on whom he depends, as the rule of his conduct: not indeed in every particular, but in all those points wherein his dependance consists. This principle therefore has more or less extent and effect, in proportion as the superiority of the one and the dependance of the other is greater or less, absolute or limited. And consequently as man depends absolutely upon his maker for every thing, it is necessary that he should in all points conform to his maker's will.

THIS will of his maker is called the law of nature. For as God, when he created matter, and endued it with a principle of mobility, established certain rules for the perpetual direction of that motion; so, when he created man, and endued him with freewill to conduct himself in all parts of life, he laid down certain immutable laws of human nature, whereby that freewill is in some degree regulated and restrained, and gave him also the faculty of reason to discover the purport of those laws.

CONSIDERING the creator only as a being of infinite *power*, he was able unquestionably to have prescribed whatever laws he pleased to his creature, man, however unjust or severe. But as he is also a being of infinite *wisdom*, he has laid down only such laws as were founded in those relations of justice, that existed in the nature of things antecedent to any positive precept. These are the eternal, immutable laws of good and evil, to which the creator himself in all his dispensations conforms; and which he has enabled human reason to discover, so far as they are necessary for the conduct of human actions. Such among others are these principles: that we should live honestly, should hurt nobody, and should render to every one it's due; to which three general precepts Justinian has reduced the whole doctrine of law.

BUT if the discovery of these first principles of the law of nature depended only upon the due exertion of right reason, and could not otherwise be attained than by a chain of metaphysical disquisitions, mankind would have wanted some inducement to have quickened their inquiries, and the greater part of the world would have rested content in mental indolence, and ignorance it's inseparable companion. As therefore the creator is a being, not only of infinite *power*, and *wisdom*, but also of infinite *goodness*, he has been pleased so to contrive the constitution and frame of humanity, that we should want no other prompter to enquire after and pursue the rule of right, but only our own self-love, that universal principle of action. For he has so intimately connected, so inseparably interwoven the laws of eternal justice with the happiness of each individual, that the latter cannot be attained but by observing the former; and, if the former be punctually obeyed, it cannot but induce the latter. In consequence of which mutual connection of justice and human felicity, he has not perplexed the law of nature with a multitude of abstracted rules and precepts, referring merely to the fitness or unfitness of things, as some have vainly surmised; but has graciously reduced the rule of obedience to this one paternal precept, "that man should pursue his own happiness." This is the foundation of what we call ethics, or natural law. For the several articles into which it is branched in our systems, amount to no more than demonstrating, that this or that action tends to man's real happiness, and therefore very justly concluding that the performance of it is a part of the law of nature; or, on the other hand, that this or that action is destructive of man's real happiness, and therefore that the law of nature forbids it.

THIS law of nature, being co-eval with mankind and dictated by God himself, is of course superior in obligation to any other. It is binding over all the globe, in all countries, and at all times: no human laws are of any validity, if contrary to this; and such of them as are valid derive all their force, and all their authority, mediately or immediately, from this original.

BUT in order to apply this to the particular exigencies of each individual, it is still necessary to have recourse to reason; whose office it is to discover, as was before observed, what the law of nature directs in every circumstance of life; by considering, what method will tend the most effectually to our own substantial happiness. And if our reason were always, as in our first ancestor before his transgression, clear and perfect, unruffled by passions, unclouded by prejudice, unimpaired by disease or intemperance, the task would be pleasant and easy; we should need no other guide but this. But every man now finds the contrary in his own experience; that his reason is corrupt, and his understanding full of ignorance and error.

T H I S has given manifold occasion for the benign interposition of divine providence; which, in companion to the frailty, the imperfection, and the blindness of human reason, hath been pleased, at sundry times and in divers manners, to discover and enforce it's laws by an immediate and direct revelation. The doctrines thus delivered we call the revealed or divine law, and they are to be found only in the holy scriptures. These precepts, when revealed, are found upon comparison to be really a part of the original law of nature, as they tend in all their consequences to man's felicity. But we are not from thence to conclude that the knowlege of these truths was attainable by reason, in it's present corrupted state; since we find that, until they were revealed, they were hid from the wisdom of ages. As then the moral precepts of this law are indeed of the same original with those of the law of nature, so their intrinsic obligation is of equal strength and perpetuity. Yet undoubtedly the revealed law is (humanly speaking) of infinitely more authority than what we generally call the natural law. Because one is the law of nature, expressly declared so to be by God himself; the other is only what, by the assistance of human reason, we imagine to be that law. If we could be as certain of the latter as we are of the former, both would have an equal authority; but, till then, they can never be put in any competition together.

U P O N these two foundations, the law of nature and the law of revelation, depend all human laws; that is to say, no human laws should be suffered to contradict these. There is, it is true, a great number of indifferent points, in which both the divine law and the natural leave a man at his own liberty; but which are found necessary for the benefit of society to be restrained within certain limits. And herein it is that human laws have their greatest force and efficacy; for, with regard to such points as are not indifferent, human laws are only declaratory of, and act in subordination to, the former. To instance in the case of murder: this is expressly forbidden by the divine, and demonstrably by the natural law; and from these prohibitions arises the true unlawfulness of this crime. Those human laws, that annex a punishment to it, do not at all increase it's moral guilt, or superadd any fresh obligation *in foro conscientiae* to abstain from it's perpetration. Nay, if any human law should allow or injoin us to commit it, we are bound to transgress that human law, or else we must offend both the natural and the divine. But with regard to matters that are in themselves indifferent, and are not commanded or forbidden by those superior laws; such, for instance, as exporting of wool into foreign countries; here the inferior legislature has scope and opportunity to interpose, and to make that action unlawful which before was not so.

IF man were to live in a state of nature, unconnected with other individuals, there would be no occasion for any other laws, than the law of nature, and the law of God. Neither could any other law possibly exist; for a law always supposes some superior who is to make it; and in a state of nature we are all equal, without any other superior but him who is the author of our being. But man was formed for society; and, as is demonstrated by the writers on this subject, is neither capable of living alone, nor indeed has the courage to do it. However, as it is impossible for the whole race of mankind to be united in one great society, they must necessarily divide into many; and form separate states, commonwealths, and nations; entirely independent of each other, and yet liable to a mutual intercourse. Hence arises a third kind of law to regulate this mutual intercourse, called "the law of nations;" which, as none of these states will acknowlege a superiority in the other, cannot be dictated by either; but depends entirely upon the rules of natural law, or upon mutual compacts, treaties, leagues, and agreements between these several communities: in the construction also of which compacts we have no other rule to resort to, but the law of nature; being the only one to which both communities are equally subject: and therefore the civil law very justly observes, that *quod naturalis ratio inter omnes homines constituit, vocatur jus gentium.*

THUS much I thought it necessary to premise concerning the law of nature, the revealed law, and the law of nations, before I proceeded to treat more fully of the principal subject of this section, municipal or civil law; that is, the rule by which particular districts, communities, or nations are governed; being thus defined by Justinian, "*jus civile est quod quisque sibi populus constituit.*" I call it *municipal* law, in compliance with common speech; for, tho' strictly that expression denotes the particular customs of one single *municipium* or free town, yet it may with sufficient propriety be applied to any one state or nation, which is governed by the same laws and customs.

MUNICIPAL law, thus understood, is properly defined to be "a rule of civil conduct prescribed by the supreme power in a state, commanding what is right and prohibiting what is wrong." Let us endeavour to explain it's several properties, as they arise out of this definition.

AND, first, it is a *rule*; not a transient sudden order from a superior to or concerning a particular person; but something permanent, uniform, and universal. Therefore a particular act of the legislature to confiscate the goods of Titius, or to attaint him of high treason, does not enter into the idea of a municipal law: for the operation of this act is spent upon Titius only, and has no relation to the community in general; it is rather a sentence than a law. But an act to declare that the crime of which Titius is accused shall be deemed high treason; this has permanency, uniformity, and universality, and therefore is properly a *rule*. It is also called a *rule*, to distinguish it from *advice* or *counsel*, which we are at liberty to follow or not, as we see proper; and to judge upon the reasonableness or unreasonableness of the thing advised. Whereas our obedience to the *law* depends not upon *our approbation*, but upon the *maker's will.* Counsel is only matter of persuasion, law is matter of injunction; counsel acts only upon the willing, law upon the unwilling also.

I T is also called a *rule*, to distinguish it from a *compact* or *agreement*; for a compact is a promise proceeding *from* us, law is a command directed *to* us. The language of a compact is, "I will, or will not, do this;" that of a law is, "thou shalt, or shalt not, do it." It is true there is an obligation which a compact carries with it, equal in point of conscience to that of a law; but then the original of the obligation is different. In compacts, we ourselves determine and promise what shall be done, before we are obliged to do it; in laws, we are obliged to act, without ourselves determining or promising any thing at all. Upon these accounts law is defined to be "*a rule.*"

M U N I C I P A L law is also "a rule *of civil conduct.*" This distinguishes municipal law from the natural, or revealed; the former of which is the rule of *moral* conduct, and the latter not only the rule of moral conduct, but also the rule of faith. These regard man as a creature, and point out his duty to God, to himself, and to his neighbour, considered in the light of an individual. But municipal or civil law regards him also as a citizen, and bound to other duties towards his neighbour, than those of mere nature and religion: duties, which he has engaged in by enjoying the benefits of the common union; and which amount to no more, than that he do contribute, on his part, to the subsistence and peace of the society.

I T is likewise "a rule *prescribed.*" Because a bare resolution, confined in the breast of the legislator, without manifesting itself by some external sign, can never be properly a law. It is requisite that this resolution be notified to the people who are to obey it. But the manner in which this notification is to be made, is matter of very great indifference. It may be notified by universal tradition and long practice, which supposes a previous publication, and is the case of the common law of England. It may be notified, *viva voce*, by officers appointed for that purpose, as is done with regard to proclamations, and such acts of parliament as are appointed to be publicly read in churches and other assemblies. It may lastly be notified by writing, printing, or the like; which is the general course taken with all our acts of parliament. Yet, whatever way is made use of, it is incumbent on the promulgators to do it in the most public and perspicuous manner; not like Caligula, who (according to Dio Cassius) wrote his laws in a very small character, and hung them up upon high pillars, the more effectually to ensnare the people. There is still a more unreasonable method than this, which is called making of laws *ex post facto*, when *after* an action is committed, the legislator then for the first time declares it to have been a crime, and inflicts a punishment upon the person who has committed it; here it is impossible that the party could foresee that an action, innocent when it was done, should be afterwards converted to guilt by a subsequent law; he had therefore no cause to abstain from it; and all punishment for not abstaining must of consequence be cruel and unjust. All laws should be therefore made to commence *in futuro*, and be notified before their commencement; which is implied in the term "*prescribed.*" But when this rule is in the usual manner notified, or prescribed, it is then the subject's business to be thoroughly acquainted therewith; for if ignorance, of what he *might* know, were admitted as a legitimate excuse, the laws would be of no effect, but might always be eluded with impunity.

B U T farther: municipal law is "a rule of civil conduct prescribed *by the supreme power in a state*." For legislature, as was before observed, is the greatest act of superiority that can be exercised by one being over another. Wherefore it is requisite to the very essence of a law, that it be made by the supreme power. Sovereignty and legislature are indeed convertible terms; one cannot subsist without the other.

T H I S will naturally lead us into a short enquiry concerning the nature of society and civil government; and the natural, inherent right that belongs to the sovereignty of a state, wherever that sovereignty be lodged, of making and enforcing laws.

T H E only true and natural foundations of society are the wants and the fears of individuals. Not that we can believe, with some theoretical writers, that there ever was a time when there was no such thing as society; and that, from the impulse of reason, and through a sense of their wants and weaknesses, individuals met together in a large plain, entered into an original contract, and chose the tallest man present to be their governor. This notion, of an actually existing unconnected state of nature, is too wild to be seriously admitted; and besides it is plainly contradictory to the revealed accounts of the primitive origin of mankind, and their preservation two thousand years afterwards; both which were effected by the means of single families. These formed the first society, among themselves; which every day extended it's limits, and when it grew too large to subsist with convenience in that pastoral state, wherein the patriarchs appear to have lived, it necessarily subdivided itself by various migrations into more. Afterwards, as agriculture increased, which employs and can maintain a much greater number of hands, migrations became less frequent; and various tribes, which had formerly separated, re-united again; sometimes by compulsion and conquest, sometimes by accident, and sometimes perhaps by compact. But though society had not it's formal beginning from any convention of individuals, actuated by their wants and their fears; yet it is the *sense* of their weakness and imperfection that *keeps* mankind together; that demonstrates the necessity of this union; and that therefore is the solid and natural foundation, as well as the cement, of society. And this is what we mean by the original contract of society; which, though perhaps in no instance it has ever been formally expressed at the first institution of a state, yet in nature and reason must always be understood and implied, in the very act of associating together: namely, that the whole should protect all it's parts, and that every part should pay obedience to the will of the whole; or, in other words, that the community should guard the rights of each individual member, and that (in return for this protection) each individual should submit to the laws of the community; without which submission of all it was impossible that protection could be certainly extended to any.

F O R when society is once formed, government results of course, as necessary to preserve and to keep that society in order. Unless some superior were constituted, whose commands and decisions all the members are bound to obey, they would still remain as in a state of nature, without any judge upon earth to define their several rights, and redress their several wrongs. But, as all the members of society are naturally equal, it may be asked, in whose hands are the reins of government to be entrusted? To this the general answer is easy; but the application of it to particular cases has occasioned one half of those mischiefs which are apt to proceed from misguided political zeal. In general, all mankind will agree that government should be reposed in such persons, in whom those qualities are most likely to be found, the perfection of which are among the attributes of him who is emphatically stiled the supreme being; the three grand requisites, I mean, of wisdom, of goodness, and of power: wisdom, to discern the real interest of the community; goodness, to endeavour always to pursue that real interest; and strength, or power, to carry this knowlege and intention into action. These are the natural foundations of sovereignty, and these are the requisites that ought to be found in every well constituted frame of government.

H O W the several forms of government we now see in the world at first actually began, is matter of great uncertainty, and has occasioned infinite disputes. It is not my business or intention to enter into any of them. However they began, or by what right soever they subsist, there is and must be in all of them a supreme, irresistible, absolute, uncontrolled authority, in which the *jura summi imperii*, or the rights of sovereignty, reside. And this authority is placed in those hands, wherein (according to the opinion of the founders of such respective states, either expressly given, or collected from their tacit approbation) the qualities requisite for supremacy, wisdom, goodness, and power, are the most likely to be found.

T H E political writers of antiquity will not allow more than three regular forms of government; the first, when the sovereign power is lodged in an aggregate assembly consisting of all the members of a community, which is called a democracy; the second, when it is lodged in a council, composed of select members, and then it is stiled an aristocracy; the last, when it is entrusted in the hands of a single person, and then it takes the name of a monarchy. All other species of government, they say, are either corruptions of, or reducible to, these three.

B Y the sovereign power, as was before observed, is meant the making of laws; for wherever that power resides, all others must conform to, and be directed by it, whatever appearance the outward form and administration of the government may put on. For it is at any time in the option of the legislature to alter that form and administration by a new edict or rule, and to put the execution of the laws into whatever hands it pleases: and all the other powers of the state must obey the legislative power in the execution of their several functions, or else the constitution is at an end.

I N a democracy, where the right of making laws resides in the people at large, public virtue, or goodness of intention, is more likely to be found, than either of the other qualities of government. Popular assemblies are frequently foolish in their contrivance, and weak in their execution; but generally mean to do the thing that is right and just, and have always a degree of patriotism or public spirit. In aristocracies there is more wisdom to be found, than in the other frames of government; being composed, or intended to be composed, of the most experienced citizens; but there is less honesty than in a republic, and less strength than in a monarchy. A monarchy is indeed the most powerful of any, all the sinews of government being knit together, and united in the hand of the prince; but then there is imminent danger of his employing that strength to improvident or oppressive purposes.

T H U S these three species of government have, all of them, their several perfections and imperfections. Democracies are usually the best calculated to direct the end of a law; aristocracies to invent the means by which that end shall be obtained; and monarchies to carry those means into execution. And the antients, as was observed, had in general no idea of any other permanent form of government but these three; for though Cicero declares himself of opinion, "*esse optime constitutam rempublicam, quae ex tribus generibus illis, regali, optimo, et populari, sit modice confusa*;" yet Tacitus treats this notion of a mixed government, formed out of them all, and partaking of the advantages of each, as a visionary whim; and one that, if effected, could never be lasting or secure.

B U T happily for us of this island, the British constitution has long remained, and I trust will long continue, a standing exception to the truth of this observation. For, as with us the executive power of the laws is lodged in a single person, they have all the advantages of strength and dispatch, that are to be found in the most absolute monarchy; and, as the legislature of the kingdom is entrusted to three distinct powers, entirely independent of each other; first, the king; secondly, the lords spiritual and temporal, which is an aristocratical assembly of persons selected for their piety, their birth, their wisdom, their valour, or their property; and, thirdly, the house of commons, freely chosen by the people from among themselves, which makes it a kind of democracy; as this aggregate body, actuated by different springs, and attentive to different interests, composes the British parliament, and has the supreme disposal of every thing; there can no inconvenience be attempted by either of the three branches, but will be withstood by one of the other two; each branch being armed with a negative power, sufficient to repel any innovation which it shall think inexpedient or dangerous.

H E R E then is lodged the sovereignty of the British constitution; and lodged as beneficially as is possible for society. For in no other shape could we be so certain of finding the three great qualities of government so well and so happily united. If the supreme power were lodged in any one of the three branches separately, we must be exposed to the inconveniences of either absolute monarchy, aristocracy, or democracy; and so want two of the three principal ingredients of good polity, either virtue, wisdom, or power. If it were lodged in any two of the branches; for instance, in the king and house of lords, our laws might be providently made, and well executed, but they might not always have the good of the people in view: if lodged in the king and commons, we should want that circumspection and mediatory caution, which the wisdom of the peers is to afford: if the supreme rights of legislature were lodged in the two houses only, and the king had no negative upon their proceedings, they might be tempted to encroach upon the royal prerogative, or perhaps to abolish the kingly office, and thereby weaken (if not totally destroy) the strength of the executive power. But the constitutional government of this island is so admirably tempered and compounded, that nothing can endanger or hurt it, but destroying the equilibrium of power between one branch of the legislature and the rest. For if ever it should happen that the independence of any one of the three should be lost, or that it should become subservient to the views of either of the other two, there would soon be an end of our constitution. The legislature would be changed from that, which was originally set up by the general consent and fundamental act of the society; and such a change, however effected, is according to Mr Locke (who perhaps carries his theory too far) at once an entire dissolution of the bands of government; and the people would be reduced to a state of anarchy, with liberty to constitute to themselves a new legislative power.

HAVING thus cursorily considered the three usual species of government, and our own singular constitution, selected and compounded from them all, I proceed to observe, that, as the power of making laws constitutes the supreme authority, so wherever the supreme authority in any state resides, it is the right of that authority to make laws; that is, in the words of our definition, *to prescribe the rule of civil action*. And this may be discovered from the very end and institution of civil states. For a state is a collective body, composed of a multitude of individuals, united for their safety and convenience, and intending to act together as one man. If it therefore is to act as one man, it ought to act by one uniform will. But, inasmuch as political communities are made up of many natural persons, each of whom has his particular will and inclination, these several wills cannot by any *natural* union be joined together, or tempered and disposed into a lasting harmony, so as to constitute and produce that one uniform will of the whole. It can therefore be no otherwise produced than by a *political* union; by the consent of all persons to submit their own private wills to the will of one man, or of one or more assemblies of men, to whom the supreme authority is entrusted: and this will of that one man, or assemblage of men, is in different states, according to their different constitutions, understood to be *law*.

THUS far as to the *right* of the supreme power to make laws; but farther, it is it's *duty* likewise. For since the respective members are bound to conform themselves to the will of the state, it is expedient that they receive directions from the state declaratory of that it's will. But since it is impossible, in so great a multitude, to give injunctions to every particular man, relative to each particular action, therefore the state establishes general rules, for the perpetual information and direction of all persons in all points, whether of positive or negative duty. And this, in order that every man may know what to look upon as his own, what as another's; what absolute and what relative duties are required at his hands; what is to be esteemed honest, dishonest, or indifferent; what degree every man retains of his natural liberty; what he has given up as the price of the benefits of society; and after what manner each person is to moderate the use and exercise of those rights which the state assigns him, in order to promote and secure the public tranquillity.

F R O M what has been advanced, the truth of the former branch of our definition, is (I trust) sufficiently evident; that "*municipal law is a rule of civil conduct prescribed by the supreme power in a state.*" I proceed now to the latter branch of it; that it is a rule so prescribed, "*commanding what is right, and prohibiting what is wrong.*"

N O W in order to do this completely, it is first of all necessary that the boundaries of right and wrong be established and ascertained by law. And when this is once done, it will follow of course that it is likewise the business of the law, considered as a rule of civil conduct, to enforce these rights and to restrain or redress these wrongs. It remains therefore only to consider in what manner the law is said to ascertain the boundaries of right and wrong; and the methods which it takes to command the one and prohibit the other.

F O R this purpose every law may be said to consist of several parts: one, *declaratory*, whereby the rights to be observed, and the wrongs to be eschewed, are clearly defined and laid down: another, *directory*, whereby the subject is instructed and enjoined to observe those rights, and to abstain from the commission of those wrongs: a third, *remedial*, whereby a method is pointed out to recover a man's private rights, or redress his private wrongs: to which may be added a fourth, usually termed the *sanction*, or *vindicatory* branch of the law; whereby it is signified what evil or penalty shall be incurred by such as commit any public wrongs, and transgress or neglect their duty.

W I T H regard to the first of these, the *declaratory* part of the municipal law, this depends not so much upon the law of revelation or of nature, as upon the wisdom and will of the legislator. This doctrine, which before was slightly touched, deserves a more particular explication. Those rights then which God and nature have established, and are therefore called natural rights, such as are life and liberty, need not the aid of human laws to be more effectually invested in every man than they are; neither do they receive any additional strength when declared by the municipal laws to be inviolable. On the contrary, no human legislature has power to abridge or destroy them, unless the owner shall himself commit some act that amounts to a forfeiture. Neither do divine or natural *duties* (such as, for instance, the worship of God, the maintenance of children, and the like) receive any stronger sanction from being also declared to be duties by the law of the land. The case is the same as to crimes and misdemesnors, that are forbidden by the superior laws, and therefore stiled *mala in se*, such as murder, theft, and perjury; which contract no additional turpitude from being declared unlawful by the inferior legislature. For that legislature in all these cases acts only, as was before observed, in subordination to the great lawgiver, transcribing and publishing his precepts. So that, upon the whole, the declaratory part of the municipal law has no force or operation at all, with regard to actions that are naturally and intrinsically right or wrong.

BUT with regard to things in themselves indifferent, the case is entirely altered. These become either right or wrong, just or unjust, duties or misdemesnors, according as the municipal legislator sees proper, for promoting the welfare of the society, and more effectually carrying on the purposes of civil life. Thus our own common law has declared, that the goods of the wife do instantly upon marriage become the property and right of the husband; and our statute law has declared all monopolies a public offence: yet that right, and this offence, have no foundation in nature; but are merely created by the law, for the purposes of civil society. And sometimes, where the thing itself has it's rise from the law of nature, the particular circumstances and mode of doing it become right or wrong, as the laws of the land shall direct. Thus, for instance, in civil duties; obedience to superiors is the doctrine of revealed as well as natural religion: but who those superiors shall be, and in what circumstances, or to what degrees they shall be obeyed, is the province of human laws to determine. And so, as to injuries or crimes, it must be left to our own legislature to decide, in what cases the seising another's cattle shall amount to the crime of robbery; and where it shall be a justifiable action, as when a landlord takes them by way of distress for rent.

THUS much for the *declaratory* part of the municipal law: and the *directory* stands much upon the same footing; for this virtually includes the former, the declaration being usually collected from the direction. The law that says, "thou shalt not steal," implies a declaration that stealing is a crime. And we have seen that, in things naturally indifferent, the very essence of right and wrong depends upon the direction of the laws to do or to omit it.

THE *remedial* part of a law is so necessary a consequence of the former two, that laws must be very vague and imperfect without it. For in vain would rights be declared, in vain directed to be observed, if there were no method of recovering and asserting those rights, when wrongfully withheld or invaded. This is what we mean properly, when we speak of the protection of the law. When, for instance, the *declaratory* part of the law has said "that the field or inheritance, which belonged to Titius's father, is vested by his death in Titius;" and the *directory* part has "forbidden any one to enter on another's property without the leave of the owner;" if Gaius after this will presume to take possession of the land, the *remedial* part of the law will then interpose it's office; will make Gaius restore the possession to Titius, and also pay him damages for the invasion.

WITH regard to the *sanction* of laws, or the evil that may attend the breach of public duties; it is observed, that human legislators have for the most part chosen to make the sanction of their laws rather *vindicatory* than *remuneratory*, or to consist rather in punishments, than in actual particular rewards. Because, in the first place, the quiet enjoyment and protection of all our civil rights and liberties, which are the sure and general consequence of obedience to the municipal law, are in themselves the best and most valuable of all rewards. Because also, were the exercise of every virtue to be enforced by the proposal of particular rewards, it were impossible for any state to furnish stock enough for so profuse a bounty. And farther, because the dread of evil is a much more forcible principle of human actions than the prospect of good. For which reasons, though a prudent bestowing of rewards is sometimes of exquisite use, yet we find that those civil laws, which enforce and enjoin our duty, do seldom, if ever, propose any privilege or gift to such as obey the law; but do constantly come armed with a penalty denounced against transgressors, either expressly defining the nature and quantity of the punishment, or else leaving it to the discretion of the judges, and those who are entrusted with the care of putting the laws in execution.

O F all the parts of a law the most effectual is the *vindicatory*. For it is but lost labour to say, "do this, or avoid that," unless we also declare, "this shall be the consequence of your noncompliance." We must therefore observe, that the main strength and force of a law consists in the penalty annexed to it. Herein is to be found the principal obligation of human laws.

L E G I S L A T O R S and their laws are said to *compel* and *oblige*; not that by any natural violence they so constrain a man, as to render it impossible for him to act otherwise than as they direct, which is the strict sense of obligation: but because, by declaring and exhibiting a penalty against offenders, they bring it to pass that no man can easily choose to transgress the law; since, by reason of the impending correction, compliance is in a high degree preferable to disobedience. And, even where rewards are proposed as well as punishments threatened, the obligation of the law seems chiefly to consist in the penalty: for rewards, in their nature, can only *persuade* and *allure*; nothing is *compulsory* but punishment.

I T is held, it is true, and very justly, by the principal of our ethical writers, that human laws are binding upon mens consciences. But if that were the only, or most forcible obligation, the good only would regard the laws, and the bad would set them at defiance. And, true as this principle is, it must still be understood with some restriction. It holds, I apprehend, as to *rights*; and that, when the law has determined the field to belong to Titius, it is matter of conscience no longer to withhold or to invade it. So also in regard to *natural duties*, and such offences as are *mala in se*: here we are bound in conscience, because we are bound by superior laws, before those human laws were in being, to perform the one and abstain from the other. But in relation to those laws which enjoin only *positive duties*, and forbid only such things as are not *mala in se* but *mala prohibita* merely, annexing a penalty to noncompliance, here I apprehend conscience is no farther concerned, than by directing a submission to the penalty, in case of our breach of those laws: for otherwise the multitude of penal laws in a state would not only be looked upon as an impolitic, but would also be a very wicked thing; if every such law were a snare for the conscience of the subject. But in these cases the alternative is offered to every man; "either abstain from this, or submit to such a penalty;" and his conscience will be clear, whichever side of the alternative he thinks proper to embrace. Thus, by the statutes for preserving the game, a penalty is denounced against every unqualified person that kills a hare. Now this prohibitory law does not make the transgression a moral offence: the only obligation in conscience is to submit to the penalty if levied.

I HAVE now gone through the definition laid down of a municipal law; and have shewn that it is "a rule—of civil conduct—prescribed—by the supreme power in a state—commanding what is right, and prohibiting what is wrong:" in the explication of which I have endeavoured to interweave a few useful principles, concerning the nature of civil government, and the obligation of human laws. Before I conclude this section, it may not be amiss to add a few observations concerning the *interpretation* of laws.

W H E N any doubt arose upon the construction of the Roman laws, the usage was to state the case to the emperor in writing, and take his opinion upon it. This was certainly a bad method of interpretation. To interrogate the legislature to decide particular disputes, is not only endless, but affords great room for partiality and oppression. The answers of the emperor were called his rescripts, and these had in succeeding cases the force of perpetual laws; though they ought to be carefully distinguished, by every rational civilian, from those general constitutions, which had only the nature of things for their guide. The emperor Macrinus, as his historian Capitolinus informs us, had once resolved to abolish these rescripts, and retain only the general edicts; he could not bear that the hasty and crude answers of such princes as Commodus and Caracalla should be reverenced as laws. But Justinian thought otherwise, and he has preserved them all. In like manner the canon laws, or decretal epistles of the popes, are all of them rescripts in the strictest sense. Contrary to all true forms of reasoning, they argue from particulars to generals.

T H E fairest and most rational method to interpret the will of the legislator, is by exploring his intentions at the time when the law was made, by *signs* the most natural and probable. And these signs are either the words, the context, the subject matter, the effects and consequence, or the spirit and reason of the law. Let us take a short view of them all.

I. W O R D S are generally to be understood in their usual and most known signification; not so much regarding the propriety of grammar, as their general and popular use. Thus the law mentioned by Puffendorf, which forbad a layman to *lay hands* on a priest, was adjudged to extend to him, who had hurt a priest with a weapon. Again; terms of art, or technical terms, must be taken according to the acceptation of the learned in each art, trade, and science. So in the act of settlement, where the crown of England is limited "to the princess Sophia, and the heirs of her body, being protestants," it becomes necessary to call in the assistance of lawyers, to ascertain the precise idea of the words "*heirs of her body*," which in a legal sense comprize only certain of her lineal descendants. Lastly, where words are clearly *repugnant* in two laws, the later law takes place of the elder: *leges posteriores priores contrarias abrogant* is a maxim of universal law, as well as of our own constitutions. And accordingly it was laid down by a law of the twelve tables at Rome, *quod populus postremum jussit, id jus ratum esto.*

L. of N. and N. 5. 12. 3.

2. I F words happen to be still dubious, we may establish their meaning from the context; with which it may be of singular use to compare a word, or a sentence, whenever they are ambiguous, equivocal, or intricate. Thus the proeme, or preamble, is often called in to help the construction of an act of parliament. Of the same nature and use is the comparison of a law with other laws, that are made by the same legislator, that have some affinity with the subject, or that expressly relate to the same point. Thus, when the law of England declares murder to be felony without benefit of clergy, we must resort to the same law of England to learn what the benefit of clergy is: and, when the common law censures simoniacal contracts, it affords great light to the subject to consider what the canon law has adjudged to be simony.

3. A S to the subject matter, words are always to be understood as having a regard thereto; for that is always supposed to be in the eye of the legislator, and all his expressions directed to that end. Thus, when a law of our Edward III. forbids all ecclesiastical persons to purchase *provisions* at Rome, it might seem to prohibit the buying of grain and other victual; but when we consider that the statute was made to repress the usurpations of the papal see, and that the nominations to vacant benefices by the pope were called *provisions*, we shall see that the restraint is intended to be laid upon such provisions only.

4. A S to the effects and consequence, the rule is, where words bear either none, or a very absurd signification, if literally understood, we must a little deviate from the received sense of them. Therefore the Bolognian law, mentioned by Puffendorf, which enacted "that whoever drew blood in the streets should be punished with the utmost severity," was held after long debate not to extend to the surgeon, who opened the vein of a person that fell down in the street with a fit.

5. B U T , lastly, the most universal and effectual way of discovering the true meaning of a law, when the words are dubious, is by considering the reason and spirit of it; or the cause which moved the legislator to enact it. For when this reason ceases, the law itself ought likewise to cease with it. An instance of this is given in a case put by Cicero, or whoever was the author of the rhetorical treatise inscribed to Herennius. There was a law, that those who in a storm forsook the ship should forfeit all property therein; and the ship and lading should belong entirely to those who staid in it. In a dangerous tempest all the mariners forsook the ship, except only one sick passenger, who by reason of his disease was unable to get out and escape. By chance the ship came safe to port. The sick man kept possession and claimed the benefit of the law. Now here all the learned agree, that the sick man is not within the reason of the law; for the reason of making it was, to give encouragement to such as should venture their lives to save the vessel: but this is a merit, which he could never pretend to, who neither staid in the ship upon that account, nor contributed any thing to it's preservation.

F R O M this method of interpreting laws, by the reason of them, arises what we call *equity*; which is thus defined by Grotius, "the correction of that, wherein the law (by reason of its universality) is deficient." For since in laws all cases cannot be foreseen or expressed, it is necessary, that when the general decrees of the law come to be applied to particular cases, there should be somewhere a power vested of excepting those circumstances, which (had they been foreseen) the legislator himself would have excepted. And these are the cases, which, as Grotius expresses it, "*lex non exacte definit, sed arbitrio boni viri permittit.*"

EQUITY thus depending, essentially, upon the particular circumstances of each individual case, there can be no established rules and fixed precepts of equity laid down, without destroying it's very essence, and reducing it to a positive law. And, on the other hand, the liberty of considering all cases in an equitable light must not be indulged too far, lest thereby we destroy all law, and leave the decision of every question entirely in the breast of the judge. And law, without equity, tho' hard and disagreeable, is much more desirable for the public good, than equity without law; which would make every judge a legislator, and introduce most infinite confusion; as there would then be almost as many different rules of action laid down in our courts, as there are differences of capacity and sentiment in the human mind.

SECTION THE THIRD.

OF THE LAWS OF ENGLAND.

THE municipal law of England, or the rule of civil conduct prescribed to the inhabitants of this kingdom, may with sufficient propriety be divided into two kinds; the *lex non scripta*, the unwritten, or common law; and the *lex scripta*, the written, or statute law.

THE *lex non scripta*, or unwritten law, includes not only *general customs*, or the common law properly so called; but also the *particular customs* of certain parts of the kingdom; and likewise those *particular laws*, that are by custom observed only in certain courts and jurisdictions.

WHEN I call these parts of our law *leges non scriptae*, I would not be understood as if all those laws were at present merely *oral*, or communicated from the former ages to the present solely by word of mouth. It is true indeed that, in the profound ignorance of letters which formerly overspread the whole western world, all laws were intirely traditional, for this plain reason, that the nations among which they prevailed had but little idea of writing. Thus the British as well as the Gallic druids committed all their laws as well as learning to memory; and it is said of the primitive Saxons here, as well as their brethren on the continent, that *leges sola memoria et usu retinebant*. But with us at present the monuments and evidences of our legal customs are contained in the records of the several courts of justice, in books of reports and judicial decisions, and in the treatises of learned sages of the profession, preserved and handed down to us from the times of highest antiquity. However I therefore stile these parts of our law *leges non scriptae*, because their original institution and authority are not set down in writing, as acts of parliament are, but they receive their binding power, and the force of laws, by long and immemorial usage, and by their universal reception throughout the kingdom. In like manner as Aulus Gellius defines the *jus non scriptum* to be that, which is "*tacito et illiterato hominum consensu et moribus expressum*."

O U R antient lawyers, and particularly Fortescue, insist with abundance of warmth, that these customs are as old as the primitive Britons, and continued down, through the several mutations of government and inhabitants, to the present time, unchanged and unadulterated. This may be the case as to some; but in general, as Mr Selden in his notes observes, this assertion must be understood with many grains of allowance; and ought only to signify, as the truth seems to be, that there never was any formal exchange of one system of laws for another: though doubtless by the intermixture of adventitious nations, the Romans, the Picts, the Saxons, the Danes, and the Normans, they must have insensibly introduced and incorporated many of their own customs with those that were before established: thereby in all probability improving the texture and wisdom of the whole, by the accumulated wisdom of divers particular countries. Our laws, saith lord Bacon, are mixed as our language: and as our language is so much the richer, the laws are the more complete.

A N D indeed our antiquarians and first historians do all positively assure us, that our body of laws is of this compounded nature. For they tell us, that in the time of Alfred the local customs of the several provinces of the kingdom were grown so various, that he found it expedient to compile his *dome-book* or *liber judicialis*, for the general use of the whole kingdom. This book is said to have been extant so late as the reign of king Edward the fourth, but is now unfortunately lost. It contained, we may probably suppose, the principal maxims of the common law, the penalties for misdemesnors, and the forms of judicial proceedings. Thus much may at least be collected from that injunction to observe it, which we find in the laws of king Edward the elder, the son of Alfred. "*Omnibus qui reipublicae praesunt, etiam atque etiam mando, ut omnibus aequos se praebeant judices, perinde ac in judiciali libro* (*Saxonice,*) *scriptum habetur; nec quicquam formident quin jus commune* (*Saxonice,*) *audacter libereque dicant*."

B U T the irruption and establishment of the Danes in England which followed soon after, introduced new customs and caused this code of Alfred in many provinces to fall into disuse; or at least to be mixed and debased with other laws of a coarser alloy. So that about the beginning of the eleventh century there were three principal systems of laws prevailing in different districts. 1. The *Mercen-Lage*, or Mercian laws, which were observed in many of the midland counties, and those bordering on the principality of Wales; the retreat of the antient Britons; and therefore very probably intermixed with the British or Druidical customs. 2. The *West-Saxon-Lage*, or laws of the west Saxons, which obtained in the counties to the south and west of the island, from Kent to Devonshire. These were probably much the same with the laws of Alfred abovementioned, being the municipal law of the far most considerable part of his dominions, and particularly including Berkshire, the seat of his peculiar residence. 3. The *Dane-Lage*, or Danish law, the very name of which speaks it's original and composition. This was principally maintained in the rest of the midland counties, and also on the eastern coast, the seat of that piratical people. As for the very northern provinces, they were at that time under a distinct government.

O U T of these three laws, Roger Hoveden and Ranulphus Cestrensis inform us, king Edward the confessor extracted one uniform law or digest of laws, to be observed throughout the whole kingdom; though Hoveden and the author of an old manuscript chronicleassure us likewise, that this work was projected and begun by his grandfather king Edgar. And indeed a general digest of the same nature has been constantly found expedient, and therefore put in practice by other great nations, formed from an assemblage of little provinces, governed by peculiar customs. As in Portugal, under king Edward, about the beginning of the fifteenth century. In Spain under Alonzo X, who about the year 1250 executed the plan of his father St. Ferdinand, and collected all the provincial customs into one uniform law, in the celebrated code entitled *las partidas*. And in Sweden about the same aera, a universal body of common law was compiled out of the particular customs established by the laghman of every province, and intitled the *land's lagh*, being analogous to the*common law* of England.

B O T H these undertakings, of king Edgar and Edward the confessor, seem to have been no more than a new edition, or fresh promulgation, of Alfred's code or dome-book, with such additions and improvements as the experience of a century and an half had suggested. For Alfred is generally stiled by the same historians the *legum Anglicanarum conditor*, as Edward the confessor is the*restitutor*. These however are the laws which our histories so often mention under the name of the laws of Edward the confessor; which our ancestors struggled so hardly to maintain, under the first princes of the Norman line; and which subsequent princes so frequently promised to keep and to restore, as the most popular act they could do, when pressed by foreign emergencies or domestic discontents. These are the laws, that so vigorously withstood the repeated attacks of the civil law; which established in the twelfth century a new Roman empire over most of the states on the continent: states that have lost, and perhaps upon that account, their political liberties; while the free constitution of England, perhaps upon the same account, has been rather improved than debased. These, in short, are the laws which gave rise and original to that collection of maxims and customs, which is now known by the name of the common law. A name either given to it, in contradistinction to other laws, as the statute law, the civil law, the law merchant, and the like; or, more probably, as a law *common* to all the realm, the *jus commune* or *folcright* mentioned by king Edward the elder, after the abolition of the several provincial customs and particular laws beforementioned.

B U T though this is the most likely foundation of this collection of maxims and customs, yet the maxims and customs, so collected, are of higher antiquity than memory or history can reach: nothing being more difficult than to ascertain the precise beginning and first spring of an antient and long established custom. Whence it is that in our law the goodness of a custom depends upon it's having been used time out of mind; or, in the solemnity of our legal phrase, time whereof the memory of man runneth not to the contrary. This it is that gives it it's weight and authority; and of this nature are the maxims and customs which compose the common law, or *lex non scripta*, of this kingdom.

T H I S unwritten, or common, law is properly distinguishable into three kinds: 1. General customs; which are the universal rule of the whole kingdom, and form the common law, in it's stricter and more usual signification. 2. Particular customs; which for the most part affect only the inhabitants of particular districts. 3. Certain particular laws; which by custom are adopted and used by some particular courts, of pretty general and extensive jurisdiction.

I. A S to general customs, or the common law, properly so called; this is that law, by which proceedings and determinations in the king's ordinary courts of justice are guided and directed. This, for the most part, settles the course in which lands descend by inheritance; the manner and form of acquiring and transferring property; the solemnities and obligation of contracts; the rules of expounding wills, deeds, and acts of parliament; the respective remedies of civil injuries; the several species of temporal offences, with the manner and degree of punishment; and an infinite number of minuter particulars, which diffuse themselves as extensively as the ordinary distribution of common justice requires. Thus, for example, that there shall be four superior courts of record, the chancery, the king's bench, the common pleas, and the exchequer;—that the eldest son alone is heir to his ancestor;—that property may be acquired and transferred by writing;—that a deed is of no validity unless sealed;—that wills shall be construed more favorably, and deeds more strictly;—that money lent upon bond is recoverable by action of debt;—that breaking the public peace is an offence, and punishable by fine and imprisonment;—all these are doctrines that are not set down in any written statute or ordinance, but depend merely upon immemorial usage, that is, upon common law, for their support.

S O M E have divided the common law into two principal grounds or foundations: 1. established customs; such as that where there are three brothers, the eldest brother shall be heir to the second, in exclusion of the youngest: and 2. established rules and maxims; as, "that the king can do no wrong, that no man shall be bound to accuse himself," and the like. But I take these to be one and the same thing. For the authority of these maxims rests entirely upon general reception and usage; and the only method of proving, that this or that maxim is a rule of the common law, is by shewing that it hath been always the custom to observe it.

B U T here a very natural, and very material, question arises: how are these customs or maxims to be known, and by whom is their validity to be determined? The answer is, by the judges in the several courts of justice. They are the depository of the laws; the living oracles, who must decide in all cases of doubt, and who are bound by an oath to decide according to the law of the land. Their knowlege of that law is derived from experience and study; from the "*viginti annorum lucubrationes*," which Fortescue mentions; and from being long personally accustomed to the judicial decisions of their predecessors. And indeed these judicial decisions are the principal and most authoritative evidence, that can be given, of the existence of such a custom as shall form a part of the common law. The judgment itself, and all the proceedings previous thereto, are carefully registered and preserved, under the name of *records*, in publick repositories set apart for that particular purpose; and to them frequent recourse is had, when any critical question arises, in the determination of which former precedents may give light or assistance. And therefore, even so early as the conquest, we find the "*praeteritorum memoria eventorum*" reckoned up as one of the chief qualifications of those who were held to be "*legibus patriae optime instituti.*" For it is an established rule to abide by former precedents, where the same points come again in litigation; as well to keep the scale of justice even and steady, and not liable to waver with every new judge's opinion; as also because the law in that case being solemnly declared and determined, what before was uncertain, and perhaps indifferent, is now become a permanent rule, which it is not in the breast of any subsequent judge to alter or vary from, according to his private sentiments: he being sworn to determine, not according to his own private judgment, but according to the known laws and customs of the land; not delegated to pronounce a new law, but to maintain and expound the old one. Yet this rule admits of exception, where the former determination is most evidently contrary to reason; much more if it be contrary to the divine law. But even in such cases the subsequent judges do not pretend to make a new law, but to vindicate the old one from misrepresentation. For if it be found that the former decision is manifestly absurd or unjust, it is declared, not that such a sentence was *bad law*, but that it was *not law*; that is, that it is not the established custom of the realm, as has been erroneously determined. And hence it is that our lawyers are with justice so copious in their encomiums on the reason of the common law; that they tell us, that the law is the perfection of reason, that it always intends to conform thereto, and that what is not reason is not law. Not that the particular reason of every rule in the law can at this distance of time be always precisely assigned; but it is sufficient that there be nothing in the rule flatly contradictory to reason, and then the law will presume it to be well founded. And it hath been an antient observation in the laws of England, that whenever a standing rule of law, of which the reason perhaps could not be remembered or discerned, hath been wantonly broke in upon by statutes or new resolutions, the wisdom of the rule hath in the end appeared from the inconveniences that have followed the innovation.

THE doctrine of the law then is this: that precedents and rules must be followed, unless flatly absurd or unjust: for though their reason be not obvious at first view, yet we owe such a deference to former times as not to suppose they acted wholly without consideration. To illustrate this doctrine by examples. It has been determined, time out of mind, that a brother of the half blood (i.e. where they have only one parent the same, and the other different) shall never succeed as heir to the estate of his half brother, but it shall rather escheat to the king, or other superior lord. Now this is a positive law, fixed and established by custom, which custom is evidenced by judicial decisions; and therefore can never be departed from by any modern judge without a breach of his oath and the law. For herein there is nothing repugnant to natural justice; though the reason of it, drawn from the feodal law, may not be quite obvious to every body. And therefore, on account of a supposed hardship upon the half brother, a modern judge might wish it had been otherwise settled; yet it is not in his power to alter it. But if any court were now to determine, that an elder brother of the half blood might enter upon and seise any lands that were purchased by his younger brother, no subsequent judges would scruple to declare that such prior determination was unjust, was unreasonable, and therefore was *not law*. So that *the law*, and the *opinion of the judge* are not always convertible terms, or one and the same thing; since it sometimes may happen that the judge may *mistake* the law. Upon the whole however, we may take it as a general rule, "that the decisions of courts of justice are the evidence of what is common law:" in the same manner as, in the civil law, what the emperor had once determined was to serve for a guide for the future.

T H E decisions therefore of courts are held in the highest regard, and are not only preserved as authentic records in the treasuries of the several courts, but are handed out to public view in the numerous volumes of *reports* which furnish the lawyer's library. These reports are histories of the several cases, with a short summary of the proceedings, which are preserved at large in the record; the arguments on both sides; and the reasons the court gave for their judgment; taken down in short notes by persons present at the determination. And these serve as indexes to, and also to explain, the records; which always, in matters of consequence and nicety, the judges direct to be searched. The reports are extant in a regular series from the reign of king Edward the second inclusive; and from his time to that of Henry the eighth were taken by the prothonotaries, or chief scribes of the court, at the expence of the crown, and published *annually*, whence they are known under the denomination of the *year books*. And it is much to be wished that this beneficial custom had, under proper regulations, been continued to this day: for, though king James the first at the instance of lord Bacon appointed two reporters with a handsome stipend for this purpose, yet that wise institution was soon neglected, and from the reign of Henry the eighth to the present time this task has been executed by many private and cotemporary hands; who sometimes through haste and inaccuracy, sometimes through mistake and want of skill, have published very crude and imperfect (perhaps contradictory) accounts of one and the same determination. Some of the most valuable of the antient reports are those published by lord chief justice Coke; a man of infinite learning in his profession, though not a little infected with the pedantry and quaintness of the times he lived in, which appear strongly in all his works. However his writings are so highly esteemed, that they are generally cited without the author's name.

B E S I D E S these reporters, there are also other authors, to whom great veneration and respect is paid by the students of the common law. Such are Glanvil and Bracton, Britton and Fleta, Littleton and Fitzherbert, with some others of antient date, whose treatises are cited as authority; and are evidence that cases have formerly happened in which such and such points were determined, which are now become settled and first principles. One of the last of these methodical writers in point of time, whose works are of any intrinsic authority in the courts of justice, and do not entirely depend on the strength of their quotations from older authors, is the same learned judge we have just mentioned, sir Edward Coke; who hath written four volumes of institutes, as he is pleased to call them, though they have little of the institutional method to warrant such a title. The first volume is a very extensive comment upon a little excellent treatise of tenures, compiled by judge Littleton in the reign of Edward the fourth. This comment is a rich mine of valuable common law learning, collected and heaped together from the antient reports and year books, but greatly defective in method. The second volume is a comment upon many old acts of parliament, without any systematical order; the third a more methodical treatise of the pleas of the crown; and the fourth an account of the several species of courts.

A N D thus much for the first ground and chief corner stone of the laws of England, which is, general immemorial custom, or common law, from time to time declared in the decisions of the courts of justice; which decisions are preserved among our public records, explained in our reports, and digested for general use in the authoritative writings of the venerable sages of the law.

T H E Roman law, as practised in the times of it's liberty, paid also a great regard to custom; but not so much as our law: it only then adopting it, when the written law is deficient. Though the reasons alleged in the digest will fully justify our practice, in making it of equal authority with, when it is not contradicted by, the written law. "For since, says Julianus, the written law binds us for no other reason but because it is approved by the judgment of the people, therefore those laws which the people hath approved without writing ought also to bind every body. For where is the difference, whether the people declare their assent to a law by suffrage, or by a uniform course of acting accordingly?" Thus did they reason while Rome had some remains of her freedom; but when the imperial tyranny came to be fully established, the civil laws speak a very different language. "*Quod principi placuit legis habet vigorem, cum populus ei et in eum omne suum imperium et potestatem conferat,*" says Ulpian. "*Imperator solus et conditor et interpres legis existimatur,*" says the code. And again, "*sacrilegii instar est rescripto principis obviare.*" And indeed it is one of the characteristic marks of English liberty, that our common law depends upon custom; which carries this internal evidence of freedom along with it, that it probably was introduced by the voluntary consent of the people.

II. T H E second branch of the unwritten laws of England are particular customs, or laws which affect only the inhabitants of particular districts.

T H E S E particular customs, or some of them, are without doubt the remains of that multitude of local customs before mentioned, out of which the common law, as it now stands, was collected at first by king Alfred, and afterwards by king Edgar and Edward the confessor: each district mutually sacrificing some of it's own special usages, in order that the whole kingdom might enjoy the benefit of one uniform and universal system of laws. But, for reasons that have been now long forgotten, particular counties, cities, towns, manors, and lordships, were very early indulged with the privilege of abiding by their own customs, in contradistinction to the rest of the nation at large: which privilege is confirmed to them by several acts of parliament.

S U C H is the custom of gavelkind in Kent and some other parts of the kingdom (though perhaps it was also general till the Norman conquest) which ordains, among other things, that not the eldest son only of the father shall succeed to his inheritance, but all the sons alike: and that, though the ancestor be attainted and hanged, yet the heir shall succeed to his estate, without any escheat to the lord.—Such is the custom that prevails in divers antient boroughs, and therefore called borough-english, that the youngest son shall inherit the estate, in preference to all his elder brothers.—Such is the custom in other boroughs that a widow shall be intitled, for her dower, to all her husband's lands; whereas at the common law she shall be endowed of one third part only.—Such also are the special and particular customs of manors, of which every one has more or less, and which bind all the copyhold-tenants that hold of the said manors.—Such likewise is the custom of holding divers inferior courts, with power of trying causes, in cities and trading towns; the right of holding which, when no royal grant can be shewn, depends entirely upon immemorial and established usage.—Such, lastly, are many particular customs within the city of London, with regard to trade, apprentices, widows, orphans, and a variety of other matters; which are all contrary to the general law of the land, and are good only by special custom, though those of London are also confirmed by act of parliament.

T O this head may most properly be referred a particular system of customs used only among one set of the king's subjects, called the custom of merchants or *lex mercatoria*; which, however different from the common law, is allowed for the benefit of trade, to be of the utmost validity in all commercial transactions; the maxim of law being, that "*cuilibet in sua arte credendum est.*"

T H E rules relating to particular customs regard either the proof of their existence; their legality when proved; or their usual method of allowance. And first we will consider the rules of proof.

A S to gavelkind, and borough-english, the law takes particular notice of them, and there is no occasion to prove that such customs actually exist, but only that the lands in question are subject thereto. All other private customs must be particularly pleaded, and as well the existence of such customs must be shewn, as that the thing in dispute is within the custom alleged. The trial in both cases (both to shew the existence of the custom, as, "that in the manor of Dale lands shall descend only to the heirs male, and never to the heirs female;" and also to shew that the lands in question are within that manor) is by a jury of twelve men, and not by the judges, except the same particular custom has been before tried, determined, and recorded in the same court.

T H E customs of London differ from all others in point of trial: for, if the existence of the custom be brought in question, it shall not be tried by a jury, but by certificate from the lord mayor and aldermen by the mouth of their recorder; unless it be such a custom as the corporation is itself interested in, as a right of taking toll, &c., for then the law permits them not to certify on their own behalf.

WHEN a custom is actually proved to exist, the next enquiry is into the legality of it; for if it is not a good custom it ought to be no longer used. "*Malus usus abolendus est*" is an established maxim of the law. To make a particular custom good, the following are necessary requisites.

1. THAT it have been used so long, that the memory of man runneth not to the contrary. So that if any one can shew the beginning of it, it is no good custom. For which reason no custom can prevail against an express act of parliament; since the statute itself is a proof of a time when such a custom did not exist.

2. IT must have been *continued*. Any interruption would cause a temporary ceasing: the revival gives it a new beginning, which will be within time of memory, and thereupon the custom will be void. But this must be understood with regard to an interruption of the *right*; for an interruption of the *possession* only, for ten or twenty years, will not destroy the custom. As if I have a right of way by custom over another's field, the custom is not destroyed, though I do not pass over it for ten years; it only becomes more difficult to prove: but if the *right* be any how discontinued for a day, the custom is quite at an end.

3. IT must have been *peaceable*, and acquiesced in; not subject to contention and dispute. For as customs owe their original to common consent, their being immemorially disputed either at law or otherwise is a proof that such consent was wanting.

4. CUSTOMS must be *reasonable*; or rather, taken negatively, they must not be unreasonable. Which is not always, as sir Edward Coke says, to be understood of every unlearned man's reason, but of artificial and legal reason, warranted by authority of law. Upon which account a custom may be good, though the particular reason of it cannot be assigned; for it sufficeth, if no good legal reason can be assigned against it. Thus a custom in a parish, that no man shall put his beasts into the common till the third of october, would be good; and yet it would be hard to shew the reason why that day in particular is fixed upon, rather than the day before or after. But a custom that no cattle shall be put in till the lord of the manor has first put in his, is unreasonable, and therefore bad: for peradventure the lord will never put in his; and then the tenants will lose all their profits.

5. CUSTOMS ought to be *certain*. A custom, that lands shall descend to the most worthy of the owner's blood, is void; for how shall this worth be determined? But a custom to descend to the next male of the blood, exclusive of females, is certain, and therefore good. A custom, to pay two pence an acre in lieu of tythes, is good; but to pay sometimes two pence and sometimes three pence, as the occupier of the land pleases, is bad for it's uncertainty. Yet a custom, to pay a year's improved value for a fine on a copyhold estate, is good: though the

value is a thing uncertain. For the value may at any time be ascertained; and the maxim of law is, *id certum est, quod certum reddi potest.*

1 Roll. Abr. 565.

6. C U S T O M S , though established by consent, must be (when established) *compulsory*; and not left to the option of every man, whether he will use them or no. Therefore a custom, that all the inhabitants shall be rated toward the maintenance of a bridge, will be good; but a custom, that every man is to contribute thereto at his own pleasure, is idle and absurd, and, indeed, no custom at all.

7. L A S T L Y , customs must be *consistent* with each other: one custom cannot be set up in opposition to another. For if both are really customs, then both are of equal antiquity, and both established by mutual consent: which to say of contradictory customs is absurd. Therefore, if one man prescribes that by custom he has a right to have windows looking into another's garden; the other cannot claim a right by custom to stop up or obstruct those windows: for these two contradictory customs cannot both be good, nor both stand together. He ought rather to deny the existence of the former custom.

9 Rep. 58.

N E X T , as to the allowance of special customs. Customs, in derogation of the common law, must be construed strictly. Thus, by the custom of gavelkind, an infant of fifteen years may by one species of conveyance (called a deed of feoffment) convey away his lands in fee simple, or for ever. Yet this custom does not impower him to use any other conveyance, or even to lease them for seven years: for the custom must be strictly pursued. And, moreover, all special customs must submit to the king's prerogative. Therefore, if the king purchases lands of the nature of gavelkind, where all the sons inherit equally; yet, upon the king's demise, his eldest son shall succeed to those lands alone. And thus much for the second part of the *leges non scriptae*, or those particular customs which affect particular persons or districts only.

III. T H E third branch of them are those peculiar laws, which by custom are adopted and used only in certain peculiar courts and jurisdictions. And by these I understand the civil and canon laws.

I T may seem a little improper at first view to rank these laws under the head of *leges non scriptae*, or unwritten laws, seeing they are set forth by authority in their pandects, their codes, and their institutions; their councils, decrees, and decretals; and enforced by an immense number of expositions, decisions, and treatises of the learned in both branches of the law. But I do this, after the example of sir Matthew Hale, because it is most plain, that it is not on account of their being *written* laws, that either the canon law, or the civil law, have any obligation within this kingdom; neither do their force and efficacy depend upon their own intrinsic authority; which is the case of our written laws, or acts of parliament. They bind not the subjects of England, because their materials were collected from popes or emperors; were digested by Justinian, or declared to be authentic by Gregory. These considerations give them no authority here: for the legislature of England doth not, nor ever did, recognize any foreign power, as superior or equal to it in this kingdom; or as having the right to give law to any, the meanest, of it's subjects. But all the strength that either the papal or imperial laws have obtained in this realm, or indeed in any other kingdom in Europe, is only because they have been admitted and received by immemorial usage and custom in some particular cases, and some particular courts; and then they form a branch of the *leges non scriptae*, or customary law: or else, because they are in some other cases introduced by consent of parliament, and then they owe their validity to the *leges scriptae*, or statute law. This is expressly declared in those remarkable words of the statute 25 Hen. VIII. c. 21. addressed to the king's royal majesty.—"This your grace's realm, recognizing no superior under God but only your grace, hath been and is free from subjection to any man's laws, but only to such as have been devised, made, and ordained *within* this realm for the wealth of the same; or to such other, as by sufferance of your grace and your progenitors, the people of this your realm, have taken at their free liberty, by their own consent, to be used among them; and have bound themselves by long use and custom to the observance of the same: not as to the observance of the laws of any foreign prince, potentate, or prelate; but as to the *customed* and antient laws of this realm, originally established as laws of the same, by the said sufferance, consents, and custom; and none otherwise."

B Y the civil law, absolutely taken, is generally understood the civil or municipal law of the Roman empire, as comprized in the institutes, the code, and the digest of the emperor Justinian, and the novel constitutions of himself and some of his successors. Of which, as there will frequently be occasion to cite them, by way of illustrating our own laws, it may not be amiss to give a short and general account.

T H E Roman law (founded first upon the regal constitutions of their antient kings, next upon the twelve tables of the *decemviri*, then upon the laws or statutes enacted by the senate or people, the edicts of the praetor, and the *responsa prudentum* or opinions of learned lawyers, and lastly upon the imperial decrees, or constitutions of successive emperors) had grown to so great a bulk, or as Livy expresses it, "*tam immensus aliarum super alias acervatarum legum cumulus*," that they were computed to be many camels' load by an author who preceded Justinian. This was in part remedied by the collections of three private lawyers, Gregorius, Hermogenes, and Papirius; and then by the emperor Theodosius the younger, by whose orders a code was compiled, *A.D.* 438, being a methodical collection of all the imperial constitutions then in force: which Theodosian code was the only book of civil law received as authentic in the western part of Europe till many centuries after; and to this it is probable that the Franks and Goths might frequently pay some regard, in framing legal constitutions for their newly erected kingdoms. For Justinian commanded only in the eastern remains of the empire; and it was under his auspices, that the present body of civil law was compiled and finished by Tribonian and other lawyers, about the year 533.

THIS consists of, 1. The institutes, which contain the elements or first principles of the Roman law, in four books. 2. The digests, or pandects, in fifty books, containing the opinions and writings of eminent lawyers, digested in a systematical method. 3. A new code, or collection of imperial constitutions, the lapse of a whole century having rendered the former code, of Theodosius, imperfect. 4. The novels, or new constitutions, posterior in time to the other books, and amounting to a supplement to the code; containing new decrees of successive emperors, as new questions happened to arise. These form the body of Roman law, or *corpus juris civilis*, as published about the time of Justinian: which however fell soon into neglect and oblivion, till about the year 1130, when a copy of the digests was found at Amalfi in Italy; which accident, concurring with the policy of the Romish ecclesiastics, suddenly gave new vogue and authority to the civil law, introduced it into several nations, and occasioned that mighty inundation of voluminous comments, with which this system of law, more than any other, is now loaded.

THE canon law is a body of Roman ecclesiastical law, relative to such matters as that church either has, or pretends to have, the proper jurisdiction over. This is compiled from the opinions of the antient Latin fathers, the decrees of general councils, the decretal epistles and bulles of the holy see. All which lay in the same disorder and confusion as the Roman civil law, till about the year 1151, one Gratian an Italian monk, animated by the discovery of Justinian's pandects at Amalfi, reduced them into some method in three books, which he entitled *concordia discordantium canonum*, but which are generally known by the name of *decretum Gratiani*. These reached as low as the time of pope Alexander III. The subsequent papal decrees, to the pontificate of Gregory IX, were published in much the same method under the auspices of that pope, about the year 1230, in five books entitled *decretalia Gregorii noni*. A sixth book was added by Boniface VIII, about the year 1298, which is called *sextus decretalium*. The Clementine constitutions, or decrees of Clement V, were in like manner authenticated in 1317 by his successor John XXII; who also published twenty constitutions of his own, called the *extravagantes Joannis*: all which in some measure answer to the novels of the civil law. To these have been since added some decrees of later popes in five books, called *extravagantes communes*. And all these together, Gratian's decree, Gregory's decretals, the sixth decretal, the Clementine constitutions, and the extravagants of John and his successors, form the *corpus juris canonici*, or body of the Roman canon law.

BESIDES these pontifical collections, which during the times of popery were received as authentic in this island, as well as in other parts of christendom, there is also a kind of national canon law, composed of *legatine* and *provincial* constitutions, and adapted only to the exigencies of this church and kingdom. The *legatine* constitutions were ecclesiastical laws, enacted in national synods, held under the cardinals Otho and Othobon, legates from pope Gregory IX and pope Adrian IV, in the reign of king Henry III about the years 1220 and 1268. The *provincial* constitutions are principally the decrees of provincial synods, held under divers arch-bishops of Canterbury, from Stephen Langton in the reign of Henry III to Henry Chichele in the reign of Henry V; and adopted also by the province of York in the reign of

Henry VI. At the dawn of the reformation, in the reign of king Henry VIII, it was enacted in parliament that a review should be had of the canon law; and, till such review should be made, all canons, constitutions, ordinances, and synodals provincial, being then already made, and not repugnant to the law of the land or the king's prerogative, should still be used and executed. And, as no such review has yet been perfected, upon this statute now depends the authority of the canon law in England.

A S for the canons enacted by the clergy under James I, in the year 1603, and never confirmed in parliament, it has been solemnly adjudged upon the principles of law and the constitution, that where they are not merely declaratory of the antient canon law, but are introductory of new regulations, they do not bind the laity; whatever regard the clergy may think proper to pay them.

T H E R E are four species of courts in which the civil and canon laws are permitted under different restrictions to be used. 1. The courts of the arch-bishops and bishops and their derivative officers, usually called in our law courts christian, *curiae christianitatis*, or the ecclesiastical courts. 2. The military courts. 3. The courts of admiralty. 4. The courts of the two universities. In all, their reception in general, and the different degrees of that reception, are grounded intirely upon custom; corroborated in the latter instance by act of parliament, ratifying those charters which confirm the customary law of the universities. The more minute consideration of these will fall properly under that part of these commentaries which treats of the jurisdiction of courts. It will suffice at present to remark a few particulars relative to them all, which may serve to inculcate more strongly the doctrine laid down concerning them.

1. A N D , first, the courts of common law have the superintendency over these courts; to keep them within their jurisdictions, to determine wherein they exceed them, to restrain and prohibit such excess, and (in case of contumacy) to punish the officer who executes, and in some cases the judge who enforces, the sentence so declared to be illegal.

2. T H E common law has reserved to itself the exposition of all such acts of parliament, as concern either the extent of these courts or the matters depending before them. And therefore if these courts either refuse to allow these acts of parliament, or will expound them in any other sense than what the common law puts upon them, the king's courts at Westminster will grant prohibitions to restrain and control them.

3. A N appeal lies from all these courts to the king, in the last resort; which proves that the jurisdiction exercised in them is derived from the crown of England, and not from any foreign potentate, or intrinsic authority of their own.—And, from these three strong marks and ensigns of superiority, it appears beyond a doubt that the civil and canon laws, though admitted in some cases by custom in some courts, are only subordinate and *leges sub graviori lege*; and that, thus admitted, restrained, altered, new-modelled, and amended, they are by no means with us a distinct independent species of laws, but are inferior branches of the

customary or unwritten laws of England, properly called, the king's ecclesiastical, the king's military, the king's maritime, or the king's academical, laws.

L E T us next proceed to the *leges scriptae*, the written laws of the kingdom, which are statutes, acts, or edicts, made by the king's majesty by and with the advice and content of the lords spiritual and temporal and commons in parliament assembled. The oldest of these now extant, and printed in our statute books, is the famous *magna carta*, as confirmed in parliament 9 Hen. III: though doubtless there were many acts before that time, the records of which are now lost, and the determinations of them perhaps at present currently received for the maxims of the old common law.

T H E manner of making these statutes will be better considered hereafter, when we examine the constitution of parliaments. At present we will only take notice of the different kinds of statutes; and of some general rules with regard to their construction.

F I R S T , as to their several kinds. Statutes are either *general* or *special*, *public* or *private*. A general or public act is an universal rule, that regards the whole community; and of these the courts of law are bound to take notice judicially and *ex officio*, without the statute being particularly pleaded, or formally set forth by the party who claims an advantage under it. Special or private acts are rather exceptions than rules, being those which only operate upon particular persons, and private concerns; such as the Romans intitled *senatus-decreta*, in contradistinction to the *senatus-consulta*, which regarded the whole community: and of these the judges are not bound to take notice, unless they be formally shewn and pleaded. Thus, to shew the distinction, the statute 13 Eliz. c. 10. to prevent spiritual persons from making leases for longer terms than twenty one years, or three lives, is a public act; it being a rule prescribed to the whole body of spiritual persons in the nation: but an act to enable the bishop of Chester to make a lease to A.B. for sixty years, is an exception to this rule; it concerns only the parties and the bishop's successors; and is therefore a private act.

S T A T U T E S also are either *declaratory* of the common law, or *remedial* of some defects therein. Declaratory, where the old custom of the kingdom is almost fallen into disuse, or become disputable; in which case the parliament has thought proper, *in perpetuum rei testimonium*, and for avoiding all doubts and difficulties, to declare what the common law is and ever hath been. Thus the statute of treasons, 25 Edw. III. cap. 2. doth not make any new species of treasons; but only, for the benefit of the subject, declares and enumerates those several kinds of offence, which before were treason at the common law. Remedial statutes are those which are made to supply such defects, and abridge such superfluities, in the common law, as arise either from the general imperfection of all human laws, from change of time and circumstances, from the mistakes and unadvised determinations of unlearned judges, or from any other cause whatsoever. And, this being done either by enlarging the common law where it was too narrow and circumscribed, or by restraining it where it was too lax and luxuriant, this has occasioned another subordinate division of remedial acts of parliament into *enlarging* and *restraining* statutes. To instance again in the case of treason. Clipping the current coin of the kingdom was an offence not sufficiently guarded against by the common law: therefore it was thought expedient by statute 5 Eliz. c. 11. to make it high treason, which it was not at the common law: so that this was an *enlarging* statute. At common law also spiritual corporations might lease out their estates for any term of years, till prevented by the statute 13 Eliz. beforementioned: this was therefore a *restraining* statute.

SECONDLY, the rules to be observed with regard to the construction of statutes are principally these which follow.

1. THERE are three points to be considered in the construction of all remedial statutes; the old law, the mischief, and the remedy: that is, how the common law stood at the making of the act; what the mischief was, for which the common law did not provide; and what remedy the parliament hath provided to cure this mischief. And it is the business of the judges so to construe the act, as to suppress the mischief and advance the remedy. Let us instance again in the same restraining statute of the 13 Eliz. By the common law ecclesiastical corporations might let as long leases as they thought proper: the mischief was, that they let long and unreasonable leases, to the impoverishment of their successors: the remedy applied by the statute was by making void all leases by ecclesiastical bodies for longer terms than three lives or twenty one years. Now in the construction of this statute it is held, that leases, though for a longer term, if made by a bishop, are not void during the bishop's life; or, if made by a dean with concurrence of his chapter, they are not void during the life of the dean: for the act was made for the benefit and protection of the successor. The mischief is therefore sufficiently suppressed by vacating them after the death of the grantor; but the leases, during their lives, being not within the mischief, are not within the remedy.

2. A STATUTE, which treats of things or persons of an inferior rank, cannot by any *general words* be extended to those of a superior. So a statute, treating of "deans, prebendaries, parsons, vicars, *and others having spiritual promotion*," is held not to extend to bishops, though they have spiritual promotion; deans being the highest persons named, and bishops being of a still higher order.

3. PENAL statutes must be construed strictly. Thus a statute 1 Edw. VI. having enacted that those who are convicted of stealing *horses* should not have the benefit of clergy, the judges conceived that this did not extend to him that should steal but *one horse*, and therefore procured a new act for that purpose in the following year. And, to come nearer our own times, by the statute 14 Geo. II. c. 6. stealing sheep, *or other cattle*, was made felony without benefit of clergy. But these general words, "or other cattle," being looked upon as much too loose to create a capital offence, the act was held to extend to nothing but mere sheep. And therefore, in the next sessions, it was found necessary to make another statute, 15 Geo. II. c. 34. extending the former to bulls, cows, oxen, steers, bullocks, heifers, calves, and lambs, by name.

4. STATUTES against frauds are to be liberally and beneficially expounded. This may seem a contradiction to the last rule; most statutes against frauds being in their consequences penal.

But this difference is here to be taken: where the statute acts upon the offender, and inflicts a penalty, as the pillory or a fine, it is then to be taken strictly: but when the statute acts upon the offence, by setting aside the fraudulent transaction, here it is to be construed liberally. Upon this footing the statute of 13 Eliz. c. 5. which avoids all gifts of goods, &c., made to defraud creditors *and others*, was held to extend by the general words to a gift made to defraud the queen of a forfeiture.

5. O N E part of a statute must be so construed by another, that the whole may if possible stand: *ut res magis valeat, quam pereat*. As if land be vested in the king and his heirs by act of parliament, saving the right of A; and A has at that time a lease of it for three years: here A shall hold it for his term of three years, and afterwards it shall go to the king. For this interpretation furnishes matter for every clause of the statute to work and operate upon. But

6. A S A V I N G , totally repugnant to the body of the act, is void. If therefore an act of parliament vests land in the king and his heirs, saving the right of all persons whatsoever; or vests the land of A in the king, saving the right of A: in either of these cases the saving is totally repugnant to the body of the statute, and (if good) would render the statute of no effect or operation; and therefore the saving is void, and the land vests absolutely in the king.

7. W H E R E the common law and a statute differ, the common law gives place to the statute; and an old statute gives place to a new one. And this upon the general principle laid down in the last section, that "*leges posteriores priores contrarias abrogant*." But this is to be understood, only when the latter statute is couched in negative terms, or by it's matter necessarily implies a negative. As if a former act says, that a juror upon such a trial shall have twenty pounds a year; and a new statute comes and says, he shall have twenty marks: here the latter statute, though it does not express, yet necessarily implies a negative, and virtually repeals the former. For if twenty marks be made qualification sufficient, the former statute which requires twenty pounds is at an end. But if both acts be merely affirmative, and the substance such that both may stand together, here the latter does not repeal the former, but they shall both have a concurrent efficacy. If by a former law an offence be indictable at the quarter sessions, and a latter law makes the same offence indictable at the assises; here the jurisdiction of the sessions is not taken away, but both have a concurrent jurisdiction, and the offender may be prosecuted at either; unless the new statute subjoins express negative words, as, that the offence shall be indictable at the assises, *and not elsewhere*.

8. I F a statute, that repeals another, is itself repealed afterwards, the first statute is hereby revived, without any formal words for that purpose. So when the statutes of 26 and 35 Hen. VIII, declaring the king to be the supreme head of the church, were repealed by a statute 1 & 2 Ph. and Mary, and this latter statute was afterwards repealed by an act of 1 Eliz. there needed not any express words of revival in queen Elizabeth's statute, but these acts of king Henry were impliedly and virtually revived.

9. A C T S of parliament derogatory from the power of subsequent parliaments bind not. So the statute 11 Hen. VII. c. 1. which directs, that no person for assisting a king *de facto* shall be attainted of treason by act of parliament or otherwise, is held to be good only as to common prosecutions for high treason; but will not restrain or clog any parliamentary attainder. Because the legislature, being in truth the sovereign power, is always of equal, always of absolute authority: it acknowleges no superior upon earth, which the prior legislature must have been, if it's ordinances could bind the present parliament. And upon the same principle Cicero, in his letters to Atticus, treats with a proper contempt these restraining clauses which endeavour to tie up the hands of succeeding legislatures. "When you repeal the law itself, says he, you at the same time repeal the prohibitory clause, which guards against such repeal."

10. L A S T L Y , acts of parliament that are impossible to be performed are of no validity; and if there arise out of them collaterally any absurd consequences, manifestly contradictory to common reason, they are, with regard to those collateral consequences, void. I lay down the rule with these restrictions; though I know it is generally laid down more largely, that acts of parliament contrary to reason are void. But if the parliament will positively enact a thing to be done which is unreasonable, I know of no power that can control it: and the examples usually alleged in support of this sense of the rule do none of them prove, that where the main object of a statute is unreasonable the judges are at liberty to reject it; for that were to set the judicial power above that of the legislature, which would be subversive of all government. But where some collateral matter arises out of the general words, and happens to be unreasonable; there the judges are in decency to conclude that this consequence was not foreseen by the parliament, and therefore they are at liberty to expound the statute by equity, and only *quoad hoc* disregard it. Thus if an act of parliament gives a man power to try all causes, that arise within his manor of Dale; yet, if a cause should arise in which he himself is party, the act is construed not to extend to that; because it is unreasonable that any man should determine his own quarrel. But, if we could conceive it possible for the parliament to enact, that he should try as well his own causes as those of other persons, there is no court that has power to defeat the intent of the legislature, when couched in such evident and express words, as leave no doubt whether it was the intent of the legislature or no.

T H E S E are the several grounds of the laws of England: over and above which, equity is also frequently called in to assist, to moderate, and to explain it. What equity is, and how impossible in it's very essence to be reduced to stated rules, hath been shewn in the preceding section. I shall therefore only add, that there are courts of this kind established for the benefit of the subject, to correct and soften the rigor of the law, when through it's generality it bears too hard in particular cases; to detect and punish latent frauds, which the law is not minute enough to reach; to enforce the execution of such matters of trust and confidence, as are binding in conscience, though perhaps not strictly legal; to deliver from such dangers as are owing to misfortune or oversight; and, in short, to relieve in all such cases as are,*bona fide*, objects of relief. This is the business of our courts of equity, which however are only conversant in matters of property. For the freedom of our constitution will not permit, that in criminal cases a power should be lodged in any judge, to construe the law otherwise than according to the letter. This caution, while it admirably protects the public liberty, can never bear hard upon individuals. A man cannot suffer *more* punishment than the law assigns, but he may suffer *less*. The laws cannot be strained by partiality to inflict a penalty beyond what the letter will warrant; but in cases where the letter induces any apparent hardship, the crown has the power to pardon.

SECTION THE FOURTH.

OF THE COUNTRIES SUBJECT TO THE

LAWS OF ENGLAND.

TH E kingdom of England, over which our municipal laws have jurisdiction, includes not, by the common law, either Wales, Scotland, or Ireland, or any other part of the king's dominions, except the territory of England only. And yet the civil laws and local customs of this territory do now obtain, in part or in all, with more or less restrictions, in these and many other adjacent countries; of which it will be proper first to take a review, before we consider the kingdom of England itself, the original and proper subject of these laws.

W A L E S had continued independent of England, unconquered and uncultivated, in the primitive pastoral state which Caesar and Tacitus ascribe to Britain in general, for many centuries; even from the time of the hostile invasions of the Saxons, when the ancient and christian inhabitants of the island retired to those natural intrenchments, for protection from their pagan visitants. But when these invaders themselves were converted to christianity, and settled into regular and potent governments, this retreat of the antient Britons grew every day narrower; they were overrun by little and little, gradually driven from one fastness to another, and by repeated losses abridged of their wild independence. Very early in our history we find their princes doing homage to the crown of England; till at length in the reign of Edward the first, who may justly be stiled the conqueror of Wales, the line of their antient princes was abolished, and the king of England's eldest son became, as a matter of course, their titular prince: the territory of Wales being then entirely annexed to the dominion of the crown of England, or, as the statute of Rutland expresses it, "*terra Walliae cum incolis suis, prius regi jure feodali subjecta*, (of which homage was the sign) *jam in proprietatis dominium totaliter et cum integritate conversa est, et coronae regni Angliae tanquam pars corporis ejusdem annexa et unita.*" By the statute also of Wales very material alterations were made in divers parts of their laws, so as to reduce them nearer to the English standard, especially in the forms of their judicial proceedings: but they still retained very much of their original polity, particularly their rule of inheritance, viz. that their lands were divided equally among all the issue male, and did not descend to the eldest son alone. By other subsequent statutes their provincial immunities were still farther abridged: but the finishing stroke to their independency, was given by the statute 27 Hen. VIII. c. 26. which at the same time gave the utmost advancement to their civil prosperity, by admitting them to a thorough communication of laws with the subjects of England. Thus were this brave people gradually conquered into the enjoyment of true liberty; being insensibly put upon the same footing, and made fellow-citizens with their conquerors. A generous method of triumph, which the republic of Rome practised with great success; till she reduced all Italy to her obedience, by admitting the vanquished states to partake of the Roman privileges.

I T is enacted by this statute 27 Hen. VIII, 1. That the dominion of Wales shall be for ever united to the kingdom of England. 2. That all Welchmen born shall have the same liberties as other the king's subjects. 3. That lands in Wales shall be inheritable according to the English tenures and rules of descent. 4. That the laws of England, and no other, shall be used in Wales: besides many other regulations of the police of this principality. And the statute 34 & 35 Hen. VIII. c. 26. confirms the same, adds farther regulations, divides it into twelve shires, and, in short, reduces it into the same order in which it stands at this day; differing from the kingdom of England in only a few particulars, and those too of the nature of privileges, (such as having courts within itself, independent of the process of Westminster hall) and some other immaterial peculiarities, hardly more than are to be found in many counties of England itself.

T H E kingdom of Scotland, notwithstanding the union of the crowns on the accession of their king James VI to that of England, continued an entirely separate and distinct kingdom for above a century, though an union had been long projected; which was judged to be the more easy to be done, as both kingdoms were antiently under the same government, and still retained a very great resemblance, though far from an identity, in their laws. By an act of parliament 1 Jac. I. c. 1. it is declared, that these two, mighty, famous, and antient kingdoms were formerly one. And sir Edward Coke observes, how marvellous a conformity there was, not only in the religion and language of the two nations, but also in their antient laws, the descent of the crown, their parliaments, their titles of nobility, their officers of state and of justice, their writs, their customs, and even the language of their laws. Upon which account he supposes the common law of each to have been originally the same, especially as their most antient and authentic book, called *regiam majestatem* and containing the rules of *their* antient common law, is extremely similar that of Glanvil, which contains the principles of *ours*, as it stood in the reign of Henry II. And the many diversities, subsisting between the two laws at present, may be well enough accounted for, from a diversity of practice in two large and uncommunicating jurisdictions, and from the acts of two distinct and independent parliaments, which have in many points altered and abrogated the old common law of both kingdoms.

HOWEVER sir Edward Coke, and the politicians of that time, conceived great difficulties in carrying on the projected union: but these were at length overcome, and the great work was happily effected in 1707, 5 Anne; when twenty five articles of union were agreed to by the parliaments of both nations: the purport of the most considerable being as follows:

1. THAT on the first of May 1707, and for ever after, the kingdoms of England and Scotland, shall be united into one kingdom, by the name of Great Britain.

2. THE succession to the monarchy of Great Britain shall be the same as was before settled with regard to that of England.

3. THE united kingdom shall be represented by one parliament.

4. THERE shall be a communication of all rights and privileges between the subjects of both kingdoms, except where it is otherwise agreed.

9. WHEN England raises 2,000,000*l.* by a land tax, Scotland shall raise 48,000*l.*

16, 17. THE standards of the coin, of weights, and of measures, shall be reduced to those of England, throughout the united kingdoms.

18. THE laws relating to trade, customs, and the excise, shall be the same in Scotland as in England. But all the other laws of Scotland shall remain in force; but alterable by the parliament of Great Britain. Yet with this caution; that laws relating to public policy are alterable at the discretion of the parliament; laws relating to private rights are not to be altered but for the evident utility of the people of Scotland.

22. SIXTEEN peers are to be chosen to represent the peerage of Scotland in parliament, and forty five members to sit in the house of commons.

23. THE sixteen peers of Scotland shall have all privileges of parliament: and all peers of Scotland shall be peers of Great Britain, and rank next after those of the same degree at the time of the union, and shall have all privileges of peers, except sitting in the house of lords and voting on the trial of a peer.

THESE are the principal of the twenty five articles of union, which are ratified and confirmed by statute 5 Ann. c. 8. in which statute there are also two acts of parliament recited; the one of Scotland, whereby the church of Scotland, and also the four universities of that kingdom, are established for ever, and all succeeding sovereigns are to take an oath inviolably to maintain the same; the other of England, 5 Ann. c. 6. whereby the acts of uniformity of 13 Eliz. and 13 Car. II. (except as the same had been altered by parliament at that time) and all other acts then in force for the preservation of the church of England, are declared perpetual; and it is stipulated, that every subsequent king and queen shall take an oath inviolably to maintain the same within England, Ireland, Wales, and the town of Berwick upon Tweed.

And it is enacted, that these two acts "shall for ever be observed as fundamental and essential conditions of the union."

UPON these articles, and act of union, it is to be observed, 1. That the two kingdoms are now so inseparably united, that nothing can ever disunite them again, but an infringement of those points which, when they were separate and independent nations, it was mutually stipulated should be "fundamental and essential conditions of the union." 2. That whatever else may be deemed "fundamental and essential conditions," the preservation of the two churches, of England and Scotland, in the same state that they were in at the time of the union, and the maintenance of the acts of uniformity which establish our common prayer, are expressly declared so to be. 3. That therefore any alteration in the constitutions of either of those churches, or in the liturgy of the church of England, would be an infringement of these "fundamental and essential conditions," and greatly endanger the union. 4. That the municipal laws of Scotland are ordained to be still observed in that part of the island, unless altered by parliament; and, as the parliament has not yet thought proper, except in a few instances, to alter them, they still (with regard to the particulars unaltered) continue in full force. Wherefore the municipal or common laws of England are, generally speaking, of no force or validity in Scotland; and, of consequence, in the ensuing commentaries, we shall have very little occasion to mention, any farther than sometimes by way of illustration, the municipal laws of that part of the united kingdoms.

THE town of Berwick upon Tweed, though subject to the crown of England ever since the conquest of it in the reign of Edward IV, is not part of the kingdom of England, nor subject to the common law; though it is subject to all acts of parliament, being represented by burgesses therein. And therefore it was declared by statute 20 Geo. II. c. 42. that where England only is mentioned in any act of parliament, the same notwithstanding shall be deemed to comprehend the dominion of Wales, and town of Berwick upon Tweed. But the general law there used is the Scots law, and the ordinary process of the courts of Westminster-hall is there of no authority.

AS to Ireland, that is still a distinct kingdom; though a dependent, subordinate kingdom. It was only entitled the dominion or lordship of Ireland, and the king's stile was no other than *dominus Hiberniae*, lord of Ireland, till the thirty third year of king Henry the eighth; when he assumed the title of king, which is recognized by act of parliament 35 Hen. VIII. c. 3. But, as Scotland and England are now one and the same kingdom, and yet differ in their municipal laws; so England and Ireland are, on the other hand, distinct kingdoms, and yet in general agree in their laws. The inhabitants of Ireland are, for the most part, descended from the English, who planted it as a kind of colony, after the conquest of it by king Henry the second, at which time they carried over the English laws along with them. And as Ireland, thus conquered, planted, and governed, still continues in a state of dependence, it must necessarily conform to, and be obliged by such laws as the superior state thinks proper to prescribe.

Stat. Hiberniae. 14 Hen. III.

A T the time of this conquest the Irish were governed by what they called the Brehon law, so stiled from the Irish name of judges, who were denominated Brehons. But king John in the twelfth year of his reign went into Ireland, and carried over with him many able sages of the law; and there by his letters patent, in right of the dominion of conquest, is said to have ordained and established that Ireland should be governed by the laws of England: which letters patent sir Edward Coke apprehends to have been there confirmed in parliament. But to this ordinance many of the Irish were averse to conform, and still stuck to their Brehon law: so that both Henry the third and Edward the first were obliged to renew the injunction; and at length in a parliament holden at Kilkenny, 40 Edw. III, under Lionel duke of Clarence, the then lieutenant of Ireland, the Brehon law was formally abolished, it being unanimously declared to be indeed no law, but a lewd custom crept in of later times. And yet, even in the reign of queen Elizabeth, the wild natives still kept and preserved their Brehon law; which is described to have been "a rule of right unwritten, but delivered by tradition from one to another, in which oftentimes there appeared great shew of equity in determining the right between party and party, but in many things repugnant quite both to God's law and man's." The latter part of which character is alone allowed it under Edward the first and his grandson.

B U T as Ireland was a distinct dominion, and had parliaments of it's own, it is to be observed, that though the immemorial customs, or common law, of England were made the rule of justice in Ireland also, yet no acts of the English parliament, since the twelfth of king John, extended into that kingdom; unless it were specially named, or included under general words, such as, "within any of the king's dominions." And this is particularly expressed, and the reason given in the year book: "Ireland hath a parliament of it's own, and maketh and altereth laws; and our statutes do not bind them, because they do not send representatives to our parliament: but their persons are the king's subjects, like as the inhabitants of Calais, Gascoigny, and Guienne, while they continued under the king's subjection." The method made use of in Ireland, as stated by sir Edward Coke, of making statutes in their parliaments, according to Poynings' law, of which hereafter, is this: 1. The lord lieutenant and council of Ireland must certify to the king under the great seal of Ireland the acts proposed to be passed. 2. The king and council of England are to consider, approve, alter, or reject the said acts; and certify them back again under the great seal of England. And then, 3. They are to be proposed, received, or rejected in the parliament of Ireland. By this means nothing was left to the parliament in Ireland, but a bare negative or power of rejecting, not of proposing, any law. But the usage now is, that bills are often framed in either house of parliament under the denomination of heads for a bill or bills; and in that shape they are offered to the consideration of the lord lieutenant and privy council, who then reject them at pleasure, without transmitting them to England.

B U T the Irish nation, being excluded from the benefit of the English statutes, were deprived of many good and profitable laws, made for the improvement of the common law: and, the measure of justice in both kingdoms becoming thereby no longer uniform, therefore in the 10 Hen. VII. a set of statutes passed in Ireland, (sir Edward Poynings being then lord deputy, whence it is called Poynings' law) by which it was, among other things, enacted, that all acts of parliament before made in England, should be of force within the realm of Ireland. But, by the same rule that no laws made in England, between king John's time and Poynings' law, were then binding in Ireland, it follows that no acts of the English parliament made since the 10 Hen. VII. do now bind the people of Ireland, unless specially named or included under general words. And on the other hand it is equally clear, that where Ireland is particularly named, or is included under general words, they are bound by such acts of parliament. For this follows from the very nature and constitution of a dependent state: dependence being very little else, but an obligation to conform to the will or law of that superior person or state, upon which the inferior depends. The original and true ground of this superiority is the right of conquest: a right allowed by the law of nations, if not by that of nature; and founded upon a compact either expressly or tacitly made between the conqueror and the conquered, that if they will acknowlege the victor for their master, he will treat them for the future as subjects, and not as enemies.

B U T this state of dependence being almost forgotten, and ready to be disputed by the Irish nation, it became necessary some years ago to declare how that matter really stood: and therefore by statute 6 Geo. I. c. 5. it is declared, that the kingdom of Ireland ought to be subordinate to, and dependent upon, the imperial crown of Great Britain, as being inseparably united thereto; and that the king's majesty, with the consent of the lords and commons of Great Britain in parliament, hath power to make laws to bind the people of Ireland.

T H U S we see how extensively the laws of Ireland communicate with those of England: and indeed such communication is highly necessary, as the ultimate resort from the courts of justice in Ireland is, as in Wales, to those in England; a writ of error (in the nature of an appeal) lying from the king's bench in Ireland to the king's bench in England, as the appeal from all other courts in Ireland lies immediately to the house of lords here: it being expressly declared, by the same statute 6 Geo. I. c. 5. that the peers of Ireland have no jurisdiction to affirm or reverse any judgments or decrees whatsoever. The propriety, and even necessity, in all inferior dominions, of this constitution, "that, though justice be in general administred by courts of their own, yet that the appeal in the last resort ought to be to the courts of the superior state," is founded upon these two reasons. 1. Because otherwise the law, appointed or permitted to such inferior dominion, might be insensibly changed within itself, without the assent of the superior. 2. Because otherwise judgments might be given to the disadvantage or diminution of the superiority; or to make the dependence to be only of the person of the king, and not of the crown of England.

W I T H regard to the other adjacent islands which are subject to the crown of Great Britain, some of them (as the isle of Wight, of Portland, of Thanet, &c.) are comprized within some neighbouring county, and are therefore to be looked upon as annexed to the mother island, and part of the kingdom of England. But there are others, which require a more particular consideration.

A N D , first, the isle of Man is a distinct territory from England and is not governed by our laws; neither doth any act of parliament extend to it, unless it be particularly named therein; and then an act of parliament is binding there. It was formerly a subordinate feudatory kingdom, subject to the kings of Norway; then to king John and Henry III of England; afterwards to the kings of Scotland; and then again to the crown of England: and at length we find king Henry IV claiming the island by right of conquest, and disposing of it to the earl of Northumberland; upon whose attainder it was granted (by the name of the lordship of Man) to sir John de Stanley by letters patent 7 Hen. IV. In his lineal descendants it continued for eight generations, till the death of Ferdinando earl of Derby, *A.D.* 1594; when a controversy arose concerning the inheritance thereof, between his daughters and William his surviving brother: upon which, and a doubt that was started concerning the validity of the original patent, the island was seised into the queen's hands, and afterwards various grants were made of it by king James the first; all which being expired or surrendered, it was granted afresh in 7 Jac. I. to William earl of Derby, and the heirs male of his body, with remainder to his heirs general; which grant was the next year confirmed by act of parliament, with a restraint of the power of alienation by the said earl and his issue male. On the death of James earl of Derby, *A.D.* 1735, the male line of earl William failing, the duke of Atholl succeeded to the island as heir general by a female branch. In the mean time, though the title of king had long been disused, the earls of Derby, as lords of Man, had maintained a sort of royal authority therein; by assenting or dissenting to laws, and exercising an appellate jurisdiction. Yet, though no English writ, or process from the courts of Westminster, was of any authority in Man, an appeal lay from a decree of the lord of the island to the king of Great Britain in council. But, the distinct jurisdiction of this little subordinate royalty being found inconvenient for the purposes of public justice, and for the revenue, (it affording a convenient asylum for debtors, outlaws, and smugglers) authority was given to the treasury by statute 12 Geo. I. c. 28. to purchase the interest of the then proprietors for the use of the crown: which purchase hath at length been completed in this present year 1765, and confirmed by statutes 5 Geo. III. c. 26, & 39. whereby the whole island and all it's dependencies, so granted as aforesaid, (except the landed property of the Atholl family, their manerial rights and emoluments, and the patronage of the bishoprick and other ecclesiastical benefices) are unalienably vested in the crown, and subjected to the regulations of the British excise and customs.

T H E islands of Jersey, Guernsey, Sark, Alderney, and their appendages, were parcel of the duchy of Normandy, and were united to the crown of England by the first princes of the Norman line. They are governed by their own laws, which are for the most part the ducal customs of Normandy, being collected in an antient book of very great authority, entituled, *le grand coustumier*. The king's writ, or process from the courts of Westminster, is there of no force; but his commission is. They are not bound by common acts of our parliaments, unless particularly named. All causes are originally determined by their own officers, the bailiffs and jurats of the islands; but an appeal lies from them to the king in council, in the last resort.

BESIDES these adjacent islands, our more distant plantations in America, and elsewhere, are also in some respects subject to the English laws. Plantations, or colonies in distant countries, are either such where the lands are claimed by right of occupancy only, by finding them desart and uncultivated, and peopling them from the mother country; or where, when already cultivated, they have been either gained by conquest, or ceded to us by treaties. And both these rights are founded upon the law of nature, or at least upon that of nations. But there is a difference between these two species of colonies, with respect to the laws by which they are bound. For it is held, that if an uninhabited country be discovered and planted by English subjects, all the English laws are immediately there in force. For as the law is the birthright of every subject, so wherever they go they carry their laws with them. But in conquered or ceded countries, that have already laws of their own, the king may indeed alter and change those laws; but, till he does actually change them, the antient laws of the country remain, unless such as are against the law of God, as in the case of an infidel country.

OUR American plantations are principally of this latter sort, being obtained in the last century either by right of conquest and driving out the natives (with what natural justice I shall not at present enquire) or by treaties. And therefore the common law of England, as such, has no allowance or authority there; they being no part of the mother country, but distinct (though dependent) dominions. They are subject however to the control of the parliament; though (like Ireland, Man, and the rest) not bound by any acts of parliament, unless particularly named. The form of government in most of them is borrowed from that of England. They have a governor named by the king, (or in some proprietary colonies by the proprietor) who is his representative or deputy. They have courts of justice of their own, from whose decisions an appeal lies to the king in council here in England. Their general assemblies which are their house of commons, together with their council of state being their upper house, with the concurrence of the king or his representative the governor, make laws suited to their own emergencies. But it is particularly declared by statute 7 & 8 W. III. c. 22. That all laws, by-laws, usages, and customs, which shall be in practice in any of the plantations, repugnant to any law, made or to be made in this kingdom relative to the said plantations, shall be utterly void and of none effect.

THESE are the several parts of the dominions of the crown of Great Britain, in which the municipal laws of England are not of force or authority, merely *as* the municipal laws of England. Most of them have probably copied the spirit of their own law from this original; but then it receives it's obligation, and authoritative force, from being the law of the country.

AS to any foreign dominions which may belong to the person of the king by hereditary descent, by purchase, or other acquisition, as the territory of Hanover, and his majesty's other property in Germany; as these do not in any wise appertain to the crown of these kingdoms, they are entirely unconnected with the laws of England, and do not communicate with this nation in any respect whatsoever. The English legislature had wisely remarked the inconveniences that had formerly resulted from dominions on the continent of Europe; from the Norman territory which William the conqueror brought with him, and held in conjunction with the English throne; and from Anjou, and it's appendages, which fell to Henry the second by hereditary descent. They had seen the nation engaged for near four hundred years together in ruinous wars for defence of these foreign dominions; till, happily for this country, they were lost under the reign of Henry the sixth. They observed that from that time the maritime interests of England were better understood and more closely pursued: that, in consequence of this attention, the nation, as soon as she had rested from her civil wars, began at this period to flourish all at once; and became much more considerable in Europe than when her princes were possessed of a larger territory, and her counsels distracted by foreign interests. This experience and these considerations gave birth to a conditional clause in the act of settlement, which vested the crown in his present majesty's illustrious house, "That in case the crown and imperial dignity of this realm shall hereafter come to any person not being a native of this kingdom of England, this nation shall not be obliged to engage in any war for the defence of any dominions or territories which do not belong to the crown of England, without consent of parliament."

W E come now to consider the kingdom of England in particular, the direct and immediate subject of those laws, concerning which we are to treat in the ensuing commentaries. And this comprehends not only Wales, of which enough has been already said, but also part of the sea. The main or high seas are part of the realm of England, for thereon our courts of admiralty have jurisdiction, as will be shewn hereafter; but they are not subject to the common law. This main sea begins at the low-water-mark. But between the high-water-mark, and the low-water-mark, where the sea ebbs and flows, the common law and the admiralty have *divisum imperium*, an alternate jurisdiction; one upon the water, when it is full sea; the other upon the land, when it is an ebb.

T H E territory of England is liable to two divisions; the one ecclesiastical, the other civil.

I. T H E ecclesiastical division is, primarily, into two provinces, those of Canterbury and York. A province is the circuit of an arch-bishop's jurisdiction. Each province contains divers dioceses, or sees of suffragan bishops; whereof Canterbury includes twenty one, and York three; besides the bishoprick of the isle of Man, which was annexed to the province of York by king Henry VIII. Every diocese is divided into archdeaconries, whereof there are sixty in all; each archdeaconry into rural deanries, which are the circuit of the archdeacon's and rural dean's jurisdiction, of whom hereafter; and every deanry is divided into parishes.

A P A R I S H is that circuit of ground in which the souls under the care of one parson or vicar do inhabit. These are computed to be near ten thousand in number. How antient the division of parishes is, may at present be difficult to ascertain; for it seems to be agreed on all hands, that in the early ages of christianity in this island, parishes were unknown, or at least signified the same that a diocese does now. There was then no appropriation of ecclesiastical dues to any particular church; but every man was at liberty to contribute his tithes to whatever priest or church he pleased, provided only that he did it to some: or, if he made no special appointment or appropriation thereof, they were paid into the hands of the bishop, whose duty it was to distribute them among the clergy and for other pious purposes according to his own discretion.

M R Camden says England was divided into parishes by arch-bishop Honorius about the year 630. Sir Henry Hobart lays it down that parishes were first erected by the council of Lateran, which was held *A.D.* 1179. Each widely differing from the other, and both of them perhaps from the truth; which will probably be found in the medium between the two extremes. For Mr Selden has clearly shewn, that the clergy lived in common without any division of parishes, long after the time mentioned by Camden. And it appears from the Saxon laws, that parishes were in being long before the date of that council of Lateran, to which they are ascribed by Hobart.

W E find the distinction of parishes, nay even of mother-churches, so early as in the laws of king Edgar, about the year 970. Before that time the consecration of tithes was in general *arbitrary*; that is, every man paid his own (as was before observed) to what church or parish he pleased. But this being liable to be attended with either fraud, or at least caprice, in the persons paying; and with either jealousies or mean compliances in such as were competitors for receiving them; it was now ordered by the law of king Edgar, that "*dentur omnes decimae primariae ecclesiae ad quam parochia pertinet.*" However, if any thane, or great lord, had a church within his own demesnes, distinct from the mother-church, in the nature of a private chapel; then, provided such church had a coemitery or consecrated place of burial belonging to it, he might allot one third of his tithes for the maintenance of the officiating minister: but, if it had no coemitery, the thane must himself have maintained his chaplain by some other means; for in such case *all* his tithes were ordained to be paid to the *primariae ecclesiae* or mother-church.

T H I S proves that the kingdom was then universally divided into parishes; which division happened probably not all at once, but by degrees. For it seems pretty clear and certain that the boundaries of parishes were originally ascertained by those of a manor or manors: since it very seldom happens that a manor extends itself over more parishes than one, though there are often many manors in one parish. The lords, as christianity spread itself, began to build churches upon their own demesnes or wastes, to accommodate their tenants in one or two adjoining lordships; and, in order to have divine service regularly performed therein, obliged all their tenants to appropriate their tithes to the maintenance of the one officiating minister, instead of leaving them at liberty to distribute them among the clergy of the diocese in general: and this tract of land, the tithes whereof were so appropriated, formed a distinct parish. Which will well enough account for the frequent intermixture of parishes one with another. For if a lord had a parcel of land detached from the main of his estate, but not sufficient to form a parish of itself, it was natural for him to endow his newly erected church with the tithes of those disjointed lands; especially if no church was then built in any lordship adjoining to those out-lying parcels.

T H U S parishes were gradually formed, and parish churches endowed with the tithes that arose within the circuit assigned. But some lands, either because they were in the hands of irreligious and careless owners, or were situate in forests and desart places, or for other now unsearchable reasons, were never united to any parish, and therefore continue to this day extraparochial; and their tithes are now by immemorial custom payable to the king instead of the bishop, in trust and confidence that he will distribute them, for the general good of the church. And thus much for the ecclesiastical division of this kingdom.2. T H E civil division of the territory of England is into counties, of those counties into hundreds, of those hundreds into tithings or towns. Which division, as it now stands, seems to owe it's original to king Alfred; who, to prevent the rapines and disorders which formerly prevailed in the realm, instituted tithings; so called, from the Saxon, because *ten* freeholders with their families composed one. These all dwelt together, and were sureties or free pledges to the king for the good behaviour of each other; and, if any offence were committed in their district, they were bound to have the offender forthcoming. And therefore antiently no man was suffered to abide in England above forty days, unless he were enrolled in some tithing or decennary. One of the principal inhabitants of the tithing is annually appointed to preside over the rest, being called the tithing-man, the headborough, (words which speak their own etymology) and in some countries the borsholder, or borough's-ealder, being supposed the discreetest man in the borough, town, or tithing.

T I T H I N G S , towns, or vills, are of the same signification in law; and had, each of them, originally a church and celebration of divine service, sacraments, and burials; which to have, or have had, separate to itself, is the essential distinction of a town, according to sir Edward Coke. The word *town* or *vill* is indeed, by the alteration of times and language, now become a generical term, comprehending under it the several species of cities, boroughs, and common towns. A city is a town incorporated, which is or hath been the see of a bishop; and though the bishoprick be dissolved, as at Westminster, yet still it remaineth a city. A borough is now understood to be a town, either corporate or not, that sendeth burgesses to parliament. Other towns there are, to the number sir Edward Coke says of 8803, which are neither cities nor boroughs; some of which have the privileges of markets, and others not; but both are equally towns in law. To several of these towns there are small appendages belonging, called hamlets; which are taken notice of in the statute of Exeter, which makes frequent mention of entire vills, demi-vills, and hamlets. Entire vills sir Henry Spelmanconjectures to have consisted of ten freemen, or frank-pledges, demi-vills of five, and hamlets of less than five. These little collections of houses are sometimes under the same administration as the town itself, sometimes governed by separate officers; in which last case it is, to some purposes in law, looked upon as a distinct township. These towns, as was before hinted, contained each originally but one parish, and one tithing; though many of them now, by the encrease of inhabitants, are divided into several parishes and tithings: and sometimes, where there is but one parish there are two or more vills or tithings.A S ten families of freeholders made up a town or tithing, so ten tithings composed a superior division, called a hundred, as consisting of ten times ten families. The hundred is governed by an high constable or bailiff, and formerly there was regularly held in it the hundred court for the trial of causes, though now fallen into disuse. In some of the more northern counties these hundreds are called wapentakes.

T H E subdivision of hundreds into tithings seems to be most peculiarly the invention of Alfred: the institution of hundreds themselves he rather introduced than invented. For they seem to have obtained in Denmark: and we find that in France a regulation of this sort was made above two hundred years before; set on foot by Clotharius and Childebert, with a view of obliging each district to answer for the robberies committed in it's own division. These divisions were, in that country, as well military as civil; and each contained a hundred freemen; who were subject to an officer called the *centenarius*; a number of which *centenarii* were themselves subject to a superior officer called the count or *comes*. And indeed this institution of hundreds may be traced back as far as the antient Germans, from whom were derived both the Franks who became masters of Gaul, and the Saxons who settled in England. For we read in Tacitus, that both the thing and the name were well known to that warlike people. "*Centeni ex singulis pagis sunt, idque ipsum inter suos vocantur; et quod primo numerus fuit, jam nomen et honor est.*"

A N indefinite number of these hundreds make up a county or shire. Shire is a Saxon word signifying a division; but a county, *comitatus*, is plainly derived from *comes*, the count of the Franks; that is, the earl, or alderman (as the Saxons called him) of the shire, to whom the government of it was intrusted. This he usually exercised by his deputy, still called in Latin *vice-comes*, and in English the sheriff, shrieve, or shire-reeve, signifying the officer of the shire; upon whom by process of time the civil administration of it is now totally devolved. In some counties there is an intermediate division, between the shire and the hundreds, as lathes in Kent, and rapes in Sussex, each of them containing about three or four hundreds apiece. These had formerly their lathe-reeves and rape-reeves, acting in subordination to the shire-reeve. Where a county is divided into *three* of these intermediate jurisdictions, they are called trithings, which were antiently governed by a trithing-reeve. These trithings still subsist in the large county of York, where by an easy corruption they are denominated ridings; the north, the east, and the west-riding. The number of counties in England and Wales have been different at different times: at present there are forty in England, and twelve in Wales.

T H R E E of these counties, Chester, Durham, and Lancaster, are called counties palatine. The two former are such by prescription, or immemorial custom; or, at least as old as the Norman conquest: the latter was created by king Edward III, in favour of Henry Plantagenet, first earl and then duke of Lancaster, whose heiress John of Gant the king's son had married; and afterwards confirmed in parliament, to honour John of Gant himself; whom, on the death of his father-in-law, he had also created duke of Lancaster. Counties palatine are so called *a palatio*, because the owners thereof, the earl of Chester, the bishop of Durham, and the duke of Lancaster, had in those counties *jura regalia*, as fully as the king hath in his palace; *regalem potestatem in omnibus*, as Bracton expresses it. They might pardon treasons, murders, and felonies; they appointed all judges and justices of the peace; all writs and indictments ran in their names, as in other counties in the king's; and all offences were said to be done against their peace, and not, as in other places, *contra pacem domini regis*. And indeed by the antient law, in all peculiar jurisdictions, offences were said to be done against his peace in whose court they were tried; in a court leet, *contra pacem domini*; in the court of a corporation, *contra pacem ballivorum*; in the sheriff's court or tourn, *contra pacem vice-comitis*. These palatine privileges were in all probability originally granted to the counties of Chester and Durham, because they bordered upon enemies countries, Wales and Scotland; in order that the owners, being encouraged by so large an authority, might be the more watchful in it's defence; and that the inhabitants, having justice administered at home, might not be obliged to go out of the county, and leave it open to the enemies incursions. And upon this account also there were formerly two other counties palatine, Pembrokeshire and Hexamshire, the latter now united with Northumberland: but these were abolished by parliament, the former in 27 Hen. VIII, the latter in 14 Eliz. And in 27 Hen. VIII likewise, the powers beforementioned of owners of counties palatine were abridged; the reason for their continuance in a manner ceasing: though still all writs are witnessed in their names, and all forfeitures for treason by the common law accrue to them.

O F these three, the county of Durham is now the only one remaining in the hands of a subject. For the earldom of Chester, as Camden testifies, was united to the crown by Henry III, and has ever since given title to the king's eldest son. And the county palatine, or duchy, of Lancaster was the property of Henry of Bolinbroke, the son of John of Gant, at the time when he wrested the crown from king Richard II, and assumed the title of Henry IV. But he was too prudent to suffer this to be united to the crown, lest, if he lost one, he should lose the other also. For, as Plowden and sir Edward Coke observe, "he knew he had the duchy of Lancaster by sure and indefeasible title, but that his title to the crown was not so assured: for that after the decease of Richard II the right of the crown was in the heir of Lionel duke of Clarence, *second* son of Edward III; John of Gant, father to this Henry IV, being but the *fourth* son." And therefore he procured an act of parliament, in the first year of his reign, to keep it distinct and separate from the crown, and so it descended to his son, and grandson, Henry V, and Henry VI. Henry VI being attainted in 1 Edw. IV, this duchy was declared in parliament to have become forfeited to the crown, and at the same time an act was made to keep it still distinct and separate from other inheritances of the crown. And in 1 Hen. VII another act was made to vest the inheritance thereof in Henry VII and his heirs; and in this state, say sir Edward Coke and Lambard, viz. in the natural heirs or posterity of Henry VII, did the right of the duchy remain to their days; a separate and distinct inheritance from that of the crown of England.

THERE are also counties *corporate*, which are certain cities and towns, some with more, some with less territory annexed to them; to which out of special grace and favour the kings of England have granted to be counties of themselves, and not to be comprized in any other county; but to be governed by their own sheriffs and other magistrates, so that no officers of the county at large have any power to intermeddle therein. Such are London, York, Bristol, Norwich, Coventry, and many others. And thus much of the countries subject to the laws of England.

Chapter the first.

Of the absolute RIGHTS of INDIVIDUALS.

THE objects of the laws of England are so very numerous and extensive, that, in order to consider them with any tolerable ease and perspicuity, it will be necessary to distribute them methodically, under proper and distinct heads; avoiding as much as possible divisions too large and comprehensive on the one hand, and too trifling and minute on the other; both of which are equally productive of confusion.

NOW, as municipal law is a rule of civil conduct, commanding what is right, and prohibiting what is wrong; or, as Cicero, and after him our Bracton, has expressed it, *sanctio justa, jubens honesta et prohibens contraria*; it follows, that the primary and principal objects of the law are RIGHTS, and WRONGS. In the prosecution therefore of these commentaries, I shall follow this very simple and obvious division; and shall in the first place consider the *rights* that are commanded, and secondly the *wrongs* that are forbidden by the laws of England.

RIGHTS are however liable to another subdivision; being either, first, those which concern, and are annexed to the persons of men, and are then called *jura personarum* or the *rights of persons*; or they are, secondly, such as a man may acquire over external objects, or things unconnected with his person, which are stiled *jura rerum* or the *rights of things*. Wrongs also are divisible into, first, *private wrongs*, which, being an infringement merely of particular rights, concern individuals only, and are called civil injuries; and secondly, *public wrongs*, which, being a breach of general and public rights, affect the whole community, and are called crimes and misdemesnors.

THE objects of the laws of England falling into this fourfold division, the present commentaries will therefore consist of the four following parts: 1. *The rights of persons*, with the means whereby such rights may be either acquired or lost. 2. *The rights of things*, with the means also of acquiring and losing them. 3. *Private wrongs*, or civil injuries; with the means of redressing them by law. 4. *Public wrongs*, or crimes and misdemesnors; with the means of prevention and punishment.

WE are now, first, to consider *the rights of persons*, with the means of acquiring and losing them.

NOW the rights of persons that are commanded to be observed by the municipal law are of two sorts; first, such as are due *from* every citizen, which are usually called civil *duties*; and, secondly, such as belong *to* him, which is the more popular acceptation of *rights* or *jura*. Both may indeed be comprized in this latter division; for, as all social duties are of a relative nature, at the same time that they are due *from* one man, or set of men, they must also be

I

due *to* another. But I apprehend it will be more clear and easy, to consider many of them as duties required from, rather than as rights belonging to, particular persons. Thus, for instance, allegiance is usually, and therefore most easily, considered as the duty of the people, and protection as the duty of the magistrate; and yet they are, reciprocally, the rights as well as duties of each other. Allegiance is the right of the magistrate, and protection the right of the people.

P E R S O N S also are divided by the law into either natural persons, or artificial. Natural persons are such as the God of nature formed us: artificial are such as created and devised by human laws for the purposes of society and government; which are called corporations or bodies politic.

T H E rights of persons considered in their natural capacities are also of two sorts, absolute, and relative. Absolute, which are such as appertain and belong to particular men, merely as individuals or single persons: relative, which are incident to them as members of society, and standing in various relations to each other. The first, that is, absolute rights, will be the subject of the present chapter.

B Y the absolute *rights* of individuals we mean those which are so in their primary and strictest sense; such as would belong to their persons merely in a state of nature, and which every man is intitled to enjoy whether out of society or in it. But with regard to the absolute *duties*, which man is bound to perform considered as a mere individual, it is not to be expected that any human municipal laws should at all explain or enforce them. For the end and intent of such laws being only to regulate the behaviour of mankind, as they are members of society, and stand in various relations to each other, they have consequently no business or concern with any but social or relative duties. Let a man therefore be ever so abandoned in his principles, or vitious in his practice, provided he keeps his wickedness to himself, and does not offend against the rules of public decency, he is out of the reach of human laws. But if he makes his vices public, though they be such as seem principally to affect himself, (as drunkenness, or the like) they then become, by the bad example they set, of pernicious effects to society; and therefore it is then the business of human laws to correct them. Here the circumstance of publication is what alters the nature of the case. *Public* sobriety is a relative duty, and therefore enjoined by our laws: *private* sobriety is an absolute duty, which, whether it be performed or not, human tribunals can never know; and therefore they can never enforce it by any civil sanction. But, with respect to *rights*, the case is different. Human laws define and enforce as well those rights which belong to a man considered as an individual, as those which belong to him considered as related to others.

F O R the principal aim of society is to protect individuals in the enjoyment of those absolute rights, which were vested in them by the immutable laws of nature; but which could not be preserved in peace without that mutual assistance and intercourse, which is gained by the institution of friendly and social communities. Hence it follows, that the first and primary end of human laws is to maintain and regulate these *absolute* rights of individuals. Such rights as are social and *relative* result from, and are posterior to, the formation of states and societies: so that to maintain and regulate these, is clearly a subsequent consideration. And therefore the principal view of human laws is, or ought always to be, to explain, protect, and enforce such rights as are absolute, which in themselves are few and simple; and, then, such rights as are relative, which arising from a variety of connexions, will be far more numerous and more complicated. These will take up a greater space in any code of laws, and hence may appear to be more attended to, though in reality they are not, than the rights of the former kind. Let us therefore proceed to examine how far all laws ought, and how far the laws of England actually do, take notice of these absolute rights, and provide for their lasting security.

THE absolute rights of man, considered as a free agent, endowed with discernment to know good from evil, and with power of choosing those measures which appear to him to be most desirable, are usually summed up in one general appellation, and denominated the natural liberty of mankind. This natural liberty consists properly in a power of acting as one thinks fit, without any restraint or control, unless by the law of nature: being a right inherent in us by birth, and one of the gifts of God to man at his creation, when he endued him with the faculty of freewill. But every man, when he enters into society, gives up a part of his natural liberty, as the price of so valuable a purchase; and, in consideration of receiving the advantages of mutual commerce, obliges himself to conform to those laws, which the community has thought proper to establish. And this species of legal obedience and conformity is infinitely more desirable, than that wild and savage liberty which is sacrificed to obtain it. For no man, that considers a moment, would wish to retain the absolute and uncontroled power of doing whatever he pleases; the consequence of which is, that every other man would also have the same power; and then there would be no security to individuals in any of the enjoyments of life. Political therefore, or civil, liberty, which is that of a member of society, is no other than natural liberty so far restrained by human laws (and no farther) as is necessary and expedient for the general advantage of the publick. Hence we may collect that the law, which restrains a man from doing mischief to his fellow citizens, though it diminishes the natural, increases the civil liberty of mankind: but every wanton and causeless restraint of the will of the subject, whether practiced by a monarch, a nobility, or a popular assembly, is a degree of tyranny. Nay, that even laws themselves, whether made with or without our consent, if they regulate and constrain our conduct in matters of mere indifference, without any good end in view, are laws destructive of liberty: whereas if any public advantage can arise from observing such precepts, the control of our private inclinations, in one or two particular points, will conduce to preserve our general freedom in others of more importance; by supporting that state, of society, which alone can secure our independence. Thus the statute of king Edward IV, which forbad the fine gentlemen of those times (under the degree of a lord) to wear pikes upon their shoes or boots of more than two inches in length, was a law that savoured of oppression; because, however ridiculous the fashion then in use might appear, the restraining it by pecuniary penalties could serve no purpose of common utility. But the statute of king Charles II, which prescribes a thing seemingly as indifferent; viz. a dress for the dead, who are all ordered to be buried in woollen; is a law consistent with public liberty, for it encourages the staple trade, on which in great measure depends the universal good of the nation. So that laws, when prudently framed, are by no means subversive but rather introductive of liberty; for (as Mr Locke has well observed) where there is no law, there is no freedom. But then, on the other hand, that constitution or frame of government, that system of laws, is alone calculated to maintain civil liberty, which leaves the subject entire master of his own conduct, except in those points wherein the public good requires some direction or restraint.

T H E idea and practice of this political or civil liberty flourish in their highest vigour in these kingdoms, where it falls little short of perfection, and can only be lost or destroyed by the folly or demerits of it's owner: the legislature, and of course the laws of England, being peculiarly adapted to the preservation of this inestimable blessing even in the meanest subject. Very different from the modern constitutions of other states, on the continent of Europe, and from the genius of the imperial law; which in general are calculated to vest an arbitrary and despotic power of controlling the actions of the subject in the prince, or in a few grandees. And this spirit of liberty is so deeply implanted in our constitution, and rooted even in our very soil, that a slave or a negro, the moment he lands in England, falls under the protection of the laws, and with regard to all natural rights becomes *eo instanti* a freeman.

T H E absolute rights of every Englishman (which, taken in a political and extensive sense, are usually called their liberties) as they are founded on nature and reason, so they are coeval with our form of government; though subject at times to fluctuate and change: their establishment (excellent as it is) being still human. At some times we have seen them depressed by overbearing and tyrannical princes; at others so luxuriant as even to tend to anarchy, a worse state than tyranny itself, as any government is better than none at all. But the vigour of our free constitution has always delivered the nation from these embarrassments, and, as soon as the convulsions consequent on the struggle have been over, the ballance of our rights and liberties has settled to it's proper level; and their fundamental articles have been from time to time asserted in parliament, as often as they were thought to be in danger.

F I R S T , by the great charter of liberties, which was obtained, sword in hand, from king John; and afterwards, with some alterations, confirmed in parliament by king Henry the third, his son. Which charter contained very few new grants; but, as sir Edward Cokeobserves, was for the most part declaratory of the principal grounds of the fundamental laws of England. Afterwards by the statute called*confirmatio cartarum*, whereby the great charter is directed to be allowed as the common law; all judgments contrary to it are declared void; copies of it are ordered to be sent to all cathedral churches, and read twice a year to the people; and sentence of excommunication is directed to be as constantly denounced against all those that by word, deed, or counsel act contrary thereto, or in any degree infringe it. Next by a multitude of subsequent corroborating statutes, (sir Edward Coke, I think, reckons thirty two,) from the first Edward to Henry the fourth. Then, after a long interval, by *the petition of right*; which was a parliamentary declaration of the liberties of the people, assented to by king Charles the first in the beginning of his reign. Which was closely followed by the still more ample concessions made by that unhappy prince to his parliament, before the fatal rupture between them; and by the many salutary laws, particularly the *habeas corpus* act, passed under Charles the second. To these succeeded *the bill of rights*, or declaration delivered by the lords and commons to the prince and princess of Orange 13 February 1688; and afterwards enacted in parliament, when they became king and queen: which declaration concludes in these remarkable words; "and they do claim, demand, and insist upon all and singular the premises, as their undoubted rights and liberties." And the act of parliament itself recognizes "all and singular the rights and liberties asserted and claimed in the said declaration to be the true, antient, and indubitable rights of the people of this kingdom." Lastly, these liberties were again asserted at the commencement of the present century, in the *act of settlement*, whereby the crown is limited to his present majesty's illustrious house, and some new provisions were added at the same fortunate aera for better securing our religion, laws, and liberties; which the statute declares to be "the birthright of the people of England;" according to the antient doctrine of the common law.

THUS much for the *declaration* of our rights and liberties. The rights themselves thus defined by these several statutes, consist in a number of private immunities; which will appear, from what has been premised, to be indeed no other, than either that *residuum* of natural liberty, which is not required by the laws of society to be sacrificed to public convenience; or else those civil privileges, which society hath engaged to provide, in lieu of the natural liberties so given up by individuals. These therefore were formerly, either by inheritance or purchase, the rights of all mankind; but, in most other countries of the world being now more or less debased and destroyed, they at present may be said to remain, in a peculiar and emphatical manner, the rights of the people of England. And these may be reduced to three principal or primary articles; the right of personal security, the right of personal liberty; and the right of private property: because as there is no other known method of compulsion, or of abridging man's natural free will, but by an infringement or diminution of one or other of these important rights, the preservation of these, inviolate, may justly be said to include the preservation of our civil immunities in their largest and most extensive sense.

I. THE right of personal security consists in a person's legal and uninterrupted enjoyment of his life, his limbs, his body, his health, and his reputation.

1. LIFE is the immediate gift of God, a right inherent by nature in every individual; and it begins in contemplation of law as soon as an infant is able to stir in the mother's womb. For if a woman is quick with child, and by a potion, or otherwise, killeth it in her womb; or if any one beat her, whereby the child dieth in her body, and she is delivered of a dead child; this, though not murder, was by the antient law homicide or manslaughter. But at present it is not looked upon in quite so atrocious a light, though it remains a very heinous misdemesnor.

5

A N infant *in ventre sa mere*, or in the mother's womb, is supposed in law to be born for many purposes. It is capable of having a legacy, or a surrender of a copyhold estate made to it. It may have a guardian assigned to it; and it is enabled to have an estate limited to it's use, and to take afterwards by such limitation, as if it were then actually born. And in this point the civil law agrees with ours.

2. A M A N ' S limbs, (by which for the present we only understand those members which may be useful to him in fight, and the loss of which only amounts to mayhem by the common law) are also the gift of the wise creator; to enable man to protect himself from external injuries in a state of nature. To these therefore he has a natural inherent right; and they cannot be wantonly destroyed or disabled without a manifest breach of civil liberty.

B O T H the life and limbs of a man are of such high value, in the estimation of the law of England, that it pardons even homicide if committed *se defendendo*, or in order to preserve them. For whatever is done by a man, to save either life or member, is looked upon as done upon the highest necessity and compulsion. Therefore if a man through fear of death or mayhem is prevailed upon to execute a deed, or do any other legal act; these, though accompanied with all other the requisite solemnities, are totally void in law, if forced upon him by a well-grounded apprehension of losing his life, or even his limbs, in case of his non-compliance. And the same is also a sufficient excuse for the commission of many misdemesnors, as will appear in the fourth book. The constraint a man is under in these circumstances is called in law *duress*, from the Latin *durities*, of which there are two sorts; duress of imprisonment, where a man actually loses his liberty, of which we shall presently speak; and duress *per minas*, where the hardship is only threatened and impending, which is that we are now discoursing of. Duress *per minas* is either for fear of loss of life, or else for fear of mayhem, or loss of limb. And this fear must be upon sufficient reason; "*non*," as Bracton expresses it, "*suspicio cujuslibet vani et meticulosi hominis, sed talis qui possit cadere in virum constantem; talis enim debet esse metus, qui in se contineat vitae periculum, aut corporis cruciatum.*" A fear of battery, or being beaten, though never so well grounded, is no duress; neither is the fear of having one's house burnt, or one's goods taken away and destroyed; because in these cases, should the threat be performed, a man may have satisfaction by recovering equivalent damages: but no suitable atonement can be made for the loss of life, or limb. And the indulgence shewn to a man under this, the principal, sort of duress, the fear of losing his life or limbs, agrees also with that maxim of the civil law; *ignoscitur ei qui sanguinem suum qualiter qualiter redemptum voluit.*

T H E law not only regards life and member, and protects every man in the enjoyment of them, but also furnishes him with every thing necessary for their support. For there is no man so indigent or wretched, but he may demand a supply sufficient for all the necessities of life, from the more opulent part of the community, by means of the several statutes enacted for the relief of the poor, of which in their proper places. A humane provision; yet, though dictated by the principles of society, discountenanced by the Roman laws. For the edicts of the emperor Constantine, commanding the public to maintain the children of those who were unable to provide for them, in order to prevent the murder and exposure of infants, an institution founded on the same principle as our foundling hospitals, though comprized in the Theodosian code, were rejected in Justinian's collection.

T H E S E rights, of life and member, can only be determined by the death of the person; which is either a civil or natural death. The civil death commences if any man be banished the realm by the process of the common law, or enters into religion; that is, goes into a monastery, and becomes there a monk professed: in which cases he is absolutely dead in law, and his next heir shall have his estate. For, such banished man is entirely cut off from society; and such a monk, upon his profession, renounces solemnly all secular concerns: and besides, as the popish clergy claimed an exemption from the duties of civil life, and the commands of the temporal magistrate, the genius of the English law would not suffer those persons to enjoy the benefits of society, who secluded themselves from it, and refused to submit to it's regulations. A monk is therefore accounted *civiliter mortuus*, and when he enters into religion may, like other dying men, make his testament and executors; or, if he makes none, the ordinary may grant administration to his next of kin, as if he were actually dead intestate. And such executors and administrators shall have the same power, and may bring the same actions for debts due *to* the religious, and are liable to the same actions for those due *from* him, as if he were naturally deceased. Nay, so far has this principle been carried, that when one was bound in a bond to an abbot and his successors, and afterwards made his executors and professed himself a monk of the same abbey, and in process of time was himself made abbot thereof; here the law gave him, in the capacity of abbot, an action of debt against his own executors to recover the money due. In short, a monk or religious is so effectually dead in law, that a lease made even to a third person, during the life (generally) of one who afterwards becomes a monk, determines by such his entry into religion: for which reason leases, and other conveyances, for life, are usually made to have and to hold for the term of one's *natural* life.

T H I S natural life being, as was before observed, the immediate donation of the great creator, cannot legally be disposed of or destroyed by any individual, neither by the person himself nor by any other of his fellow creatures, merely upon their own authority. Yet nevertheless it may, by the divine permission, be frequently forfeited for the breach of those laws of society, which are enforced by the sanction of capital punishments; of the nature, restrictions, expedience, and legality of which, we may hereafter more conveniently enquire in the concluding book of these commentaries. At present, I shall only observe, that whenever the *constitution* of a state vests in any man, or body of men, a power of destroying at pleasure, without the direction of laws, the lives or members of the subject, such constitution is in the highest degree tyrannical: and that whenever any *laws* direct such destruction for light and trivial causes, such laws are likewise tyrannical, though in an inferior degree; because here the subject is aware of the danger he is exposed to, and may by prudent caution provide against it. The statute law of

7

England does therefore very seldom, and the common law does never, inflict any punishment extending to life or limb, unless upon the highest necessity: and the constitution is an utter stranger to any arbitrary power of killing or maiming the subject without the express warrant of law. "*Nullus liber homo*, says the great charter, *aliquo modo destruatur, nisi per legale judicium parium suorum aut per legem terrae.*" Which words, "*aliquo modo destruatur,*" according to sir Edward Coke, include a prohibition not only of *killing*, and *maiming*, but also of *torturing* (to which our laws are strangers) and of every oppression by colour of an illegal authority. And it is enacted by the statute 5 Edw. III. c. 9. that no man shall be forejudged of life or limb, contrary to the great charter and the law of the land: and again, by statute 28 Ed. III. c. 3. that no man shall be put to death, without being brought to answer by due process of law.

3. B E S I D E S those limbs and members that may be necessary to man, in order to defend himself or annoy his enemy, the rest of his person or body is also entitled by the same natural right to security from the corporal insults of menaces, assaults, beating, and wounding; though such insults amount not to destruction of life or member.

4. T H E preservation of a man's health from such practices as may prejudice or annoy it, and

5. T H E security of his reputation or good name from the arts of detraction and slander, are rights to which every man is intitled, by reason and natural justice; since without these it is impossible to have the perfect enjoyment of any other advantage or right. But these three last articles (being of much less importance than those which have gone before, and those which are yet to come) it will suffice to have barely mentioned among the rights of persons; referring the more minute discussion of their several branches, to those parts of our commentaries which treat of the infringement of these rights, under the head of personal wrongs.

II. N E X T to personal security, the law of England regards, asserts, and preserves the personal liberty of individuals. This personal liberty consists in the power of loco-motion, of changing situation, or removing one's person to whatsoever place one's own inclination may direct; without imprisonment or restraint, unless by due course of law. Concerning which we may make the same observations as upon the preceding article; that it is a right strictly natural; that the laws of England have never abridged it without sufficient cause; and, that in this kingdom it cannot ever be abridged at the mere discretion of the magistrate, without the explicit permission of the laws. Here again the language of the great charter is, that no freeman shall be taken or imprisoned, but by the lawful judgment of his equals, or by the law of the land. And many subsequent old statutes expressly direct, that no man shall be taken or imprisoned by suggestion or petition to the king, or his council, unless it be by legal indictment, or the process of the common law. By the petition of right, 3 Car. I, it is enacted, that no freeman shall be imprisoned or detained without cause shewn, to which he may make answer according to law. By 16 Car. I. c. 10. if any person be restrained of his liberty by order or decree of any illegal court, or by command of the king's majesty in person, or by warrant of the council board, or of any of the privy council; he shall, upon demand of his counsel, have a writ of *habeas corpus*, to bring his body before the court of king's bench or common pleas; who shall determine whether the cause of his commitment be just, and thereupon do as to justice shall appertain. And by 31 Car. II. c. 2. commonly called *the habeas corpus act*, the methods of obtaining this writ are so plainly pointed out and enforced, that, so long as this statute remains unimpeached, no subject of England can be long detained in prison, except in those cases in which the law requires and justifies such detainer. And, lest this act should be evaded by demanding unreasonable bail, or sureties for the prisoner's appearance, it is declared by 1 W. & M. st. 2. c. 2. that excessive bail ought not to be required.

O F great importance to the public is the preservation of this personal liberty: for if once it were left in the power of any, the highest, magistrate to imprison arbitrarily whomever he or his officers thought proper, (as in France it is daily practiced by the crown) there would soon be an end of all other rights and immunities. Some have thought, that unjust attacks, even upon life, or property, at the arbitrary will of the magistrate, are less dangerous to the commonwealth, than such as are made upon the personal liberty of the subject. To bereave a man of life, or by violence to confiscate his estate, without accusation or trial, would be so gross and notorious an act of despotism, as must at once convey the alarm of tyranny throughout the whole kingdom. But confinement of the person, by secretly hurrying him to gaol, where his sufferings are unknown or forgotten; is a less public, a less striking, and therefore a more dangerous engine of arbitrary government. And yet sometimes, when the state is in real danger, even this may be a necessary measure. But the happiness of our constitution is, that it is not left to the executive power to determine when the danger of the state is so great, as to render this measure expedient. For the parliament only, or legislative power, whenever it sees proper, can authorize the crown, by suspending the *habeas corpus* act for a short and limited time, to imprison suspected persons without giving any reason for so doing. As the senate of Rome was wont to have recourse to a dictator, a magistrate of absolute authority, when they judged the republic in any imminent danger. The decree of the senate, which usually preceded the nomination of this magistrate, "*dent operam consules, nequid respublica detrimenti capiat*," was called the *senatus consultum ultimae necessitatis.* In like manner this experiment ought only to be tried in cases of extreme emergency; and in these the nation parts with it's liberty for a while, in order to preserve it for ever.

T H E confinement of the person, in any wise, is an imprisonment. So that the keeping a man against his will in a private house, putting him in the stocks, arresting or forcibly detaining him in the street, is an imprisonment. And the law so much discourages unlawful confinement, that if a man is under *duress of imprisonment*, which we before explained to mean a compulsion by an illegal restraint of liberty, until he seals a bond or the like; he may alledge this duress, and avoid the extorted bond. But if a man be lawfully imprisoned, and either to procure his discharge, or on any other fair account, seals a bond or a deed, this is not by duress of imprisonment, and he is not at liberty to avoid it. To make imprisonment lawful, it must either be, by process from the courts of judicature, or by warrant from some legal officer, having authority to commit to prison; which warrant must be in writing, under the hand and seal of the magistrate, and express the causes of the commitment, in order to be examined into (if necessary) upon a *habeas corpus*. If there be no cause expressed, the goaler is not bound to detain the prisoner. For the law judges in this respect, saith sir Edward Coke, like Festus the Roman governor; that it is unreasonable to send a prisoner, and not to signify withal the crimes alleged against him.

A NATURAL and regular consequence of this personal liberty, is, that every Englishman may claim a right to abide in his own country so long as he pleases; and not to be driven from it unless by the sentence of the law. The king indeed, by his royal prerogative, may issue out his writ *ne exeat regnum*, and prohibit any of his subjects from going into foreign parts without licence. This may be necessary for the public service, and safeguard of the commonwealth. But no power on earth, except the authority of parliament, can send any subject of England *out of* the land against his will; no not even a criminal. For exile, or transportation, is a punishment unknown to the common law; and, wherever it is now inflicted, it is either by the choice of the criminal himself, to escape a capital punishment, or else by the express direction of some modern act of parliament. To this purpose the great charter declares that no freeman shall be banished, unless by the judgment of his peers, or by the law of the land. And by the *habeas corpus* act, 31 Car. II. c. 2. (that second *magna carta*, and stable bulwark of our liberties) it is enacted, that no subject of this realm, who is an inhabitant of England, Wales, or Berwick, shall be sent prisoner into Scotland, Ireland, Jersey, Guernsey, or places beyond the seas; (where they cannot have the benefit and protection of the common law) but that all such imprisonments shall be illegal; that the person, who shall dare to commit another contrary to this law, shall be disabled from bearing any office, shall incur the penalty of a praemunire, and be incapable of receiving the king's pardon: and the party suffering shall also have his private action against the person committing, and all his aiders, advisers and abettors, and shall recover treble costs; besides his damages, which no jury shall assess at less than five hundred pounds.

THE law is in this respect so benignly and liberally construed for the benefit of the subject, that, though *within* the realm the king may command the attendance and service of all his liege-men, yet he cannot send any man *out of* the realm, even upon the public service: he cannot even constitute a man lord deputy or lieutenant of Ireland against his will, nor make him a foreign embassador. For this might in reality be no more than an honorable exile.

III. THE third absolute right, inherent in every Englishman, is that of property; which consists in the free use, enjoyment, and disposal of all his acquisitions, without any control or diminution, save only by the laws of the land. The original of private property is probably founded in nature, as will be more fully explained in the second book of the ensuing commentaries: but certainly the modifications under which we at present find it, the method of conserving it in the present owner, and of translating it from man to man, are entirely derived from society; and are some of those civil advantages, in exchange for which every individual has resigned a part of his natural liberty. The laws of England are therefore, in point of honor and justice, extremely watchful in ascertaining and protecting this right. Upon this principle the great charter has declared that no freeman shall be disseised, or divested, of his freehold, or of his liberties, or free customs, but by the judgment of his peers, or by the law of the land. And by a variety of antient statutes it is enacted, that no man's lands or goods shall be seised into the king's hands, against the great charter, and the law of the land; and that no man shall be disinherited, nor put out of his franchises or freehold, unless he be duly brought to answer, and be forejudged by course of law; and if any thing be done to the contrary, it shall be redressed, and holden for none.

S O great moreover is the regard of the law for private property, that it will not authorize the least violation of it; no, not even for the general good of the whole community. If a new road, for instance, were to be made through the grounds of a private person, it might perhaps be extensively beneficial to the public; but the law permits no man, or set of men, to do this without consent of the owner of the land. In vain may it be urged, that the good of the individual ought to yield to that of the community; for it would be dangerous to allow any private man, or even any public tribunal, to be the judge of this common good, and to decide whether it be expedient or no. Besides, the public good is in nothing more essentially interested, than in the protection of every individual's private rights, as modelled by the municipal law. In this, and similar cases the legislature alone can, and indeed frequently does, interpose, and compel the individual to acquiesce. But how does it interpose and compel? Not by absolutely stripping the subject of his property in an arbitrary manner; but by giving him a full indemnification and equivalent for the injury thereby sustained. The public is now considered as an individual, treating with an individual for an exchange. All that the legislature does is to oblige the owner to alienate his possessions for a reasonable price; and even this is an exertion of power, which the legislature indulges with caution, and which nothing but the legislature can perform.

N O R is this the only instance in which the law of the land has postponed even public necessity to the sacred and inviolable rights of private property. For no subject of England can be constrained to pay any aids or taxes, even for the defence of the realm or the support of government, but such as are imposed by his own consent, or that of his representatives in parliament. By the statute 25 Edw. I. c. 5 and 6. it is provided, that the king shall not take any aids or tasks, but by the common assent of the realm. And what that common assent is, is more fully explained by 34 Edw. I. st. 4. cap. 1. which enacts, that no talliage or aid shall be taken without assent of the arch-bishops, bishops, earls, barons, knights, burgesses, and other freemen of the land: and again by 14 Edw. III. st. 2. c. 1. the prelates, earls, barons, and commons, citizens, burgesses, and merchants shall not be charged to make any aid, if it be not by the common assent of the great men and commons in parliament. And as this fundamental law had been shamefully evaded under many succeeding princes, by compulsive loans, and benevolences extorted without a real and voluntary consent, it was made an article in the petition of right 3 Car. l, that no man shall be compelled to yield any gift, loan, or benevolence, tax, or such like charge, without common consent by act of parliament. And, lastly, by the statute 1 W. & M. st. 2. c. 2. it is declared, that levying money for or to the use of the crown, by pretence of prerogative, without grant of parliament; or for longer time, or in other manner, than the same is or shall be granted, is illegal.

I N the three preceding articles we have taken a short view of the principal absolute rights which appertain to every Englishman. But in vain would these rights be declared, ascertained, and protected by the dead letter of the laws, if the constitution had provided no other method to secure their actual enjoyment. It has therefore established certain other auxiliary subordinate rights of the subject, which serve principally as barriers to protect and maintain inviolate the three great and primary rights, of personal security, personal liberty, and private property. These are,

1. T H E constitution, powers, and privileges of parliament, of which I shall treat at large in the ensuing chapter.

2. T H E limitation of the king's prerogative, by bounds so certain and notorious, that it is impossible he should exceed them without the consent of the people. Of this also I shall treat in it's proper place. The former of these keeps the legislative power in due health and vigour, so as to make it improbable that laws should be enacted destructive of general liberty: the latter is a guard upon the executive power, by restraining it from acting either beyond or in contradiction to the laws, that are framed and established by the other.

3. A T H I R D subordinate right of every Englishman is that of applying to the courts of justice for redress of injuries. Since the law is in England the supreme arbiter of every man's life, liberty, and property, courts of justice must at all times be open to the subject, and the law be duly administred therein. The emphatical words of *magna carta*, spoken in the person of the king, who in judgment of law (says sir Edward Coke) is ever present and repeating them in all his courts, are these; "*nulli vendemus, nulli negabimus, aut differemus rectum vel justitiam*: and therefore every subject," continues the same learned author, "for injury done to him *in bonis, in terris, vel persona*, by any other subject, be he ecclesiastical or temporal without any exception, may take his remedy by the course of the law, and have justice and right for the injury done to him, freely without sale, fully without any denial, and speedily without delay." It were endless to enumerate all the *affirmative* acts of parliament wherein justice is directed to be done according to the law of the land: and what that law is, every subject knows; or may know if he pleases: for it depends not upon the arbitrary will of any judge; but is permanent, fixed, and unchangeable, unless by authority of parliament. I shall however just mention a few *negative* statutes, whereby abuses, perversions, or delays of justice, especially by the prerogative, are restrained. It is ordained by *magna carta*, that no freeman shall be outlawed, that is, put out of the protection and benefit of the laws, but

according to the law of the land. By 2 Edw. III. c. 8. and 11 Ric. II. c. 10. it is enacted, that no commands or letters shall be sent under the great seal, or the little seal, the signet, or privy seal, in disturbance of the law; or to disturb or delay common right: and, though such commandments should come, the judges shall not cease to do right. And by 1 W. & M. st. 2. c. 2. it is declared, that the pretended power of suspending, or dispensing with laws, or the execution of laws, by regal authority without consent of parliament, is illegal.

NOT only the substantial part, or judicial decisions, of the law, but also the formal part, or method of proceeding, cannot be altered but by parliament: for if once those outworks were demolished, there would be no inlet to all manner of innovation in the body of the law itself. The king, it is true, may erect new courts of justice; but then they must proceed according to the old established forms of the common law. For which reason it is declared in the statute 16 Car. I. c. 10. upon the dissolution of the court of starchamber, that neither his majesty, nor his privy council, have any jurisdiction, power, or authority by English bill, petition, articles, libel (which were the course of proceeding in the starchamber, borrowed from the civil law) or by any other arbitrary way whatsoever, to examine, or draw into question, determine or dispose of the lands or goods of any subjects of this kingdom; but that the same ought to be tried and determined in the ordinary courts of justice, and by *course of law*.

4. IF there should happen any uncommon injury, or infringement of the rights beforementioned, which the ordinary course of law is too defective to reach, there still remains a fourth subordinate right appertaining to every individual, namely, the right of petitioning the king, or either house of parliament, for the redress of grievances. In Russia we are told that the czar Peter established a law, that no subject might petition the throne, till he had first petitioned two different ministers of state. In case he obtained justice from neither, he might then present a third petition to the prince; but upon pain of death, if found to be in the wrong. The consequence of which was, that no one dared to offer such third petition; and grievances seldom falling under the notice of the sovereign, he had little opportunity to redress them. The restrictions, for some there are, which are laid upon petitioning in England, are of a nature extremely different; and while they promote the spirit of peace, they are no check upon that of liberty. Care only must be taken, lest, under the pretence of petitioning, the subject be guilty of any riot or tumult; as happened in the opening of the memorable parliament in 1640: and, to prevent this, it is provided by the statute 13 Car. II. st. 1. c. 5. that no petition to the king, or either house of parliament, for any alterations in church or state, shall be signed by above twenty persons, unless the matter thereof be approved by three justices of the peace or the major part of the grand jury, in the country; and in London by the lord mayor, aldermen, and common council; nor shall any petition be presented by more than two persons at a time. But under these regulations, it is declared by the statute 1 W. & M. st. 2. c. 2. that the subject hath a right to petition; and that all commitments and prosecutions for such petitioning are illegal.

5. T H E fifth and last auxiliary right of the subject, that I shall at present mention, is that of having arms for their defence, suitable to their condition and degree, and such as are allowed by law. Which is also declared by the same statute 1 W. & M. st. 2. c. 2. and is indeed a public allowance, under due restrictions, of the natural right of resistance and self-preservation, when the sanctions of society and laws are found insufficient to restrain the violence of oppression.

I N these several articles consist the rights, or, as they are frequently termed, the liberties of Englishmen: liberties more generally talked of, than thoroughly understood; and yet highly necessary to be perfectly known and considered by every man of rank or property, lest his ignorance of the points whereon it is founded should hurry him into faction and licentiousness on the one hand, or a pusillanimous indifference and criminal submission on the other. And we have seen that these rights consist, primarily, in the free enjoyment of personal security, of personal liberty, and of private property. So long as these remain inviolate, the subject is perfectly free; for every species of compulsive tyranny and oppression must act in opposition to one or other of these rights, having no other object upon which it can possibly be employed. To preserve these from violation, it is necessary that the constitution of parliaments be supported in it's full vigor; and limits certainly known, be set to the royal prerogative. And, lastly, to vindicate these rights, when actually violated or attacked, the subjects of England are entitled, in the first place, to the regular administration and free course of justice in the courts of law; next to the right of petitioning the king and parliament for redress of grievances; and lastly to the right of having and using arms for self-preservation and defence. And all these rights and liberties it is our birthright to enjoy entire; unless where the laws of our country have laid them under necessary restraints. Restraints in themselves so gentle and moderate, as will appear upon farther enquiry, that no man of sense or probity would wish to see them slackened. For all of us have it in our choice to do every thing that a good man would desire to do; and are restrained from nothing, but what would be pernicious either to ourselves or our fellow citizens. So that this review of our situation may fully justify the observation of a learned French author, who indeed generally both thought and wrote in the spirit of genuine freedom; and who hath not scrupled to profess, even in the very bosom of his native country, that the English is the only nation in the world, where political or civil liberty is the direct end of it's constitution. Recommending therefore to the student in our laws a farther and more accurate search into this extensive and important title, I shall close my remarks upon it with the expiring wish of the famous father Paul to his country, "E S T O   P E R P E T U A !"

CHAPTER THE SECOND.

OF THE PARLIAMENT.

WE are next to treat of the rights and duties of persons, as they are members of society, and stand in various relations to each other. These relations are either public or private: and we will first consider those that are public.

THE most universal public relation, by which men are connected together, is that of government; namely, as governors and governed, or, in other words, as magistrates and people. Of magistrates also some are *supreme*, in whom the sovereign power of the state resides; others are *subordinate*, deriving all their authority from the supreme magistrate, accountable to him for their conduct, and acting in an inferior secondary sphere.

IN all tyrannical governments the supreme magistracy, or the right both of *making* and of *enforcing* the laws, is vested in one and the same man, or one and the same body of men; and wherever these two powers are united together, there can be no public liberty. The magistrate may enact tyrannical laws, and execute them in a tyrannical manner, since he is possessed, in quality of dispenser of justice, with all the power which he as legislator thinks proper to give himself. But, where the legislative and executive authority are in distinct hands, the former will take care not to entrust the latter with so large a power, as may tend to the subversion of it's own independence, and therewith of the liberty of the subject. With us therefore in England this supreme power is divided into two branches; the one legislative, to wit, the parliament, consisting of king, lords, and commons; the other executive, consisting of the king alone. It will be the business of this chapter to consider the British parliament; in which the legislative power, and (of course) the supreme and absolute authority of the state, is vested by our constitution.

THE original or first institution of parliaments is one of those matters that lie so far hidden in the dark ages of antiquity, that the tracing of it out is a thing equally difficult and uncertain. The word, *parliament*, itself (or *colloquium*, as some of our historians translate it) is comparatively of modern date, derived from the French, and signifying the place where they met and conferred together. It was first applied to general assemblies of the states under Louis VII in France, about the middle of the twelfth century. But it is certain that, long before the introduction of the Norman language into England, all matters of importance were debated and settled in the great councils of the realm. A practice, which seems to have been universal among the northern nations, particularly the Germans; and carried by them into all the countries of Europe, which they overran at the dissolution of the Roman empire. Relics of which constitution, under various modifications and changes, are still to be met with in the diets of Poland, Germany, and Sweden, and the assembly of the estates in France; for what is there now called the parliament is only the supreme court of justice, composed of judges and advocates; which neither is in practice, nor is supposed to be in theory, a general council of the realm.

WITH us in England this general council hath been held immemorially, under the several names of *michel-synoth*, or great council, *michel-gemote* or great meeting, and more frequently *wittena-gemote* or the meeting of wise men. It was also stiled in Latin, *commune concilium regni*, *magnum concilium regis*, *curia magna*, *conventus magnatum vel procerum*, *assisa generalis*, and sometimes *communitas regni Angliae*. We have instances of it's meeting to order the affairs of the kingdom, to make new laws, and to amend the old, or, as Fleta expresses it, "*novis injuriis emersis nova constituere remedia*," so early as the reign of Ina king of the west Saxons, Offa king of the Mercians, and Ethelbert king of Kent, in the several realms of the heptarchy. And, after their union, the mirrour informs us, that king Alfred ordained for a perpetual usage, that these councils should meet twice in the year, or oftener, if need be, to treat of the government of God's people; how they should keep themselves from sin, should live in quiet, and should receive right. Our succeeding Saxon and Danish monarchs held frequent councils of this sort, as appears from their respective codes of laws; the titles whereof usually speak them to be enacted, either by the king with the advice of his wittena-gemote, or wise men, as, "*haec sunt instituta, quae Edgarus rex consilio sapientum suorum instituit*," or to be enacted by those sages with the advice of the king, as, "*haec sunt judicia, quae sapientes consilio regis Ethelstani instituerunt*," or lastly, to be enacted by them both together, as; "*hae sunt institutiones, quas rex Edmundus et episcopi sui cum sapientibus suis instituerunt*."

THERE is also no doubt but these great councils were held regularly under the first princes of the Norman line. Glanvil, who wrote in the reign of Henry the second, speaking of the particular amount of an amercement in the sheriff's court, says, it had never yet been ascertained by the general assise, or assembly, but was left to the custom of particular counties. Here the general assise is spoken of as a meeting well known, and it's statutes or decisions are put in a manifest contradistinction to customs, or the common law. And in Edward the third's time an act of parliament, made in the reign of William the conqueror, was pleaded in the case of the abbey of St Edmund's-bury, and judicially allowed by the court.

HENCE it indisputably appears, that parliaments, or general councils, are coeval with the kingdom itself. How those parliaments were constituted and composed, is another question, which has been matter of great dispute among our learned antiquarians; and, particularly, whether the commons were summoned at all; or, if summoned, at what period they began to form a distinct assembly. But it is not my intention here to enter into controversies of this sort. I hold it sufficient that it is generally agreed, that in the main the constitution of parliament, as it now stands, was marked out so long ago as the seventeenth year of king John, *A.D.* 1215, in the great charter granted by that prince; wherein he promises to summon all arch-bishops, bishops, abbots, earls, and greater barons, personally; and all other tenants in chief under the crown, by the sheriff and bailiffs; to meet at a certain place, with forty days notice, to assess aids and scutages when necessary. And this constitution has subsisted in fact at least from the year 1266, 49 Hen. III: there being still extant writs of that date, to summon knights, citizens, and burgesses to parliament. I proceed therefore to enquire wherein consists this constitution of parliament, as it now stands, and has stood for the space of five hundred years. And in the prosecution of this enquiry, I shall consider, first, the manner and time of it's assembling: secondly, it's constituent parts: thirdly, the laws and customs relating to parliament, considered as one aggregate body: fourthly and fifthly, the laws and customs relating to each house, separately and distinctly taken: sixthly, the methods of proceeding, and of making statutes, in both houses: and lastly, the manner of the parliament's adjournment, prorogation, and dissolution.

I. A S to the manner and time of assembling. The parliament is regularly to be summoned by the king's writ or letter, issued out of chancery by advice of the privy council, at least forty days before it begins to sit. It is a branch of the royal prerogative, that no parliament can be convened by it's own authority, or by the authority of any, except the king alone. And this prerogative is founded upon very good reason. For, supposing it had a right to meet spontaneously, without being called together, it is impossible to conceive that all the members, and each of the houses, would agree unanimously upon the proper time and place of meeting: and if half of the members met, and half absented themselves, who shall determine which is really the legislative body, the part assembled, or that which stays away? It is therefore necessary that the parliament should be called together at a determinate time and place; and highly becoming it's dignity and independence, that it should be called together by none but one of it's own constituent parts; and, of the three constituent parts, this office can only appertain to the king; as he is a single person, whose will may be uniform and steady; the first person in the nation, being superior to both houses in dignity; and the only branch of the legislature that has a separate existence, and is capable of performing any act at a time when no parliament is in being. Nor is it an exception to this rule that, by some modern statutes, on the demise of a king or queen, if there be then no parliament in being, the last parliament revives, and is to sit again for six months, unless dissolved by the successor: for this revived parliament must have been originally summoned by the crown.

I T is true, that by a statute, 16 Car. I. c. I. it was enacted, that if the king neglected to call a parliament for three years, the peers might assemble and issue out writs for the choosing one; and, in case of neglect of the peers, the constituents might meet and elect one themselves. But this, if ever put in practice, would have been liable to all the inconveniences I have just now stated; and the act itself was esteemed so highly detrimental and injurious to the royal prerogative, that it was repealed by statute 16 Car. II. c. I. From thence therefore no precedent can be drawn.

I T is also true, that the convention-parliament, which restored king Charles the second, met above a month before his return; the lords by their own authority, and the commons in pursuance of writs issued in the name of the keepers of the liberty of England by authority of parliament: and that the said parliament sat till the twenty ninth of December, full seven months after the restoration; and enacted many laws, several of which are still in force. But this was for the necessity of the thing, which supersedes all law; for if they had not so met, it was morally impossible that the kingdom should have been settled in peace. And the first thing done after the king's return, was to pass an act declaring this to be a good parliament, notwithstanding the defect of the king's writs. So that, as the royal prerogative was chiefly wounded by their so meeting, and as the king himself, who alone had a right to object, consented to wave the objection, this cannot be drawn into an example in prejudice of the rights of the crown. Besides we should also remember, that it was at that time a great doubt among the lawyers, whether even this healing act made it a good parliament; and held by very many in the negative: though it seems to have been too nice a scruple.

I T is likewise true, that at the time of the revolution, *A.D.* 1688, the lords and commons by their own authority, and upon the summons of the prince of Orange, (afterwards king William) met in a convention and therein disposed of the crown and kingdom. But it must be remembered, that this assembling was upon a like principle of necessity as at the restoration; that is, upon an apprehension that king James the second had abdicated the government, and that the throne was thereby vacant: which apprehension of theirs was confirmed by their concurrent resolution, when they actually came together. And in such a case as the palpable vacancy of a throne, it follows *ex necessitate rei,* that the form of the royal writs must be laid aside, otherwise no parliament can ever meet again. For, let us put another possible case, and suppose, for the sake of argument, that the whole royal line should at any time fail, and become extinct, which would indisputably vacate the throne: in this situation it seems reasonable to presume, that the body of the nation, consisting of lords and commons, would have a right to meet and settle the government; otherwise there must be no government at all. And upon this and no other principle did the convention in 1688 assemble. The vacancy of the throne was precedent to their meeting without any royal summons, not a consequence of it. They did not assemble without writ, and then make the throne vacant; but the throne being previously vacant by the king's abdication, they assembled without writ, as they must do if they assembled at all. Had the throne been full, their meeting would not have been regular; but, as it was really empty, such meeting became absolutely necessary. And accordingly it is declared by statute 1 W. & M. st. 1. c. 1. that this convention was really the two houses of parliament, notwithstanding the want of writs or other defects of form. So that, notwithstanding these two capital exceptions, which were justifiable only on a principle of necessity, (and each of which, by the way, induced a revolution in the government) the rule laid down is in general certain, that the king, only, can convoke a parliament.

A N D this by the antient statutes of the realm, he is bound to do every year, or oftener, if need be. Not that he is, or ever was, obliged by these statutes to call a *new* parliament every year; but only to permit a parliament to sit annually for the redress of grievances, and dispatch of business, *if need be.* These last words are so loose and vague, that such of our monarchs as were enclined to govern without parliaments, neglected the convoking them, sometimes for a very considerable period, under pretence that there was no need of them. But, to remedy this, by the statute 16 Car. II. c. 1. it is enacted, that the sitting and holding of parliaments shall not be intermitted above three years at the most. And by the statute 1 W. & M. st. 2. c. 2. it is declared to be one of the rights of the people, that for redress of all grievances, and for the amending, strengthening, and preserving the laws, parliaments ought to be held *frequently*. And this indefinite *frequency* is again reduced to a certainty by statute 6 W. & M. c. 2. which enacts, as the statute of Charles the second had done before, that a new parliament shall be called within three years after the determination of the former.

II. T H E constituent parts of a parliament are the next objects of our enquiry. And these are, the king's majesty, sitting there in his royal political capacity, and the three estates of the realm; the lords spiritual, the lords temporal, (who sit, together with, the king, in one house) and the commons, who sit by themselves in another. And the king and these three estates, together, form the great corporation or body politic of the kingdom, of which the king is said to be *caput, principium, et finis*. For upon their coming together the king meets them, either in person or by representation; without which there can be no beginning of a parliament; and he also has alone the power of dissolving them.

I T is highly necessary for preserving the ballance of the constitution, that the executive power should be a branch, though not the whole, of the legislature. The total union of them, we have seen, would be productive of tyranny; the total disjunction of them for the present, would in the end produce the same effects, by causing that union, against which it seems to provide. The legislature would soon become tyrannical, by making continual encroachments, and gradually assuming to itself the rights of the executive power. Thus the long parliament of Charles the first, while it acted in a constitutional manner, with the royal concurrence, redressed many heavy grievances and established many salutary laws. But when the two houses assumed the power of legislation, in exclusion of the royal authority, they soon after assumed likewise the reins of administration; and, in consequence of these united powers, overturned both church and state, and established a worse oppression than any they pretended to remedy. To hinder therefore any such encroachments, the king is himself a part of the parliament: and, as this is the reason of his being so, very properly therefore the share of legislation, which the constitution has placed in the crown, consists in the power of *rejecting*, rathar than *resolving*; this being sufficient to answer the end proposed. For we may apply to the royal negative, in this instance, what Cicero observes of the negative of the Roman tribunes, that the crown has not any power of *doing* wrong, but merely of *preventing* wrong from being done. The crown cannot begin of itself any alterations in the present established law; but it may approve or disapprove of the alterations suggested and consented to by the two houses. The legislative therefore cannot abridge the executive power of any rights which it now has by law, without it's own consent; since the law must perpetually stand as it now does, unless all the powers will agree to alter it. And herein indeed consists the true excellence of the English government, that all the parts of it form a mutual check upon each other. In the legislature, the people are a check upon the nobility, and the nobility a check upon the people; by the mutual privilege of rejecting what the other has resolved: while the king is a check upon both, which preserves the executive power from encroachments. And this very executive power is again checked, and kept within due bounds by the two houses, through the privilege they have of enquiring into, impeaching, and punishing the conduct (not indeed of the king, which would destroy his constitutional independence; but, which is more beneficial to the public) of his evil and pernicious counsellors. Thus every branch of our civil polity supports and is supported, regulates and is regulated, by the rest; for the two houses naturally drawing in two directions of opposite interest, and the prerogative in another still different from them both, they mutually keep each other from exceeding their proper limits; while the whole is prevented from separation, and artificially connected together by the mixed nature of the crown, which is a part of the legislative, and the sole executive magistrate. Like three distinct powers in mechanics, they jointly impel the machine of government in a direction different from what either, acting by themselves, would have done; but at the same time in a direction partaking of each, and formed out of all; a direction which constitutes the true line of the liberty and happiness of the community.

L E T us now consider these constituent parts of the sovereign power, or parliament, each in a separate view. The king's majesty will be the subject of the next, and many subsequent chapters, to which we must at present refer.

T H E next in order are the spiritual lords. These consist of two arch-bishops, and twenty four bishops; and, at the dissolution of monasteries by Henry VIII, consisted likewise of twenty six mitred abbots, and two priors: a very considerable body, and in those times equal in number to the temporal nobility. All these hold, or are supposed to hold, certain antient baronies under the king: for William the conqueror thought proper to change the spiritual tenure, of frankalmoign or free alms, under which the bishops held their lands during the Saxon government, into the feodal or Norman tenure by barony; which subjected their estates to all civil charges and assessments, from which they were before exempt: and, in right of succession to those baronies, the bishops obtained their seat in the house of lords. But though these lords spiritual are in the eye of the law a distinct estate from the lords temporal, and are so distinguished in all our acts of parliament, yet in practice they are usually blended together under the one name of *the lords*; they intermix in their votes; and the majority of such intermixture binds both estates. For if a bill should pass their house, there is no doubt of it's being effectual, though every lord spiritual should vote against it; of which Selden, and sir Edward Coke, give many instances: as, on the other hand, I presume it would be equally good, if the lords temporal present were inferior to the bishops in number, and every one of those temporal lords gave his vote to reject the bill; though this sir Edward Coke seems to doubt of.

T H E lords temporal consist of all the peers of the realm (the bishops not being in strictness held to be such, but merely lords of parliament) by whatever title of nobility distinguished; dukes, marquisses, earls, viscounts, or barons; of which dignities we shall speak more hereafter. Some of these sit by descent, as do all antient peers; some by creation, as do all new-made ones; others, since the union with Scotland, by election, which is the case of the sixteen peers, who represent the body of the Scots nobility. Their number is indefinite, and may be encreased at will by the power of the crown: and once, in the reign of queen Anne, there was an instance of creating no less than twelve together; in contemplation of which, in the reign of king George the first, a bill passed the house of lords, and was countenanced by the then ministry, for limiting the number of the peerage. This was thought by some to promise a great acquisition to the constitution, by restraining the prerogative from gaining the ascendant in that august assembly, by pouring in at pleasure an unlimited number of new created lords. But the bill was ill-relished and miscarried in the house of commons, whose leading members were then desirous to keep the avenues to the other house as open and easy as possible.

T H E distinction of rank and honours is necessary in every well-governed state; in order to reward such as are eminent for their services to the public, in a manner the most desirable to individuals, and yet without burthen to the community; exciting thereby an ambitious yet laudable ardor, and generous emulation in others. And emulation, or virtuous ambition, is a spring of action which, however dangerous or invidious in a mere republic or under a despotic sway, will certainly be attended with good effects under a free monarchy; where, without destroying it's existence, it's excesses may be continually restrained by that superior power, from which all honour is derived. Such a spirit, when nationally diffused, gives life and vigour to the community; it sets all the wheels of government in motion, which under a wise regulator, may be directed to any beneficial purpose; and thereby every individual may be made subservient to the public good, while he principally means to promote his own particular views. A body of nobility is also more peculiarly necessary in our mixed and compounded constitution, in order to support the rights of both the crown and the people, by forming a barrier to withstand the encroachments of both. It creates and preserves that gradual scale of dignity, which proceeds from the peasant to the prince; rising like a pyramid from a broad foundation, and diminishing to a point as it rises. It is this ascending and contracting proportion that adds stability to any government; for when the departure is sudden from one extreme to another, we may pronounce that state to be precarious. The nobility therefore are the pillars, which are reared from among the people, more immediately to support the throne; and if that falls, they must also be buried under it's ruins. Accordingly, when in the last century the commons had determined to extirpate monarchy, they also voted the house of lords to be useless and dangerous. And since titles of nobility are thus expedient in the state, it is also expedient that their owners should form an independent and separate branch of the legislature. If they were confounded with the mass of the people, and like them had only a vote in electing representatives, their privileges would soon be borne down and overwhelmed by the popular torrent, which would effectually level all distinctions. It is therefore highly necessary that the body of nobles should have a distinct assembly, distinct deliberations, and distinct powers from the commons.

THE commons consist of all such men of any property in the kingdom as have not seats in the house of lords; every one of which has a voice in parliament, either personally, or by his representatives. In a free state, every man, who is supposed a free agent, ought to be, in some measure, his own governor; and therefore a branch at least of the legislative power should reside in the whole body of the people. And this power, when the territories of the state are small and it's citizens easily known, should be exercised by the people in their aggregate or collective capacity, as was wisely ordained in the petty republics of Greece, and the first rudiments of the Roman state. But this will be highly inconvenient, when the public territory is extended to any considerable degree, and the number of citizens is encreased. Thus when, after the social war, all the burghers of Italy were admitted free citizens of Rome, and each had a vote in the public assemblies, it became impossible to distinguish the spurious from the real voter, and from that time all elections and popular deliberations grew tumultuous and disorderly; which paved the way for Marius and Sylla, Pompey and Caesar, to trample on the liberties of their country, and at last to dissolve the commonwealth. In so large a state as ours it is therefore very wisely contrived, that the people should do that by their representatives, which it is impracticable to perform in person: representatives, chosen by a number of minute and separate districts, wherein all the voters are, or easily may be, distinguished. The counties are therefore represented by knights, elected by the proprietors of lands; the cities and boroughs are represented by citizens and burgesses, chosen by the mercantile part or supposed trading interest of the nation; much in the same manner as the burghers in the diet of Sweden are chosen by the corporate towns, Stockholm sending four, as London does with us, other cities two, and some only one. The number of English representatives is 513, and of Scots 45; in all 558. And every member, though chosen by one particular district, when elected and returned serves for the whole realm. For the end of his coming thither is not particular, but general; not barely to advantage his constituents, but the *common*wealth; to advise his majesty (as appears from the writ of summons) "*de communi consilio super negotiis quibusdam arduis et urgentibus, regem, statum et defensionem regni Angliae et ecclesiae Anglicanae concernentibus.*" And therefore he is not bound, like a deputy in the united provinces, to consult with, or take the advice, of his constituents upon any particular point, unless he himself thinks it proper or prudent so to do.

THESE are the constituent parts of a parliament, the king, the lords spiritual and temporal, and the commons. Parts, of which each is so necessary, that the consent of all three is required to make any new law that shall bind the subject. Whatever is enacted for law by one, or by two only, of the three is no statute; and to it no regard is due, unless in matters relating to their own privileges. For though, in the times of madness and anarchy, the commons once passed a vote, "that whatever is enacted or declared for law by the commons in parliament assembled hath the force of law; and all the people of this nation are concluded thereby, although the consent and concurrence of the king or house of peers be not had thereto;" yet, when the constitution was restored in all it's forms, it was particularly enacted by statute 13 Car. II. c. 1. that if any person shall maliciously or advisedly affirm, that both or either of the houses of parliament have any legislative authority without the king, such person shall incur all the penalties of a praemunire.

III. W E are next to examine the laws and customs relating to parliament, thus united together and considered as one aggregate body.

T H E power and jurisdiction of parliament, says sir Edward Coke, is so transcendent and absolute, that it cannot be confined, either for causes or persons, within any bounds. And of this high court he adds, it may be truly said "*si antiquitatem spectes, est vetustissima; si dignitatem, est honoratissima; si juridictionem, est capacissima.*" It hath sovereign and uncontrolable authority in making, confirming, enlarging, restraining, abrogating, repealing, reviving, and expounding of laws, concerning matters of all possible denominations, ecclesiastical, or temporal, civil, military, maritime, or criminal: this being the place where that absolute despotic power, which must in all governments reside somewhere, is entrusted by the constitution of these kingdoms. All mischiefs and grievances, operations and remedies, that transcend the ordinary course of the laws, are within the reach of this extraordinary tribunal. It can regulate or new model the succession to the crown; as was done in the reign of Henry VIII and William III. It can alter the established religion of the land; as was done in a variety of instances, in the reigns of king Henry VIII and his three children. It can change and create afresh even the constitution of the kingdom and of parliaments themselves; as was done by the act of union, and the several statutes for triennial and septennial elections. It can, in short, do every thing that is not naturally impossible; and therefore some have not scrupled to call it's power, by a figure rather too bold, the omnipotence of parliament. True it is, that what they do, no authority upon earth can undo. So that it is a matter most essential to the liberties of this kingdom, that such members be delegated to this important trust, as are most eminent for their probity, their fortitude, and their knowlege; for it was a known apothegm of the great lord treasurer Burleigh, "thatEngland could never be ruined but by a parliament:" and, as sir Matthew Hale observes, this being the highest and greatest court, over which none other can have jurisdiction in the kingdom, if by any means a misgovernment should any way fall upon it, the subjects of this kingdom are left without all manner of remedy. To the same purpose the president Montesquieu, though I trust too hastily, presages; that as Rome, Sparta, and Carthage have lost their liberty and perished, so the constitution of England will in time lose it's liberty, will perish: it will perish, whenever the legislative power shall become more corrupt than the executive.

I T must be owned that Mr Locke, and other theoretical writers, have held, that "there remains still inherent in the people a supreme power to remove or alter the legislative, when they find the legislative act contrary to the trust reposed in them: for when such trust is abused, it is thereby forfeited, and devolves to those who gave it." But however just this conclusion may be in theory, we cannot adopt it, nor argue from it, under any dispensation of government at present actually existing. For this devolution of power, to the people at large, includes in it a dissolution of the whole form of government established by that people, reduces all the members to their original state of equality, and by annihilating the sovereign power repeals all positive laws whatsoever before enacted. No human laws will therefore suppose a case, which at once must destroy all law, and compel men to build afresh upon a new foundation; nor will they make provision for so desperate an event, as must render all legal provisions ineffectual. So long therefore as the English constitution lasts, we may venture to affirm, that the power of parliament is absolute and without control.

I N order to prevent the mischiefs that might arise, by placing this extensive authority in hands that are either incapable, or else improper, to manage it, it is provided that no one shall sit or vote in either house of parliament, unless he be twenty one years of age. This is expressly declared by statute 7 & 8 W. III. c. 25. with regard to the house of commons; though a minor was incapacitated before from sitting in either house, by the law and custom of parliament. To prevent crude innovations in religion and government, it is enacted by statute 30 Car. II. st. 2. and 1 Geo. I. c. 13. that no member shall vote or sit in either house, till he hath in the presence of the house taken the oaths of allegiance, supremacy, and abjuration, and subscribed and repeated the declaration against transubstantiation, and invocation of saints, and the sacrifice of the mass. To prevent dangers that may arise to the kingdom from foreign attachments, connexions, or dependencies, it is enacted by the 12 & 13 W. III. c. 2. that no alien, born out of the dominions of the crown of Great Britain, even though he be naturalized, shall be capable of being a member of either house of parliament.

F A R T H E R : as every court of justice hath laws and customs for it's direction, some the civil and canon, some the common law, others their own peculiar laws and customs, so the high court of parliament hath also it's own peculiar law, called the *lex et consuetudo parliamenti*; a law which sir Edward Coke observes, is "*ab omnibus quaerenda, a multis ignorata, a paucis cognita.*" It will not therefore be expected that we should enter into the examination of this law, with any degree of minuteness; since, as the same learned author assures us, it is much better to be learned out of the rolls of parliament, and other records, and by precedents, and continual experience, than can be expressed by any one man. It will be sufficient to observe, that the whole of the law and custom of parliament has it's original from this one maxim; "that whatever matter arises concerning either house of parliament, ought to be examined, discussed, and adjudged in that house to which it relates, and not elsewhere." Hence, for instance, the lords will not suffer the commons to interfere in settling a claim of peerage; the commons will not allow the lords to judge of the election of a burgess; nor will either house permit the courts of law to examine the merits of either case. But the maxims upon which they proceed, together with their method of proceeding, rest entirely in the breast of the parliament itself; and are not defined and ascertained by any particular stated laws.

T H E *privileges* of parliament are likewise very large and indefinite; which has occasioned an observation, that the principal privilege of parliament consisted in this, that it's privileges were not certainly known to any but the parliament itself. And therefore when in 31 Hen. VI the house of lords propounded a question to the judges touching the privilege of parliament, the chief justice, in the name of his brethren, declared, "that they ought not to make answer to that question; for it hath not been used aforetime that the justices should in any wise determine the privileges of the high court of parliament; for it is so high and mighty in his nature, that it may make law; and that which is law, it may make no law; and the determination and knowlege of that privilege belongs to the lords of parliament, and not to the justices." Privilege of parliament was principally established, in order to protect it's members not only from being molested by their fellow-subjects, but also more especially from being oppressed by the power of the crown. If therefore all the privileges of parliament were once to be set down and ascertained, and no privilege to be allowed but what was so defined and determined, it were easy for the executive power to devise some new case, not within the line of privilege, and under pretence thereof to harass any refractory member and violate the freedom of parliament. The dignity and independence of the two houses are therefore in great measure preserved by keeping their privileges indefinite. Some however of the more notorious privileges of the members of either house are, privilege of speech, of person, of their domestics, and of their lands and goods. As to the first, privilege of speech, it is declared by the statute 1 W. & M. st. 2. c. 2. as one of the liberties of the people, "that the freedom of speech, and debates, and proceedings in parliament, ought not to be impeached or questioned in any court or place out of parliament." And this freedom of speech is particularly demanded of the king in person, by the speaker of the house of commons, at the opening of every new parliament. So likewise are the other privileges, of person, servants, lands and goods; which are immunities as antient as Edward the confessor, in whose laws we find this precept. "*Ad synodos venientibus, sive summoniti sint, sive per se quid agendum habuerint, sit summa pax.*" and so too, in the old Gothic constitutions, "*extenditur haec pax et securitas ad quatuordecim dies, convocato regni senatu.*" This includes not only privilege from illegal violence, but also from legal arrests, and seisures by process from the courts of law. To assault by violence a member of either house, or his menial servants, is a high contempt of parliament, and there punished with the utmost severity. It has likewise peculiar penalties annexed to it in the courts of law, by the statutes 5 Hen. IV. c. 6. and 11 Hen. VI. c. 11. Neither can any member of either house be arrested and taken into custody, nor served with any process of the courts of law; nor can his menial servants be arrested; nor can any entry be made on his lands; nor can his goods be distrained or seised; without a breach of the privilege of parliament. These privileges however, which derogate from the common law, being only indulged to prevent the member's being diverted from the public business, endure no longer than the session of parliament, save only as to the freedom of his person: which in a peer is for ever sacred and inviolable; and in a commoner for forty days after every prorogation, and forty days before the next appointed meeting; which is now in effect as long as the parliament subsists, it seldom being prorogued for more than fourscore days at a time. But this privilege of person does not hold in crimes of such public malignity as treason, felony, or breach of the peace; or rather perhaps in such crimes for which surety of the peace may be required. As to all other privileges which obstruct the ordinary course of justice, they cease by the statutes 12 W. III. c. 3. and 11 Geo. II. c. 24. immediately after the dissolution or prorogation of the parliament, or adjournment of the houses for above a fortnight; and during these recesses a peer, or member of the house of commons, may be sued like an ordinary subject, and in consequence of such suits may be dispossessed of his lands and goods. In these cases the king has also his prerogative: he may sue for his debts, though not arrest the person of a member, during the sitting of parliament; and by statute 2 & 3 Ann. c. 18. a member may be sued during the sitting of parliament for any misdemesnor or breach of trust in a public office. Likewise, for the benefit of commerce, it is provided by statute 4 Geo. III. c. 33, that any trader, having privilege of parliament, may be served with legal process for any just debt, (to the amount of 100*l.*) and unless he makes satisfaction within two months, it shall be deemed an act of bankruptcy; and that commissions of bankrupt may be issued against such privileged traders, in like manner as against any other.

T H E S E are the general heads of the laws and customs relating to parliament, considered as one aggregate body. We will next proceed to

IV. T H E laws and customs relating to the house of lords in particular. These, if we exclude their judicial capacity, which will be more properly treated of in the third and fourth books of these commentaries, will take up but little of our time.

O N E very antient privilege is that declared by the charter of the forest, confirmed in parliament 9 Hen. III; viz. that every lord spiritual or temporal summoned to parliament, and passing through the king's forests, may, both in going and returning, kill one or two of the king's deer without warrant; in view of the forester, if he be present; or on blowing a horn if he be absent, that he may not seem to take the king's venison by stealth.

I N the next place they have a right to be attended, and constantly are, by the judges of the court of king's bench and commonpleas, and such of the barons of the exchequer as are of the degree of the coif, or have been made serjeants at law; as likewise by the masters of the court of chancery; for their advice in point of law, and for the greater dignity of their proceedings. The secretaries of state, the attorney and solicitor general, and the rest of the king's learned counsel being serjeants, were also used to attend the house of peers, and have to this day their regular writs of summons issued out at the beginning of every parliament: but, as many of them have of late years been members of the house of commons, their attendance is fallen into disuse.

A N O T H E R privilege is, that every peer, by licence obtained from the king, may make another lord of parliament his proxy, to vote for him in his absence. A privilege which a member of the other house can by no means have, as he is himself but a proxy for a multitude of other people.

E A C H peer has also a right, by leave of the house, when a vote passes contrary to his sentiments, to enter his dissent on the journals of the house, with the reasons for such dissent; which is usually stiled his protest.

ALL bills likewise, that may in their consequences any way affect the rights of the peerage, are by the custom of parliament to have their first rise and beginning in the house of peers, and to suffer no changes or amendments in the house of commons.

THERE is also one statute peculiarly relative to the house of lords; 6 Ann. c. 23. which regulates the election of the sixteen representative peers of North Britain, in consequence of the twenty second and twenty third articles of the union: and for that purpose prescribes the oaths, &c., to be taken by the electors; directs the mode of balloting; prohibits the peers electing from being attended in an unusual manner; and expressly provides, that no other matter shall be treated of in that assembly, save only the election, on pain of incurring a praemunire.

V. THE peculiar laws and customs of the house of commons relate principally to the raising of taxes, and the elections of members to serve in parliament.

FIRST, with regard to taxes: it is the antient indisputable privilege and right of the house of commons, that all grants of subsidies or parliamentary aids do begin in their house, and are first bestowed by them; although their grants are not effectual to all intents and purposes, until they have the assent of the other two branches of the legislature. The general reason, given for this exclusive privilege of the house of commons, is, that the supplies are raised upon the body of the people, and therefore it is proper that they alone should have the right of taxing themselves. This reason would be unanswerable, if the commons taxed none but themselves: but it is notorious, that a very large share of property is in the possession of the house of lords; that this property is equally taxable, and taxed, as the property of the commons; and therefore the commons not being the *sole* persons taxed, this cannot be the reason of their having the *sole* right of raising and modelling the supply. The true reason, arising from the spirit of our constitution, seems to be this. The lords being a permanent hereditary body, created at pleasure by the king, are supposed more liable to be influenced by the crown, and when once influenced to continue so, than the commons, who are a temporary elective body, freely nominated by the people. It would therefore be extremely dangerous, to give them any power of framing new taxes for the subject: it is sufficient, that they have a power of rejecting, if they think the commons too lavish or improvident in their grants. But so reasonably jealous are the commons of this valuable privilege, that herein they will not suffer the other house to exert any power but that of rejecting; they will not permit the least alteration or amendment to be made by the lords to the mode of taxing the people by a money bill; under which appellation are included all bills, by which money is directed to be raised upon the subject, for any purpose or in any shape whatsoever; either for the exigencies of government, and collected from the kingdom in general, as the land tax; or for private benefit, and collected in any particular district; as by turnpikes, parish rates, and the like. Yet sir Matthew Hale mentions one case, founded on the practice of parliament in the reign of Henry VI, wherein he thinks the lords may alter a money bill; and that is, if the commons grant a tax, as that of tonnage and poundage, for *four* years; and the lords alter it to a less time, as for *two* years; here, he says, the bill need not be sent back to the commons for their concurrence, but may receive the royal assent without farther ceremony; for the alteration of the lords is consistent with the grant of the commons. But such an experiment will hardly be repeated by the lords, under the present improved idea of the privilege of the house of commons: and, in any case where a money bill is remanded to the commons, all amendments in the mode of taxation are sure to be rejected.

N E X T , with regard to the elections of knights, citizens, and burgesses; we may observe that herein consists the exercise of the democratical part of our constitution: for in a democracy there can be no exercise of sovereignty but by suffrage, which is the declaration of the people's will. In all democracies therefore it is of the utmost importance to regulate by whom, and in what manner, the suffrages are to be given. And the Athenians were so justly jealous of this prerogative, that a stranger, who interfered in the assemblies of the people, was punished by their laws with death: because such a man was esteemed guilty of high treason, by usurping those rights of sovereignty, to which he had no title. In England, where the people do not debate in a collective body but by representation, the exercise of this sovereignty consists in the choice of representatives. The laws have therefore very strictly guarded against usurpation or abuse of this power, by many salutary provisions; which may be reduced to these three points, 1. The qualifications of the electors. 2. The qualifications of the elected. 3. The proceedings at elections.

1. A S to the qualifications of the electors. The true reason of requiring any qualification, with regard to property, in voters, is to exclude such persons as are in so mean a situation that they are esteemed to have no will of their own. If these persons had votes, they would be tempted to dispose of them under some undue influence or other. This would give a great, an artful, or a wealthy man, a larger share in elections than is consistent with general liberty. If it were probable that every man would give his vote freely, and without influence of any kind, then, upon the true theory and genuine principles of liberty, every member of the community, however poor, should have a vote in electing those delegates, to whose charge is committed the disposal of his property, his liberty, and his life. But, since that can hardly be expected in persons of indigent fortunes, or such as are under the immediate dominion of others, all popular states have been obliged to establish certain qualifications; whereby some, who are suspected to have no will of their own, are excluded from voting, in order to set other individuals, whose wills may be supposed independent, more thoroughly upon a level with each other.

A N D this constitution of suffrages is framed upon a wiser principle than either of the methods of voting, by centuries, or by tribes, among the Romans. In the method by centuries, instituted by Servius Tullius, it was principally property, and not numbers that turned the scale: in the method by tribes, gradually introduced by the tribunes of the people, numbers only were regarded and property entirely overlooked. Hence the laws passed by the former method had usually too great a tendency to aggrandize the patricians or rich nobles; and those by the latter had too much of a levelling principle. Our constitution steers between the two extremes. Only such as are entirely excluded, as can have no will of their own: there is hardly a free agent to be found, but what is entitled to a vote in some place or other in the kingdom. Nor is comparative wealth, or property, entirely disregarded in elections; for though the richest man has only one vote at one place, yet if his property be at all diffused, he has probably a right to vote at more places than one, and therefore has many representatives. This is the spirit of our constitution: not that I assert it is in fact quite so perfect as I have here endeavoured to describe it; for, if any alteration might be wished or suggested in the present frame of parliaments, it should be in favour of a more complete representation of the people.

B U T to return to our qualifications; and first those of electors for knights of the shire. 1. By statute 8 Hen. VI. c. 7. and 10 Hen. VI. c. 2. The knights of the shires shall be chosen of people dwelling in the same counties; whereof every man shall have freehold to the value of forty shillings by the year within the county; which by subsequent statutes is to be clear of all charges and deductions, except parliamentary and parochial taxes. The knights of shires are the representatives of the landholders, or landed interest, of the kingdom: their electors must therefore have estates in lands or tenements, within the county represented: these estates must be freehold, that is, for term of life at least; because beneficial leases for long terms of years were not in use at the making of these statutes, and copyholders were then little better than villeins, absolutely dependent upon their lord: this freehold must be of forty shillings annual value; because that sum would then, with proper industry, furnish all the necessaries of life, and render the freeholder, if he pleased, an independent man. For bishop Fleetwood, in his *chronicon pretiosum* written about sixty years since, has fully proved forty shillings in the reign of Henry VI to have been equal to twelve pounds *per annum* in the reign of queen Anne; and, as the value of money is very considerably lowered since the bishop wrote, I think we may fairly conclude, from this and other circumstances, that what was equivalent to twelve pounds in his days is equivalent to twenty at present. The other less important qualifications of the electors for counties in England and Wales may be collected from the statutes cited in the margin; which direct, 2. That no person under twenty one years of age shall be capable of voting for any member. This extends to all sorts of members, as well for boroughs as counties; as does also the next, viz. 3. That no person convicted of perjury, or subornation of perjury, shall be capable of voting in any election. 4. That no person shall vote in right of any freehold, granted to him fraudulently to qualify him to vote. Fraudulent grants are such as contain an agreement to reconvey, or to defeat the estate granted; which agreements are made void, and the estate is absolutely vested in the person to whom it is so granted. And, to guard the better against such frauds, it is farther provided, 5. That every voter shall have been in the actual possession, or receipt of the profits, of his freehold to his own use for twelve calendar months before; except it came to him by descent, marriage, marriage settlement, will, or promotion to a benefice or office. 6. That no person shall vote in respect of an annuity or rentcharge, unless registered with the clerk of the peace twelve calendar months before. 7. That in mortgaged or trust-estates, the person in possession, under the abovementioned restrictions, shall have the vote. 8. That only one person shall be admitted to vote for any one house or tenement, to prevent the splitting of freeholds. 9. That no estate shall qualify a voter, unless the estate has been assessed to some land tax aid, at least twelve months before the election. 10. That no tenant by copy of court roll shall be permitted to vote as a freeholder. Thus much for the electors in counties.

A S for the electors of citizens and burgesses, these are supposed to be the mercantile part or trading interest of this kingdom. But as trade is of a fluctuating nature, and seldom long fixed in a place, it was formerly left to the crown to summon, *pro re nata*, the most flourishing towns to send representatives to parliament. So that as towns encreased in trade, and grew populous, they were admitted to a share in the legislature. But the misfortune is, that the deserted boroughs continued to be summoned, as well as those to whom their trade and inhabitants were transferred; except a few which petitioned to be eased of the expence, then usual, of maintaining their members: four shillings a day being allowed for a knight of the shire, and two shillings for a citizen or burgess; which was the rate of wages established in the reign of Edward III. Hence the members for boroughs now bear above a quadruple proportion to those for counties, and the number of parliament men is increased since Fortescue's time, in the reign of Henry the sixth, from 300 to upwards of 500, exclusive of those for Scotland. The universities were in general not empowered to send burgesses to parliament; though once, in 28 Edw. I. when a parliament was summoned to consider of the king's right to Scotland, there were issued writs, which required the university of Oxford to send up four or five, and that of Cambridge two or three, of their most discreet and learned lawyers for that purpose. But it was king James the first, who indulged them with the permanent privilege to send constantly two of their own body; to serve for those students who, though useful members of the community, were neither concerned in the landed nor the trading interest; and to protect in the legislature the rights of the republic of letters. The right of election in boroughs is various, depending entirely on the several charters, customs, and constitutions of the respective places, which has occasioned infinite disputes; though now by statute 2 Geo. II. c. 24. the right of voting for the future shall be allowed according to the last determination of the house of commons concerning it. And by statute 3 Geo. III. c. 15. no freeman of any city or borough (other than such as claim by birth, marriage, or servitude) shall be intitled to vote therein unless he hath been admitted to his freedom twelve calendar months before.

2. O U R second point is the qualification of persons to be elected members of the house of commons. This depends upon the law and custom of parliaments, and the statutes referred to in the margin. And from these it appears, 1. That they must not be aliens born, or minors. 2. That they must not be any of the twelve judges, because they sit in the lords' house; nor of the clergy, for they sit in the convocation; nor persons attainted of treason or felony, for they are unfit to sit any where. 3. That sheriffs of counties, and mayors and bailiffs of boroughs, are not eligible in their respective jurisdictions, as being returning officers; but that sheriffs of one county are eligible to be knights of another. 4. That, in strictness, all members ought to be inhabitants of the places for which they are chosen: but this is intirely disregarded. 5. That no persons concerned in the management of any duties or taxes created since 1692, except the

commissioners of the treasury, nor any of the officers following, (viz. commissioners of prizes, transports, sick and wounded, wine licences, navy, and victualling; secretaries or receivers of prizes; comptrollers of the army accounts; agents for regiments; governors of plantations and their deputies; officers of Minorca or Gibraltar; officers of the excise and customs; clerks or deputies in the several offices of the treasury, exchequer, navy, victualling, admiralty, pay of the army or navy, secretaries of state, salt, stamps, appeals, wine licences, hackney coaches, hawkers and pedlars) nor any persons that hold any new office under the crown created since 1705, are capable of being elected members. 6. That no person having a pension under the crown during pleasure, or for any term of years, is capable of being elected. 7. That if any member accepts an office under the crown, except an officer in the army or navy accepting a new commission, his seat is void; but such member is capable of being re-elected. 8. That all knights of the shire shall be actual knights, or such notable esquires and gentlemen, as have estates sufficient to be knights, and by no means of the degree of yeomen. This is reduced to a still greater certainty, by ordaining, 9. That every knight of a shire shall have a clear estate of freehold or copyhold to the value of six hundred pounds *per annum*, and every citizen and burgess to the value of three hundred pounds; except the eldest sons of peers, and of persons qualified to be knights of shires, and except the members for the two universities: which somewhat ballances the ascendant which the boroughs have gained over the counties, by obliging the trading interest to make choice of landed men: and of this qualification the member must make oath, and give in the particulars in writing, at the time of his taking his seat. But, subject to these restrictions and disqualifications, every subject of the realm is eligible of common right. It was therefore an unconstitutional prohibition, which was inserted in the king's writs, for the parliament holden at Coventry, 6 Hen. IV, that no apprentice or other man of the law should be elected a knight of the shire therein: in return for which, our law books and historians have branded this parliament with the name of *parliamentum indoctum*, or the lack-learning parliament; and sir Edward Coke observes with some spleen, that there was never a good law made thereat.

3. T H E third point regarding elections, is the method of proceeding therein. This is also regulated by the law of parliament, and the several statutes referred to in the margin; all which I shall endeavour to blend together, and extract out of them a summary account of the method of proceeding to elections.

A S soon as the parliament is summoned, the lord chancellor, (or if a vacancy happens during parliament, the speaker, by order of the house) sends his warrant to the clerk of the crown in chancery; who thereupon issues out writs to the sheriff of every county, for the election of all the members to serve for that county, and every city and borough therein. Within three days after the receipt of this writ, the sheriff is to send his precept, under his seal, to the proper returning officers of the cities and boroughs, commanding them to elect their members; and the said returning officers are to proceed to election within eight days from the receipt of the precept, giving four days notice of the same; and to return the persons chosen, together with the precept, to the sheriff.

B U T elections of knights of the shire must be proceeded to by the sheriffs themselves in person, at the next county court that shall happen after the delivery of the writ. The county court is a court held every month or oftener by the sheriff, intended to try little causes not exceeding the value of forty shillings, in what part of the county he pleases to appoint for that purpose: but for the election of knights of the shire, it must be held at the most usual place. If the county court falls upon the day of delivering the writ, or within six days after, the sheriff may adjourn the court and election to some other convenient time, not longer than sixteen days, nor shorter than ten; but he cannot alter the place, without the consent of all the candidates; and in all such cases ten days public notice must be given of the time and place of the election.

A N D , as it is essential to the very being of parliament that elections should be absolutely free, therefore all undue influences upon the electors are illegal, and strongly prohibited. For Mr Locke ranks it among those breaches of trust in the executive magistrate, which according to his notions amount to a dissolution of the government, "if he employs the force, treasure, and offices of the society to corrupt the representatives, or openly to preingage the electors, and prescribe what manner of persons shall be chosen. For thus to regulate candidates and electors, and new model the ways of election, what is it, says he, but to cut up the government by the roots, and poison the very fountain of public security?" As soon therefore as the time and place of election, either in counties or boroughs, are fixed, all soldiers quartered in the place are to remove, at least one day before the election, to the distance of two miles or more; and not return till one day after the poll is ended. Riots likewise have been frequently determined to make an election void. By vote also of the house of commons, to whom alone belongs the power of determining contested elections, no lord of parliament, or lord lieutenant of a county, hath any right to interfere in the election of commoners; and, by statute, the lord warden of the cinque ports shall not recommend any members there. If any officer of the excise, customs, stamps, or certain other branches of the revenue, presumes to intermeddle in elections, by persuading any voter or dissuading him, he forfeits 100l, and is disabled to hold any office.

T H U S are the electors of one branch of the legislature secured from any undue influence from either of the other two, and from all external violence and compulsion. But the greatest danger is that in which themselves co-operate, by the infamous practice of bribery and corruption. To prevent which it is enacted that no candidate shall, after the date (usually called the *teste*) of the writs, or after the vacancy, give any money or entertainment to his electors, or promise to give any, either to particular persons, or to the place in general, in order to his being elected; on pain of being incapable to serve for that place in parliament. And if any money, gift, office, employment, or reward be given or promised to be given to any voter, at any time, in order to influence him to give or withhold his vote, both he that takes and he that offers such bribe forfeits 500l, and is for ever disabled from voting and holding any office in any corporation; unless, before conviction, he will discover some other offender of the same kind, and then he is indemnified for his own offence. The first instance that occurs of election bribery, was so early as 13 Eliz. when one Thomas Longe (being a simple man and of small capacity to serve in parliament) acknowleged that he had given the returning officer and others of the borough of Westbury four pounds to be returned member, and was for that premium elected. But for this offence the borough was amerced, the member was removed, and the officer fined and imprisoned. But, as this practice hath since taken much deeper and more universal root, it hath occasioned the making of these wholesome statutes; to complete the efficacy of which, there is nothing wanting but resolution and integrity to put them in strict execution.

U N D U E influence being thus (I wish the depravity of mankind would permit me to say, effectually) guarded against, the election is to be proceeded to on the day appointed; the sheriff or other returning officer first taking an oath against bribery, and for the due execution of his office. The candidates likewise, if required, must swear to their qualification; and the electors in counties to theirs; and the electors both in counties and boroughs are also compellable to take the oath of abjuration and that against bribery and corruption. And it might not be amiss, if the members elected were bound to take the latter oath, as well as the former; which in all probability would be much more effectual, than administring it only to the electors.

T H E election being closed, the returning officer in boroughs returns his precept to the sheriff, with the persons elected by the majority: and the sheriff returns the whole, together with the writ for the county and the knights elected thereupon, to the clerk of the crown in chancery; before the day of meeting, if it be a new parliament, or within fourteen days after the election, if it be an occasional vacancy; and this under penalty of 500*l.* If the sheriff does not return such knights only as are duly elected, he forfeits, by the old statutes of Henry VI, 100*l*; and the returning officer in boroughs for a like false return 40*l*; and they are besides liable to an action, in which double damages shall be recovered, by the later statutes of king William: and any person bribing the returning officer shall alio forfeit 300*l.* But the members returned by him are the sitting members, until the house of commons, upon petition, shall adjudge the return to be false and illegal. And this abstract of the proceedings at elections of knights, citizens, and burgesses, concludes our enquiries into the laws and customs more peculiarly relative to the house of commons.

VI. I P R O C E E D now, sixthly, to the method of making laws; which is much the same in both houses: and I shall touch it very briefly, beginning in the house of commons. But first I must premise, that for dispatch of business each house of parliament has it's speaker. The speaker of the house of lords is the lord chancellor, or keeper of the king's great seal; whose office it is to preside there, and manage the formality of business. The speaker of the house of commons is chosen by the house; but must be approved by the king. And herein the usage of the two houses differs, that the speaker of the house of commons cannot give his opinion or argue any question in the house; but the speaker of the house of lords may. In each house the act of the majority binds the whole; and this majority is declared by votesopenly and publickly given: not as at Venice, and many other senatorial assemblies, privately or by ballot. This latter method may be serviceable, to prevent intrigues and unconstitutional combinations: but is impossible to be practiced with us; at least in the house of commons, where every member's conduct is subject to the future censure of his constituents, and therefore should be openly submitted to their inspection.

T O bring a bill into the house, if the relief sought by it is of a private nature, it is first necessary to prefer a petition; which must be presented by a member, and usually sets forth the grievance desired to be remedied. This petition (when founded on facts that may be in their nature disputed) is referred to a committee of members, who examine the matter alleged, and accordingly report it to the house; and then (or, otherwise, upon the mere petition) leave is given to bring in the bill. In public matters the bill is brought in upon motion made to the house, without any petition at all. Formerly, all bills were drawn in the form of petitions, which were entered upon the *parliament rolls*, with the king's answer thereunto subjoined; not in any settled form of words, but as the circumstances of the case required: and at the end of each parliament the judges drew them into the form of a statute, which was entered on the *statute-rolls*. In the reign of Henry V, to prevent mistakes and abuses, the statutes were drawn up by the judges before the end of the parliament; and, in the reign of Henry VI, bills in the form of acts, according to the modern custom, were first introduced.

T H E persons, directed to bring in the bill, present it in a competent time to the house, drawn out on paper, with a multitude of blanks, or void spaces, where any thing occurs that is dubious, or necessary to be settled by the parliament itself; (such, especially, as the precise date of times, the nature and quantity of penalties, or of any sums of money to be raised) being indeed only the sceleton of the bill. In the house of lords, if the bill begins there, it is (when of a private nature) perused by two of the judges, who settle all points of legal propriety. This is read a first time, and at a convenient distance a second time; and after each reading the speaker opens to the house the substance of the bill, and puts the question, whether it shall proceed any farther. The introduction of the bill may be originally opposed, as the bill itself may at either of the readings; and, if the opposition succeeds, the bill must be dropt for that sessions; as it must also, if opposed with success in any of the subsequent stages.

A F T E R the second reading it is committed, that is, referred to a committee; which is either selected by the house in matters of small importance, or else, upon a bill of consequence, the house resolves itself into a committee of the whole house. A committee of the whole house is composed of every member; and, to form it, the speaker quits the chair, (another member being appointed chairman) and may sit and debate as a private member. In these committees the bill is debated clause by clause, amendments made, the blanks filled up, and sometimes the bill entirely new modelled. After it has gone through the committee, the chairman reports it to the house with such amendments as the committee have made; and then the house reconsider the whole bill again, and the question is repeatedly put upon every clause and amendment. When the house have agreed or disagreed to the amendments of the committee, and sometimes added new amendments of their own, the bill is then ordered to be engrossed, or written in a strong gross hand, on one or more long rolls of parchment sewed together. When this is finished, it is read a third time, and amendments are sometimes then made to it; and, if a new clause be added, it is done by tacking a separate piece of parchment on the bill, which is called a ryder. The speaker then again opens the contents; and, holding it up in his hands, puts the question, whether the bill shall pass. If this is agreed to, one of the members is directed to carry it to the lords, and desire their concurrence; who, attended by several more, carries it to the bar of the house of peers, and there delivers it to their speaker, who comes down from his woolsack to receive it.

I T there passes through the same forms as in the other house, (except engrossing, which is already done) and, if rejected, no more notice is taken, but it passes *sub silentio*, to prevent unbecoming altercations. But if it is agreed to, the lords send a message by two masters in chancery (or sometimes two of the judges) that they have agreed to the same: and the bill remains with the lords, if they have made no amendment to it. But if any amendments are made, such amendments are sent down with the bill to receive the concurrence of the commons. If the commons disagree to the amendments, a conference usually follows between members deputed from each house; who for the most part settle and adjust the difference: but, if both houses remain inflexible, the bill is dropped. If the commons agree to the amendments, the bill is sent back to the lords by one of the members, with a message to acquaint them therewith. The same forms are observed, *mutatis mutandis*, when the bill begins in the house of lords. And when both houses have done with the bill, it always is deposited in the house of peers, to wait the royal assent.

T H I S may be given two ways: 1. In person; when the king comes to the house of peers, in his crown and royal robes, and sending for the commons to the bar, the titles of all the bills that have passed both houses are read; and the king's answer is declared by the clerk of the parliament in Norman-French: a badge, it must be owned, (now the only one remaining) of conquest; and which one could wish to see fall into total oblivion; unless it be reserved as a solemn memento to remind us that our liberties are mortal, having once been destroyed by a foreign force. If the king consents to a public bill, the clerk usually declares, "*le roy le veut*, the king wills it so to be;" if to a private bill, "*soit fait come il est desirè*, be it as it is desired." If the king refuses his assent, it is in the gentle language of "*le roy s'avisera*, the king will advise upon it." 2. By statute 33 Hen. VIII. c. 21. the king may give his assent by letters patent under his great seal, signed with his hand, and notified, in his absence, to both houses assembled together in the high house. And, when the bill has received the royal assent in either of these ways, it is then, and not before, a statute or act of parliament.

T H I S statute or act is placed among the records of the kingdom; there needing no formal promulgation to give it the force of a law, as was necessary by the civil law with regard to the emperors edicts: because every man in England is, in judgment of law, party to the making of an act of parliament, being present thereat by his representatives. However, a copy thereof is usually printed at the king's press, for the information of the whole land. And formerly, before the invention of printing, it was used to be published by the sheriff of every county; the king's writ being sent to him at the end of every session, together with a transcript of all the acts made at that session, commanding him "*ut statuta illa, et omnes articulos in eisdem contentos, in singulis locis ubi expedire viderit, publice proclamari, et firmiter teneri et observari faciat.*" And the usage was to proclaim them at his county court, and there to keep them, that whoever would might read or take copies thereof; which custom continued till the reign of Henry the seventh.

A N act of parliament, thus made, is the exercise of the highest authority that this kingdom acknowleges upon earth. It hath power to bind every subject in the land, and the dominions thereunto belonging; nay, even the king himself, if particularly named therein. And it cannot be altered, amended, dispensed with, suspended, or repealed, but in the same forms and by the same authority of parliament: for it is a maxim in law, that it requires the same strength to dissolve, as to create an obligation. It is true it was formerly held, that the king might in many cases dispense with penal statutes: but now by statute 1 W. & M. st. 2. c. 2. it is declared, that the suspending or dispensing with laws by regal authority, without consent of parliament, is illegal.

VII. T H E R E remains only, in the seventh and last place, to add a word or two concerning the manner in which parliaments may be adjourned, prorogued, or dissolved.

A N adjournment is no more than a continuance of the session from one day to another, as the word itself signifies: and this is done by the authority of each house separately every day; and sometimes for a fortnight or a month together, as at Christmas or Easter, or upon other particular occasions. But the adjournment of one house is no adjournment of the other. It hath also been usual, when his majesty hath signified his pleasure that both or either of the houses should adjourn themselves to a certain day, to obey the king's pleasure so signified, and to adjourn accordingly. Otherwise, besides the indecorum of a refusal, a prorogation would assuredly follow; which would often be very inconvenient to both public and private business. For prorogation puts an end to the session; and then such bills, as are only begun and not perfected, must be resumed *de novo* (if at all) in a subsequent session: whereas, after an adjournment, all things continue in the same state as at the time of the adjournment made, and may be proceeded on without any fresh commencement.

A P R O R O G A T I O N is the continuance of the parliament from one session to another, as an adjournment is a continuation of the session from day to day. This is done by the royal authority, expressed either by the lord chancellor in his majesty's presence, or by commission from the crown, or frequently by proclamation. Both houses are necessarily prorogued at the same time; it not being a prorogation of the house of lords, or commons, but of the parliament. The session is never understood to be at an end, until a prorogation: though, unless some act be passed or some judgment given in parliament, it is in truth no session at all. And formerly the usage was, for the king to give the royal assent to all such bills as he approved, at the end of every session, and then to prorogue the parliament; though sometimes only for a day or two: after which all business then depending in the houses was to be begun again. Which custom obtained so strongly, that it once became a question, whether giving the royal assent to a single bill did not of course put an end to the session. And, though it was then resolved in the negative, yet the notion was so deeply rooted, that the statute 1 Car. I. c. 7. was passed to declare, that the king's assent to that and some other acts should not put an end to the session; and, even so late as the restoration of Charles II, we find a proviso tacked to the first bill then enacted that his majesty's assent thereto should not determine the session of parliament. But it now seems to be allowed, that a prorogation must be expressly made, in order to determine the session. And, if at the time of an actual rebellion, or imminent danger of invasion, the parliament shall be separated by adjournment or prorogation, the king is empowered to call them together by proclamation, with fourteen days notice of the time appointed for their reassembling.

A DISSOLUTION is the civil death of the parliament; and this may be effected three ways: 1. By the king's will, expressed either in person or by representation. For, as the king has the sole right of convening the parliament, so also it is a branch of the royal prerogative, that he may (whenever he pleases) prorogue the parliament for a time, or put a final period to it's existence. If nothing had a right to prorogue or dissolve a parliament but itself, it might happen to become perpetual. And this would be extremely dangerous, if at any time it should attempt to encroach upon the executive power: as was fatally experienced by the unfortunate king Charles the first; who, having unadvisedly passed an act to continue the parliament then in being till such time as it should please to dissolve itself, at last fell a sacrifice to that inordinate power, which he himself had consented to give them. It is therefore extremely necessary that the crown should be empowered to regulate the duration of these assemblies, under the limitations which the English constitution has prescribed: so that, on the one hand, they may frequently and regularly come together, for the dispatch of business and redress of grievances; and may not, on the other, even with the consent of the crown, be continued to an inconvenient or unconstitutional length.

2. A PARLIAMENT may be dissolved by the demise of the crown. This dissolution formerly happened immediately upon the death of the reigning sovereign, for he being considered in law as the head of the parliament, (*caput, principium, et finis*) that failing, the whole body was held to be extinct. But, the calling a new parliament immediately on the inauguration of the successor being found inconvenient, and dangers being apprehended from having no parliament in being in case of a disputed succession, it was enacted by the statutes 7 & 8 W. III. c. 15. and 6 Ann. c. 7. that the parliament in being shall continue for six months after the death of any king or queen, unless sooner prorogued or dissolved by the successor: that, if the parliament be, at the time of the king's death, separated by adjournment

or prorogation, it shall notwithstanding assemble immediately: and that, if no parliament is then in being, the members of the last parliament shall assemble, and be again a parliament.

3. L A S T L Y , a parliament may be dissolved or expire by length of time. For if either the legislative body were perpetual; or might last for the life of the prince who convened them, as formerly; and were so to be supplied, by occasionally filling the vacancies with new representatives; in these cases, if it were once corrupted, the evil would be past all remedy: but when different bodies succeed each other, if the people see cause to disapprove of the present, they may rectify it's faults in the next. A legislative assembly also, which is sure to be separated again, (whereby it's members will themselves become private men, and subject to the full extent of the laws which they have enacted for others) will think themselves bound, in interest as well as duty, to make only such laws as are good. The utmost extent of time that the same parliament was allowed to sit, by the statute 6 W. & M. c. 2. was *three* years; after the expiration of which, reckoning from the return of the first summons, the parliament was to have no longer continuance. But by the statute 1 Geo. I. st. 2. c. 38. (in order, professedly, to prevent the great and continued expenses of frequent elections, and the violent heats and animosities consequent thereupon, and for the peace and security of the government then just recovering from the late rebellion) this term was prolonged to *seven* years; and, what alone is an instance of the vast authority of parliament, the very same house, that was chosen for three years, enacted it's own continuance for seven. So that, as our constitution now stands, the parliament must expire, or die a natural death, at the end of every seventh year; if not sooner dissolved by the royal prerogative.

CHAPTER THE THIRD.

OF THE KING, AND HIS TITLE.

THE supreme executive power of these kingdoms is vested by our laws in a single person, the king or queen: for it matters not to which sex the crown descends; but the person entitled to it, whether male or female, is immediately invested with all the ensigns, rights, and prerogatives of sovereign power; as is declared by statute 1 Mar. st. 3. c. 1.

IN discoursing of the royal rights and authority, I shall consider the king under six distinct views: 1. With regard to his title. 2. His royal family. 3. His councils. 4. His duties. 5. His prerogative. 6. His revenue. And, first, with regard to his title.

THE executive power of the English nation being vested in a single person, by the general consent of the people, the evidence of which general consent is long and immemorial usage, it became necessary to the freedom and peace of the state, that a rule should be laid down, uniform, universal, and permanent; in order to mark out with precision, *who* is that single person, to whom are committed (in subservience to the law of the land) the care and protection of the community; and to whom, in return, the duty and allegiance of every individual are due. It is of the highest importance to the public tranquillity, and to the consciences of private men, that this rule should be clear and indisputable: and our constitution has not left us in the dark upon this material occasion. It will therefore be the endeavour of this chapter to trace out the constitutional doctrine of the royal succession, with that freedom and regard to truth, yet mixed with that reverence and respect, which the principles of liberty and the dignity of the subject require.

THE grand fundamental maxim upon which the *jus coronae*, or right of succession to the throne of these kingdoms, depends, I take to be this: "that the crown is, by common law and constitutional custom, hereditary; and this in a manner peculiar to itself: but that the right of inheritance may from time to time be changed or limited by act of parliament; under which limitations the crown still continues hereditary." And this proposition it will be the business of this chapter to prove, in all it's branches: first, that the crown is hereditary; secondly, that it is hereditary in a manner peculiar to itself; thirdly, that this inheritance is subject to limitation by parliament; lastly, that when it is so limited, it is hereditary in the new proprietor.

I. FIRST, it is in general *hereditary*, or descendible to the next heir, on the death or demise of the last proprietor. All regal governments must be either hereditary or elective: and, as I believe there is no instance wherein the crown of England has ever been asserted to be elective, except by the regicides at the infamous and unparalleled trial of king Charles I, it must of consequence be hereditary. Yet while I assert an hereditary, I by no means intend a *jure divino*, title to the throne. Such a title may be allowed to have subsisted under the theocratic establishments of the children of Israel in Palestine: but it never yet subsisted in any other country; save only so far as kingdoms, like other human fabrics, are subject to the general and ordinary dispensations of providence. Nor indeed have a *jure divino* and an *hereditary* right any necessary connexion with each other; as some have very weakly imagined. The titles of David and Jehu were equally *jure divino*, as those of either Solomon or Ahab; and yet David slew the sons of his predecessor, and Jehu his predecessor himself. And when our kings have the same warrant as they had, whether it be to sit upon the throne of their fathers, or to destroy the house of the preceding sovereign, they will then, and not before, possess the crown of England by a right like theirs, *immediately* derived from heaven. The hereditary right, which the laws of England acknowlege, owes it's origin to the founders of our constitution, and to them only. It has no relation to, nor depends upon, the civil laws of the Jews, the Greeks, the Romans, or any other nation upon earth: the municipal laws of one society having no connexion with, or influence upon, the fundamental polity of another. The founders of our English monarchy might perhaps, if they had thought proper, have made it an elective monarchy: but they rather chose, and upon good reason, to establish originally a succession by inheritance. This has been acquiesced in by general consent; and ripened by degrees into common law: the very same title that every private man has to his own estate. Lands are not naturally descendible any more than thrones: but the law has thought proper, for the benefit and peace of the public, to establish hereditary succession in one as well as the other.

I T must be owned, an elective monarchy seems to be the most obvious, and best suited of any to the rational principles of government, and the freedom of human nature: and accordingly we find from history that, in the infancy and first rudiments of almost every state, the leader, chief magistrate, or prince, hath usually been elective. And, if the individuals who compose that state could always continue true to first principles, uninfluenced by passion or prejudice, unassailed by corruption, and unawed by violence, elective succession were as much to be desired in a kingdom, as in other inferior communities. The best, the wisest, and the bravest man would then be sure of receiving that crown, which his endowments have merited; and the sense of an unbiassed majority would be dutifully acquiesced in by the few who were of different opinions. But history and observation will inform us, that elections of every kind (in the present state of human nature) are too frequently brought about by influence, partiality, and artifice: and, even where the case is otherwise, these practices will be often suspected, and as constantly charged upon the successful, by a splenetic disappointed minority. This is an evil, to which all societies are liable; as well those of a private and domestic kind, as the great community of the public, which regulates and includes the rest. But in the former there is this advantage; that such suspicions, if false, proceed no farther than jealousies and murmurs, which time will effectually suppress; and, if true, the injustice may be remedied by legal means, by an appeal to those tribunals to which every member of society has (by becoming such) virtually engaged to submit. Whereas, in the great and independent society, which every nation composes, there is no superior to resort to but the law of nature; no method to redress the infringements of that law, but the actual exertion of private force. As therefore between two nations, complaining of mutual injuries, the quarrel can only be decided by the law of arms; so in one and the same nation, when the fundamental principles of their common union are supposed to be invaded, and more especially when the appointment of their chief magistrate is alleged to be unduly made, the only tribunal to which the complainants can appeal is that of the God of battels, the only process by which the appeal can be carried on is that of a civil and intestine war. An hereditary succession to the crown is therefore now established, in this and most other countries, in order to prevent that periodical bloodshed and misery, which the history of antient imperial Rome, and the more modern experience of Poland and Germany, may shew us are the consequences of elective kingdoms.

2. B U T , secondly, as to the particular mode of inheritance, it in general corresponds with the feodal path of descents, chalked out by the common law in the succession to landed estates; yet with one or two material exceptions. Like them, the crown will descend lineally to the issue of the reigning monarch; as it did from king John to Richard II, through a regular pedigree of six lineal descents. As in them, the preference of males to females, and the right of primogeniture among the males, are strictly adhered to. Thus Edward V succeeded to the crown, in preference to Richard his younger brother and Elizabeth his elder sister. Like them, on failure of the male line, it descends to the issue female; according to the antient British custom remarked by Tacitus, "*solent foeminarum ductu bellare, et sexum in imperiis non discernere.*" Thus Mary I succeeded to Edward VI; and the line of Margaret queen of Scots, the daughter of Henry VII, succeeded on failure of the line of Henry VIII, his son. But, among the females, the crown descends by right of primogeniture to the eldest daughter only and her issue; and not, as in common inheritances, to all the daughters at once; the evident necessity of a sole succession to the throne having occasioned the royal law of descents to depart from the common law in this respect: and therefore queen Mary on the death of her brother succeeded to the crown alone, and not in partnership with her sister Elizabeth. Again: the doctrine of representation prevails in the descent of the crown, as it does in other inheritances; whereby the lineal descendants of any person deceased stand in the same place as their ancestor, if living, would have done. Thus Richard II succeeded his grandfather Edward III, in right of his father the black prince; to the exclusion of all his uncles, his grandfather's younger children. Lastly, on failure of lineal descendants, the crown goes to the next collateral relations of the late king; provided they are lineally descended from the blood royal, that is, from that royal stock which originally acquired the crown. Thus Henry I succeeded to William II, John to Richard I, and James I to Elizabeth; being all derived from the conqueror, who was then the only regal stock. But herein there is no objection (as in the case of common descents) to the succession of a brother, an uncle, or other collateral relation, of the *half* blood; that is, where the relationship proceeds not from the same *couple* of ancestors (which constitutes a kinsman of the *whole* blood) but from a *single* ancestor only; as when two persons are derived from the same father, and not from the same mother, or *vice versa*: provided only, that the one ancestor, from whom both are descended, be he from whose veins the blood royal is communicated to each. Thus Mary I inherited to Edward VI, and Elizabeth inherited to Mary; all born of the same father, king Henry VIII, but all by different mothers.

The reason of which diversity, between royal and common descents, will be better understood hereafter, when we examine the nature of inheritances in general.

3. T H E doctrine of *hereditary* right does by no means imply an *indefeasible* right to the throne. No man will, I think, assert this, that has considered our laws, constitution, and history, without prejudice, and with any degree of attention. It is unquestionably in the breast of the supreme legislative authority of this kingdom, the king and both houses of parliament, to defeat this hereditary right; and, by particular entails, limitations, and provisions, to exclude the immediate heir, and vest the inheritance in any one else. This is strictly consonant to our laws and constitution; as may be gathered from the expression so frequently used in our statute book, of "the king's majesty, his heirs, and successors." In which we may observe, that as the word, "heirs," necessarily implies an inheritance or hereditary right, generally subsisting in the royal person; so the word, "successors," distinctly taken, must imply that this inheritance may sometimes be broke through; or, that there may be a successor, without being the heir, of the king. And this is so extremely reasonable, that without such a power, lodged somewhere, our polity would be very defective. For, let us barely suppose so melancholy a case, as that the heir apparent should be a lunatic, an ideot, or otherwise incapable of reigning: how miserable would the condition of the nation be, if he were also incapable of being set aside!—It is therefore necessary that this power should be lodged somewhere: and yet the inheritance, and regal dignity, would be very precarious indeed, if this power were *expressly* and *avowedly* lodged in the hands of the subject only, to be exerted whenever prejudice, caprice, or discontent should happen to take the lead. Consequently it can no where be so properly lodged as in the two houses of parliament, by and with the consent of the reigning king; who, it is not to be supposed, will agree to any thing improperly prejudicial to the rights of his own descendants. And therefore in the king, lords, and commons, in parliament assembled, our laws have expressly lodged it.

4. B U T , fourthly; however the crown maybe limited or transferred, it still retains it's descendible quality, and becomes hereditary in the wearer of it: and hence in our law the king is said never to die, in his political capacity; though, in common with other men, he is subject to mortality in his natural: because immediately upon the natural death of Henry, William, or Edward, the king survives in his successor; and the right of the crown vests, *eo instanti*, upon his heir; either the *haeres natus*, if the course of descent remains unimpeached, or the *haeres factus*, if the inheritance be under any particular settlement. So that there can be no *interregnum*; but as sir Matthew Hale observes, the right of sovereignty is fully invested in the successor by the very descent of the crown. And therefore, however acquired, it becomes in him absolutely hereditary, unless by the rules of the limitation it is otherwise ordered and determined. In the same manner as landed estates, to continue our former comparison, are by the law hereditary, or descendible to the heirs of the owner; but still there exists a power, by which the property of those lands may be transferred to another person. If this transfer be made simply and absolutely, the lands will be hereditary in the new owner, and descend to his

heirs at law: but if the transfer be clogged with any limitations, conditions, or entails, the lands must descend in that chanel, so limited and prescribed, and no other.

I N these four points consists, as I take it, the constitutional notion of hereditary right to the throne: which will be still farther elucidated, and made clear beyond all dispute, from a short historical view of the successions to the crown of England, the doctrines of our antient lawyers, and the several acts of parliament that have from time to time been made, to create, to declare, to confirm, to limit, or to bar, the hereditary title to the throne. And in the pursuit of this enquiry we shall find, that from the days of Egbert, the first sole monarch of this kingdom, even to the present, the four cardinal maxims above mentioned have ever been held the constitutional canons of succession. It is true, this succession, through fraud, or force, or sometimes through necessity, when in hostile times the crown descended on a minor or the like, has been very frequently suspended; but has always at last returned back into the old hereditary chanel, though sometimes a very considerable period has intervened. And, even in those instances where the succession has been violated, the crown has ever been looked upon as hereditary in the wearer of it. Of which the usurpers themselves were so sensible, that they for the most part endeavoured to vamp up some feeble shew of a title by descent, in order to amuse the people, while they gained the possession of the kingdom. And, when possession was once gained, they considered it as the purchase or acquisition of a new estate of inheritance, and transmitted or endeavoured to transmit it to their own posterity, by a kind of hereditary right of usurpation.

K I N G Egbert about the year 800, found himself in possession of the throne of the west Saxons, by a long and undisturbed descent from his ancestors of above three hundred years. How his ancestors acquired their title, whether by force, by fraud, by contract, or by election, it matters not much to enquire; and is indeed a point of such high antiquity, as must render all enquiries at best but plausible guesses. His right must be supposed indisputably good, because we know no better. The other kingdoms of the heptarchy he acquired, some by consent, but most by a voluntary submission. And it is an established maxim in civil polity, and the law of nations, that when one country is united to another in such a manner, as that one keeps it's government and states, and the other loses them; the latter entirely assimilates or is melted down in the former, and must adopt it's laws and customs. And in pursuance of this maxim there hath ever been, since the union of the heptarchy in king Egbert, a general acquiescence under the hereditary monarchy of the west Saxons, through all the united kingdoms.

F R O M Egbert to the death of Edmund Ironside, a period of above two hundred years, the crown descended regularly, through a succession of fifteen princes, without any deviation or interruption; save only that king Edred, the uncle of Edwy, mounted the throne for about nine years, in the right of his nephew a minor, the times being very troublesome and dangerous. But this was with a view to preserve, and not to destroy, the succession; and accordingly Edwy succeeded him.

KING Edmund Ironside was obliged, by the hostile irruption of the Danes, at first to divide his kingdom with Canute, king of Denmark; and Canute, after his death, seised the whole of it, Edmund's sons being driven into foreign countries. Here the succession was suspended by actual force, and a new family introduced upon the throne: in whom however this new acquired throne continued hereditary for three reigns; when, upon the death of Hardiknute, the antient Saxon line was restored in the person of Edward the confessor.

HE was not indeed the true heir to the crown, being the younger brother of king Edmund Ironside, who had a son Edward, sirnamed (from his exile) the outlaw, still living. But this son was then in Hungary; and, the English having just shaken off the Danish yoke, it was necessary that somebody on the spot should mount the throne; and the confessor was the next of the royal line then in England. On his decease without issue, Harold II usurped the throne, and almost at the same instant came on the Norman invasion: the right to the crown being all the time in Edgar, sirnamed Atheling, (which signifies in the Saxon language the first of the blood royal) who was the son of Edward the outlaw, and grandson of Edmund Ironside; or, as Matthew Paris well expresses the sense of our old constitution, "*Edmundus autem latusferreum, rex naturalis de stirpe regum, genuit Edwardum; et Edwardus genuit Edgarum, cui de jure debebatur regnum Anglorum.*"

WILLIAM the Norman claimed the crown by virtue of a pretended grant from king Edward the confessor; a grant which, if real, was in itself utterly invalid: because it was made, as Harold well observed in his reply to William's demand, "*absque generali senatus et populi conventu et edicto;*" which also very plainly implies, that it then was generally understood that the king, with consent of the general council, might dispose of the crown and change the line of succession. William's title however was altogether as good as Harold's, he being a mere private subject, and an utter stranger to the royal blood. Edgar Atheling's undoubted right was overwhelmed by the violence of the times; though frequently asserted by the English nobility after the conquest, till such time as he died without issue: but all their attempts proved unsuccessful, and only served the more firmly to establish the crown in the family which had newly acquired it.

THIS conquest then by William of Normandy was, like that of Canute before, a forcible transfer of the crown of England into a new family: but, the crown being so transferred, all the inherent properties of the crown were with it transferred also. For, the victory obtained at Hastings not being a victory over the nation collectively, but only over the person of Harold, the only right that the conqueror could pretend to acquire thereby, was the right to possess the crown of England, not to alter the nature of the government. And therefore, as the English laws still remained in force, he must necessarily take the crown subject to those laws, and with all it's inherent properties; the first and principal of which was it's descendibility. Here then we must drop our race of Saxon kings, at least for a while, and derive our descents from William the conqueror as from a new stock, who acquired by right of war (such as it is, yet still the *dernier resort* of kings) a strong and undisputed title to the inheritable crown of England.

ACCORDINGLY it descended from him to his sons William II and Henry I. Robert, it must be owned, his eldest son, was kept out of possession by the arts and violence of his brethren; who proceeded upon a notion, which prevailed for some time in the law of descents, that when the eldest son was already provided for (as Robert was constituted duke of Normandy by his father's will) in such a case the next brother was entitled to enjoy the rest of their father's inheritance. But, as he died without issue, Henry at last had a good title to the throne, whatever he might have at first.

STEPHEN of Blois, who succeeded him, was indeed the grandson of the conqueror, by Adelicia his daughter, and claimed the throne by a feeble kind of hereditary right; not as being the nearest of the male line, but as the nearest male of the blood royal. The real right was in the empress Matilda or Maud, the daughter of Henry I; the rule of succession being (where women are admitted at all) that the daughter of a son shall be preferred to the son of a daughter. So that Stephen was little better than a mere usurper; and the empress Maud did not fail to assert her right by the sword: which dispute was attended with various success, and ended at last in a compromise, that Stephen should keep the crown, but that Henry the son of Maud should succeed him; as he afterwards accordingly did.

HENRY, the second of that name, was the undoubted heir of William the conqueror; but he had also another connexion in blood, which endeared him still farther to the English. He was lineally descended from Edmund Ironside, the last of the Saxon race of hereditary kings. For Edward the outlaw, the son of Edmund Ironside, had (besides Edgar Atheling, who died without issue) a daughter Margaret, who was married to Malcolm king of Scotland; and in her the Saxon hereditary right resided. By Malcolm she had several children, and among the rest Matilda the wife of Henry I, who by him had the empress Maud, the mother of Henry II. Upon which account the Saxon line is in our histories frequently said to have been restored in his person: though in reality that right subsisted in the *sons* of Malcolm by queen Margaret; king Henry's best title being as heir to the conqueror.

FROM Henry II the crown descended to his eldest son Richard I, who dying childless, the right vested in his nephew Arthur, the son of Geoffrey his next brother; but John, the youngest son of king Henry, seised the throne; claiming, as appears from his charters, the crown by hereditary right: that is to say, he was next of kin to the deceased king, being his surviving brother; whereas Arthur was removed one degree farther, being his brother's son, though by right of representation he stood in the place of his father Geoffrey. And however flimzey this title, and those of William Rufus and Stephen of Blois, may appear at this distance to us, after the law of descents hath now been settled for so many centuries, they were sufficient to puzzle the understandings of our brave, but unlettered, ancestors. Nor indeed can we wonder at the number of partizans, who espoused the pretensions of king John in particular; since even in the reign of his father, king Henry II, it was a point undetermined, whether, even in common inheritances, the child of an elder brother should succeed to the land in right of representation, or the younger surviving brother in right of proximity of blood. Nor is it to this day decided in the collateral succession to the fiefs of the empire, whether the order of the stocks, or the proximity of degree shall take place. However, on the death of Arthur and his sister Eleanor without issue, a clear and indisputable title vested in Henry III the son of John: and from him to Richard the second, a succession of six generations, the crown descended in the true hereditary line. Under one of which race of princes, we find it declared in parliament, "that the law of the crown of England is, and always hath been, that the children of the king of England, whether born in England, or elsewhere, ought to bear the inheritance after the death of their ancestors. Which law, our sovereign lord the king, the prelates, earls, and barons, and other great men, together with all the commons, in parliament assembled, do approve and affirm for ever."

UPON Richard the second's resignation of the crown, he having no children, the right resulted to the issue of his grandfather Edward III. That king had many children, besides his eldest, Edward the black prince of Wales, the father of Richard II: but to avoid confusion I shall only mention three; William his second son, who died without issue; Lionel duke of Clarence, his third son; and John of Gant duke of Lancaster, his fourth. By the rules of succession therefore the posterity of Lionel duke of Clarence were entitled to the throne, upon the resignation of king Richard; and had accordingly been declared by the king, many years before, the presumptive heirs of the crown; which declaration was also confirmed in parliament. But Henry duke of Lancaster, the son of John of Gant, having then a large army in the kingdom, the pretence of raising which was to recover his patrimony from the king, and to redress the grievances of the subject, it was impossible for any other title to be asserted with any safety; and he became king under the title of Henry IV. But, as sir Matthew Hale remarks, though the people unjustly assisted Henry IV in his usurpation of the crown, yet he was not admitted thereto, until he had declared that he claimed, not as a conqueror, (which he very much inclined to do) but as a successor, descended by right line of the blood royal; as appears from the rolls of parliament in those times. And in order to this he set up a shew of two titles: the one upon the pretence of being the first of the blood royal in the intire male line, whereas the duke of Clarence left only one daughter Philippa; from which female branch, by a marriage with Edmond Mortimer earl of March, the house of York descended: the other, by reviving an exploded rumour, first propagated by John of Gant, that Edmond earl of Lancaster (to whom Henry's mother was heiress) was in reality the elder brother of king Edward I; though his parents, on account of his personal deformity, had imposed him on the world for the younger: and therefore Henry would be intitled to the crown, either as successor to Richard II, in case the intire male line was allowed a preference to the female; or, even prior to that unfortunate prince, if the crown could descend through a female, while an intire male line was existing.

H O W E V E R , as in Edward the third's time we find the parliament approving and affirming the right of the crown, as before stated, so in the reign of Henry IV they actually exerted their right of new-settling the succession to the crown. And this was done by the statute 7 Hen. IV. c. 2. whereby it is enacted, "that the inheritance of the crown and realms of England and France, and all other the king's dominions, shall be *set and remain* in the person of our sovereign lord the king, and in the heirs of his body issuing;" and prince Henry is declared heir apparent to the crown, to hold to him and the heirs of his body issuing, with remainder to lord Thomas, lord John, and lord Humphry, the king's sons, and the heirs of their bodies respectively. Which is indeed nothing more than the law would have done before, provided Henry the fourth had been a rightful king. It however serves to shew that it was then generally understood, that the king and parliament had a right to new-model and regulate the succession to the crown. And we may observe, with what caution and delicacy the parliament then avoided declaring any sentiment of Henry's original title. However sir Edward Coke more than once expressly declares, that at the time of passing this act the right of the crown was in the descent from Philippa, daughter and heir of Lionel duke of Clarence.

N E V E R T H E L E S S the crown descended regularly from Henry IV to his son and grandson Henry V and VI; in the latter of whose reigns the house of York asserted their dormant title; and, after imbruing the kingdom in blood and confusion for seven years together, at last established it in the person of Edward IV. At his accession to the throne, after a breach of the succession that continued for three descents, and above threescore years, the distinction of a king *de jure*, and a king *de facto* began to be first taken; in order to indemnify such as had submitted to the late establishment, and to provide for the peace of the kingdom by confirming all honors conferred, and all acts done, by those who were now called the usurpers, not tending to the disherison of the rightful heir. In statute 1 Edw. IV. c. 1. the three Henrys are stiled, "late kings of England successively in dede, and not of ryght." And, in all the charters which I have met with of king Edward, wherever he has occasion to speak of any of the line of Lancaster, he calls them "*nuper de facto, et non de jure, reges Angliae.*"

E D W A R D IV left two sons and a daughter; the eldest of which sons, king Edward V, enjoyed the regal dignity for a very short time, and was then deposed by Richard his unnatural uncle; who immediately usurped the royal dignity, having previously insinuated to the populace a suspicion of bastardy in the children of Edward IV, to make a shew of some hereditary title: after which he is generally believed to have murdered his two nephews; upon whose death the right of the crown devolved to their sister Elizabeth.

T H E tyrannical reign of king Richard III gave occasion to Henry earl of Richmond to assert his title to the crown. A title the most remote and unaccountable that was ever set up, and which nothing could have given success to, but the universal detestation of the then usurper Richard. For, besides that he claimed under a descent from John of Gant, whose title was now exploded, the claim (such as it was) was through John earl of Somerset, a bastard son, begotten by John of Gant upon Catherine Swinford. It is true, that, by an act of parliament 20 Ric. II, this son was, with others, legitimated and made inheritable to all lands, offices, and dignities, as if he had been born in wedlock: but still, with an express reservation of the crown, "*excepta dignitate regali.*"

N O T W I T H S T A N D I N G all this, immediately after the battle of Bosworth field, he assumed the regal dignity; the right of the crown then being, as sir Edward Coke expressly declares, in Elizabeth, eldest daughter of Edward IV: and his possession was established by parliament, held the first year of his reign. In the act for which purpose, the parliament seems to have copied the caution of their predecessors in the reign of Henry IV; and therefore (as lord Bacon the historian of this reign observes) carefully avoided any recognition of Henry VII's right, which indeed was none at all; and the king would not have it by way of new law or ordinance, whereby a right might seem to be created and conferred upon him; and therefore a middle way was rather chosen, by way (as the noble historian expresses it) of *establishment*, and that under covert and indifferent words, "that the inheritance of the crown should *rest, remain*, and *abide* in king Henry VII and the heirs of his body:" thereby providing for the future, and at the same time acknowleging his present possession; but not determining either way, whether that possession was *de jure* or *de facto* merely. However he soon after married Elizabeth of York, the undoubted heiress of the conqueror, and thereby gained (as sir Edward Coke declares) by much his best title to the crown.Whereupon the act made in his favour was so much disregarded, that it never was printed in our statute books.

H E N R Y the eighth, the issue of this marriage, succeeded to the crown by clear indisputable hereditary right, and transmitted it to his three children in successive order. But in his reign we at several times find the parliament busy in regulating the succession to the kingdom. And, first, by statute 25 Hen. VIII. c. 12. which recites the mischiefs, which have and may ensue by disputed titles, because no perfect and substantial provision hath been made by law concerning the succession; and then enacts, that the crown shall be entailed to his majesty, and the sons or heirs males of his body; and in default of such sons to the lady Elizabeth (who is declared to be the king's eldest issue female, in exclusion of the lady Mary, on account of her supposed illegitimacy by the divorce of her mother queen Catherine) and to the lady Elizabeth's heirs of her body; and so on from issue female to issue female, and the heirs of their bodies, by course of inheritance according to their ages, *as the crown of England hath been accustomed and ought to go*, in case where there be heirs female of the same: and in default of issue female, then to the king's right heirs for ever. This single statute is an ample proof of all the four positions we at first set out with.

B U T , upon the king's divorce from Ann Boleyn, this statute was, with regard to the settlement of the crown, repealed by statute 28 Hen. VIII. c. 7. wherein the lady Elizabeth is also, as well as the lady Mary, bastardized, and the crown settled on the king's children by queen Jane Seymour, and his future wives; and, in defect of such children, then with this remarkable remainder, to such persons as the king by letters patent, or last will and testament, should limit and appoint the same. A vast power; but, notwithstanding, as it was regularly vested in him by the supreme legislative authority, it was therefore indisputably valid. But this power was never carried into execution; for by statute 35 Hen. VIII. c. 1. the king's two daughters are legitimated again, and the crown is limited to prince Edward by name, after that to the lady Mary, and then to the lady Elizabeth, and the heirs of their respective bodies; which succession took effect accordingly, being indeed no other than the usual course of the law, with regard to the descent of the crown.

B U T lest there should remain any doubt in the minds of the people, through this jumble of acts for limiting the succession, by statute 1 Mar. p. 2. c. 1. queen Mary's hereditary right to the throne is acknowleged and recognized in these words: "the crown of these realms is most lawfully, justly, and rightly *descended* and come to the queen's highness that now is, being the very, true, and undoubted heir and inheritrix thereof." And again, upon the queen's marriage with Philip of Spain, in the statute which settles the preliminaries of that match, the hereditary right to the crown is thus asserted and declared: "as touching the right of the queen's inheritance in the realm and dominions of England, the children, whether male or female, shall succeed in them, according to the known laws, statutes, and customs of the same." Which determination of the parliament, that the succession *shall* continue in the usual course, seems tacitly to imply a power of new-modelling and altering it, in case the legislature had thought proper.

O N queen Elizabeth's accession, her right is recognized in still stronger terms than her sister's; the parliament acknowleging, "that the queen's highness is, and in very deed and of most mere right ought to be, by the laws of God, and the laws and statutes of this realm, our most lawful and rightful sovereign liege lady and queen; and that her highness is rightly, lineally, and lawfully descended and come of the blood royal of this realm of England; in and to whose princely person, and to the heirs of her body lawfully to be begotten, after her, the imperial crown and dignity of this realm doth belong." And in the same reign, by statute 13 Eliz. c. 1. we find the right of parliament to direct the succession of the crown asserted in the most explicit words. "If any person shall hold, affirm, or maintain that the common laws of this realm, not altered by parliament, ought not to direct the right of the crown of England; or that the queen's majesty, with and by the authority of parliament, is not able to make laws and statutes of sufficient force and validity, to limit and bind the crown of this realm, and the descent, limitation, inheritance, and government thereof;—such person, so holding, affirming, or maintaining, shall during the life of the queen be guilty of high treason; and after her decease shall be guilty of a misdemesnor, and forfeit his goods and chattels."

O N the death of queen Elizabeth, without issue, the line of Henry VIII became extinct. It therefore became necessary to recur to the other issue of Henry VII, by Elizabeth of York his queen: whose eldest daughter Margaret having married James IV king of Scotland, king James the sixth of Scotland, and of England the first, was the lineal descendant from that alliance. So that in his person, as clearly as in Henry VIII, centered all the claims of different competitors from the conquest downwards, he being indisputably the lineal heir of the conqueror. And, what is still more remarkable, in his person also centered the right of the Saxon monarchs, which had been suspended from the conquest till his accession. For, as was formerly observed, Margaret the sister of Edgar Atheling, the daughter of Edward the outlaw, and granddaughter of king Edmund Ironside, was the person in whom the hereditary right of the Saxon kings, supposing it not abolished by the conquest, resided. She married Malcolm king of Scotland; and Henry II, by a descent from Matilda their daughter, is generally called the restorer of the Saxon line. But it must be remembered, that Malcolm by his Saxon queen had sons as well as daughters; and that the royal family of Scotland from that time downwards were the offspring of Malcolm and Margaret. Of this royal family king James the first was the direct lineal heir, and therefore united in his person every possible claim by hereditary right to the English, as well as Scottish throne, being the heir both of Egbert and William the conqueror.

A N D it is no wonder that a prince of more learning than wisdom, who could deduce an hereditary title for more than eight hundred years, should easily be taught by the flatterers of the times to believe there was something divine in this right, and that the finger of providence was visible in it's preservation. Whereas, though a wise institution, it was clearly a human institution; and the right inherent in him no natural, but a positive right. And in this and no other light was it taken by the English parliament; who by statute 1 Jac. 1. c. 1. did "recognize and acknowlege, that immediately upon the dissolution and decease of Elizabeth late queen of England, the imperial crown thereof did by inherent birthright, and lawful and undoubted succession, descend and come to his most excellent majesty, as being lineally, justly, and lawfully, next and sole heir of the blood royal of this realm." Not a word here of any right immediately derived from heaven: which, if it existed any where, must be sought for among the *aborigines* of the island, the antient Britons; among whose princes indeed some have gone to search it for him.

B U T, wild and absurd as the doctrine of divine right most undoubtedly is, it is still more astonishing, that when so many human hereditary rights had centered in this king, his son and heir king Charles the first should be told by those infamous judges, who pronounced his unparalleled sentence, that he was an elective prince; elected by his people, and therefore accountable to them, in his own proper person, for his conduct. The confusion, instability, and madness, which followed the fatal catastrophe of that pious and unfortunate prince, will be a standing argument in favour of hereditary monarchy to all future ages; as they proved at last to the then deluded people: who, in order to recover that peace and happiness which for twenty years together they had lost, in a solemn parliamentary convention of the states restored the right heir of the crown. And in the proclamation for that purpose, which was drawn up and attended by both houses, they declared, "that, according to their duty and allegiance, they did heartily, joyfully, and unanimously acknowlege and proclaim, that immediately upon the decease of our late sovereign lord king Charles, the imperial crown of these realms did by inherent birthright and lawful and undoubted succession descend and come to his most excellent majesty Charles the second, as being lineally, justly, and lawfully, next heir of the blood royal of this realm: and thereunto they most humbly and faithfully did submit and oblige themselves, their heirs and posterity for ever."

T H U S I think it clearly appears, from the highest authority this nation is acquainted with, that the crown of England hath been ever an hereditary crown; though subject to limitations by parliament. The remainder of this chapter will consist principally of those instances, wherein the parliament has asserted or exercised this right of altering and limiting the succession; a right which, we have seen, was before exercised and asserted in the reigns of Henry IV, Henry VII, Henry VIII, queen Mary, and queen Elizabeth.

T H E first instance, in point of time, is the famous bill of exclusion, which raised such a ferment in the latter end of the reign of king Charles the second. It is well known, that the purport of this bill was to have set aside the king's brother and presumptive heir, the duke of York, from the succession, on the score of his being a papist; that it passed the house of commons, but was rejected by the lords; the king having also declared beforehand, that he never would be brought to consent to it. And from this transaction we may collect two things: 1. That the crown was universally acknowleged to be hereditary; and the inheritance indefeasible unless by parliament: else it had been needless to prefer such a bill. 2. That the parliament had a power to have defeated the inheritance: else such a bill had been ineffectual. The commons acknowleged the hereditary right then subsisting; and the lords did not dispute the power, but merely the propriety, of an exclusion. However, as the bill took no effect, king James the second succeeded to the throne of his ancestors; and might have enjoyed it during the remainder of his life, but for his own infatuated conduct, which (with other concurring circumstances) brought on the revolution in 1688.

T H E true ground and principle, upon which that memorable event proceeded, was an entirely new case in politics, which had never before happened in our history; the abdication of the reigning monarch, and the vacancy of the throne thereupon. It was not a defeazance of the right of succession, and a new limitation of the crown, by the king and both houses of parliament: it was the act of the nation alone, upon an apprehension that there was no king in being. For in a full assembly of the lords and commons, met in convention upon this apprehended vacancy, both houses came to this resolution; "that king James the second, having endeavoured to subvert the constitution of the kingdom, by breaking the original contract between king and people; and, by the advice of jesuits and other wicked persons, having violated the fundamental laws; and having withdrawn himself out of this kingdom; has abdicated the government, and that the throne is thereby vacant." Thus ended at once, by this sudden and unexpected vacancy of the throne, the old line of succession; which from the conquest had lasted above six hundred years, and from the union of the heptarchy in king Egbert almost nine hundred. The facts themselves thus appealed to, the king's endeavours to subvert the constitution by breaking the original contract, his violation of the fundamental laws, and his withdrawing himself out of the kingdom, were evident and notorious: and the consequences drawn from these facts (namely, that they amounted to an abdication of the government; which abdication did not affect only the person of the king himself, but also all his heirs, and rendered the throne absolutely and completely vacant) it belonged to our ancestors to determine. For, whenever a question arises between the society at large and any magistrate vested with powers originally delegated by that society, it must be decided by the voice of the society itself: there is not upon earth any other tribunal to resort to. And that these consequences were fairly deduced from these facts, our ancestors have solemnly determined, in a full parliamentary convention representing the whole society. The reasons upon which they decided may be found at large in the parliamentary proceedings of the times; and may be matter of instructive amusement for us to contemplate, as a speculative point of history. But care must be taken not to carry this enquiry farther, than merely for instruction or amusement. The idea, that the consciences of posterity were concerned in the rectitude of their ancestors' decisions, gave birth to those dangerous political heresies, which so long distracted the state, but at length are all happily extinguished. I therefore rather chuse to consider this great political measure, upon the solid footing of authority, than to reason in it's favour from it's justice, moderation, and expedience: because that might imply a right of dissenting or revolting from it, in case we should think it unjust, oppressive, or inexpedient. Whereas, our ancestors having most indisputably a competent jurisdiction to decide this great and important question, and having in fact decided it, it is now become our duty at this distance of time to acquiesce in their determination; being born under that establishment which was built upon this foundation, and obliged by every tie, religious as well as civil, to maintain it.

BUT, while we rest this fundamental transaction, in point of authority, upon grounds the least liable to cavil, we are bound both in justice and gratitude to add, that it was conducted with a temper and moderation which naturally arose from it's equity; that, however it might in some respects go beyond the letter of our antient laws, (the reason of which will more fully appear hereafter) it was agreeable to the spirit of our constitution, and the rights of human nature; and that though in other points (owing to the peculiar circumstances of things and persons) it was not altogether so perfect as might have been wished, yet from thence a new aera commenced, in which the bounds of prerogative and liberty have been better defined, the principles of government more thoroughly examined and understood, and the rights of the subject more explicitly guarded by legal provisions, than in any other period of the English history. In particular, it is worthy observation that the convention, in this their judgment, avoided with great wisdom the wild extremes into which the visionary theories of some zealous republicans would have led them. They held that this misconduct of king James amounted to an *endeavour* to subvert the constitution, and not to an actual subversion, or total dissolution of the government, according to the principles of Mr Locke: which would have reduced the society almost to a state of nature; would have levelled all distinctions of honour, rank, offices, and property; would have annihilated the sovereign power, and in consequence have repealed all positive laws; and would have left the people at liberty to have erected a new system of state upon a new foundation of polity. They therefore very prudently voted it to amount to no more than an abdication of the government, and a consequent vacancy of the throne; whereby the government was allowed to subsist, though the executive magistrate was gone, and the kingly office to remain, though king James was no longer king. And thus the constitution was kept intire; which upon every sound principle of government must otherwise have fallen to pieces, had so principal and constituent a part as the royal authority been abolished, or even suspended.

THIS single postulatum, the vacancy of the throne, being once established, the rest that was then done followed almost of course. For, if the throne be at any time vacant (which may happen by other means besides that of abdication; as if all the bloodroyal should fail, without any successor appointed by parliament;) if, I say, a vacancy by any means whatsoever should happen, the right of disposing of this vacancy seems naturally to result to the lords and commons, the trustees and representatives of the nation. For there are no other hands in which it can so properly be intrusted; and there is a necessity of it's being intrusted somewhere, else the whole frame of government must be dissolved and perish. The lords and commons having therefore determined this main fundamental article, that there was a vacancy of the throne, they proceeded to fill up that vacancy in such manner as they judged the most proper. And this was done by their declaration of 12 February 1688, in the following manner: "that William and Mary, prince and princess of Orange, be, and be declared king and queen, to hold the crown and royal dignity during their lives, and the life of the survivor of them; and that the sole and full exercise of the regal power be only in, and executed by, the said prince of Orange, in the names of the said prince and princess, during their joint lives; and after their deceases the said crown and royal dignity to be to the heirs of the body of the said princess; and for default of such issue to the princess Anne of Denmark and the heirs of her body; and for default of such issue to the heirs of the body of the said prince of Orange."

PERHAPS, upon the principles before established, the convention might (if they pleased) have vested the regal dignity in a family intirely new, and strangers to the royal blood: but they were too well acquainted with the benefits of hereditary succession, and the influence which it has by custom over the minds of the people, to depart any farther from the antient line than temporary necessity and self-preservation required. They therefore settled the crown, first on king William and queen Mary, king James's eldest daughter, for their *joint* lives; then on the survivor of them; and then on the issue of queen Mary: upon

53

failure of such issue, it was limited to the princess Anne, king James's second daughter, and her issue; and lastly, on failure of that, to the issue of king William, who was the grandson of Charles the first, and nephew as well as son in law of king James the second, being the son of Mary his only sister. This settlement included all the protestant posterity of king Charles I, except such other issue as king James might at any time have, which was totally omitted through fear of a popish succession. And this order of succession took effect accordingly.

T H E S E three princes therefore, king William, queen Mary, and queen Anne, did not take the crown by hereditary right or *descent*, but by way of donation or *purchase*, as the lawyers call it; by which they mean any method of acquiring an estate otherwise than by descent. The new settlement did not merely consist in excluding king James, and the person pretended to be prince of Wales, and then suffering the crown to descend in the old hereditary chanel: for the usual course of descent was in some instances broken through; and yet the convention still kept it in their eye, and paid a great, though not total, regard to it. Let us see how the succession would have stood, if no abdication had happened, and king James had left no other issue than his two daughters queen Mary and queen Anne. It would have stood thus: queen Mary and her issue; queen Anne and her issue; king William and his issue. But we may remember, that queen Mary was only nominally queen, jointly with her husband king William, who alone had the regal power; and king William was absolutely preferred to queen Anne, though his issue was postponed to hers. Clearly therefore these princes were successively in possession of the crown by a title different from the usual course of descent.

I T was towards the end of king William's reign, when all hopes of any surviving issue from any of these princes died with the duke of Glocester, that the king and parliament thought it necessary again to exert their power of limiting and appointing the succession, in order to prevent another vacancy of the throne; which must have ensued upon their deaths, as no farther provision was made at the revolution, than for the issue of king William, queen Mary, and queen Anne. The parliament had previously by the statute of 1 W. & M. st. 2. c. 2. enacted, that every person who should be reconciled to, or hold communion with, the see of Rome, should profess the popish religion, or should marry a papist, should be excluded and for ever incapable to inherit, possess, or enjoy, the crown; and that in such case the people should be absolved from their allegiance, and the crown should descend to such persons, being protestants, as would have inherited the same, in case the person so reconciled, holding communion, professing, or marrying, were naturally dead. To act therefore consistently with themselves, and at the same time pay as much regard to the old hereditary line as their former resolutions would admit, they turned their eyes on the princess Sophia, electress and duchess dowager of Hanover, the most accomplished princess of her age. For, upon the impending extinction of the protestant posterity of Charles the first, the old law of regal descent directed them to recur to the descendants of James the first; and the princess Sophia, being the daughter of Elizabeth queen of Bohemia, who was the youngest daughter of James the first, was the nearest of the antient blood royal, who was not incapacitated by professing the popish religion. On her therefore, and the heirs of her body, being protestants, the remainder

54

of the crown, expectant on the death of king William and queen Anne without issue, was settled by statute 12 & 13 W. III. c. 2. And at the same time it was enacted, that whosoever should hereafter come to the possession of the crown, should join in the communion of the church of England as by law established.

T H I S is the last limitation of the crown that has been made by parliament: and these several actual limitations, from the time of Henry IV to the present, do clearly prove the power of the king and parliament to new-model or alter the succession. And indeed it is now again made highly penal to dispute it: for by the statute 6 Ann. c. 7. it is enacted, that if any person maliciously, advisedly, and directly, shall maintain by writing or printing, that the kings of this realm with the authority of parliament are not able to make laws to bind the crown and the descent thereof, he shall be guilty of high treason; or if he maintains the same by only preaching, teaching, or advised speaking, he shall incur the penalties of a praemunire.

T H E princess Sophia dying before queen Anne, the inheritance thus limited descended on her son and heir king George the first; and, having on the death of the queen taken effect in his person, from him it descended to his late majesty king George the second; and from him to his grandson and heir, our present gracious sovereign, king George the third.

H E N C E it is easy to collect, that the title to the crown is at present hereditary, though not quite so absolutely hereditary as formerly; and the common stock or ancestor, from whom the descent must be derived, is also different. Formerly the common stock was king Egbert; then William the conqueror; afterwards in James the first's time the two common stocks united, and so continued till the vacancy of the throne in 1688: now it is the princess Sophia, in whom the inheritance was vested by the new king and parliament. Formerly the descent was absolute, and the crown went to the next heir without any restriction: but now, upon the new settlement, the inheritance is conditional, being limited to such heirs only, of the body of the princess Sophia, as are protestant members of the church of England, and are married to none but protestants.

A N D in this due medium consists, I apprehend, the true constitutional notion of the right of succession to the imperial crown of these kingdoms. The extremes, between which it steers, are each of them equally destructive of those ends for which societies were formed and are kept on foot. Where the magistrate, upon every succession, is elected by the people, and may by the express provision of the laws be deposed (if not punished) by his subjects, this may sound like the perfection of liberty, and look well enough when delineated on paper; but in practice will be ever productive of tumult, contention, and anarchy. And, on the other hand, divine indefeasible hereditary right, when coupled with the doctrine of unlimited passive obedience, is surely of all constitutions the most thoroughly slavish and dreadful. But when such an hereditary right, as our laws have created and vested in the royal stock, is closely interwoven with those liberties, which, we have seen in a former chapter, are equally the inheritance of the subject; this union will form a constitution, in theory the most beautiful of any, in practice the most approved, and, I trust, in duration the most permanent. It was the duty of an expounder of our laws to lay this constitution before the student in it's true and genuine light: it is the duty of every good Englishman to understand, to revere, to defend it.

CHAPTER THE FOURTH.

OF THE KING'S ROYAL FAMILY.

THE first and most considerable branch of the king's royal family, regarded by the laws of England, is the queen.

THE queen of England is either queen *regent*, queen *consort*, or queen *dowager*. The queen *regent*, *regnant*, or *sovereign*, is she who holds the crown in her own right; as the first (and perhaps the second) queen Mary, queen Elizabeth, and queen Anne; and such a one has the same powers, prerogatives, rights, dignities, and duties, as if she had been a king. This was observed in the entrance of the last chapter, and is expressly declared by statute 1 Mar. I. st. 3. c. 1. But the queen *consort* is the wife of the reigning king; and she by virtue of her marriage is participant of divers prerogatives above other women. AND, first, she is a public person, exempt and distinct from the king; and not, like other married women, so closely connected as to have lost all legal or separate existence so long as the marriage continues. For the queen is of ability to purchase lands, and to convey them, to make leases, to grant copyholds, and do other acts of ownership, without the concurrence of her lord; which no other married woman can do: a privilege as old as the Saxon aera. She is also capable of taking a grant from the king, which no other wife is from her husband; and in this particular she agrees with the *augusta*, or *piissima regina conjux divi imperatoris* of the Roman laws; who, according to Justinian, was equally capable of making a grant to, and receiving one from, the emperor. The queen of England hath separate courts and officers distinct from the king's, not only in matters of ceremony, but even of law; and her attorney and solicitor general are intitled to a place within the bar of his majesty's courts, together with the king's counsel. She may also sue and be sued alone, without joining her husband. She may also have a separate property in goods as well as lands, and has a right to dispose of them by will. In short, she is in all legal proceedings looked upon as a feme sole, and not as a feme covert; as a single, not as a married woman. For which the reason given by Sir Edward Coke is this: because the wisdom of the common law would not have the king (whose continual care and study is for the public, and *circa ardua regni*) to be troubled and disquieted on account of his wife's domestic affairs; and therefore it vests in the queen a power of transacting her own concerns, without the intervention of the king, as if she was an unmarried woman.

THE queen hath also many exemptions, and minute prerogatives. For instance: she pays no toll; nor is she liable to any amercement in any court. But in general, unless where the law has expressly declared her exempted, she is upon the same footing with other subjects; being to all intents and purposes the king's subject, and not his equal: in like manner as, in the imperial law, "*augusta legibus soluta non est.*"

THE queen hath also some pecuniary advantages, which form her a distinct revenue: as, in the first place, she is intitled to an antient perquisite called queen-gold or *aurum reginae*; which is a royal revenue, belonging to every queen consort during her marriage with the king, and due from every person who hath made a voluntary offering or fine to the king, amounting to ten marks or upwards, for and in consideration of any privileges, grants, licences, pardons, or other matter of royal favour conferred upon him by the king: and it is due in the proportion of one tenth part more, over and above the intire offering or fine made to the king; and becomes an actual debt of record to the queen's majesty by the mere recording the fine. As, if an hundred marks of silver be given to the king for liberty to take in mortmain, or to have a fair, market, park, chase, or free warren; there the queen is intitled to ten marks in silver, or (what was formerly an equivalent denomination) to one mark in gold, by the name of queen-gold, or *aurum reginae*. But no such payment is due for any aids or subsidies granted to the king in parliament or convocation; nor for fines imposed by courts on offenders, against their will; nor for voluntary presents to the king, without any consideration moving from him to the subject; nor for any sale or contract whereby the present revenues or possessions of the crown are granted away or diminished.

T H E revenue of our antient queens, before and soon after the conquest, seems to have consisted in certain reservations or rents out of the demesne lands of the crown, which were expressly appropriated to her majesty, distinct from the king. It is frequent in domesday-book, after specifying the rent due to the crown, to add likewise the quantity of gold or other renders reserved to the queen. These were frequently appropriated to particular purposes; to buy wool for her majesty's use, to purchase oyl for her lamps, or to furnish her attire from head to foot, which was frequently very costly, as one single robe in the fifth year of Henry II stood the city of London in upwards of fourscore pounds. A practice somewhat similar to that of the eastern countries, where whole cities and provinces were specifically assigned to purchase particular parts of the queen's apparel. And, for a farther addition to her income, this duty of queen-gold is supposed to have been originally granted; those matters of grace and favour, out of which it arose, being frequently obtained from the crown by the powerful intercession of the queen. There are traces of it's payment, though obscure ones, in the book of domesday and in the great pipe-roll of Henry the first. In the reign of Henry the second the manner of collecting it appears to have been well understood, and it forms a distinct head in the antient dialogue of the exchequer written in the time of that prince, and usually attributed to Gervase of Tilbury. From that time downwards it was regularly claimed and enjoyed by all the queen consorts of England till the death of Henry VIII; though after the accession of the Tudor family the collecting of it seems to have been much neglected: and, there being no queen consort afterwards till the accession of James I, a period of near sixty years, it's very nature and quantity became then a matter of doubt: and, being referred by the king to his then chief justices and chief baron, their report of it was so very unfavorable, that queen Anne (though she claimed it) yet never thought proper to exact it. In 1635, 11 Car. I, a time fertile of expedients for raising money upon dormant precedents in our old records (of which ship-money was a fatal instance) the king, at the petition of his queen Henrietta Maria, issued out his writ for levying it; but afterwards purchased it of his consort at the price of ten thousand pounds; finding it, perhaps, too trifling and troublesome to levy. And when afterwards, at the restoration, by the abolition of the military tenures, and the fines that were consequent upon them, the little that legally remained of this revenue was reduced to almost nothing at all, in vain did Mr Prynne, by a treatise which does honour to his abilities as a painful and judicious antiquarian, endeavour to excite queen Catherine to revive this antiquated claim.

A N O T H E R antient perquisite belonging to the queen consort, mentioned by all our old writers, and, therefore only, worthy notice, is this: that on the taking of a whale on the coasts, which is a royal fish, it shall be divided between the king and queen; the head only being the king's property, and the tail of it the queen's. "*De sturgione observetur, quod rex illum habebit integrum: de balena vero sufficit, si rex habeat caput, et regina caudam.*" The reason of this whimsical division, as assigned by our antient records, was, to furnish the queen's wardrobe with whalebone.

B U T farther: though the queen is in all respects a subject, yet, in point of the security of her life and person, she is put on the same footing with the king. It is equally treason (by the statute 25 Edw. III.) to compass or imagine the death of our lady the king's companion, as of the king himself: and to violate, or defile, the queen consort, amounts to the same high crime; as well in the person committing the fact, as in the queen herself, if consenting. A law of Henry the eighth made it treason also for any woman, who was not a virgin, to marry the king without informing him thereof. But this law was soon after repealed; it trespassing too strongly, as well on natural justice, as female modesty. If however the queen be accused of any species of treason, she shall (whether consort or dowager) be tried by the house of peers, as queen Ann Boleyn was in 28 Hen. VIII.

T H E husband of a queen regnant, as prince George of Denmark was to queen Anne, is her subject; and may be guilty of high treason against her: but, in the instance of conjugal fidelity, he is not subjected to the same penal restrictions. For which the reason seems to be, that, if a queen consort is unfaithful to the royal bed, this may debase or bastardize the heirs to the crown; but no such danger can be consequent on the infidelity of the husband to a queen regnant.

A Q U E E N *dowager* is the widow of the king, and as such enjoys most of the privileges belonging to her as queen consort. But it is not high treason to conspire her death; or to violate her chastity, for the same reason as was before alleged, because the succession to the crown is not thereby endangered. Yet still, *pro dignitate regali*, no man can marry a queen dowager without special licence from the king, on pain of forfeiting his lands and goods. This sir Edward Coke tells us was enacted in parliament in 6 Hen. IV, though the statute be not in print. But she, though an alien born, shall still be intitled to dower after the king's demise, which no other alien is. A queen dowager, when married again to a subject, doth not lose her regal dignity, as peeresses dowager do their peerage when they marry commoners. For Katherine, queen dowager of Henry V, though she married a private gentleman, Owen ap Meredith ap Theodore, commonly called Owen Tudor; yet, by the name of Katherine queen of England, maintained an action against the bishop of Carlisle. And so the queen of Navarre marrying with Edmond, brother to king Edward the first, maintained an action of dower by the name of queen of Navarre.

THE prince of Wales, or heir apparent to the crown, and also his royal consort, and the princess royal, or eldest daughter of the king, are likewise peculiarly regarded by the laws. For, by statute 25 Edw. III, to compass or conspire the death of the former, or to violate the chastity of either of the latter, are as much high treason, as to conspire the death of the king, or violate the chastity of the queen. And this upon the same reason, as was before given; because the prince of Wales is next in succession to the crown, and to violate his wife might taint the blood royal with bastardy: and the eldest daughter of the king is also alone inheritable to the crown, in failure of issue male, and therefore more respected by the laws than any of her younger sisters; insomuch that upon this, united with other (feodal) principles, while our military tenures were in force, the king might levy an aid for marrying his eldest daughter, and her only. The heir apparent to the crown is usually made prince of Wales and earl of Chester, by special creation, and investiture; but, being the king's eldest son, he is by inheritance duke of Cornwall, without any new creation.

THE younger sons and daughters of the king, who are not in the immediate line of succession, are little farther regarded by the laws, than to give them precedence before all peers and public officers as well ecclesiastical as temporal. This is done by the statute 31 Hen. VIII. c. 10. which enacts that no person, except the king's children, shall presume to sit or have place at the side of the cloth of estate in the parliament chamber; and that certain great officers therein named shall have precedence above all dukes, except only such as shall happen to be the king's son, brother, uncle, nephew (which sir Edward Coke explains to signify grandson or *nepos*) or brother's or sister's son. And in 1718, upon a question referred to all the judges by king George I, it was resolved by the opinion of ten against the other two, that the education and care of all the king's grandchildren while minors, and the care and approbation of their marriages, when grown up, did belong of right to his majesty as king of this realm, during their father's life. And this may suffice for the notice, taken by law, of his majesty's royal family.

CHAPTER THE FIFTH.

OF THE COUNCILS BELONGING TO THE KING.

THE third point of view, in which we are to consider the king, is with regard to his councils. For, in order to assist him in the discharge of his duties, the maintenance of his dignity, and the exertion of his prerogative, the law hath assigned him a diversity of councils to advise with.

1. THE first of these is the high court of parliament, whereof we have already treated at large.

2. SECONDLY, the peers of the realm are by their birth hereditary counsellors of the crown, and may be called together by the king to impart their advice in all matters of importance to the realm, either in time of parliament, or, which hath been their principal use, when there is no parliament in being. Accordingly Bracton, speaking of the nobility of his time, says they might properly be called "*consules, a consulendo; reges enim tales sibi associant ad consulendum.*" And in our law books it is laid down, that peers are created for two reasons; 1. *Ad consulendum,* 2. *Ad defendendum regem:* for which reasons the law gives them certain great and high privileges; such as freedom from arrests, &c., even when no parliament is sitting: because the law intends, that they are always assisting the king with their counsel for the commonwealth; or keeping the realm in safety by their prowess and valour.

INSTANCES of conventions of the peers, to advise the king, have been in former times very frequent; though now fallen into disuse, by reason of the more regular meetings of parliament. Sir Edward Coke gives us an extract of a record, 5 Hen. IV, concerning an exchange of lands between the king and the earl of Northumberland, wherein the value of each was agreed to be settled by advice of parliament (if any should be called before the feast of St Lucia) or otherwise by advice of the grand council (of peers) which the king promises to assemble before the said feast, in case no parliament shall be called. Many other instances of this kind of meeting are to be found under our antient kings: though the formal method of convoking them had been so long left off, that when king Charles I in 1640 issued out writs under the great seal to call a great council of all the peers of England to meet and attend his majesty at York, previous to the meeting of the long parliament, the earl of Clarendon mentions it as a new invention, not before heard of; that is, as he explains himself, so old, that it had not been practiced in some hundreds of years. But, though there had not so long before been an instance, nor has there been any since, of assembling them in so solemn a manner, yet, in cases of emergency, our princes have at several times thought proper to call for and consult as many of the nobility as could easily be got together: as was particularly the case with king James the second, after the landing of the prince of Orange; and with the prince of Orange himself, before he called that convention parliament, which afterwards called him to the throne.

B E S I D E S this general meeting, it is usually looked upon to be the right of each particular peer of the realm, to demand an audience of the king, and to lay before him, with decency and respect, such matters as he shall judge of importance to the public weal. And therefore, in the reign of Edward II, it was made an article of impeachment in parliament against the two Hugh Spencers, father and son, for which they were banished the kingdom, "that they by their evil covin would not suffer the great men of the realm, the king's good counsellors, to speak with the king, or to come near him; but only in the presence and hearing of the said Hugh the father and Hugh the son, or one of them, and at their will, and according to such things as pleased them."

3. A T H I R D council belonging the king, are, according to sir Edward Coke, his judges of the courts of law, for law matters. And this appears frequently in our statutes, particularly 14 Ed. III. c. 5. and in other books of law. So that when the king's council is mentioned generally, it must be defined, particularized, and understood, *secundum subjectam materiam*; and, if the subject be of a legal nature, then by the king's council is understood his council for matters of law; namely, his judges. Therefore when by statute 16 Ric. II. c. 5. it was made a high offence to import into this kingdom any papal bulles, or other processes from Rome; and it was enacted, that the offenders should be attached by their bodies, and brought before the king and his *council* to answer for such offence; here, by the expression of king's *council*, were understood the king's judges of his courts of justice, the subject matter being legal: this being the general way of interpreting the word, *council*.

4. B U T the principal council belonging to the king is his privy council, which is generally called, by way of eminence, *the council*. And this, according to sir Edward Coke's description of it, is a noble, honorable, and reverend assembly, of the king and such as he wills to be of his privy council, in the king's court or palace. The king's will is the sole constituent of a privy counsellor; and this also regulates their number, which of antient time was twelve or thereabouts. Afterwards it increased to so large a number, that it was found inconvenient for secrecy and dispatch; and therefore king Charles the second in 1679 limited it to thirty: whereof fifteen were to be the principal officers of state, and those to be counsellors, *virtute officii*; and the other fifteen were composed of ten lords and five commoners of the king's choosing. But since that time the number has been much augmented, and now continues indefinite. At the same time also, the antient office of lord president of the council was revived in the person of Anthony earl of Shaftsbury; an officer, that by the statute of 31 Hen. VIII. c. 10. has precedence next after the lord chancellor and lord treasurer.

P R I V Y counsellors are *made* by the king's nomination, without either patent or grant; and, on taking the necessary oaths, they become immediately privy counsellors during the life of the king that chooses them, but subject to removal at his discretion.

T H E *duty* of a privy counsellor appears from the oath of office, which consists of seven articles: 1. To advise the king according to the best of his cunning and discretion. 2. To advise for the king's honour and good of the public, without partiality through affection, love, meed, doubt, or dread. 3. To keep the king's counsel secret. 4. To avoid corruption. 5. To help and strengthen the execution of what shall be there resolved. 6. To withstand all persons who would attempt the contrary. And, lastly, in general, 7. To observe, keep, and do all that a good and true counsellor ought to do to his sovereign lord.

T H E *power* of the privy council is to enquire into all offences against the government, and to commit the offenders into custody, in order to take their trial in some of the courts of law. But their jurisdiction is only to enquire, and not to punish: and the persons committed by them are entitled to their *habeas corpus* by statute 16 Car. I. c. 10. as much as if committed by an ordinary justice of the peace. And, by the same statute, the court of starchamber, and the court of requests, both of which consisted of privy counsellors, were dissolved; and it was declared illegal for them to take cognizance of any matter of property, belonging to the subjects of this kingdom. But, in plantation or admiralty causes, which arise out of the jurisdiction of this kingdom, and in matters of lunacy and ideocy (being a special flower of the prerogative) with regard to these, although they may eventually involve questions of extensive property, the privy council continues to have cognizance, being the court of appeal in such causes: or, rather, the appeal lies to the king's majesty himself, assisted by his privy council.

A S to the *qualifications* of members to sit this board: any natural born subject of England is capable of being a member of the privy council; taking the proper oaths for security of the government, and the test for security of the church. But, in order to prevent any persons under foreign attachments from insinuating themselves into this important trust, as happened in the reign of king William in many instances, it is enacted by the act of settlement, that no person born out of the dominions of the crown of England, unless born of English parents, even though naturalized by parliament, shall be capable of being of the privy council.

T H E *privileges* of privy counsellors, as such, consist principally in the security which the law has given them against attempts and conspiracies to destroy their lives. For, by statute 3 Hen. VII. c. 14. if any of the king's servants of his houshold, conspire or imagine to take away the life of a privy counsellor, it is felony, though nothing be done upon it. And the reason of making this statute, sir Edward Coke tells us, was because such servants have greater and readier means, either by night or by day, to destroy such as be of great authority, and near about the king: and such a conspiracy was, just before this parliament, made by some of king Henry the seventh's houshold servants, and great mischief was like to have ensued thereupon. This extends only to the king's menial servants. But the statute 9 Ann. c. 16. goes farther, and enacts, that *any persons* that shall unlawfully attempt to kill, or shall unlawfully assault, and strike, or wound, any privy counsellor in the execution of his office, shall be felons, and suffer death as such. This statute was made upon the daring attempt of the sieur Guiscard, who stabbed Mr Harley, afterwards earl of Oxford, with a penknife, when under examination for high crimes in a committee of the privy council.

T H E *dissolution* of the privy council depends upon the king's pleasure; and he may, whenever he thinks proper, discharge any particular member, or the whole of it, and appoint another. By the common law also it was dissolved *ipso facto* by the king's demise; as deriving all it's authority from him. But now, to prevent the inconveniences of having no council in being at the accession of a new prince, it is enacted by statute 6 Ann. c. 7. that the privy council shall continue for six months after the demise of the crown, unless sooner determined by the successor.

Chapter the Sixth.

Of the KING'S DUTIES.

I PROCEED next to the duties, incumbent on the king by our constitution; in consideration of which duties his dignity and prerogative are established by the laws of the land: it being a maxim in the law, that protection and subjection are reciprocal. And these reciprocal duties are what, I apprehend, were meant by the convention in 1688, when they declared that king James had broken the *original contract* between king and people. But however, as the terms of that original contract were in some measure disputed, being alleged to exist principally in theory, and to be only deducible by reason and the rules of natural law; in which deduction different understandings might very considerably differ; it was, after the revolution, judged proper to declare these duties expressly; and to reduce that contract to a plain certainty. So that, whatever doubts might be formerly raised by weak and scrupulous minds about the existence of such an original contract, they must now entirely cease; especially with regard to every prince, who has reigned since the year 1688.

THE principal duty of the king is, to govern his people according to law. *Nec regibus infinita aut libera potestas*, was the constitution of our German ancestors on the continent. And this is not only consonant to the principles of nature, of liberty, of reason, and of society, but has always been esteemed an express part of the common law of England, even when prerogative was at the highest. "The king," saith Bracton, who wrote under Henry III, "ought not to be subject to man, but to God, and to the law; for the law maketh the king. Let the king therefore render to the law, what the law has invested in him with regard to others; dominion, and power: for he is not truly king, where will and pleasure rules, and not the law." And again; "the king also hath a superior, namely God, and also the law, by which he was made a king." Thus Bracton: and Fortescue also, having first well distinguished between a monarchy absolutely and despotically regal, which is introduced by conquest and violence, and a political or civil monarchy, which arises from mutual consent; (of which last species he asserts the government of England to be) immediately lays it down as a principle, that "the king of England must rule his people according to the decrees of the laws thereof: insomuch that he is bound by an oath at his coronation to the observance and keeping of his own laws." But, to obviate all doubts and difficulties concerning this matter, it is expressly declared by statute 12 & 13 W. III. c. 2. that "the laws of England are the birthright of the people thereof; and all the kings and queens who shall ascend the throne of this realm ought to administer the government of the same according to the said laws; and all their officers and ministers ought to serve them respectively according to the same: and therefore all the laws and statutes of this realm, for securing the established religion, and the rights and liberties of the people thereof, and all other laws and statutes of the same now in force, are by his majesty, by and with the advice and consent of the lords spiritual and temporal and commons, and by authority of the same, ratified and confirmed accordingly."

A N D , as to the terms of the original contract between king and people, these I apprehend to be now couched in the coronation oath, which by the statute 1 W. & M. st. 1. c. 6. is to be administred to every king and queen, who shall succeed to the imperial crown of these realms, by one of the archbishops or bishops of the realm, in the presence of all the people; who on their parts do reciprocally take the oath of allegiance to the crown. This coronation oath is conceived in the following terms:

"*The archbishop or bishop shall say*, Will you solemnly promise and swear to govern the people of this kingdom of England, and the dominions thereto belonging, according to the statutes in parliament agreed on, and the laws and customs of the same?—*The king or queen shall say*, I solemnly promise so to do.

"*Archbishop or bishop.* Will you to your power cause law and justice, in mercy, to be executed in all your judgments?—*King or queen.* I will.

"*Archbishop or bishop.* Will you to the utmost of your power maintain the laws of God, the true profession of the gospel, and the protestant reformed religion established by the law? And will you preserve unto the bishops and clergy of this realm, and to the churches committed to their charge, all such rights and privileges as by law do or shall appertain unto them, or any of them?—*King or queen.* All this I promise to do.

"*After this the king or queen, laying his or her hand upon the holy gospels, shall say*, The things which I have here before promised I will perform and keep: so help me God. *And then shall kiss the book.*"

T H I S is the form of the coronation oath, as it is now prescribed by our laws: the principal articles of which appear to be at least as antient as the mirror of justices, and even as the time of Bracton: but the wording of it was changed at the revolution, because (as the statute alleges) the oath itself had been framed in doubtful words and expressions, with relation to antient laws and constitutions at this time unknown. However, in what form soever it be conceived, this is most indisputably a fundamental and original express contract; though doubtless the duty of protection is impliedly as much incumbent on the sovereign before coronation as after: in the same manner as allegiance to the king becomes the duty of the subject immediately on the descent of the crown, before he has taken the oath of allegiance, or whether he ever takes it at all. This reciprocal duty of the subject will be considered in it's proper place. At present we are only to observe, that in the king's part of this original contract are expressed all the duties that a monarch can owe to his people; viz. to govern according to law: to execute judgment in mercy: and to maintain the established religion.

CHAPTER THE SEVENTH.

OF THE KING'S PREROGATIVE.

IT was observed in a former chapter, that one of the principal bulwarks of civil liberty, or (in other words) of the British constitution, was the limitation of the king's prerogative by bounds so certain and notorious, that it is impossible he should ever exceed them, without the consent of the people, on the one hand; or without, on the other, a violation of that original contract, which in all states impliedly, and in ours most expressly, subsists between the prince and the subject. It will now be our business to consider this prerogative minutely; to demonstrate it's necessity in general; and to mark out in the most important instances it's particular extent and restrictions: from which considerations this conclusion will evidently follow, that the powers which are vested in the crown by the laws of England, are necessary for the support of society; and do not intrench any farther on our *natural* liberties, than is expedient for the maintenance of our *civil*.

THERE cannot be a stronger proof of that genuine freedom, which is the boast of this age and country, than the power of discussing and examining, with decency and respect, the limits of the king's prerogative. A topic, that in some former ages was thought too delicate and sacred to be profaned by the pen of a subject. It was ranked among the *arcana imperii*; and, like the mysteries of the *bona dea*, was not suffered to be pried into by any but such as were initiated in it's service: because perhaps the exertion of the one, like the solemnities of the other, would not bear the inspexion of a rational and sober enquiry. The glorious queen Elizabeth herself made no scruple to direct her parliaments to abstain from discoursing of matters of state; and it was the constant language of this favorite princess and her ministers, that even that august assembly "ought not to deal, to judge, or to meddle, with her majesty's prerogative royal." And her successor, king James the first, who had imbibed high notions of the divinity of regal sway, more than once laid it down in his speeches, that "as it is atheism and blasphemy in a creature to dispute what the deity may do, so it is presumption and sedition in a subject to dispute what a king may do in the height of his power: good christians, he adds, will be content with God's will, revealed in his word; and good subjects will rest in the king's will, revealed in *his* law."

BUT, whatever might be the sentiments of some of our princes, this was never the language of our antient constitution and laws. The limitation of the regal authority was a first and essential principle in all the Gothic systems of government established in Europe; though gradually driven out and overborne, by violence and chicane, in most of the kingdoms on the continent. We have seen, in the preceding chapter, the sentiments of Bracton and Fortescue, at the distance of two centuries from each other. And sir Henry Finch, under Charles the first, after the lapse of two centuries more, though he lays down the law of prerogative in very strong and emphatical terms, yet qualifies it with a general restriction, in regard to the liberties of the people. "The king hath a prerogative in all things, that are not injurious to the subject; for in them all it must be remembered, that the king's prerogative stretcheth not to the doing of any wrong." *Nihil enim aliud potest rex, nisi id solum quod de jure potest.* And here it may be some satisfaction to remark, how widely the civil law differs from our own, with regard to the authority of the laws over the prince, or (as a civilian would rather have expressed it) the authority of the prince over the laws. It is a maxim of the English law, as we have seen from Bracton, that "*rex debet esse sub lege, quia lex facit regem:*" the imperial law will tell us, that "*in omnibus, imperatoris excipitur fortuna; cui ipsas leges Deus subjecit.*" We shall not long hesitate to which of them to give the preference, as most conducive to those ends for which societies were framed, and are kept together; especially as the Roman lawyers themselves seem to be sensible of the unreasonableness of their own constitution. "*Decet tamen principem,*" says Paulus, "*servare leges, quibus ipse solutus est.*" This is at once laying down the principle of despotic power, and at the same time acknowleging it's absurdity.

BY the word prerogative we usually understand that special pre-eminence, which the king hath, over and above all other persons, and out of the ordinary course of the common law, in right of his regal dignity. It signifies, in it's etymology, (from *prae* and *rogo*) something that is required or demanded before, or in preference to, all others. And hence it follows, that it must be in it's nature singular and eccentrical; that it can only be applied to those rights and capacities which the king enjoys alone, in contradistinction to others, and not to those which he enjoys in common with any of his subjects: for if once any one prerogative of the crown could be held in common with the subject, it would cease to be prerogative any longer. And therefore Finch lays it down as a maxim, that the prerogative is that law in case of the king, which is law in no case of the subject.

PREROGATIVES are either *direct* or *incidental.* The *direct* are such positive substantial parts of the royal character and authority, as are rooted in and spring from the king's political person, considered merely by itself, without reference to any other extrinsic circumstance; as, the right of sending embassadors, of creating peers, and of making war or peace. But such prerogatives as are *incidental* bear always a relation to something else, distinct from the king's person; and are indeed only exceptions, in favour of the crown, to those general rules that are established for the rest of the community: such as, that no costs shall be recovered against the king; that the king can never be a joint-tenant; and that his debt shall be preferred before a debt to any of his subjects. These, and an infinite number of other instances, will better be understood, when we come regularly to consider the rules themselves, to which these incidental prerogatives are exceptions. And therefore we will at present only dwell upon the king's substantive or direct prerogatives.

THESE substantive or direct prerogatives may again be divided into three kinds: being such as regard, first, the king's royal *character;* secondly, his royal *authority;* and, lastly, his royal *income.* These are necessary, to secure reverence to his person, obedience to his commands, and an affluent supply for the ordinary expenses of government; without all of which it is impossible to maintain the executive power in due independence and vigour. Yet, in every branch of this large and extensive dominion, our free constitution has interposed such seasonable checks and restrictions, as may curb it from trampling on those liberties, which it was meant to secure and establish. The enormous weight of prerogative (if left to itself, as in arbitrary government it is) spreads havoc and destruction among all the inferior movements: but, when balanced and bridled (as with us) by it's proper counterpoise, timely and judiciously applied, it's operations are then equable and regular, it invigorates the whole machine, and enables every part to answer the end of it's construction.

I N the present chapter we shall only consider the two first of these divisions, which relate to the king's political *character* and *authority*; or, in other words, his *dignity* and regal *power*; to which last the name of prerogative is frequently narrowed and confined. The other division, which forms the royal *revenue*, will require a distinct examination; according to the known distribution of the feodal writers, who distinguish the royal prerogatives into the *majora* and *minora regalia*, in the latter of which classes the rights of the revenue are ranked. For, to use their own words, "*majora regalia imperii praeeminentiam spectant; minora vero ad commodum pecuniarium immediate attinent; et haec proprie fiscalia sunt, et ad jus fisci pertinent.*"

F I R S T , then, of the royal dignity. Under every monarchical establishment, it is necessary to distinguish the prince from his subjects, not only by the outward pomp and decorations of majesty, but also by ascribing to him certain qualities, as inherent in his royal capacity, distinct from and superior to those of any other individual in the nation. For, though a philosophical mind will consider the royal person merely as one man appointed by mutual consent to preside over many others, and will pay him that reverence and duty which the principles of society demand, yet the mass of mankind will be apt to grow insolent and refractory, if taught to consider their prince as a man of no greater perfection than themselves. The law therefore ascribes to the king, in his high political character, not only large powers and emoluments which form his prerogative and revenue, but likewise certain attributes of a great and transcendent nature; by which the people are led to consider him in the light of a superior being, and to pay him that awful respect, which may enable him with greater ease to carry on the business of government. This is what I understand by the royal dignity, the several branches of which we will now proceed to examine.

I. A N D , first, the law ascribes to the king the attribute of *sovereignty,* or pre-eminence. "*Rex est vicarius,*" says Bracton, "*et minister Dei in terra: omnis quidem sub eo est, et ipse sub nullo, nisi tantum sub Deo.*" He is said to have *imperial* dignity, and in charters before the conquest is frequently stiled *basileus* and *imperator,* the titles respectively assumed by the emperors of the east and west. His realm is declared to be an *empire,* and his crown imperial, by many acts of parliament, particularly the statutes 24 Hen. VIII. c. 12. and 25 Hen. VIII. c. 28; which at the same time declare the king to be the supreme head of the realm in matters both civil and ecclesiastical, and of consequence inferior to no man upon earth, dependent on no man, accountable to no man. Formerly there prevailed a ridiculous notion, propagated by the German and Italian civilians, that an emperor could do many things which a king could not, (as the creation of notaries and the like) and that all kings were in some degree subordinate and subject to the emperor of Germany or Rome. The meaning therefore of the legislature, when it uses these terms of *empire* and *imperial*, and applies them to the realm of England, is only to assert that our king is equally sovereign and independent within these his dominions, as any emperor is in his empire; and owes no kind of subjection to any other potentate upon earth. Hence it is, that no suit or action can be brought against the king, even in civil matters, because no court can have jurisdiction over him. For all jurisdiction implies superiority of power: authority to try would be vain and idle, without an authority to redress; and the sentence of a court would be contemptible, unless that court had power to command the execution of it: but who, says Finch, shall command the king? Hence it is likewise, that by law the person of the king is sacred, even though the measures pursued in his reign be completely tyrannical and arbitrary: for no jurisdiction upon earth has power to try him in a criminal way; much less to condemn him to punishment. If any foreign jurisdiction had this power, as was formerly claimed by the pope, the independence of the kingdom would be no more: and, if such a power were vested in any domestic tribunal, there would soon be an end of the constitution, by destroying the free agency of one of the constituent parts of the sovereign legislative power.

A R E then, it may be asked, the subjects of England totally destitute of remedy, in case the crown should invade their rights, either by private injuries, or public oppressions? To this we may answer, that the law has provided a remedy in both cases.

A N D , first, as to private injuries; if any person has, in point of property, a just demand upon the king, he must petition him in his court of chancery, where his chancellor will administer right as a matter of grace, though not upon compulsion. And this is entirely consonant to what is laid down by the writers on natural law. "A subject, says Puffendorf, so long as he continues a subject, hath no way to *oblige* his prince to give him his due, when he refuses it; though no wise prince will ever refuse to stand to a lawful contract. And, if the prince gives the subject leave to enter an action against him, upon such contract, in his own courts, the action itself proceeds rather upon natural equity, than upon the municipal laws." For the end of such action is not to *compel* the prince to observe the contract, but to *persuade* him. And, as to personal wrongs; it is well observed by Mr Locke, "the harm which the sovereign can do in his own person not being likely to happen often, nor to extend itself far; nor being able by his single strength to subvert the laws, nor oppress the body of the people, (should any prince have so much weakness and ill nature as to endeavour to do it)—the inconveniency therefore of some particular mischiefs, that may happen sometimes, when a heady prince comes to the throne, are well recompensed by the peace of the public and security of the government, in the person of the chief magistrate being thus set out of the reach of danger."

N E X T , as to cases of ordinary public oppression, where the vitals of the constitution are not attacked, the law hath also assigned a remedy. For, as a king cannot misuse his power, without the advice of evil counsellors, and the assistance of wicked ministers, these men may be examined and punished. The constitution has therefore provided, by means of indictments, and parliamentary impeachments, that no man shall dare to assist the crown in contradiction to the laws of the land. But it is at the same time a maxim in those laws, that the king himself can do no wrong; since it would be a great weakness and absurdity in any system of positive law, to define any possible wrong, without any possible redress.

F O R, as to such public oppressions as tend to dissolve the constitution, and subvert the fundamentals of government, they are cases which the law will not, out of decency, suppose; being incapable of distrusting those, whom it has invested with any part of the supreme power; since such distrust would render the exercise of that power precarious and impracticable. For, whereever the law expresses it's distrust of abuse of power, it always vests a superior coercive authority in some other hand to correct it; the very notion of which destroys the idea of sovereignty. If therefore (for example) the two houses of parliament, or either of them, had avowedly a right to animadvert on the king, or each other, or if the king had a right to animadvert on either of the houses, that branch of the legislature, so subject to animadversion, would instantly cease to be part of the supreme power; the ballance of the constitution would be overturned; and that branch or branches, in which this jurisdiction resided, would be completely sovereign. The supposition of *law* therefore is, that neither the king nor either house of parliament (collectively taken) is capable of doing any wrong; since in such cases the law feels itself incapable of furnishing any adequate remedy. For which reason all oppressions, which may happen to spring from any branch of the sovereign power, must necessarily be out of the reach of any *stated rule*, or *express legal* provision: but, if ever they unfortunately happen, the prudence of the times must provide new remedies upon new emergencies.

I N D E E D, it is found by experience, that whenever the unconstitutional oppressions, even of the sovereign power, advance with gigantic strides and threaten desolation to a state, mankind will not be reasoned out of the feelings of humanity; nor will sacrifice their liberty by a scrupulous adherence to those political maxims, which were originally established to preserve it. And therefore, though the positive laws are silent, experience will furnish us with a very remarkable case, wherein nature and reason prevailed. When king James the second invaded the fundamental constitution of the realm, the convention declared an abdication, whereby the throne was rendered vacant, which induced a new settlement of the crown. And so far as this precedent leads, and no farther, we may now be allowed to lay down the *law* of redress against public oppression. If therefore any future prince should endeavour to subvert the constitution by breaking the original contract between king and people, should violate the fundamental laws, and should withdraw himself out of the kingdom; we are now authorized to declare that this conjunction of circumstances would amount to an abdication, and the throne would be thereby vacant. But it is not for us to say, that any one, or two, of these ingredients would amount to such a situation; for there our precedent would fail us. In these therefore, or other circumstances, which a fertile imagination may furnish, since both law and history are silent, it becomes us to be silent too; leaving to future generations, whenever necessity and the safety of the whole shall require it, the exertion of those inherent (though latent) powers of society, which no climate, no time, no constitution, no contract, can ever destroy or diminish.

II. B E S I D E S the attribute of sovereignty, the law also ascribes to the king, in his political capacity, absolute *perfection*. The king can do no wrong. Which antient and fundamental maxim is not to be understood, as if every thing transacted by the government was of course just and lawful, but means only two things. First, that whatever is exceptionable in the conduct of public affairs is not to be imputed to the king, nor is he answerable for it personally to his people: for this doctrine would totally destroy that constitutional independence of the crown, which is necessary for the balance of power, in our free and active, and therefore compounded, constitution. And, secondly, it means that the prerogative of the crown extends not to do any injury: it is created for the benefit of the people, and therefore cannot be exerted to their prejudice.

T H E king, moreover, is not only incapable of *doing* wrong, but even of *thinking* wrong: he can never mean to do an improper thing: in him is no folly or weakness. And therefore, if the crown should be induced to grant any franchise or privilege to a subject contrary to reason, or in any wise prejudicial to the commonwealth, or a private person, the law will not suppose the king to have meant either an unwise or an injurious action, but declares that the king was deceived in his grant; and thereupon such grant is rendered void, merely upon the foundation of fraud and deception, either by or upon those agents, whom the crown has thought proper to employ. For the law will not cast an imputation on that magistrate whom it entrusts with the executive power, as if he was capable of intentionally disregarding his trust: but attributes to mere imposition (to which the most perfect of sublunary beings must still continue liable) those little inadvertencies, which, if charged on the will of the prince, might lessen him in the eyes of his subjects.

Y E T still, notwithstanding this personal perfection, which the law attributes to the sovereign, the constitution has allowed a latitude of supposing the contrary, in respect to both houses of parliament; each of which, in it's turn, hath exerted the right of remonstrating and complaining to the king even of those acts of royalty, which are most properly and personally his own; such as messages signed by himself, and speeches delivered from the throne. And yet, such is the reverence which is paid to the royal person, that though the two houses have an undoubted right to consider these acts of state in any light whatever, and accordingly treat them in their addresses as personally proceeding from the prince, yet, among themselves, (to preserve the more perfect decency, and for the greater freedom of debate) they usually suppose them to flow from the advice of the administration. But the privilege of canvassing thus freely the personal acts of the sovereign (either directly, or even through the medium of his reputed advisers) belongs to no individual, but is confined to those august assemblies: and there too the objections must be proposed with the utmost respect and deference. One member was sent to the tower, for suggesting that his majesty's answer to the address of the commons contained "high words, to fright the members out of their duty;" and another, for saying that a part of the king's speech "seemed rather to be calculated for the meridian of Germany than Great Britain."

I N farther pursuance of this principle, the law also determines that in the king can be no negligence, or *laches*, and therefore no delay will bar his right. *Nullum tempus occurrit regi* is the standing maxim upon all occasions: for the law intends that the king is always busied for the public good, and therefore has not leisure to assert his right within the times limited to subjects. In the king also can be no stain or corruption of blood: for if the heir to the crown were attainted of treason or felony, and afterwards the crown should descend to him, this would purge the attainder *ipso facto*. And therefore when Henry VII, who as earl of Richmond stood attainted, came to the crown, it was not thought necessary to pass an act of parliament to reverse this attainder; because, as lord Bacon in his history of that prince informs us, it was agreed that the assumption of the crown had at once purged all attainders. Neither can the king in judgment of law, as king, ever be a minor or under age; and therefore his royal grants and assents to acts of parliament are good, though he has not in his natural capacity attained the legal age of twenty one. By a statute indeed, 28 Hen. VIII. c. 17. power was given to future kings to rescind and revoke all acts of parliament that should be made while they were under the age of twenty four: but this was repealed by the statute 1 Edw. VI. c. 11. so far as related to that prince; and both statutes are declared to be determined by 24 Geo. II. c. 24. It hath also been usually thought prudent, when the heir apparent has been very young, to appoint a protector, guardian, or regent, for a limited time: but the very necessity of such extraordinary provision is sufficient to demonstrate the truth of that maxim of the common law, that in the king is no minority; and therefore he hath no legal guardian.

III. A T H I R D attribute of the king's majesty is his *perpetuity*. The law ascribes to him, in his political capacity, an absolute immortality. The king never dies. Henry, Edward, or George may die; but the king survives them all. For immediately upon the decease of the reigning prince in his natural capacity, his kingship or imperial dignity, by act of law, without any *interregnum* or interval, is vested at once in his heir; who is, *eo instanti*, king to all intents and purposes. And so tender is the law of supposing even a possibility of his death, that his natural dissolution is generally called his *demise, dimissio regis, vel coronae*: an expression which signifies merely a transfer of property; for, as is observed in Plowden, when we say the demise of the crown, we mean only that in consequence of the disunion of the king's body natural from his body politic, the kingdom is transferred or demised to his successor; and so the royal dignity remains perpetual. Thus too, when Edward the fourth, in the tenth year of his reign, was driven from his throne for a few months by the house of Lancaster, this temporary transfer of his dignity was denominated his *demise*; and all process was held to be discontinued, as upon a natural death of the king.

W E are next to consider those branches of the royal prerogative, which invest this our sovereign lord, thus all-perfect and immortal in his kingly capacity, with a number of authorities and powers; in the exertion whereof consists the executive part of government. This is wisely placed in a single hand by the British constitution, for the sake of unanimity, strength and dispatch. Were it placed in many hands, it would be subject to many wills: many wills, if disunited and drawing different ways, create weakness in a government: and to unite those several wills, and reduce them to one, is a work of more time and delay than the exigencies of state will afford. The king of England is therefore not only the chief, but properly the sole, magistrate of the nation; all others acting by commission from, and in due subordination to him: in like manner as, upon the great revolution in the Roman state, all the powers of the antient magistracy of the commonwealth were concentred in the new emperor; so that, as Gravina expresses it, "*in ejus unius persona veteris reipublicae vis atque majestas per cumulatas magistratuum potestates exprimebatur.*"

AFTER what has been premised in this chapter, I shall not (I trust) be considered as an advocate for arbitrary power, when I lay it down as a principle, that in the exertion of lawful prerogative, the king is and ought to be absolute; that is, so far absolute, that there is no legal authority that can either delay or resist him. He may reject what bills, may make what treaties, may coin what money, may create what peers, may pardon what offences he pleases: unless where the constitution hath expressly, or by evident consequence, laid down some exception or boundary; declaring, that thus far the prerogative shall go and no farther. For otherwise the power of the crown would indeed be but a name and a shadow, insufficient for the ends of government, if, where it's jurisdiction is clearly established and allowed, any man or body of men were permitted to disobey it, in the ordinary course of law: I say, in the *ordinary* course of law; for I do not now speak of those *extraordinary* recourses to first principles, which are necessary when the contracts of society are in danger of dissolution, and the law proves too weak a defence against the violence of fraud or oppression. And yet the want of attending to this obvious distinction has occasioned these doctrines, of absolute power in the prince and of national resistance by the people, to be much misunderstood and perverted by the advocates for slavery on the one hand, and the demagogues of faction on the other. The former, observing the absolute sovereignty and transcendent dominion of the crown laid down (as it certainly is) most strongly and emphatically in our lawbooks, as well as our homilies, have denied that any case can be excepted from so general and positive a rule; forgetting how impossible it is, in any practical system of laws, to point out beforehand those eccentrical remedies, which the sudden emergence of national distress may dictate, and which that alone can justify. On the other hand, over-zealous republicans, feeling the absurdity of unlimited passive obedience, have fancifully (or sometimes factiously) gone over to the other extreme: and, because resistance is justifiable to the person of the prince when the being of the state is endangered, and the public voice proclaims such resistance necessary, they have therefore allowed to every individual the right of determining this expedience, and of employing private force to resist even private oppression. A doctrine productive of anarchy, and (in consequence) equally fatal to civil liberty as tyranny itself. For civil liberty, rightly understood, consists in protecting the rights of individuals by the united force of society: society cannot be maintained, and of course can exert no protection, without obedience to

74

some sovereign power: and obedience is an empty name, if every individual has a right to decide how far he himself shall obey.

IN the exertion therefore of those prerogatives, which the law has given him, the king is irresistible and absolute, according to the forms of the constitution. And yet, if the consequence of that exertion be manifestly to the grievance or dishonour of the kingdom, the parliament will call his advisers to a just and severe account. For prerogative consisting (as Mr Locke has well defined it) in the discretionary power of acting for the public good, where the positive laws are silent, if that discretionary power be abused to the public detriment, such prerogative is exerted in an unconstitutional manner. Thus the king may make a treaty with a foreign state, which shall irrevocably bind the nation; and yet, when such treaties have been judged pernicious, impeachments have pursued those ministers, by whose agency or advice they were concluded.

THE prerogatives of the crown (in the sense under which we are now considering them) respect either this nation's intercourse with foreign nations, or it's own domestic government and civil polity.

WITH regard to foreign concerns, the king is the delegate or representative of his people. It is impossible that the individuals of a state, in their collective capacity, can transact the affairs of that state with another community equally numerous as themselves. Unanimity must be wanting to their measures, and strength to the execution of their counsels. In the king therefore, as in a center, all the rays of his people are united, and form by that union a consistency, splendor, and power, that make him feared and respected by foreign potentates; who would scruple to enter into any engagements, that must afterwards be revised and ratified by a popular assembly. What is done by the royal authority, with regard to foreign powers, is the act of the whole nation: what is done without the king's concurrence is the act only of private men. And so far is this point carried by our law, that it hath been held, that should all the subjects of England make war with a king in league with the king of England, without the royal assent, such war is no breach of the league. And, by the statute 2 Hen. V. c. 6. any subject committing acts of hostility upon any nation in league with the king, was declared to be guilty of high treason: and, though that act was repealed by the statute 20 Hen. VI. c. 11. so far as relates to the making this offence high treason, yet still it remains a very great offence against the law of nations, and punishable by our laws, either capitally or otherwise, according to the circumstances of the case.

I. THE king therefore, considered as the representative of his people, has the sole power of sending embassadors to foreign states, and receiving embassadors at home. This may lead us into a short enquiry, how far the municipal laws of England intermeddle with or protect the rights of these messengers from one potentate to another, whom we call embassadors.

THE rights, the powers, the duties, and the privileges of embassadors are determined by the law of nature and nations, and not by any municipal constitutions. For, as they represent the persons of their respective masters, who owe no subjection to any laws but those of their own country, their actions are not subject to the control of the private law of that state, wherein they are appointed to reside. He that is subject to the coercion of laws is necessarily dependent on that power by whom those laws were made: but an embassador ought to be independent of every power, except that by which he is sent; and of consequence ought not to be subject to the mere municipal laws of that nation, wherein he is to exercise his functions. If he grossly offends, or makes an ill use of his character, he may be sent home and accused before his master; who is bound either to do justice upon him, or avow himself the accomplice of his crimes. But there is great dispute among the writers on the laws of nations, whether this exemption of embassadors extends to all crimes, as well natural as positive; or whether it only extends to such as are *mala prohibita*, as coining, and not to those that are *mala in se*, as murder. Our law seems to have formerly taken in the restriction, as well as the general exemption. For it has been held, both by our common lawyers and civilians, that an embassador is privileged by the law of nature and nations; and yet, if he commits any offence against the law of reason and nature, he shall lose his privilege: and that therefore, if an embassador conspires the death of the king in whose land he is, he may be condemned and executed for treason; but if he commits any other species of treason, it is otherwise, and he must be sent to his own kingdom. And these positions seem to be built upon good appearance of reason. For since, as we have formerly shewn, all municipal laws act in subordination to the primary law of nature, and, where they annex a punishment to natural crimes, are only declaratory of and auxiliary to that law; therefore to this natural, universal rule of justice embassadors, as well as other men, are subject in all countries; and of consequence it is reasonable that wherever they transgress it, there they shall be liable to make atonement. But, however these principles might formerly obtain, the general practice of Europe seems now to have adopted the sentiments of the learned Grotius, that the security of embassadors is of more importance than the punishment of a particular crime. And therefore few, if any, examples have happened within a century past, where an embassador has been punished for any offence, however atrocious in it's nature.

I N respect to civil suits, all the foreign jurists agree, that neither an embassador, nor any of his train or *comites*, can be prosecuted for any debt or contract in the courts of that kingdom wherein he is sent to reside. Yet sir Edward Coke maintains, that, if an embassador make a contract which is good *jure gentium*, he shall answer for it here. And the truth is, we find no traces in our lawbooks of allowing any privilege to embassadors or their domestics, even in civil suits, previous to the reign of queen Anne; when an embassador from Peter the great, czar of Muscovy, was actually arrested and taken out of his coach in London, in 1708, for debts which he had there contracted. This the czar resented very highly, and demanded (we are told) that the officers who made the arrest should be punished with death. But the queen (to the amazement of that despotic court) directed her minister to inform him, "that the law of England had not yet protected embassadors from the payment of their lawful debts; that therefore the arrest was no offence by the laws; and thatshe could inflict no punishment upon any, the meanest, of her subjects, unless warranted by the law of the land." To satisfy however the clamours of the foreign ministers (who made it a common cause) as well as to appease the wrath of Peter, a new statute was enacted by parliament, reciting the arrest which had been made, "in contempt of the protection granted by her majesty, contrary to the law of nations, and in prejudice of the rights and privileges, which embassadors and other public ministers have at all times been thereby possessed of, and ought to be kept sacred and inviolable:" wherefore it enacts, that for the future all process whereby the person of any embassador, or of his domestic or domestic servant, may be arrested, or his goods distreined or seised, shall be utterly null and void; and the persons prosecuting, soliciting, or executing such process shall be deemed violaters of the law of nations, and disturbers of the public repose; and shall suffer such penalties and corporal punishment as the lord chancellor and the two chief justices, or any two of them, shall think fit. But it is expressly provided, that no trader, within the description of the bankrupt laws, who shall be in the service of any embassador, shall be privileged or protected by this act; nor shall any one be punished for arresting an embassador's servant, unless his name be registred with the secretary of state, and by him transmitted to the sheriffs of London and Middlesex. Exceptions, that are strictly conformable to the rights of embassadors, as observed in the most civilized countries. And, in consequence of this statute, thus enforcing the law of nations, these privileges are now usually allowed in the courts of common law.

III. U P O N the same principle the king has also the sole prerogative of making war and peace. For it is held by all the writers on the law of nature and nations, that the right of making war, which by nature subsisted in every individual, is given up by all private persons that enter into society, and is vested in the sovereign power: and this right is given up not only by individuals, but even by the intire body of people, that are under the dominion of a sovereign. It would indeed be extremely improper, that any number of subjects should have the power of binding the supreme magistrate, and putting him against his will in a state of war. Whatever hostilities therefore may be committed by private citizens, the state ought not to be affected thereby; unless that should justify their proceedings, and thereby become partner in the guilt. Such unauthorized voluntiers in violence are not ranked among open enemies, but are treated like pirates and robbers: according to that rule of the civil law; *hostes hi sunt qui nobis, aut quibus nos, publice bellum decrevimus: caeteri latrones aut praedones sunt.* And the reason which is given by Grotius, why according to the law of nations a denunciation of war ought always to precede the actual commencement of hostilities, is not so much that the enemy may be put upon his guard, (which is matter rather of magnanimity than right) but that it may be certainly clear that the war is not undertaken by private persons, but by the will of the whole community; whose right of willing is in this case transferred to the supreme magistrate by the fundamental laws of society. So that, in order to make a war completely effectual, it is necessary with us in England that it be publicly declared and duly proclaimed by the king's authority; and, then, all parts of both the contending nations, from the highest to the lowest, are bound by it. And, wherever the right resides of beginning a national war, there also must reside the right of ending it, or the power of making peace. And the same check of parliamentary impeachment, for improper or inglorious conduct, in beginning, conducting, or concluding a national war, is in general sufficient to restrain the ministers of the crown from a wanton or injurious exertion of this great prerogative.

IV. B U T , as the delay of making war may sometimes be detrimental to individuals who have suffered by depredations from foreign potentates, our laws have in some respect armed the subject with powers to impel the prerogative; by directing the ministers of the crown to issue letters of marque and reprisal upon due demand: the prerogative of granting which is nearly related to, and plainly derived from, that other of making war; this being indeed only an incomplete state of hostilities, and generally ending in a formal denunciation of war. These letters are grantable by the law of nations, whenever the subjects of one state are oppressed and injured by those of another; and justice is denied by that state to which the oppressor belongs. In this case letters of marque and reprisal (words in themselves synonimous and signifying a taking in return) may be obtained, in order to seise the bodies or goods of the subjects of the offending state, until satisfaction be made, wherever they happen to be found. Indeed this custom of reprisals seems dictated by nature herself; and accordingly we find in the most antient times very notable instances of it. But here the necessity is obvious of calling in the sovereign power, to determine when reprisals may be made; else every private sufferer would be a judge in his own cause. And, in pursuance of this principle, it is with us declared by the statute 4 Hen. V. c. 7. that, if any subjects of the realm are oppressed in time of truce by any foreigners, the king will grant marque in due form, to all that feel themselves grieved. Which form is thus directed to be observed: the sufferer must first apply to the lord privy-seal, and he shall make out letters of request under the privy seal; and, if, after such request of satisfaction made, the party required do not within convenient time make due satisfaction or restitution to the party grieved, the lord chancellor shall make him out letters of marque under the great seal; and by virtue of these he may attack and seise the property of the aggressor nation, without hazard of being condemned as a robber or pirate.

V. U P O N exactly the same reason stands the prerogative of granting safe-conducts, without which by the law of nations no member of one society has a right to intrude into another. And therefore Puffendorf very justly resolves, that it is left in the power of all states, to take such measures about the admission of strangers, as they think convenient; those being ever excepted who are driven on the coasts by necessity, or by any cause that deserves pity or compassion. Great tenderness is shewn by our laws, not only to foreigners in distress (as will appear when we come to speak of shipwrecks) but with regard also to the admission of strangers who come spontaneously. For so long as their nation continues at peace with ours, and they themselves behave peaceably, they are under the king's protection; though liable to be sent home whenever the king sees occasion. But no subject of a nation at war with us can, by the law of nations, come into the realm, nor can travel himself upon the high seas, or send his goods and merchandize from one place to another, without danger of being seized by our subjects, unless he has letters of safe-conduct; which by divers antient statutes must be granted under the king's great seal and inrolled in chancery, or else are of no effect: the king being supposed the best judge of such emergencies, as may deserve exception from the general law of arms.

INDEED the law of England, as a commercial country, pays a very particular regard to foreign merchants in innumerable instances. One I cannot omit to mention: that by *magna carta* it is provided, that all merchants (unless publickly prohibited beforehand) shall have safe conduct to depart from, to come into, to tarry in, and to go through England, for the exercise of merchandize, without any unreasonable imposts, except in time of war: and, if a war breaks out between us and their country, they shall be attached (if in England) without harm of body or goods, till the king or his chief justiciary be informed how our merchants are treated in the land with which we are at war; and, if ours be secure in that land, they shall be secure in ours. This seems to have been a common rule of equity among all the northern nations; for we learn from Stiernhook, that it was a maxim among the Goths and Swedes, "*quam legem exteri nobis posuere, eandem illis ponemus.*" But it is somewhat extraordinary, that it should have found a place in *magna carta*, a mere interior treaty between the king and his natural-born subjects; which occasions the learned Montesquieu to remark with a degree of admiration, "that the English have made the protection of *foreign* merchants one of the articles of their *national* liberty." But indeed it well justifies another observation which he has made, "that the English know better than any other people upon earth, how to value at the same time these three great advantages, religion, liberty, and commerce." Very different from the genius of the Roman people; who in their manners, their constitution, and even in their laws, treated commerce as a dishonorable employment, and prohibited the exercise thereof to persons of birth, or rank, or fortune: and equally different from the bigotry of the canonists, who looked on trade as inconsistent with christianity, and determined at the council of Melfi, under pope Urban II, *A.D.* 1090, that it was impossible with a safe conscience to exercise any traffic, or follow the profession of the law.

THESE are the principal prerogatives of the king, respecting this nation's intercourse with foreign nations; in all of which he is considered as the delegate or representative of his people. But in domestic affairs he is considered in a great variety of characters, and from thence there arises an abundant number of other prerogatives.

I. FIRST, he is a constituent part of the supreme legislative power; and, as such, has the prerogative of rejecting such provisions in parliament, as he judges improper to be passed. The expediency of which constitution has before been evinced at large. I shall only farther remark, that the king is not bound by any act of parliament, unless he be named therein by special and particular words. The most general words that can be devised ("any person or persons, bodies politic, or corporate, *&c.*") affect not him in the least, if they may tend to restrain or diminish any of his rights or interests. For it would be of most mischievous consequence to the public, if the strength of the executive power were liable to be curtailed without it's own express consent, by constructions and implications of the subject. Yet where an act of parliament is expressly made for the preservation of public rights and the suppression of public wrongs, and does not interfere with the established rights of the crown, it is said to be binding as well upon the king as upon the subject: and, likewise, the king may take the benefit of any particular act, though he be not especially named.

II. T H E king is considered, in the next place, as the generalissimo, or the first in military command, within the kingdom. The great end of society is to protect the weakness of individuals by the united strength of the community: and the principal use of government is to direct that united strength in the best and most effectual manner, to answer the end proposed. Monarchical government is allowed to be the fittest of any for this purpose: it follows therefore, from the very end of it's institution, that in a monarchy the military power must be trusted in the hands of the prince.

I N this capacity therefore, of general of the kingdom, the king has the sole power of raising and regulating fleets and armies. Of the manner in which they are raised and regulated I shall speak more, when I come to consider the military state. We are now only to consider the prerogative of enlisting and of governing them: which indeed was disputed and claimed, contrary to all reason and precedent, by the long parliament of king Charles I; but, upon the restoration of his son, was solemnly declared by the statute 13 Car. II. c. 6. to be in the king alone: for that the sole supreme government and command of the militia within all his majesty's realms and dominions, and of all forces by sea and land, and of all forts and places of strength, ever was and is the undoubted right of his majesty, and his royal predecessors, kings and queens of England; and that both or either house of parliament cannot, nor ought to, pretend to the same.

T H I S statute, it is obvious to observe, extends not only to fleets and armies, but also to forts, and other places of strength, within the realm; the sole prerogative as well of erecting, as manning and governing of which, belongs to the king in his capacity of general of the kingdom: and all lands were formerly subject to a tax, for building of castles wherever the king thought proper. This was one of the three things, from contributing to the performance of which no lands were exempted; and therefore called by our Saxon ancestors the *trinoda necessitas: sc. pontis reparatio, arcis constructio, et expeditio contra hostem.* And this they were called upon to do so often, that, as sir Edward Coke from M. Paris assures us, there were in the time of Henry II 1115 castles subsisting in England. The inconvenience of which, when granted out to private subjects, the lordly barons of those times, was severely felt by the whole kingdom; for, as William of Newbury remarks in the reign of king Stephen, "*erant in Anglia quodammodo tot reges vel potius tyranni, quot domini castellorum:*" but it was felt by none more sensibly than by two succeeding princes, king John and king Henry III. And therefore, the greatest part of them being demolished in the barons' wars, the kings of after times have been very cautious of suffering them to be rebuilt in a fortified manner: and sir Edward Coke lays it down, that no subject can build a castle, or house of strength imbatteled, or other fortress defensible, without the licence of the king; for the danger which might ensue, if every man at his pleasure might do it.

T O this branch of the prerogative may be referred the power vested in his majesty, by statutes 12 Car. II. c. 4. and 29 Geo. II. c. 16. of prohibiting the exportation of arms or ammunition out of this kingdom, under severe penalties: and likewise the right which the king has, whenever he sees proper, of confining his subjects to stay within the realm, or of recalling them when beyond the seas. By the common law, every man may go out of the realm for whatever cause he pleaseth, without obtaining the king's leave; provided he is under no injunction of staying at home: (which liberty was expressly declared in king John's great charter, though left out in that of Henry III) but, because that every man ought of right to defend the king and his realm, therefore the king at his pleasure may command him by his writ that he go not beyond the seas, or out of the realm without licence; and if he do the contrary, he shall be punished for disobeying the king's command. Some persons there antiently were, that, by reason of their stations, were under a perpetual prohibition of going abroad without licence obtained; among which were reckoned all peers, on account of their being counsellors of the crown; all knights, who were bound to defend the kingdom from invasions; all ecclesiastics, who were expressly confined by cap. 4. of the constitutions of Clarendon, on account of their attachment in the times of popery to the see of Rome; all archers and other artificers, lest they should instruct foreigners to rival us in their several trades and manufactures. This was law in the times of Britton, who wrote in the reign of Edward I: and sir Edward Coke gives us many instances to this effect in the time of Edward III. In the succeeding reign the affair of travelling wore a very different aspect: an act of parliament being made, forbidding all persons whatever to go abroad without licence; *except* only the lords and other great men of the realm; and true and notable merchants; and the king's soldiers. But this act was repealed by the statute 4 Jac. I. c. 1. And at present every body has, or at least assumes, the liberty of going abroad when he pleases. Yet undoubtedly if the king, by writ of *ne exeat regnum*, under his great seal or privy seal, thinks proper to prohibit him from so doing; or if the king sends a writ to any man, when abroad, commanding his return; and in either case the subject disobeys; it is a high contempt of the king's prerogative, for which the offender's lands shall be seised till he return; and then he is liable to fine and imprisonment.

III. A N O T H E R capacity, in which the king is considered in domestic affairs, is as the fountain of justice and general conservator of the peace of the kingdom. By the fountain of justice the law does not mean the *author* or *original*, but only the *distributor*. Justice is not derived from the king, as from his *free gift*; but he is the steward of the public, to dispense it to whom it is *due*. He is not the spring, but the reservoir; from whence right and equity are conducted, by a thousand chanels, to every individual. The original power of judicature, by the fundamental principles of society, is lodged in the society at large: but as it would be impracticable to render complete justice to every individual, by the people in their collective capacity, therefore every nation has committed that power to certain select magistrates, who with more ease and expedition can hear and determine complaints; and in England this authority has immemorially been exercised by the king or his substitutes. He therefore has alone the right of erecting courts of judicature: for, though the constitution of the kingdom hath entrusted him with the whole executive power of the laws, it is impossible, as well as improper, that he should personally carry into execution this great and extensive trust: it is consequently necessary, that courts should be erected, to assist him in executing this power; and equally necessary, that, if erected, they should be erected by his authority. And hence it is, that all jurisdictions of courts are either mediately or immediately derived from the crown, their proceedings run generally in the king's name, they pass under his seal, and are executed by his officers.

I T is probable, and almost certain, that in very early times, before our constitution arrived at it's full perfection, our kings in person often heard and determined causes between party and party. But at present, by the long and uniform usage of many ages, our kings have delegated their whole judicial power to the judges of their several courts; which are the grand depositary of the fundamental laws of the kingdom, and have gained a known and stated jurisdiction, regulated by certain and established rules, which the crown itself cannot now alter but by act of parliament. And, in order to maintain both the dignity and independence of the judges in the superior courts, it is enacted by the statute 13 W. III. c. 2. that their commissions shall be made (not, as formerly, *durante bene placito*, but) *quamdiu bene se gesserint*, and their salaries ascertained and established; but that it may be lawful to remove them on the address of both houses of parliament. And now, by the noble improvements of that law in the statute of 1 Geo. III. c. 23. enacted at the earnest recommendation of the king himself from the throne, the judges are continued in their offices during their good behaviour, notwithstanding any demise of the crown (which was formerly held immediately to vacate their seats) and their full salaries are absolutely secured to them during the continuance of their commissions: his majesty having been pleased to declare, that "he looked upon the independence and uprightness of the judges, as essential to the impartial administration of justice; as one of the best securities of the rights and liberties of his subjects; and as most conducive to the honour of the crown."

I N criminal proceedings, or prosecutions for offences, it would still be a higher absurdity, if the king personally sate in judgment; because in regard to these he appears in another capacity, that of *prosecutor*. All offences are either against the king's peace, or his crown and dignity; and are so laid in every indictment. For, though in their consequences they generally seem (except in the case of treason and a very few others) to be rather offences against the kingdom than the king; yet, as the public, which is an invisible body, has delegated all it's power and rights, with regard to the execution of the laws, to one visible magistrate, all affronts to that power, and breaches of those rights, are immediately offences against him, to whom they are so delegated by the public. He is therefore the proper person to prosecute for all public offences and breaches of the peace, being the person injured in the eye of the law. And this notion was carried so far in the old Gothic constitution, (wherein the king was bound by his coronation oath to conserve the peace) that in case of any forcible injury offered to the person of a fellow subject, the offender was accused of a kind of perjury, in having violated the king's coronation oath; *dicebatur fregisse juramentum regis juratum*. And hence also arises another branch of the prerogative, that of *pardoning* offences; for it is reasonable that he only who is injured should have the power of forgiving. And therefore, in parliamentary impeachments, the king has no prerogative of pardoning: because there the commons of Great Britain are in their own names the prosecutors, and not the crown; the offence being for the most part avowedly taken to be done against the public. Of prosecutions and pardons I shall treat more at large hereafter; and only mention them here, in this cursory manner, to shew the constitutional grounds of this power of the crown, and how regularly connected all the links are in this vast chain of prerogative.

IN this distinct and separate existence of the judicial power, in a peculiar body of men, nominated indeed, but not removeable at pleasure, by the crown, consists one main preservative of the public liberty; which cannot subsist long in any state, unless the administration of common justice be in some degree separated both from the legislative and also from the executive power. Were it joined with the legislative, the life, liberty, and property, of the subject would be in the hands of arbitrary judges, whose decisions would be then regulated only by their own opinions, and not by any fundamental principles of law; which, though legislators may depart from, yet judges are bound to observe. Were it joined with the executive, this union might soon be an over-ballance for the legislative. For which reason, by the statute of 16 Car. I. c. 10. which abolished the court of star chamber, effectual care is taken to remove all judicial power out of the hands of the king's privy council; who, as then was evident from recent instances, might soon be inclined to pronounce that for law, which was most agreeable to the prince or his officers. Nothing therefore is more to be avoided, in a free constitution, than uniting the provinces of a judge and a minister of state. And indeed, that the absolute power, claimed and exercised in a neighbouring nation, is more tolerable than that of the eastern empires, is in great measure owing to their having vested the judicial power in their parliaments, a body separate and distinct from both the legislative and executive: and, if ever that nation recovers it's former liberty, it will owe it to the efforts of those assemblies. In Turkey, where every thing is centered in the sultan or his ministers, despotic power is in it's meridian, and wears a more dreadful aspect.

A CONSEQUENCE of this prerogative is the legal *ubiquity* of the king. His majesty, in the eye of the law, is always present in all his courts, though he cannot personally distribute justice. His judges are the mirror by which the king's image is reflected. It is the regal office, and not the royal person, that is always present in court, always ready to undertake prosecutions, or pronounce judgment, for the benefit and protection of the subject. And from this ubiquity it follows, that the king can never be nonsuit; for a nonsuit is the desertion of the suit or action by the non-appearance of the plaintiff in court. For the same reason also, in the forms of legal proceedings, the king is not said to appear *by his attorney*, as other men do; for he always appears in contemplation of law in his own proper person.

F R O M the same original, of the king's being the fountain of justice, we may also deduce the prerogative of issuing proclamations, which is vested in the king alone. These proclamations have then a binding force, when (as Sir Edward Coke observes) they are grounded upon and enforce the laws of the realm. For, though the making of laws is entirely the work of a distinct part, the legislative branch, of the sovereign power, yet the manner, time, and circumstances of putting those laws in execution must frequently be left to the discretion of the executive magistrate. And therefore his constitutions or edicts, concerning these points, which we call proclamations, are binding upon the subject, where they do not either contradict the old laws, or tend to establish new ones; but only enforce the execution of such laws as are already in being, in such manner as the king shall judge necessary. Thus the established law is, that the king may prohibit any of his subjects from leaving the realm: a proclamation therefore forbidding this in general for three weeks, by laying an embargo upon all shipping in time of war, will be equally binding as an act of parliament, because founded upon a prior law. A proclamation for disarming papists is also binding, being only in execution of what the legislature has first ordained: but a proclamation for allowing arms to papists, or for disarming any protestant subjects, will not bind; because the first would be to assume a dispensing power, the latter a legislative one; to the vesting of either of which in any single person the laws of England are absolutely strangers. Indeed by the statute 31 Hen. VIII. c. 8. it was enacted, that the king's proclamations should have the force of acts of parliament: a statute, which was calculated to introduce the most despotic tyranny; and which must have proved fatal to the liberties of this kingdom, had it not been luckily repealed in the minority of his successor, about five years after.

IV. T H E king is likewise the fountain of honour, of office, and of privilege: and this in a different sense from that wherein he is stiled the fountain of justice; for here he is really the parent of them. It is impossible that government can be maintained without a due subordination of rank; that the people may know and distinguish such as are set over them, in order to yield them their due respect and obedience; and also that the officers themselves, being encouraged by emulation and the hopes of superiority, may the better discharge their functions: and the law supposes, that no one can be so good a judge of their several merits and services, as the king himself who employs them. It has therefore intrusted with him the sole power of conferring dignities and honours, in confidence that he will bestow them upon none, but such as deserve them. And therefore all degrees of nobility, of knighthood, and other titles, are received by immediate grant from the crown: either expressed in writing, by writs or letters patent, as in the creations of peers and baronets; or by corporeal investiture, as in the creation of a simple knight.

F R O M the same principle also arises the prerogative of erecting and disposing of offices: for honours and offices are in their nature convertible and synonymous. All offices under the crown carry in the eye of the law an honour along with them; because they imply a superiority of parts and abilities, being supposed to be always filled with those that are most able to execute them. And, on the other hand, all honours in their original had duties or offices annexed to them: an earl, *comes*, was the conservator or governor of a county; and a knight, *miles*, was bound to attend the king in his wars. For the same reason therefore that honours are in the disposal of the king, offices ought to be so likewise; and as the king may create new titles, so may he create new offices: but with this restriction, that he cannot create new offices with new fees annexed to them, nor annex new fees to old offices; for this would be a tax upon the subject, which cannot be imposed but by act of parliament. Wherefore, in 13 Hen. IV, a new office being created by the king's letters patent for measuring cloths, with a new fee for the same, the letters patent were, on account of the new fee, revoked and declared void in parliament.

U P O N the same, or a like reason, the king has also the prerogative of conferring privileges upon private persons. Such as granting place or precedence to any of his subjects, as shall seem good to his royal wisdom: or such as converting aliens, or persons born out of the king's dominions, into denizens; whereby some very considerable privileges of natural-born subjects are conferred upon them. Such also is the prerogative of erecting corporations; whereby a number of private persons are united and knit together, and enjoy many liberties, powers, and immunities in their politic capacity, which they were utterly incapable of in their natural. Of aliens, denizens, natural-born, and naturalized subjects, I shall speak more largely in a subsequent chapter; as also of corporations at the close of this book of our commentaries. I now only mention them incidentally, in order to remark the king's prerogative of making them; which is grounded upon this foundation, that the king, having the sole administration of the government in his hands, is the best and the only judge, in what capacities, with what privileges, and under what distinctions, his people are the best qualified to serve, and to act under him. A principle, which was carried so far by the imperial law, that it was determined to be the crime of sacrilege, even to doubt whether the prince had appointed proper officers in the state.

V. A N O T H E R light in which the laws of England consider the king with regard to domestic concerns, is as the arbiter of commerce. By commerce, I at present mean domestic commerce only. It would lead me into too large a field, if I were to attempt, to enter upon the nature of foreign trade, it's privileges, regulations, and restrictions; and would be also quite beside the purpose of these commentaries, which are confined to the laws of England. Whereas no municipal laws can be sufficient to order and determine the very extensive and complicated affairs of traffic and merchandize; neither can they have a proper authority for this purpose. For as these are transactions carried on between the subjects of independent states, the municipal laws of one will not be regarded by the other. For which reason the affairs of commerce are regulated by a law of their own, called the law merchant or *lex mercatoria*, which all nations agree in and take notice of. And in particular the law of England does in many cases refer itself to it, and leaves the causes of merchants to be tried by their own peculiar customs; and that often even in matters relating to inland trade, as for instance with regard to the drawing, the acceptance, and the transfer, of bills of exchange.

Co. Litt. 172. Ld Raym. 181. 1542.

W I T H us in England, the king's prerogative, so far as it relates to mere domestic commerce, will fall principally under the following articles:

F I R S T, the establishment of public marts, or places of buying and selling, such as markets and fairs, with the tolls thereunto belonging. These can only be set up by virtue of the king's grant, or by long and immemorial usage and prescription, which presupposes such a grant. The limitation of these public resorts, to such time and such place as may be most convenient for the neighbourhood, forms a part of oeconomics, or domestic polity; which, considering the kingdom as a large family, and the king as the master of it, he clearly has a right to dispose and order as he pleases.

2 Inst. 220.

S E C O N D L Y, the regulation of weights and measures. These, for the advantage of the public, ought to be universally the same throughout the kingdom; being the general criterions which reduce all things to the same or an equivalent value. But, as weight and measure are things in their nature arbitrary and uncertain, it is therefore expedient that they be reduced to some fixed rule or standard: which standard it is impossible to fix by any written law or oral proclamation; for no man can, by words only, give another an adequate idea of a foot-rule, or a pound-weight. It is therefore necessary to have recourse to some visible, palpable, material standard; by forming a comparison with which, all weights and measures may be reduced to one uniform size: and the prerogative of fixing this standard, our antient law vested in the crown; as in Normandy it belonged to the duke. This standard was originally kept at Winchester: and we find in the laws of king Edgar, near a century before the conquest, an injunction that the one measure, which was kept at Winchester, should be observed throughout the realm. Most nations have regulated the standard of measures of length by comparison with the parts of the human body; as the palm, the hand, the span, the foot, the cubit, the ell, (*ulna*, or arm) the pace, and the fathom. But, as these are of different dimensions in men of different proportions, our antient historians inform us, that a new standard of longitudinal measure was ascertained by king Henry the first; who commanded that the *ulna* or antient ell, which answers to the modern yard, should be made of the exact length of his own arm. And, one standard of measures of length being gained, all others are easily derived from thence; those of greater length by multiplying, those of less by subdividing, that original standard. Thus, by the statute called *compositio ulnarum et perticarum*, five yards and an half make a perch; and the yard is subdivided into three feet, and each foot into twelve inches; which inches will be each of the length of three grains of barley. Superficial measures are derived by squaring those of length; and measures of capacity by cubing them. The standard of weights was originally taken from corns of wheat, whence the lowest denomination of weights we have is still called a grain; thirty two of which are directed, by the statute called *compositio mensurarum*, to compose a penny weight, whereof twenty make an ounce, twelve ounces a pound, and so upwards. And upon these principles the first standards were made; which, being originally so fixed by the crown, their subsequent regulations have been generally made by the king in parliament. Thus, under king Richard I, in his parliament holden at Westminster, *A.D.* 1197, it was ordained that there shall be only one weight and one measure throughout the kingdom, and that the custody of the assise or standard of weights and measures shall be committed to certain persons in every city and borough; from whence the antient office of the king's aulnager seems to have been derived, whose duty it was, for a certain fee, to measure all cloths made for sale, till the office was abolished by the statute 11 & 12 W. III. c. 20. In king John's time this ordinance of king Richard was frequently dispensed with for money; which occasioned a provision to be made for inforcing it, in the great charters of king John and his son. These original standards were called *pondus regis*, and *mensura domini regis*; and are directed by a variety of subsequent statutes to be kept in the exchequer, and all weights and measures to be made conformable thereto. But, as sir Edward Coke observes, though this hath so often by authority of parliament been enacted, yet it could never be effected; so forcible is custom with the multitude, when it hath gotten an head.

THIRDLY, as money is the medium of commerce, it is the king's prerogative, as the arbiter of domestic commerce, to give it authority or make it current. Money is an universal medium, or common standard, by comparison with which the value of all merchandize may be ascertained: or it is a sign, which represents the respective values of all commodities. Metals are well calculated for this sign, because they are durable and are capable of many subdivisions: and a precious metal is still better calculated for this purpose, because it is the most portable. A metal is also the most proper for a common measure, because it can easily be reduced to the same standard in all nations: and every particular nation fixes on it it's own impression, that the weight and standard (wherein consists the intrinsic value) may both be known by inspection only.

AS the quantity of precious metals increases, that is, the more of them there is extracted from the mine, this universal medium or common sign will sink in value, and grow less precious. Above a thousand millions of bullion are calculated to have been imported into Europe from America within less than three centuries; and the quantity is daily increasing. The consequence is, that more money must be given now for the same commodity than was given an hundred years ago. And, if any accident was to diminish the quantity of gold and silver, their value would proportionably rise. A horse, that was formerly worth ten pounds, is now perhaps worth twenty; and, by any failure of current specie, the price may be reduced to what it was. Yet is the horse in reality neither dearer nor cheaper at one time than another: for, if the metal which constitutes the coin was formerly twice as scarce as at present, the commodity was then as dear at half the price, as now it is at the whole.

THE coining of money is in all states the act of the sovereign power; for the reason just mentioned, that it's value may be known on inspection. And with respect to coinage in general, there are three things to be considered therein; the materials, the impression, and the denomination.

WITH regard to the materials, sir Edward Coke lays it down, that the money of England must either be of gold or silver; and none other was ever issued by the royal authority till 1672, when copper farthings and half-pence were coined by king Charles the second, and ordered by proclamation to be current in all payments, under the value of six-pence, and not otherwise. But this copper coin is not upon the same footing with the other in many respects, particularly with regard to the offence of counterfeiting it.

S to the impression, the stamping thereof is the unquestionable prerogative of the crown: for, though divers bishops and monasteries had formerly the privilege of coining money, yet, as sir Matthew Hale observes, this was usually done by special grant from the king, or by prescription which supposes one; and therefore was derived from, and not in derogation of, the royal prerogative. Besides that they had only the profit of the coinage, and not the power of instituting either the impression or denomination; but had usually the stamp sent them from the exchequer.

THE denomination, or the value for which the coin is to pass current, is likewise in the breast of the king; and, if any unusual pieces are coined, that value must be ascertained by proclamation. In order to fix the value, the weight, and the fineness of the metal are to be taken into consideration together. When a given weight of gold or silver is of a given fineness, it is then of the true standard, and called sterling metal; a name for which there are various reasons given, but none of them entirely satisfactory. And of this sterling metal all the coin of the kingdom must be made by the statute 25 Edw. III. c. 13. So that the king's prerogative seemeth not to extend to the debasing or inhancing the value of the coin, below or above the sterling value: though sir Matthew Hale appears to be of another opinion. The king may also, by his proclamation, legitimate foreign coin, and make it current here; declaring at what value it shall be taken in payments. But this, I apprehend, ought to be by comparison with the standard of our own coin; otherwise the consent of parliament will be necessary. There is at present no such legitimated money; Portugal coin being only current by private consent, so that any one who pleases may refuse to take it in payment. The king may also at any time decry, or cry down, any coin of the kingdom, and make it no longer current.

VI. THE king is, lastly, considered by the laws of England as the head and supreme governor of the national church.

TO enter into the reasons upon which this prerogative is founded is matter rather of divinity than of law. I shall therefore only observe that by statute 26 Hen. VIII. c. 1. (reciting that the king's majesty justly and rightfully is and ought to be the supreme head of the church of England; and so had been recognized by the clergy of this kingdom in their convocation) it is enacted, that the king shall be reputed the only supreme head in earth of the church of England, and shall have, annexed to the imperial crown of this realm, as well the titles and stile thereof, as all jurisdictions, authorities, and commodities, to the said dignity of supreme head of the church appertaining. And another statute to the same purport was made, 1 Eliz. c. 1.

IN virtue of this authority the king convenes, prorogues, restrains, regulates, and dissolves all ecclesiastical synods or convocations. This was an inherent prerogative of the crown, long before the time of Henry VIII, as appears by the statute 8 Hen. VI. c. 1. and the many authors, both lawyers and historians, vouched by sir Edward Coke. So that the statute 25 Hen. VIII. c. 19. which restrains the convocation from making or putting in execution any canons repugnant to the king's prerogative, or the laws, customs, and statutes of the realm, was merely declaratory of the old common law: that part of it only being new, which makes the king's royal assent actually necessary to the validity of every canon. The convocation or ecclesiastical synod, in England, differs considerably in it's constitution from the synods of other christian kingdoms: those consisting wholly of bishops; whereas with us the convocation is the miniature of a parliament, wherein the archbishop presides with regal state; the upper house of bishops represents the house of lords; and the lower house, composed of representatives of the several dioceses at large, and of each particular chapter therein, resembles the house of commons with it's knights of the shire and burgesses. This constitution is said to be owing to the policy of Edward I; who thereby at one and the same time let in the inferior clergy to the privilege of forming ecclesiastical canons, (which before they had not) and also introduced a method of taxing ecclesiastical benefices, by consent of convocation.

FROM this prerogative also of being the head of the church arises the king's right of nomination to vacant bishopricks, and certain other ecclesiastical preferments; which will better be considered when we come to treat of the clergy. I shall only here observe, that this is now done in consequence of the statute 25 Hen. VIII. c. 20.

AS head of the church, the king is likewise the *dernier resort* in all ecclesiastical causes; an appeal lying ultimately to him in chancery from the sentence of every ecclesiastical judge: which right was restored to the crown by statute 25 Hen. VIII. c. 19. as will more fully be shewn hereafter.

CHAPTER THE EIGHTH.

OF THE KING'S REVENUE.

HAVING, in the preceding chapter, considered at large those branches of the king's prerogative, which contribute to his royal dignity, and constitute the executive power of the government, we proceed now to examine the king's *fiscal* prerogatives, or such as regard his *revenue*; which the British constitution hath vested in the royal person, in order to support his dignity and maintain his power: being a portion which each subject contributes of his property, in order to secure the remainder.

THIS revenue is either ordinary, or extraordinary. The king's ordinary revenue is such, as has either subsisted time out of mind in the crown; or else has been granted by parliament, by way of purchase or exchange for such of the king's inherent hereditary revenues, as were found inconvenient to the subject.

WHEN I say that it has subsisted time out of mind in the crown, I do not mean that the king is at present in the actual possession of the whole of this revenue. Much (nay, the greatest part) of it is at this day in the hands of subjects; to whom it has been granted out from time to time by the kings of England: which has rendered the crown in some measure dependent on the people for it's ordinary support and subsistence. So that I must be obliged to recount, as part of the royal revenue, what lords of manors and other subjects frequently look upon to be their own absolute rights, because they are and have been vested in them and their ancestors for ages, though in reality originally derived from the grants of our antient princes.

I. THE first of the king's ordinary revenues, which I shall take notice of, is of an ecclesiastical kind; (as are also the three succeeding ones) viz. the custody of the temporalties of bishops; by which are meant all the lay revenues, lands, and tenements (in which is included his barony) which belong to an archbishop's or bishop's see. And these upon the vacancy of the bishoprick are immediately the right of the king, as a consequence of his prerogative in church matters; whereby he is considered as the founder of all archbishopricks and bishopricks, to whom during the vacancy they revert. And for the same reason, before the dissolution of abbeys, the king had the custody of the temporalties of all such abbeys and priories as were of royal foundation (but not of those founded by subjects) on the death of the abbot or prior. Another reason may also be given, why the policy of the law hath vested this custody in the king; because, as the successor is not known, the lands and possessions of the see would be liable to spoil and devastation, if no one had a property therein. Therefore the law has given the king, not the temporalties themselves, but the *custody* of the temporalties, till such time as a successor is appointed; with power of taking to himself all the intermediate profits, without any account to the successor; and with the right of presenting (which the crown very frequently exercises) to such benefices and other preferments as fall within the time of vacation. This revenue is of so high a nature, that it could not be granted out to a subject, before, or even after, it accrued: but now by the statute 14 Edw. III. st. 4. c. 4 & 5. the king may, after the vacancy, lease the temporalties to the dean and chapter; saving to himself all advowsons, escheats, and the like. Our antient kings, and particularly William Rufus, were not only remarkable for keeping the bishopricks a long time vacant, for the sake of enjoying the temporalties, but also committed horrible waste on the woods and other parts of the estate; and, to crown all, would never, when the see was filled up, restore to the bishop his temporalties again, unless he purchased them at an exorbitant price. To remedy which, king Henry the first granted a charter at the beginning of his reign, promising neither to sell, nor let to farm, nor take any thing from, the domains of the church, till the successor was installed. And it was made one of the articles of the great charter, that no waste should be committed in the temporalties of bishopricks, neither should the custody of them be sold. The same is ordained by the statute of Westminster the first; and the statute 14 Edw. III. st. 4. c. 4. (which permits, as we have seen, a lease to the dean and chapter) is still more explicit in prohibiting the other exactions. It was also a frequent abuse, that the king would for trifling, or no causes, seise the temporalties of bishops, even during their lives, into his own hands: but this is guarded against by statute 1 Edw. III. st. 2. c. 2.

THIS revenue of the king, which was formerly very considerable, is now by a customary indulgence almost reduced to nothing: for, at present, as soon as the new bishop is consecrated and confirmed, he usually receives the restitution of his temporalties quite entire, and untouched, from the king; and then, and not sooner, he has a fee simple in his bishoprick, and may maintain an action for the same.

II. THE king is entitled to a corody, as the law calls it, out of every bishoprick: that is, to send one of his chaplains to be maintained by the bishop, or to have a pension allowed him till the bishop promotes him to a benefice. This is also in the nature of an acknowlegement to the king, as founder of the see; since he had formerly the same corody or pension from every abbey or priory of royal foundation. It is, I apprehend, now fallen into total disuse; though sir Matthew Hale says, that it is due of common right, and that no prescription will discharge it.

III. THE king also (as was formerly observed) is entitled to all the tithes arising in extraparochial places: though perhaps it may be doubted how far this article, as well as the last, can be properly reckoned a part of the king's own royal revenue; since a corody supports only his chaplains, and these extraparochial tithes are held under an implied trust, that the king will distribute them for the good of the clergy in general.

IV. THE next branch consists in the first-fruits, and tenths, of all spiritual preferments in the kingdom; both of which I shall consider together.

THESE were originally a part of the papal usurpations over the clergy of this kingdom; first introduced by Pandulph the pope's legate, during the reigns of king John and Henry the third, in the see of Norwich; and afterwards attempted to be made universal by the popes Clement

V and John XXII, about the beginning of the fourteenth century. The first-fruits, *primitiae*, or *annates*, were the first year's whole profits of the spiritual preferment, according to a rate or *valor* made under the direction of pope Innocent IV by Walter bishop of Norwich in 38 Hen. III, and afterwards advanced in value by commission from pope Nicholas the third, *A.D.* 1292, 20 Edw. I; which valuation of pope Nicholas is still preserved in the exchequer. The tenths, or *decimae*, were the tenth part of the annual profit of each living by the same valuation; which was also claimed by the holy see, under no better pretence than a strange misapplication of that precept of the Levitical law, which directs, "that the Levites should offer the tenth part of their tithe as a heave-offering to the Lord, and give it to Aaron the *high* priest." But this claim of the pope met with vigorous resistance from the English parliament; and a variety of acts were passed to prevent and restrain it, particularly the statute 6 Hen. IV. c. 1. which calls it a horrible mischief and damnable custom. But the popish clergy, blindly devoted to the will of a foreign master, still kept it on foot; sometimes more secretly, sometimes more openly and avowedly: so that, in the reign of Henry VIII, it was computed, that in the compass of fifty years 800000 ducats had been sent to Rome for first-fruits only. And, as the clergy expressed this willingness to contribute so much of their income to the head of the church, it was thought proper (when in the same reign the papal power was abolished, and the king was declared the head of the church of England) to annex this revenue to the crown; which was done by statute 26 Hen. VIII. c. 3. (confirmed by statute 1 Eliz. c. 4.) and a new *valor beneficiorum* was then made, by which the clergy are at present rated.

Numb. 18. 26.

B Y these lastmentioned statutes all vicarages under ten pounds a year, and all rectories under ten marks, are discharged from the payment of first-fruits: and if, in such livings as continue chargeable with this payment, the incumbent lives but half a year, he shall pay only one quarter of his first-fruits; if but one whole year, then half of them; if a year and half, three quarters; and if two years, then the whole; and not otherwise. Likewise by the statute 27 Hen. VIII. c. 8. no tenths are to be paid for the first year, for then the first-fruits are due: and by other statutes of queen Anne, in the fifth and sixth years of her reign, if a benefice be under fifty pounds *per annum* clear yearly value, it shall be discharged of the payment of first-fruits and tenths.

T H U S the richer clergy, being, by the criminal bigotry of their popish predecessors, subjected at first to a foreign exaction, were afterwards, when that yoke was shaken off, liable to a like misapplication of their revenues, through the rapacious disposition of the then reigning monarch: till at length the piety of queen Anne restored to the church what had been thus indirectly taken from it. This she did, not by remitting the tenths and first-fruits entirely; but, in a spirit of the truest equity, by applying these superfluities of the larger benefices to make up the deficiences of the smaller. And to this end she granted her royal charter, which was confirmed by the statute 2 Ann. c. 11. whereby all the revenue of first-fruits and tenths is vested in trustees for ever, to form a perpetual fund for the augmentation of poor livings. This is usually called queen Anne's bounty; which has been still farther regulated by subsequent statutes, too numerous here to recite.

V. T H E next branch of the king's ordinary revenue (which, as well as the subsequent branches, is of a lay or temporal nature) consists in the rents and profits of the demesne lands of the crown. These demesne lands, *terrae dominicales regis*, being either the share reserved to the crown at the original distribution of landed property, or such as came to it afterwards by forfeitures or other means, were antiently very large and extensive; comprizing divers manors, honors, and lordships; the tenants of which had very peculiar privileges, as will be shewn in the second book of these commentaries, when we speak of the tenure in antient demesne. At present they are contracted within a very narrow compass, having been almost entirely granted away to private subjects. This has occasioned the parliament frequently to interpose; and, particularly, after king William III had greatly impoverished the crown, an act passed, whereby all future grants or leases from the crown for any longer term than thirty one years or three lives are declared to be void; except with regard to houses, which may be granted for fifty years. And no reversionary lease can be made, so as to exceed, together with the estate in being, the same term of three lives or thirty one years: that is, where there is a subsisting lease, of which there are twenty years still to come, the king cannot grant a future interest, to commence after the expiration of the former, for any longer term than eleven years. The tenant must also be made liable to be punished for committing waste; and the usual rent must be reserved, or, where there has usually been no rent, one third of the clear yearly value. The misfortune is, that this act was made too late, after almost every valuable possession of the crown had been granted away for ever, or else upon very long leases; but may be of benefit to posterity, when those leases come to expire.

VI. H I T H E R might have been referred the advantages which were used to arise to the king from the profits of his military tenures, to which most lands in the kingdom were subject, till the statute 12 Car. II. c. 24. which in great measure abolished them all: the explication of the nature of which tenures, must be referred to the second book of these commentaries. Hither also might have been referred the profitable prerogative of purveyance and pre-emption: which was a right enjoyed by the crown of buying up provisions and other necessaries, by the intervention of the king's purveyors, for the use of his royal houshold, at an appraised valuation, in preference to all others, and even without consent of the owner; and also of forcibly impressing the carriages and horses of the subject, to do the king's business on the publick roads, in the conveyance of timber, baggage, and the like, however inconvenient to the proprietor, upon paying him a settled price. A prerogative, which prevailed pretty generally throughout Europe, during the scarcity of gold and silver, and the high valuation of money consequential thereupon. In those early times the king's houshold (as well as those of inferior lords) were supported by specific renders of corn, and other victuals, from the tenants of the respective demesnes; and there was also a continual market kept at the palace gate to furnish viands for the royal use. And this answered all purposes, in those ages of simplicity, so long as the king's court continued in any certain place. But when it removed from one part of the kingdom to another (as was formerly very frequently done) it was found necessary to send purveyors beforehand, to get together a sufficient quantity of provisions and other necessaries for the houshold: and, lest the unusual demand should raise them to an exorbitant price, the powers beforementioned were vested in these purveyors; who in process of time very greatly abused their authority, and became a great oppression to the subject though of little advantage to the crown; ready money in open market (when the royal residence was more permanent, and specie began to be plenty) being found upon experience to be the best proveditor of any. Wherefore by degrees the powers of purveyance have declined, in foreign countries as well as our own; and particularly were abolished in Sweden by Gustavus Adolphus, toward the beginning of the last century. And, with us in England, having fallen into disuse during the suspension of monarchy, king Charles at his restoration consented, by the same statute, to resign intirely these branches of his revenue and power, for the ease and convenience of his subjects: and the parliament, in part of recompense, settled on him, his heirs, and successors, for ever, the hereditary excise of fifteen pence *per* barrel on all beer and ale sold in the kingdom, and a proportionable sum for certain other liquors. So that this hereditary excise, the nature of which shall be farther explained in the subsequent part of this chapter, now forms the sixth branch of his majesty's ordinary revenue.

VII. A SEVENTH branch might also be computed to have arisen from wine licences; or the rents payable to the crown by such persons as are licensed to sell wine by retale throughout England, except in a few privileged places. These were first settled on the crown by the statute 12 Car. II. c. 25. and, together with the hereditary excise, made up the equivalent in value for the loss sustained by the prerogative in the abolition of the military tenures, and the right of pre-emption and purveyance: but this revenue was abolished by the statute 30 Geo. II. c. 19. and an annual sum of upwards of £7000 *per annum*, issuing out of the new stamp duties imposed on wine licences, was settled on the crown in it's stead.

VIII. AN eighth branch of the king's ordinary revenue is usually reckoned to consist in the profits arising from his forests. Forests are waste grounds belonging to the king, replenished with all manner of beasts of chase or venary; which are under the king's protection, for the sake of his royal recreation and delight: and, to that end, and for preservation of the king's game, there are particular laws, privileges, courts and officers belonging to the king's forests; all which will be, in their turns, explained in the subsequent books of these commentaries. What we are now to consider are only the profits arising to the king from hence; which consist principally in amercements or fines levied for offences against the forest-laws. But as few, if any courts of this kind for levying amercements have been held since 1632, 8 Car. I. and as, from the accounts given of the proceedings in that court by our histories and law books, nobody would now wish to see them again revived, it is needless (at least in this place) to pursue this enquiry any farther.

IX. THE profits arising from the king's ordinary courts of justice make a ninth branch of his revenue. And these consist not only in fines imposed upon offenders, forfeitures of recognizances, and amercements levied upon defaulters; but also in certain fees due to the crown in a variety of legal matters, as, for setting the great seal to charters, original writs, and other legal proceedings, and for permitting fines to be levied of lands in order to bar entails, or otherwise to insure their title. As none of these can be done without the immediate intervention of the king, by himself or his officers, the law allows him certain perquisites and profits, as a recompense for the trouble he undertakes for the public. These, in process of time, have been almost all granted out to private persons, or else appropriated to certain particular uses: so that, though our law-proceedings are still loaded with their payment, very little of them is now returned into the king's exchequer; for a part of whose royal maintenance they were originally intended. All future grants of them however, by the statute 1 Ann. st. 2. c. 7. are to endure for no longer time than the prince's life who grants them.

X. A TENTH branch of the king's ordinary revenue, said to be grounded on the consideration of his guarding and protecting the seas from pirates and robbers, is the right to *royal fish*, which are whale and sturgeon: and these, when either thrown ashore, or caught near the coasts, are the property of the king, on account of their superior excellence. Indeed our ancestors seem to have entertained a very high notion of the importance of this right; it being the prerogative of the kings of Denmark and the dukes of Normandy; and from one of these it was probably derived to our princes. It is expressly claimed and allowed in the statute *de praerogativa regis*: and the most antient treatises of law now extant make mention of it; though they seem to have made a distinction between whale and sturgeon, as was incidentally observed in a former chapter.

XI. ANOTHER maritime revenue, and founded partly upon the same reason, is that of shipwrecks; which are also declared to be the king's property by the same prerogative statute 17 Edw. II. c. 11. and were so, long before, at the common law. It is worthy observation, how greatly the law of wrecks has been altered, and the rigour of it gradually softened, in favour of the distressed proprietors. Wreck, by the antient common law, was where any ship was lost at sea, and the goods or cargo were thrown upon the land; in which case these goods, so wrecked, were adjudged to belong to the king: for it was held, that, by the loss of the ship, all property was gone out of the original owner. But this was undoubtedly adding sorrow to sorrow, and was consonant neither to reason nor humanity. Wherefore it was first ordained by king Henry I, that if any person escaped alive out of the ship it should be no wreck; and afterwards king Henry II, by his charter, declared, that if on the coasts of either England, Poictou, Oleron, or Gascony, any ship should be distressed, and either man or beast should escape or be found therein alive, the goods should remain to the owners, if they claimed them within three months; but otherwise should be esteemed a wreck, and should belong to the king, or other lord of the franchise. This was again confirmed with improvements by king Richard the first, who, in the second year of his reign, not only established these concessions, by ordaining that the owner, if he was shipwrecked and escaped, "*omnes res suas liberas et quietas haberet,*" but also, that, if he perished, his children, or in default of them his brethren and sisters, should retain the property; and, in default of brother or sister, then the goods should remain to the king. And the law, so long after as the reign of Henry III, seems still to have been guided by the same equitable provisions. For then if a dog (for instance) escaped, by which the owner might be discovered, or if any certain mark were set on the goods, by which they might be known again, it was held to be no wreck. And this is certainly most agreeable to reason; the rational claim of the king being only founded upon this, that the true owner cannot be ascertained. But afterwards, in the statute of Westminster the first, the law is laid down more agreeable to the charter of king Henry the second: and upon that statute hath stood the legal doctrine of wrecks to the present time. It enacts, that if any live thing escape (a man, a cat, or a dog; which, as in Bracton, are only put for examples,) in this case, and, as it seems, in this case only, it is clearly not a legal wreck: but the sheriff of the county is bound to keep the goods a year and a day (as in France for one year, agreeably to the maritime laws of Oleron, and in Holland for a year and an half) that if any man can prove a property in them, either in his own right or by right of representation, they shall be restored to him without delay; but, if no such property be proved within that time, they then shall be the king's. If the goods are of a perishable nature, the sheriff may sell them, and the money shall be liable in their stead. This revenue of wrecks is frequently granted out to lords of manors, as a royal franchise; and if any one be thus entitled to wrecks in his own land, and the king's goods are wrecked thereon, the king may claim them at any time, even after the year and day.

In like manner Constantine the great, finding that by the imperial law the revenue of wrecks was given to the prince's treasury or *fiscus*, restrained it by an edict (*Cod.* 11. 5. 1.) and ordered them to remain to the owners; adding this humane expostulation, "*Quod enim jus habet fiscus in aliena calamitate, ut de re tam luctuosa compendium sectetur?*"

I T is to be observed, that in order to constitute a legal *wreck*, the goods must come to land. If they continue at sea, the law distinguishes them by the barbarous and uncouth appellations of *jetsam*, *flotsam*, and *ligan*. Jetsam is where goods are cast into the sea, and there sink and remain under water: flotsam is where they continue swimming on the surface of the waves: ligan is where they are sunk in the sea, but tied to a cork or buoy, in order to be found again. These are also the king's, if no owner appears to claim them; but, if any owner appears, he is entitled to recover the possession. For even if they be cast overboard, without any mark or buoy, in order to lighten the ship, the owner is not by this act of necessity construed to have renounced his property: much less can things ligan be supposed to be abandoned, since the owner has done all in his power, to assert and retain his property. These three are therefore accounted so far a distinct thing from the former, that by the king's grant to a man of wrecks, things jetsam, flotsam, and ligan will not pass.

Quae enim res in tempestate, levandae navis causa, ejiciuntur, hac dominorum permanent. Quia palam est, eas non eo animo ejici, quod quis habere nolit. Inst. 2. 1. §. 48.

W R E C K S, in their legal acceptation, are at present not very frequent: it rarely happening that every living creature on board perishes; and if any should survive, it is a very great chance, since the improvement of commerce, navigation, and correspondence, but the owner will be able to assert his property within the year and day limited by law. And in order to preserve this property entire for him, and if possible to prevent wrecks at all, our laws have made many very humane regulations; in a spirit quite opposite to those savage laws, which formerly prevailed in all the northern regions of Europe, and a few years ago were still laid to subsist on the coasts of the Baltic sea, permitting the inhabitants to seize on whatever they could get as lawful prize; or, as an author of their own expresses it, "*in naufragorum miseria et calamitate tanquam vultures ad praedam currere.*" For by the statute 2 Edw. III. c. 13. if any ship be lost on the shore, and the goods come to land (so as it be not legal wreck) they shall be presently delivered to the merchants, they paying only a reasonable reward to those that saved and preserved them, which is intitled *salvage*. Also by the common law, if any persons (other than the sheriff) take any goods so cast on shore, which are not legal wreck, the owners might have a commission to enquire and find them out, and compel them to make restitution. And by statute 12 Ann. st. 2. c. 18. confirmed by 4 Geo. I. c. 12. in order to assist the distressed, and prevent the scandalous illegal practices on some of our sea coasts, (too similar to those on the Baltic) it is enacted, that all head-officers and others of towns near the sea shall, upon application made to them, summon as many hands as are necessary, and send them to the relief of any ship in distress, on forfeiture of 100*l.* and, in case of assistance given, salvage shall be paid by the owners, to be assessed by three neighbouring justices. All persons that secrete any goods shall forfeit their treble value: and if they wilfully do any act whereby the ship is lost or destroyed, by making holes in her, stealing her pumps, or otherwise, they are guilty of felony, without benefit of clergy. Lastly, by the statute 26 Geo. II. c. 19. plundering any vessel either in distress, or wrecked, and whether any living creature be on board or not, (for, whether wreck or otherwise, it is clearly not the property of the populace) such plundering, I say, or preventing the escape of any person that endeavors to save his life, or wounding him with intent to destroy him, or putting out false lights in order to bring any vessel into danger, are all declared to be capital felonies; in like manner as the destroying trees, steeples, or other stated seamarks, is punished by the statute 8 Eliz. c. 13. with a forfeiture of 200*l.* Moreover, by the statute of George II, pilfering any goods cast ashore is declared to be petty larceny; and many other salutary regulations are made, for the more effectually preserving ships of any nation in distress.

By the civil law, to destroy persons shipwrecked, or prevent their saving the ship, is capital. And to steal even a plank from a vessel in distress, or wrecked, makes the party liable to answer for the whole ship and cargo. (*Ff.* 47. 9. 3.) The laws also of the Wisigoths, and the most early Neapolitan constitutions, punished with the utmost severity all those who neglected to assist any ship in distress, or plundered any goods cast on shore. (Lindenbrog. *Cod. LL. antiq.* 146. 715.)

XII. A TWELFTH branch of the royal revenue, the right to mines, has it's original from the king's prerogative of coinage, in order to supply him with materials: and therefore those mines, which are properly royal, and to which the king is entitled when found, are only those of silver and gold. By the old common law, if gold or silver be found in mines of base metal, according to the opinion of some the whole was a royal mine, and belonged to the king; though others held that it only did so, if the quantity of gold or silver was of greater value than the quantity of base metal. But now by the statutes 1 W. & M. st. 1. c. 30. and 5 W. & M. c. 6. this difference is made immaterial; it being enacted, that no mines of copper, tin, iron, or lead, shall be looked upon as royal mines, notwithstanding gold or silver may be extracted from them in any quantities: but that the king, or persons claiming royal mines under his authority, may have theore, (other than tin-ore in the counties of Devon and Cornwall) paying for the same a price stated in the act. This was an extremely reasonable law: for now private owners are not discouraged from working mines, through a fear that they may be claimed as royal ones; neither does the king depart from the just rights of his revenue, since he may have all the precious metal contained in the ore, paying no more for it than the value of the base metal which it is supposed to be; to which base metal the land-owner is by reason and law entitled.

2 Inst. 577.

Plowd. 566.

XIII. T O the same original may in part be referred the revenue of treasure-trove (derived from the French word, *trover*, to find) called in Latin *thesaurus inventus*, which is where any money or coin, gold, silver, plate, or bullion, is found hidden *in* the earth, or other private place, the owner thereof being unknown; in which case the treasure belongs to the king: but if he that hid it be known, or afterwards found out, the owner and not the king is entitled to it. Also if it be found in the sea, or *upon* the earth, it doth not belong to the king, but the finder, if no owner appears. So that it seems it is the *hiding*, not the *abandoning* of it, that gives the king a property: Bracton defining it, in the words of the civilians, to be "*vetus depositio pecuniae.*" This difference clearly arises from the different intentions, which the law implies in the owner. A man, that hides his treasure in a secret place, evidently does not mean to relinquish his property; but reserves a right of claiming it again, when he sees occasion; and, if he dies and the secret also dies with him, the law gives it the king, in part of his royal revenue. But a man that scatters his treasure into the sea, or upon the public surface of the earth, is construed to have absolutely abandoned his property, and returned it into the common stock, without any intention of reclaiming it; and therefore it belongs, as in a state of nature, to the first occupant, or finder; unless the owner appear and assert his right, which then proves that the loss was by accident, and not with an intent to renounce his property.

F O R M E R L Y all treasure-trove belonged to the finder; as was also the rule of the civil law. Afterwards it was judged expedient for the purposes of the state, and particularly for the coinage, to allow part of what was so found to the king; which part was assigned to be all *hidden* treasure; such as is *casually lost* and unclaimed, and also such as is *designedly abandoned*, still remaining the right of the fortunate finder. And that the prince shall be entitled to this hidden treasure is now grown to be, according to Grotius, "*jus commune, et quasi gentium*:" for it is not only observed, he adds, in England, but in Germany, France, Spain, and Denmark. The finding of deposited treasure was much more frequent, and the treasures themselves more considerable, in the infancy of our constitution than at present. When the Romans, and other inhabitants of the respective countries which composed their empire, were driven out by the northern nations, they concealed their money under-ground; with a view of resorting to it again when the heat of the irruption should be over, and the invaders driven back to their desarts. But as this never happened, the treasures were never claimed; and on the death of the owners the secret also died along with them. The conquering generals, being aware of the value of these hidden mines, made it highly penal to secrete them from the public service. In England therefore, as among the feudists, the punishment of such as concealed from the king the finding of hidden treasure was formerly no less than death; but now it is only fine and imprisonment.

XIV. W A I F S , *bona waviata*, are goods stolen, and waived or thrown away by the thief in his flight, for fear of being apprehended. These are given to the king by the law, as a punishment upon the owner, for not himself pursuing the felon, and taking away his goods from him. And therefore if the party robbed do his diligence immediately to follow and apprehend the thief (which is called making fresh *suit*) or do convict him afterwards, or procure evidence to convict him, he shall have his goods again. Waived goods do also not belong to the king, till seised by somebody for his use; for if the party robbed can seise them first, though at the distance of twenty years, the king shall never have them. If the goods are hid by the thief, or left any where by him, so that he had them not about him when he fled, and therefore did not throw them away in his flight; these also are not *bona waviata*, but the owner may have them again when he pleases. The goods of a foreign merchant, though stolen and thrown away in flight, shall never be waifs: the reason whereof may be, not only for the encouragement of trade, but also because there is no wilful default in the foreign merchant's not pursuing the thief, he being generally a stranger to our laws, our usages, and our language.

XV. E S T R A Y S are such valuable animals as are found wandering in any manor or lordship, and no man knoweth the owner of them; in which case the law gives them to the king as the general owner and lord paramount of the soil, in recompence for the damage which they may have done therein; and they now most commonly belong to the lord of the manor, by special grant from the crown. But in order to vest an absolute property in the king or his grantees, they must be proclaimed in the church and two market towns next adjoining to the place where they are found; and then, if no man claims them, after proclamation and a year and a day passed, they belong to the king or his substitute without redemption; even though the owner were a minor, or under any other legal incapacity. A provision similar to which obtained in the old Gothic constitution, with regard to all things that were found, which were to be thrice proclaimed, *primum coram comitibus et viatoribus obviis, deinde in proxima villa vel pago, postremo coram ecclesia vel judicio*: and the space of a year was allowed for the owner to reclaim his property. If the owner claims them within the year and day, he must pay the charges of finding, keeping, and proclaiming them. The king or lord has no property till the year and day passed: for if a lord keepeth an estray three quarters of a year, and within the year it strayeth again, and another lord getteth it, the first lord cannot take it again. Any beast may be an estray, that is by nature tame or reclaimable, and in which there is a valuable property, as sheep, oxen, swine, and horses, which we in general call cattle; and so Fleta defines it, *pecus vagans, quod nullus petit, sequitur, vel advocat.* For animals upon which the law sets no value, as a dog or cat, and animals *ferae naturae*, as a bear or wolf, cannot be considered as estrays. So swans may be estrays, but not any other fowl; whence they are said to be royal fowl. The reason of which distinction seems to be, that, cattle and swans being of a reclaimed nature, the owner's property in them is not lost merely by their temporary escape; and they also, from their intrinsic value, are a sufficient pledge for the expense of the lord of the franchise in keeping them the year and day. For he that takes an estray is bound, so long as he keeps it, to find it in provisions and keep it from damage; and may not use it by way of labour, but is liable to an action for so doing. Yet he may milk a cow, or the like, for that tends to the preservation, and is for the benefit, of the animal.

B E S I D E S the particular reasons before given why the king should have the several revenues of royal fish, shipwrecks, treasure-trove, waifs, and estrays, there is also one general reason which holds for them all; and that is, because they are *bona vacantia*, or goods in which no one else can claim a property. And therefore by the law of nature they belonged to the first occupant or finder; and so continued under the imperial law. But, in settling the modern constitutions of most of the governments in Europe, it was thought proper (to prevent that strife and contention, which the mere title of occupancy is apt to create and continue, and to provide for the support of public authority in a manner the least burthensome to individuals) that these rights should be annexed to the supreme power by the positive laws of the state. And so it came to pass that, as Bracton expresses it, *haec, quae nullius in bonis sunt, et olim fuerunt inventoris de jure naturali, jam efficiuntur principis de jure gentium.*

XVI. T H E next branch of the king's ordinary revenue consists in forfeitures of lands and goods for offences; *bona confiscata*, as they are called by the civilians, because they belonged to the *fiscus* or imperial treasury; or, as our lawyers term them, *forisfacta*, that is, such whereof the property is gone away or departed from the owner. The true reason and only substantial ground of any forfeiture for crimes consist in this; that all property is derived from society, being one of those civil rights which are conferred upon individuals, in exchange for that degree of natural freedom, which every man must sacrifice when he enters into social communities. If therefore a member of any national community violates the fundamental contract of his association, by transgressing the municipal law, he forfeits his right to such privileges as he claims by that contract; and the state may very justly resume that portion of property, or any part of it, which the laws have before assigned him. Hence, in every offence of an atrocious kind, the laws of England have exacted a total confiscation of the moveables or personal estate; and in many cases a perpetual, in others only a temporary, loss of the offender's immoveables or landed property; and have vested them both in the king, who is the person supposed to be offended, being the one visible magistrate in whom the majesty of the public resides. The particulars of these forfeitures will be more properly recited when we treat of crimes and misdemesnors. I therefore only mention them here, for the sake of regularity, as a part of the *census regalis*; and shall postpone for the present the farther consideration of all forfeitures, excepting one species only, which arises from the misfortune rather than the crime of the owner, and is called a *deodand*.

B Y this is meant whatever personal chattel is the immediate occasion of the death of any reasonable creature; which is forfeited to the king, to be applied to pious uses, and distributed in alms by his high almoner; though formerly destined to a more superstitious purpose. It seems to have been originally designed, in the blind days of popery, as an expiation for the souls of such as were snatched away by sudden death; and for that purpose ought properly to have been given to holy church; in the same manner, as the apparel of a stranger who was found dead was applied to purchase masses for the good of his soul. And this may account for that rule of law, that no deodand is due where an infant under the years of discretion is killed by a fall *from* a cart, or horse, or the like, not being in motion; whereas, if an adult person falls from thence and is killed, the thing is certainly forfeited. For the reason given by sir Matthew Hale seems to be very inadequate, *viz.* because an infant is not able to take care of himself: for why should the owner save his forfeiture, on account of the imbecillity of the child, which ought rather to have made him more cautious to prevent any accident of mischief? The true ground of this rule seems rather to be, that the child, by reason of it's want of discretion, is presumed incapable of actual sin, and therefore needed no deodand to purchase propitiatory masses: but every adult, who dies in actual sin, stood in need of such atonement, according to the humane superstition of the founders of the English law.

T H U S stands the law, if a person be killed by a fall from a thing standing still. But if a horse, or ox, or other animal, of his own motion, kill as well an infant as an adult, or if a cart run over him, they shall in either case be forfeited as deodands; which is grounded upon this additional reason, that such misfortunes are in part owing to the negligence of the owner, and therefore he is properly punished by such forfeiture. A like punishment is in like cases inflicted by the mosaical law: "if an ox gore a man that he die, the ox shall be stoned, and his flesh shall not be eaten." And among the Athenians, whatever was the cause of a man's death, by falling upon him, was exterminated or cast out of the dominions of the republic. Where a thing, not in motion, is the occasion of a man's death, that part only which is the immediate cause is forfeited; as if a man be climbing up a wheel, and is killed by falling from it, the wheel alone is a deodand: but, wherever the thing is in motion, not only that part which immediately gives the wound, (as the wheel, which runs over his body) but all things which move with it and help to make the wound more dangerous (as the cart and loading, which increase the pressure of the wheel) are forfeited. It matters not whether the owner were concerned in the killing or not; for if a man kills another with my sword, the sword is forfeited as an accursed thing. And therefore, in all indictments for homicide, the instrument of death and the value are presented and found by the grand jury (as, that the stroke was given with a certain penknife, value sixpence) that the king or his grantee may claim the deodand:

for it is no deodand, unless it be presented as such by a jury of twelve men. No deodands are due for accidents happening upon the high sea, that being out of the jurisdiction of the common law: but if a man falls from a boat or ship in fresh water, and is drowned, the vessel and cargo are in strictness a deodand.

D E O D A N D S , and forfeitures in general, as well as wrecks, treasure trove, royal fish, mines, waifs, and estrays, may be granted by the king to particular subjects, as a royal franchise: and indeed they are for the most part granted out to the lords of manors, or other liberties; to the perversion of their original design.

XVII. A N O T H E R branch of the king's ordinary revenue arises from escheats of lands, which happen upon the defect of heirs to succeed to the inheritance; whereupon they in general revert to and vest in the king, who is esteemed, in the eye of the law, the original proprietor of all the lands in the kingdom. But the discussion of this topic more properly belongs to the second book of these commentaries, wherein we shall particularly consider the manner in which lands may be acquired or lost by escheat.

XVIII. I P R O C E E D therefore to the eighteenth and last branch of the king's ordinary revenue; which consists in the custody of idiots, from whence we shall be naturally led to consider also the custody of lunatics.

A N idiot, or natural fool, is one that hath had no understanding from his nativity; and therefore is by law presumed never likely to attain any. For which reason the custody of him and of his lands was formerly vested in the lord of the fee; (and therefore still, by special custom, in some manors the lord shall have the ordering of idiot and lunatic copyholders) but, by reason of the manifold abuses of this power by subjects, it was at last provided by common consent, that it should be given to the king, as the general conservator of his people, in order to prevent the idiot from wasting his estate, and reducing himself and his heirs to poverty and distress: This fiscal prerogative of the king is declared in parliament by statute 17 Edw. II. c. 9. which directs (in affirmance of the common law,) that the king shall have ward of the lands of natural fools, taking the profits without waste or destruction, and shall find them necessaries; and after the death of such idiots he shall render the estate to the heirs; in order to prevent such idiots from aliening their lands, and their heirs from being disherited.

B Y the old common law there is a writ *de idiota inquirendo*, to enquire whether a man be an idiot or not: which must be tried by a jury of twelve men; and if they find him *purus idiota*, the profits of his lands, and the custody of his person may be granted by the king to some subject, who has interest enough to obtain them. This branch of the revenue hath been long considered as a hardship upon private families; and so long ago as in the 8 Jac. I. it was under the consideration of parliament, to vest this custody in the relations of the party, and to settle an equivalent on the crown in lieu of it; it being then proposed to share the same fate with the slavery of the feodal tenures, which has been since abolished. Yet few instances can be given of the oppressive exertion of it, since it seldom happens that a jury finds a man an idiot *a nativitate*, but only *non compos mentis* from some particular time; which has an operation very different in point of law.

A MAN is not an idiot, if he hath any glimmering of reason, so that he can tell his parents, his age, or the like common matters. But a man who is born deaf, dumb, and blind, is looked upon by the law as in the same state with an idiot; he being supposed incapable of understanding, as wanting those senses which furnish the human mind with ideas.

A LUNATIC, or *non compos mentis*, is one who hath had understanding, but by disease, grief, or other accident hath lost the use of his reason. A lunatic is indeed properly one that hath lucid intervals; sometimes enjoying his senses, and sometimes not, and that frequently depending upon the change of the moon. But under the general name of *non compos mentis* (which sir Edward Coke says is the most legal name) are comprized not only lunatics, but persons under frenzies; or who lose their intellects by disease; those that *grow* deaf, dumb, and blind, not being *born* so; or such, in short, as are by any means rendered incapable of conducting their own affairs. To these also, as well as idiots, the king is guardian, but to a very different purpose. For the law always imagines, that these accidental misfortunes may be removed; and therefore only constitutes the crown a trustee for the unfortunate persons, to protect their property, and to account to them for all profits received, if they recover, or after their decease to their representatives. And therefore it is declared by the statute 17 Edw. II. c. 10. that the king shall provide for the custody and sustentation of lunatics, and preserve their lands and the profits of them, for their use, when they come to their right mind: and the king shall take nothing to his own use; and if the parties die in such estate, the residue shall be distributed for their souls by the advice of the ordinary, and of course (by the subsequent amendments of the law of administrations) shall now go to their executors or administrators.

THE method of proving a person *non compos* is very similar to that of proving him an idiot. The lord chancellor, to whom, by special authority from the king, the custody of idiots and lunatics is intrusted, upon petition or information, grants a commission in nature of the writ *de idiota inquirendo*, to enquire into the party's state of mind; and if he be found *non compos*, he usually commits the care of his person, with a suitable allowance for his maintenance, to some friend, who is then called his committee. However, to prevent sinister practices, the next heir is never permitted to be this committee of the person; because it is his interest that the party should die. But, it hath been said, there lies not the same objection against his next of kin, provided he be not his heir; for it is his interest to preserve the lunatic's life, in order to increase the personal estate by savings, which he or his family may hereafter be entitled to enjoy. The heir is generally made the manager or committee of the estate, it being clearly his interest by good management to keep it in condition; accountable however to the court of chancery, and to the *non compos* himself, if he recovers; or otherwise, to his administrators.

IN this care of idiots and lunatics the civil law agrees with ours; by assigning them tutors to protect their persons, and curators to manage their estates. But in another instance the

Roman law goes much beyond the English. For, if a man by notorious prodigality was in danger of wasting his estate, he was looked upon as *non compos* and committed to the care of curators or tutors by the praetor. And by the laws of Solon such prodigals were branded with perpetual infamy. But with us, when a man on an inquest of idiocy hath been returned an *unthrift* and not an *idiot*, no farther proceedings have been had. And the propriety of the practice itself seems to be very questionable. It was doubtless an excellent method of benefiting the individual and of preserving estates in families; but it hardly seems calculated for the genius of a free nation, who claim and exercise the liberty of using their own property as they please. "*Sic utere tuo, ut alienum non laedas*," is the only restriction our laws have given with regard to oeconomical prudence. And the frequent circulation and transfer of lands and other property, which cannot be effected without extravagance somewhere, are perhaps not a little conducive towards keeping our mixed constitution in it's due health and vigour.

T H I S may suffice for a short view of the king's *ordinary* revenue, or the proper patrimony of the crown; which was very large formerly, and capable of being increased to a magnitude truly formidable: for there are very few estates in the kingdom, that have not, at some period or other since the Norman conquest, been vested in the hands of the king by forfeiture, escheat, or otherwise. But, fortunately for the liberty of the subject, this hereditary landed revenue, by a series of improvident management, is sunk almost to nothing; and the casual profits, arising from the other branches of the *census regalis*, are likewise almost all of them alienated from the crown. In order to supply the deficiences of which, we are now obliged to have recourse to new methods of raising money, unknown to our early ancestors; which methods constitute the king's *extraordinary* revenue. For, the publick patrimony being got into the hands of private subjects, it is but reasonable that private contributions should supply the public service. Which, though it may perhaps fall harder upon some individuals, whose ancestors have had no share in the general plunder, than upon others, yet, taking the nation throughout, it amounts to nearly the same; provided the gain by the extraordinary, should appear to be no greater than the loss by the ordinary, revenue. And perhaps, if every gentleman in the kingdom was to be stripped of such of his lands as were formerly the property of the crown; was to be again subject to the inconveniences of purveyance and pre-emption, the oppression of forest laws, and the slavery of feodal tenures; and was to resign into the king's hands all his royal franchises of waifs, wrecks, estrays, treasure-trove, mines, deodands, forfeitures, and the like; he would find himself a greater loser, than by paying his *quota* to such taxes, as are necessary to the support of government. The thing therefore to be wished and aimed at in a land of liberty, is by no means the total abolition of taxes, which would draw after it very pernicious consequences, and the very supposition of which is the height of political absurdity. For as the true idea of government and magistracy will be found to consist in this, that some few men are deputed by many others to preside over public affairs, so that individuals may the better be enabled to attend to their private concerns; it is necessary that those individuals should be bound to contribute a portion of their private gains, in order to support that government, and reward that magistracy, which protects them in the enjoyment of their respective properties. But the things to be aimed at are wisdom and moderation, not only in granting, but also in the method of raising, the necessary supplies; by contriving to do both in such a manner as may be most conducive to the national welfare and at the same time most consistent with oeconomy and the liberty of the subject; who, when properly taxed, contributes only, as was before observed, some part of his property, in order to enjoy the rest.

T H E S E extraordinary grants are usually called by the synonymous names of aids, subsidies, and supplies; and are granted, we have formerly seen, by the commons of Great Britain, in parliament assembled: who, when they have voted a supply to his majesty, and settled the *quantum* of that supply, usually resolve themselves into what is called a committee of ways and means, to consider of the ways and means of raising the supply so voted. And in this committee every member (though it is looked upon as the peculiar province of the chancellor of the exchequer) may propose such scheme of taxation as he thinks will be least detrimental to the public. The resolutions of this committee (when approved by a vote of the house) are in general esteemed to be (as it were) final and conclusive. For, through the supply cannot be actually raised upon the subject till directed by an act of the whole parliament, yet no monied man will scruple to advance to the government any quantity of ready cash, on the credit of a bare vote of the house of commons, though no law be yet passed to establish it.

T H E taxes, which are raised upon the subject, are either annual or perpetual. The usual annual taxes are those upon land and malt.

I. T H E land tax, in it's modern shape, has superseded all the former methods of rating either property, or persons in respect of their property, whether by tenths or fifteenths, subsidies on land, hydages, scutages, or talliages; a short explication of which will greatly assist us in understanding our antient laws and history.

T E N T H S, and fifteenths, were temporary aids issuing out of personal property, and granted to the king by parliament. They were formerly the real tenth or fifteenth part of all the moveables belonging to the subject; when such moveables, or personal estates, were a very different and a much less considerable thing than what they usually are at this day. Tenths are said to have been first granted under Henry the second, who took advantage of the fashionable zeal for croisades to introduce this new taxation, in order to defray the expense of a pious expedition to Palestine, which he really or seemingly had projected against Saladine emperor of the Saracens; whence it was originally denominated the Saladine tenth. But afterwards fifteenths were more usually granted than tenths. Originally the amount of these taxes was uncertain, being levied by assessments new made at every fresh grant of the commons, a commission for which is preserved by Matthew Paris: but it was at length reduced to a certainty in the eighth of Edw. III. when, by virtue of the king's commission, new taxations were made of every township, borough, and city in the kingdom, and recorded in the exchequer; which rate was, at the time, the fifteenth part of the value of every township, the whole amounting to about 29000*l.* and therefore it still kept up the name of a fifteenth, when, by the alteration of the value of money and the encrease of personal property, things came to be in a very different situation. So that when, of later years, the commons granted the king a fifteenth, every parish in England immediately knew their proportion of it; that is, the same identical sum that was assessed by the same aid in the eighth of Edw. III; and then raised it by a rate among themselves, and returned it into the royal exchequer.

T H E other antient levies were in the nature of a modern land tax; for we may trace up the original of that charge as high as to the introduction of our military tenures; when every tenant of a knight's fee was bound, if called upon, to attend the king in his army for forty days in every year. But this personal attendance growing troublesome in many respects, the tenants found means of compounding for it, by first sending others in their stead, and in process of time by making a pecuniary satisfaction to the crown in lieu of it. This pecuniary satisfaction at last came to be levied by assessments, at so much for every knight's fee, under the name of scutages; which appear to have been levied for the first time in the fifth year of Henry the second, on account of his expedition to Toulouse, and were then (I apprehend) mere arbitrary compositions, as the king and the subject could agree. But this precedent being afterwards abused into a means of oppression, (by levying scutages on the landholders by the royal authority only, whenever our kings went to war, in order to hire mercenary troops and pay their contingent expences) it became thereupon a matter of national complaint; and king John was obliged to promise in his *magna carta*, that no scutage should be imposed without the consent of the common council of the realm. This clause was indeed omitted in the charters of Henry III, where we only find it stipulated, that scutages should be taken as they were used to be in the time of king Henry the second. Yet afterwards, by a variety of statutes under Edward I and his grandson, it was provided, that the king shall not take any aids or tasks, any talliage or tax, but by the common assent of the great men and commons in parliament.

O F the same nature with scutages upon knights-fees were the assessments of hydage upon all other lands, and of talliage upon cities and burghs. But they all gradually fell into disuse, upon the introduction of subsidies, about the time of king Richard II and king Henry IV. These were a tax, not immediately imposed upon property, but upon persons in respect of their reputed estates, after the nominal rate of 4s. in the pound for lands, and 2s. 6d. for goods; and for those of aliens in a double proportion. But this assessment was also made according to an antient valuation; wherein the computation was so very moderate, and the rental of the kingdom was supposed to be so exceeding low, that one subsidy of this sort did not, according to sir Edward Coke, amount to more than 70000l. whereas a modern land tax at the same rate produces two millions. It was antiently the rule never to grant more than one subsidy, and two fifteenths at a time; but this rule was broke through for the first time on a very pressing occasion, the Spanish invasion in 1588; when the parliament gave queen Elizabeth two subsidies and four fifteenths. Afterwards, as money sunk in value, more subsidies were given; and we have an instance in the first parliament of 1640, of the king's desiring twelve subsidies of the commons, to be levied in three years; which was looked upon as a startling proposal: though lord Clarendon tells us, that the speaker, serjeant Glanvile, made it manifest to the house, how very inconsiderable a sum twelve subsidies amounted to, by telling them he had computed what he was to pay for them; and, when he named the sum, he being known to be possessed of a great estate, it seemed not worth any farther deliberation. And indeed, upon calculation, we shall find, that the total amount of these twelve subsidies, to be raised in three years, is less than what is now raised in one year, by a land tax of two shillings in the pound.

THE grant of scutages, talliages, or subsidies by the commons did not extend to spiritual preferments; those being usually taxed at the same time by the clergy themselves in convocation; which grants of the clergy were confirmed in parliament, otherwise they were illegal, and not binding; as the same noble writer observes of the subsidies granted by the convocation, who continued sitting after the dissolution of the first parliament in 1640. A subsidy granted by the clergy was after the rate of 4s. in the pound according to the valuation of their livings in the king's books; and amounted, sir Edward Coke tells us, to about 20000l. While this custom continued, convocations were wont to sit as frequently as parliaments: but the last subsidies, thus given by the clergy, were those confirmed by statute 15 Car. II. cap. 10. since which another method of taxation has generally prevailed, which takes in the clergy as well as the laity; in recompense for which the beneficed clergy have from that period been allowed to vote at the elections of knights of the shire; and thenceforward also the practice of giving ecclesiastical subsidies hath fallen into total disuse.

THE lay subsidy was usually raised by commissioners appointed by the crown, or the great officers of state: and therefore in the beginning of the civil wars between Charles I and his parliament, the latter, having no other sufficient revenue to support themselves and their measures, introduced the practice of laying weekly and monthly assessments of a specific sum upon the several counties of the kingdom; to be levied by a pound rate on lands and personal estates: which were occasionally continued during the whole usurpation, sometimes at the rate of 120000l. a month; sometimes at inferior rates. After the restoration the antient method of granting subsidies, instead of such monthly assessments, was twice, and twice only, renewed; viz. in 1663, when four subsidies were granted by the temporalty, and four by the clergy; and in 1670, when 800000l. was raised by way of subsidy, which was the last time of raising supplies in that manner. For, the monthly assessments being now established by custom, being raised by commissioners named by parliament, and producing a more certain revenue; from that time forwards we hear no more of subsidies; but occasional assessments were granted as the national emergencies required. These periodical assessments, the subsidies which preceded them, and the more antient scutage, hydage, and talliage, were to all intents and purposes a land tax; and the assessments were sometimes expressly called so. Yet a popular opinion has prevailed, that the land tax was first introduced in the reign of king William III; because in the year 1692 a new assessment or valuation of estates was made throughout the kingdom; which, though by no means a perfect one, had this effect, that a supply of 500000l. was equal to 1s. in the pound of the value of the estates given in. And, according to this enhanced valuation, from the year 1693 to the present, a period of above seventy years, the land tax has continued an annual charge upon the subject; above half the time at 4*s*. in the pound, sometimes at 3*s*, sometimes at 2*s*, twice at 1*s*, but without any total intermission. The medium has been 3*s*.3*d*. in the pound, being equivalent to twenty three antient subsidies, and amounting annually to more than a million and an half of money. The method of raising it is by charging a particular sum upon each county, according to the valuation given in, *A.D.* 1692: and this sum is assessed and raised upon individuals (their personal estates, as well as real, being liable thereto) by commissioners appointed in the act, being the principal landholders of the county, and their officers.

II. T H E other annual tax is the malt tax; which is a sum of 750000*l*, raised every year by parliament, ever since 1697, by a duty of 6*d*.in the bushel on malt, and a proportionable sum on certain liquors, such as cyder and perry, which might otherwise prevent the consumption of malt. This is under the management of the commissioners of the excise; and is indeed itself no other than an annual excise, the nature of which species of taxation I shall presently explain: only premising at present, that in the year 1760 an additional perpetual excise of 3*d. per* bushel was laid upon malt; and in 1763 a proportionable excise was laid upon cyder and perry.

T H E perpetual taxes are,

I. T H E customs; or the duties, toll, tribute, or tariff, payable upon merchandize exported and imported. The considerations upon which this revenue (or the more antient part of it, which arose only from exports) was invested in the king, were said to be two; 1. Because he gave the subject leave to depart the kingdom, and to carry his goods along with him. 2. Because the king was bound of common right to maintain and keep up the ports and havens, and to protect the merchant from pirates. Some have imagined they are called with us customs, because they were the inheritance of the king by immemorial usage and the common law, and not granted him by any statute: but sir Edward Coke hath clearly shewn, that the king's first claim to them was by grant of parliament 3 Edw. I. though the record thereof is not now extant. And indeed this is in express words confessed by statute 25 Edw. I. c. 7. wherein the king promises to take no customs from merchants, without the common assent of the realm, "saving to us and our heirs, the customs on wools, skins, and leather, formerly granted to us by the commonalty aforesaid." These were formerly called the hereditary customs of the crown; and were due on the exportation only of the said three commodities, and of none other: which were stiled the *staple* commodities of the kingdom, because they were obliged to be brought to those ports where the king's staple was established, in order to be there first rated, and then exported. They were denominated in the barbarous Latin of our antient records, *custuma*; not *consuetudines*, which is the language of our law whenever it means merely usages. The duties on wool, sheep-skins, or woolfells, and leather, exported, were called *custuma antiqua sive magna*; and were payable by every merchant, as well native as stranger; with this difference, that merchant-strangers paid an additional toll, *viz.* half as much again as was paid by natives. The *custuma parva et nova* were an impost of 3*d*. in the pound, due from merchant-strangers only, for all commodities as well imported as exported; which was usually called the alien's duty, and was first granted in 31 Edw. I. But these antient hereditary customs, especially those on wool and woolfells, came to be of little account when the nation became sensible of the advantages of a home manufacture, and prohibited the exportation of wool by statute 11 Edw. III. c. 1.

THERE is also another antient hereditary duty belonging to the crown, called the *prisage* or *butlerage* of wines. Prisage was a right of *taking* two tons of wine from every ship importing into England twenty tons or more; which by Edward I was exchanged into a duty of 2*s.* for every ton imported by merchant-strangers; which is called butlerage, because paid to the king's butler.

OTHER customs payable upon exports and imports are distinguished into subsidies, tonnage, poundage, and other imposts. Subsidies are such as were imposed by parliament upon any of the staple commodities before mentioned, over and above the *custuma antiqua et magna*: tonnage was a duty upon all wines imported, over and above the prisage and butlerage aforesaid: poundage was a duty imposed *ad valorem*, at the rate of 12*d.* in the pound, on all other merchandize whatsoever: and the other imports were such as were occasionally laid on by parliament, as circumstances and times required. These distinctions are now in a manner forgotten, except by the officers immediately concerned in this department; their produce being in effect all blended together, under the one denomination of the customs.

BY these we understand, at present, a duty or subsidy paid by the merchant, at the quay, upon all imported as well as exported commodities, by authority of parliament; unless where, for particular national reasons, certain rewards, bounties, or drawbacks, are allowed for particular exports or imports. Those of tonnage and poundage, in particular, were at first granted, as the old statutes, and particularly 1 Eliz. c. 19. express it, for the defence of the realm, and the keeping and safeguard of the seas, and for the intercourse of merchandize safely to come into and pass out of the same. They were at first usually granted only for a stated term of years, as, for two years in 5 Ric. II; but in Henry the fifth's time, they were granted him for life by a statute in the third year of his reign; and again to Edward IV for the term of his life also: since which time they were regularly granted to all his successors, for life, sometimes at their first, sometimes at other subsequent parliaments, till the reign of Charles the first; when, as had before happened in the reign of Henry VIII and other princes, they were neglected to be asked. And yet they were imprudently and unconstitutionally levied and taken without consent of parliament, (though more than one had been assembled) for fifteen years together; which was one of the causes of those unhappy discontents, justifiable at first in too many instances, but which degenerated at last into causeless rebellion and murder. For, as in every other, so in this particular case, the king (previous to the commencement of hostilities) gave the nation ample satisfaction for the errors of his former conduct, by passing an act, whereby he renounced all power in the crown of levying the duty of tonnage and poundage, without the express consent of parliament; and also all power of imposition upon any merchandizes whatever. Upon the restoration this duty was granted to king Charles the second for life, and so it was to his two immediate successors; but now by three several statutes, 9 Ann. c. 6. 1 Geo. l. c. 12. and 3 Geo. l. c. 7. it is made perpetual and mortgaged for the debt of the publick. The customs, thus imposed by parliament, are chiefly contained in two books of rates, set forth by parliamentary authority; one signed by sir Harbottle Grimston, speaker of the house of commons in Charles the second's time; and the other an additional one signed by sir Spenser Compton, speaker in the reign of George the first; to which also subsequent additions have been made. Aliens pay a larger proportion than natural subjects, which is what is now generally understood by the aliens' duty; to be exempted from which is one principal cause of the frequent applications to parliament for acts of naturalization.

THESE customs are then, we see, a tax immediately paid by the merchant, although ultimately by the consumer. And yet these are the duties felt least by the people; and, if prudently managed, the people hardly consider that they pay them at all. For the merchant is easy, being sensible he does not pay them for himself; and the consumer, who really pays them, confounds them with the price of the commodity: in the same manner as Tacitus observes, that the emperor Nero gained the reputation of abolishing the tax on the sale of slaves, though he only transferred it from the buyer to the seller; so that it was, as he expresses it, "*remissum magis specie, quam vi: quia cum venditor pendere juberetur, in partem pretii emptoribus accrescebat.*" But this inconvenience attends it on the other hand, that these imposts, if too heavy, are a check and cramp upon trade; and especially when the value of the commodity bears little or no proportion to the quantity of the duty imposed. This in consequence gives rise also to smuggling, which then becomes a very lucrativeemployment: and it's natural and most reasonable punishment, *viz.* confiscation of the commodity, is in such cases quite ineffectual; the intrinsic value of the goods, which is all that the smuggler has paid, and therefore all that he can lose, being very inconsiderable when compared with his prospect of advantage in evading the duty. Recourse must therefore be had to extraordinary punishments to prevent it; perhaps even to capital ones: which destroys all proportion of punishment, and puts murderers upon an equal footing with such as are really guilty of no natural, but merely a positive offence.

THERE is also another ill consequence attending high imports on merchandize, not frequently considered, but indisputably certain; that the earlier any tax is laid on a commodity, the heavier it falls upon the consumer in the end: for every trader, through whose hands it passes, must have a profit, not only upon the raw material and his own labour and time in preparing it, but also upon the very tax itself, which he advances to the government; otherwise he loses the use and interest of the money which he so advances. To instance in the article of foreign paper. The merchant pays a duty upon importation, which he does not receive again till he sells the commodity, perhaps at the end of three months. He is therefore equally entitled to a profit upon that duty which he pays at the customhouse, as to a profit upon the original price which he pays to the manufacturer abroad; and considers it accordingly in the price he demands of the stationer. When the stationer sells it again, he requires a profit of the printer or bookseller upon the whole sum advanced by him to the merchant: and the bookseller does not forget to charge the full proportion to the student or ultimate consumer; who therefore does not only pay the original duty, but the profits of these three intermediate traders, who have successively advanced it for him. This might be carried much farther in any mechanical, or more complicated, branch of trade.

II. DIRECTLY opposite in it's nature to this is the excise duty; which is an inland imposition, paid sometimes upon the consumption of the commodity, or frequently upon the retail sale, which is the last stage before the consumption. This is doubtless, impartially speaking, the most oeconomical way of taxing the subject: the charges of levying, collecting, and managing the excise duties being considerably less in proportion, than in any other branch of the revenue. It also renders the commodity cheaper to the consumer, than charging it with customs to the same amount would do; for the reason just now given, because generally paid in a much later stage of it. But, at the same time, the rigour and arbitrary proceedings of excise-laws seem hardly compatible with the temper of a free nation. For the frauds that might be committed in this branch of the revenue, unless a strict watch is kept, make it necessary, wherever it is established, to give the officers a power of entring and searching the houses of such as deal in excisable commodities, at any hour of the day, and, in many cases, of the night likewise. And the proceedings in case of transgressions are so summary and sudden, that a man may be convicted in two days time in the penalty of many thousand pounds by two commissioners or justices of the peace; to the total exclusion of the trial by jury, and disregard of the common law. For which reason, though lord Clarendon tells us, that to his knowlege the earl of Bedford (who was made lord treasurer by king Charles the first, to oblige his parliament) intended to have set up the excise in England, yet it never made a part of that unfortunate prince's revenue; being first introduced, on the model of the Dutch prototype, by the parliament itself after it's rupture with the crown. Yet such was the opinion of it's general unpopularity, that when in 1642 "aspersions were cast by malignant persons upon the house of commons, that they intended to introduce excises, the house for it's vindication therein did declare, that these rumours were false and scandalous; and that their authors should be apprehended and brought to condign punishment." It's original establishment was in 1643, and it's progress was gradual; being at first laid upon those persons and commodities, where it was supposed the hardship would be least perceivable, *viz.* the makers and venders of beer, ale, cyder, and perry; and the royalists at Oxford soon followed the example of their brethren at Westminster by imposing a similar duty; both sides protesting that it should be continued no longer than to the end of the war, and then be utterly abolished. But the parliament at Westminster soon after imposed it on flesh, wine, tobacco, sugar, and such a multitude of other commodities that it might fairly be denominated general; in pursuance of the plan laid down by Mr Pymme (who seems to have been the father of the excise) in his letter to sir John Hotham, signifying, "that they had proceeded in the excise to many particulars, and intended to go on farther; but that it would be necessary to use the people to it by little and little." And afterwards, when the people had been accustomed to it for a series of years, the succeeding champions of liberty boldly and openly declared, "the impost of excise to be the most easy and indifferent levy that could be laid upon the people:" and accordingly continued it during the whole usurpation. Upon king Charles's return, it having then been long established and it's produce well known, some part of it was given to the crown, in the 12 Car. II, by way of purchase (as was before observed) for the feodal tenures and other oppressive parts of the hereditary revenue. But, from it's first original to the present time, it's very name has been odious to the people of England. It has nevertheless been imposed on abundance of other commodities in the reigns of king William III, and every succeeding prince, to support the enormous expenses occasioned by our wars on the continent. Thus brandies and other spirits are now excised at the distillery; printed silks and linens, at the printers; starch and hair powder, at the maker's; gold and silver wire, at the wiredrawer's; all plate whatsoever, first in the hands of the vendor, who pays yearly for a licence to sell it, and afterwards in the hands of the occupier, who also pays an annual duty for having it in his custody; and coaches and other wheel carriages, for which the occupier is excised; though not with the same circumstances of arbitrary strictness with regard to plate and coaches, as in the other instances. To these we may add coffee and tea, chocolate, and cocoa paste, for which the duty is paid by the retailer; all artificial wines, commonly called sweets; paper and pasteboard, first when made, and again if stained or printed; malt as before-mentioned; vinegars; and the manufacture of glass; for all which the duty is paid by the manufacturer; hops, for which the person that gathers them is answerable; candles and soap, which are paid for at the maker's; malt liquors brewed for sale, which are excised at the brewery; cyder and perry, at the mill; and leather and skins, at the tanner's. A list, which no friend to his country would wish to see farther encreased.

III. I PROCEED therefore to a third duty, namely that upon salt; which is another distinct branch of his majesty's extraordinary revenue, and consists in an excise of 3s. 4d. per bushel imposed upon all salt, by several statutes of king William and other subsequent reigns. This is not generally called an excise, because under the management of different commissioners: but the commissioners of the salt duties have by statute 1 Ann. c. 21. the same powers, and must observe the same regulations, as those of other excises. This tax had usually been only temporary; but by statute 26 Geo. II. c. 3. was made perpetual.

IV. ANOTHER very considerable branch of the revenue is levied with greater chearfulness, as, instead of being a burden, it is a manifest advantage to the public. I mean the post-office, or duty for the carriage of letters. As we have traced the original of the excise to the parliament of 1643, so it is but justice to observe that this useful invention owes it's birth to the same assembly. It is true, there existed postmasters in much earlier times: but I apprehend their business was confined to the furnishing of posthorses to persons who were desirous to travel expeditiously, and to the dispatching extraordinary pacquets upon special occasions. The outline of the present plan seems to have been originally conceived by Mr Edmond Prideaux, who was appointed attorney general to the commonwealth after the murder of king Charles. He was a chairman of a committee in 1642 for considering what rates should be set upon inland letters; and afterwards appointed postmaster by an ordinance of both the houses, in the execution of which office he first established a weekly conveyance of letters into all parts of the nation: thereby saving to the public the charge of maintaining postmasters, to the amount of 7000*l. per annum.* And, his own emoluments being probably considerable, the common council of London endeavoured to erect another post-office in opposition to his, till checked by a resolution of the commons, declaring, that the office of postmaster is and ought to be in the sole power and disposal of the parliament. This office was afterwards farmed by one Manley in 1654. But, in 1657, a regular post-office was erected by the authority of the protector and his parliament, upon nearly the same model as has been ever since adopted, with the same rates of postage as were continued till the reign of queen Anne. After the restoration a similar office, with some improvements, was established by statute 12 Car. II. c. 35. but the rates of letters were altered, and some farther regulations added, by the statutes 9 Ann. c. 10. 6 Geo. I. c. 21. 26 Geo. II. c. 12. and 5 Geo. III. c. 25. and penalties were enacted, in order to confine the carriage of letters to the public office only, except in some few cases: a provision, which is absolutely necessary; for nothing but an exclusive right can support an office of this sort: many rival independent offices would only serve to ruin one another. The privilege of letters coming free of postage, to and from members of parliament, was claimed by the house of commons in 1660, when the first legal settlement of the present post-office was made; but afterwards dropped upon a private assurance from the crown, that this privilege should be allowed the members. And accordingly a warrant was constantly issued to the postmaster-general, directing the allowance thereof, to to the extent of two ounces in weight: till at length it was expressly confirmed by statute 4 Geo. III. c. 24; which adds many new regulations, rendered necessary by the great abuses crept into the practice of franking; whereby the annual amount of franked letters had gradually increased, from 23600*l.* in the year 1715, to 170700*l.* in the year 1763. There cannot be devised a more eligible method, than this, of raising money upon the subject: for therein both the government and the people find a mutual benefit. The government acquires a large revenue; and the people do their business with greater ease, expedition, and cheapness, than they would be able to do if no such tax (and of course no such office) existed.

V. A FIFTH branch of the perpetual revenue consists in the stamp duties, which are a tax imposed upon all parchment and paper whereon any legal proceedings, or private instruments of almost any nature whatsoever, are written; and also upon licences for retailing wines, of all denominations; upon all almanacks, newspapers, advertisements, cards, dice, and pamphlets containing less than six sheets of paper. These imposts are very various, according to the nature of the thing stamped, rising gradually from a penny to ten pounds. This is also a tax, which though in some instances it may be heavily felt, by greatly increasing the expence of all mercantile as well as legal proceedings, yet (if moderately imposed) is of service to the public in general, by authenticating instruments, and rendering it much more difficult than formerly to forge deeds of any standing; since, as the officers of this branch of the revenue vary their stamps frequently, by marks perceptible to none but themselves, a man that would forge a deed of king William's time, must know and be able to counterfeit the stamp of that date also. In France and some other countries the duty is laid on the contract itself, not on the instrument in which it is contained: but this draws the subject into a thousand nice disquisitions and disputes concerning the nature of his contract, and whether taxable or not; in which the farmers of the revenue are sure to have the advantage. Our method answers the purposes of the state as well, and consults the ease of the subject much better. The first institution of the stamp duties was by statute 5 & 6 W. & M. c. 21. and they have since in many instances been encreased to five times their original amount.

VI. A SIXTH branch is the duty upon houses and windows. As early as the conquest mention is made in domesday book of fumage or fuage, vulgarly called smoke farthings; which were paid by custom to the king for every chimney in the house. And we read that Edward the black prince (soon after his successes in France) in imitation of the English custom, imposed a tax of a florin upon every hearth in his French dominions. But the first parliamentary establishment of it in England was by statute 13 & 14 Car. II. c. 10. whereby an hereditary revenue of 2*s.* for every hearth, in all houses paying to church and poor, was granted to the king for ever. And, by subsequent statutes, for the more regular assessment of this tax, the constable and two other substantial inhabitants of the parish, to be appointed yearly, were, once in every year, empowered to view the inside of every house in the parish. But, upon the revolution, by statute 1 W. & M. st. 1. c. 10. hearth-money was declared to be "not only a great oppression to the poorer sort, but a badge of slavery upon the whole people, exposing every man's house to be entered into, and searched at pleasure, by persons unknown to him; and therefore, to erect a lasting monument of their majesties' goodness in every house in the kingdom, the duty of hearth-money was taken away and abolished." This monument of goodness remains among us to this day: but the prospect of it was somewhat darkened when, in six years afterwards, by statute 7 W. III. c. 18. a tax was laid upon all houses (except cottages) of 2*s.* now advanced to 3*s. per* house, and a tax also upon all windows, if they exceed nine, in such house. Which rates have been from time to time varied, (particularly by statutes 20 Geo. II. c. 3. and 31 Geo. II. c. 22.) and power is given to surveyors, appointed by the crown, to inspect the outside of houses, and also to pass through any house two days in the year, into any court or yard to inspect the windows there.

Mod. Un. Hist. xxiii. 463. Spelm. Gloss. *tit. Fuage.*

VII. THE seventh branch of the extraordinary perpetual revenue is the duty arising from licences to hackney coaches and chairs in London, and the parts adjacent. In 1654 two hundred hackney coaches were allowed within London, Westminster, and six miles round, under the direction of the court of aldermen. By statute 13 & 14 Car. II. c. 2. four hundred were licensed; and the money arising thereby was applied to repairing the streets. This number was increased to seven hundred by statute 5 W. & M. c. 22. and the duties vested in the crown: and by the statute 9 Ann. c. 23. and other subsequent statutes, there are now eight hundred licensed coaches and four hundred chairs. This revenue is governed by commissioners of it's own, and is, in truth, a benefit to the subject; as the expense of it is felt by no individual, and it's necessary regulations have established a competent jurisdiction, whereby a very refractory race of men may be kept in some tolerable order.

VIII. T H E eighth and last branch of the king's extraordinary perpetual revenue is the duty upon offices and pensions; consisting in a payment of 1*s.* in the pound (over and above all other duties) out of all salaries, fees, and perquisites, of offices and pensions payable by the crown. This highly popular taxation was imposed by statute 31 Geo. II. c. 22. and is under the direction of the commissioners of the land tax.

T H E clear neat produce of these several branches of the revenue, after all charges of collecting and management paid, amounts annually to about seven millions and three quarters sterling; besides two millions and a quarter raised annually, at an average, by the land and malt tax. How these immense sums are appropriated, is next to be considered. And this is, first and principally, to the payment of the interest of the national debt.

I N order to take a clear and comprehensive view of the nature of this national debt, it must first be premised, that after the revolution, when our new connections with Europe introduced a new system of foreign politics, the expenses of the nation, not only in settling the new establishment, but in maintaining long wars, as principals, on the continent, for the security of the Dutch barrier, reducing the French monarchy, settling the Spanish succession, supporting the house of Austria, maintaining the liberties of the Germanic body, and other purposes, increased to an unusual degree: insomuch that it was not thought advisable to raise all the expenses of any one year by taxes to be levied within that year, lest the unaccustomed weight of them should create murmurs among the people. It was therefore the policy of the times, to anticipate the revenues of their posterity, by borrowing immense sums for the current service of the state, and to lay no more taxes upon the subject than would suffice to pay the annual interest of the sums so borrowed: by this means converting the principal debt into a new species of property, transferrable from one man to another at any time and in any quantity. A system which seems to have had it's original in the state of Florence, *A.D.* 1344: which government then owed about 60000*l.* sterling; and, being unable to pay it, formed the principal into an aggregate sum, called metaphorically a *mount* or *bank*, the shares whereof were transferrable like our stocks, with interest at 5 *per cent.* the prices varying according to the exigencies of the state. This laid the foundation of what is called the national debt: for a few long annuities created in the reign of Charles II will hardly deserve that name. And the example then set has been so closely followed during the long wars in the reign of queen Anne, and since, that the capital of the national debt, (funded and unfunded) amounted in January 1765 to upwards of 145,000,000*l.* to pay the interest of which, and the charges for management, amounting annually to about four millions and three quarters, the revenues just enumerated are in the first place mortgaged, and made perpetual by parliament. Perpetual, I say; but still redeemable by the same authority that imposed them: which, if it at any time can pay off the capital, will abolish those taxes which are raised to discharge the interest.

B Y this means the quantity of property in the kingdom is greatly encreased in idea, compared with former times; yet, if we coolly consider it, not at all encreased in reality. We may boast of large fortunes, and quantities of money in the funds. But where does this money exist? It exists only in name, in paper, in public faith, in parliamentary security: and that is undoubtedly sufficient for the creditors of the public to rely on. But then what is the pledge which the public faith has pawned for the security of these debts? The land, the trade, and the personal industry of the subject; from which the money must arise that supplies the several taxes. In these therefore, and these only, the property of the public creditors does really and intrinsically exist: and of course the land, the trade, and the personal industry of individuals, are diminished in their true value just so much as they are pledged to answer. If A's income amounts to 100*l. per annum*; and he is so far indebted to B, that he pays him 50*l. per annum* for his interest; one half of the value of A's property is transferred to B the creditor. The creditor's property exists in the demand which he has upon the debtor, and no where else; and the debtor is only a trustee to his creditor for one half of the value of his income. In short, the property of a creditor of the publick, consists in a certain portion of the national taxes: by how much therefore he is the richer, by so much the nation, which pays these taxes, is the poorer.

T H E only advantage, that can result to a nation from public debts, is the encrease of circulation by multiplying the cash of the kingdom, and creating a new species of money, always ready to be employed in any beneficial undertaking, by means of it's transferrable quality; and yet productive of some profit, even when it lies idle and unemployed. A certain proportion of debt seems therefore to be highly useful to a trading people; but what that proportion is, it is not for me to determine. Thus much is indisputably certain, that the present magnitude of our national incumbrances very far exceeds all calculations of commercial benefit, and is productive of the greatest inconveniences. For, first, the enormous taxes, that are raised upon the necessaries of life for the payment of the interest of this debt, are a hurt both to trade and manufactures, by raising the price as well of the artificer's subsistence, as of the raw material, and of course, in a much greater proportion, the price of the commodity itself. Secondly, if part of this debt be owing to foreigners, either they draw out of the kingdom annually a considerable quantity of specie for the interest; or else it is made an argument to grant them unreasonable privileges in order to induce them to reside here. Thirdly, if the whole be owing to subjects only, it is then charging the active and industrious subject, who pays his share of the taxes, to maintain the indolent and idle creditor who receives them. Lastly, and principally, it weakens the internal strength of a state, by anticipating those resources which should be reserved to defend it in case of necessity. The interest we now pay for our debts would be nearly sufficient to maintain any war, that any national motives could require. And if our ancestors in king William's time had annually paid, so long as their exigences lasted, even a less sum than we now annually raise upon their accounts, they would in the time of war have borne no greater burdens, than they have bequeathed to and settled upon their posterity in time of peace; and might have been eased the instant the exigence was over.

THE produce of the several taxes beforementioned were originally separate and distinct funds; being securities for the sums advanced on each several tax, and for them only. But at last it became necessary, in order to avoid confusion, as they multiplied yearly, to reduce the number of these separate funds, by uniting and blending them together; superadding the faith of parliament for the general security of the whole. So that there are now only three capital funds of any account, the *aggregate* fund, and the *general* fund, so called from such union and addition; and the *south sea* fund, being the produce of the taxes appropriated to pay the interest of such part of the national debt as was advanced by that company and it's annuitants. Whereby the separate funds, which were thus united, are become mutual securities for each other; and the whole produce of them, thus aggregated, is liable to pay such interest or annuities as were formerly charged upon each distinct fund; the faith of the legislature being moreover engaged to supply any casual deficiences.

THE customs, excises, and other taxes, which are to support these funds, depending on contingencies, upon exports, imports, and consumptions, must necessarily be of a very uncertain amount; but they have always been considerably more than was sufficient to answer the charge upon them. The surplusses therefore of the three great national funds, the aggregate, general, and south sea funds, over and above the interest and annuities charged upon them, are directed by statute 3 Geo. I. c. 7. to be carried together, and to attend the disposition of parliament; and are usually denominated the *sinking* fund, because originally destined to sink and lower the national debt. To this have been since added many other intire duties, granted in subsequent years; and the annual interest of the sums borrowed on their respective credits is charged on and payable out of the produce of the sinking fund. However the neat surplusses and savings, after all deductions paid, amount annually to a very considerable sum; particularly in the year ending at Christmas 1764, to about two millions and a quarter. For, as the interest on the national debt has been at several times reduced, (by the consent of the proprietors, who had their option either to lower their interest or be paid their principal) the savings from the appropriated revenues must needs be extremely large. This sinking fund is the last resort of the nation; on which alone depend all the hopes we can entertain of ever discharging or moderating our incumbrances. And therefore the prudent application of the large sums, now arising from this fund, is a point of the utmost importance, and well worthy the serious attention of parliament; which has thereby been enabled, in this present year 1765, to reduce above two millions sterling of the public debt.

BUT, before any part of the aggregate fund (the surplusses whereof are one of the chief ingredients that form the sinking fund) can be applied to diminish the principal of the public debt, it stands mortgaged by parliament to raise an annual sum for the maintenance of the king's houshold and the civil list. For this purpose, in the late reigns, the produce of certain branches of the excise and customs, the post-office, the duty on wine licences, the revenues of the remaining crown lands, the profits arising from courts of justice, (which articles include all the hereditary revenues of the crown) and also a clear annuity of 120000*l.* in money, were settled on the king for life, for the support of his majesty's houshold, and the honour and dignity of the crown. And, as the amount of these several branches was uncertain, (though in the last reign they were generally computed to raise almost a million) if they did not arise annually to 800,000*l.* the parliament engaged to make up the deficiency. But his present majesty having, soon after his accession, spontaneously signified his consent, that his own hereditary revenues might be so disposed of as might best conduce to the utility and satisfaction of the public, and having graciously accepted the limited sum of 800000*l. per annum* for the support of his civil list (and that also charged with three life annuities, to the princess of Wales, the duke of Cumberland, and the princess Amalie, to the amount of 77000*l.*) the said hereditary and other revenues are now carried into and made a part of the aggregate fund, and the aggregate fund is charged with the payment of the whole annuity to the crown of 800000*l. per annum.* Hereby the revenues themselves, being put under the same care and management as the other branches of the public patrimony, will produce more and be better collected than heretofore; and the public is a gainer of upwards of 100000*l. per annum* by this disinterested bounty of his majesty. The civil list, thus liquidated, together with the four millions and three quarters, interest of the national debt, and the two millions and a quarter produced from the sinking fund, make up the seven millions and three quarters *per annum*, neat money, which were before stated to be the annual produce of our *perpetual* taxes; besides the immense, though uncertain, sums arising from the *annual* taxes on land and malt, but which, at an average, may be calculated at more than two millions and a quarter; and, added to the preceding sum, make the clear produce of the taxes, exclusive of the charge of collecting, which are raised yearly on the people of this country, and returned into the king's exchequer, amount to upwards of ten millions sterling.

T H E expences defrayed by the civil list are those that in any shape relate to civil government; as, the expenses of the houshold; all salaries to officers of state, to the judges, and every of the king's servants; the appointments to foreign embassadors; the maintenance of the royal family; the king's private expenses, or privy purse; and other very numerous outgoings, as secret service money, pensions, and other bounties: which sometimes have so far exceeded the revenues appointed for that purpose, that application has been made to parliament to discharge the debts contracted on the civil list; as particularly in 1724, when one million was granted for that purpose by the statute 11 Geo. I. c. 17.

T H E civil list is indeed properly the whole of the king's revenue in his own distinct capacity; the rest being rather the revenue of the public, or it's creditors, though collected, and distributed again, in the name and by the officers of the crown: it now standing in the same place, as the hereditary income did formerly; and, as that has gradually diminished, the parliamentary appointments have encreased. The whole revenue of queen Elizabeth did not amount to more than 600000*l.* a year: that of king Charles I was 800000*l.* and the revenue voted for king Charles II was 1200000*l.* though it never in fact amounted to quite so much. But it must be observed, that under these sums were included all manner of public expenses, among which lord Clarendon in his speech to the parliament computed that the charge of the navy and land forces amounted annually to 800000*l.* which was ten times more than before the former troubles. The same revenue, subject to the same charges, was settled on on king James II: but by the encrease of trade, and more frugal management, it amounted on an average to a million and half *per annum*, (besides other additional customs, granted by parliament, which produced an annual revenue of 400000*l*.) out of which his fleet and army were maintained at the yearly expense of 1100000*l*.After the revolution, when the parliament took into it's own hands the annual support of the forces, both maritime and military, a civil list revenue was settled on the new king and queen, amounting, with the hereditary duties, to 700000*l*. *per annum*; and the same was continued to queen Anne and king George I. That of king George II, we have seen, was nominally augmented to 800000*l*. and in fact was considerably more. But that of his present majesty is expressly limited to that sum; and, by reason of the charges upon it, amounts at present to little more than 700000*l*. And upon the whole it is doubtless much better for the crown, and also for the people, to have the revenue settled upon the modern footing rather than the antient. For the crown; because it is more certain, and collected with greater ease: for the people; because they are now delivered from the feodal hardships, and other odious branches of the prerogative. And though complaints have sometimes been made of the encrease of the civil list, yet if we consider the sums that have been formerly granted, the limited extent under which it is now established, the revenues and prerogatives given up in lieu of it by the crown, and (above all) the diminution of the value of money compared with what it was worth in the last century, we must acknowlege these complaints to be void of any rational foundation; and that it is impossible to support that dignity, which a king of Great Britain should maintain, with an income in any degree less than what is now established by parliament. This finishes our enquiries into the fiscal prerogatives of the king; or his revenue, both ordinary and extraordinary. We have therefore now chalked out all the principal outlines of this vast title of the law, the supreme executive magistrate, or the king's majesty, considered in his several capacities and points of view. But, before we intirely dismiss this subject, it may not be improper to take a short comparative review of the power of the executive magistrate, or prerogative of the crown, as it stood in former days, and as it stands at present. And we cannot but observe, that most of the laws for ascertaining, limiting, and restraining this prerogative have been made within the compass of little more than a century past; from the petition of right in 3 Car. I. to the present time. So that the powers of the crown are now to all appearance greatly curtailed and diminished since the reign of king James the first: particularly, by the abolition of the star chamber and high commission courts in the reign of Charles the first, and by the disclaiming of martial law, and the power of levying taxes on the subject, by the same prince: by the disuse of forest laws for a century past: and by the many excellent provisions enacted under Charles the second; especially, the abolition of military tenures, purveyance, and preemption; the *habeas corpus* act; and the act to prevent the discontinuance of parliaments for above three years: and, since the revolution, by the strong and emphatical words in which our liberties are asserted in the bill of rights, and act of settlement; by the act for triennial, since turned into septennial, elections; by the exclusion of certain officers from the house of commons; by rendering the seats of the judges permanent, and their salaries independent;

and by restraining the king's pardon from operating on parliamentary impeachments. Besides all this, if we consider how the crown is impoverished and stripped of all it's antient revenues, so that it greatly depends on the liberality of parliament for it's necessary support and maintenance, we may perhaps be led to think, that the ballance is enclined pretty strongly to the popular scale, and that the executive magistrate has neither independence nor power enough left, to form that check upon the lords and commons, which the founders of our constitution intended.

B U T , on the other hand, it is to be considered, that every prince, in the first parliament after his accession, has by long usage a truly royal addition to his hereditary revenue settled upon him for his life; and has never any occasion to apply to parliament for supplies, but upon some public necessity of the whole realm. This restores to him that constitutional independence, which at his first accession seems, it must be owned, to be wanting. And then, with regard to power, we may find perhaps that the hands of government are at least sufficiently strengthened; and that an English monarch is now in no danger of being overborne by either the nobility or the people. The instruments of power are not perhaps so open and avowed as they formerly were, and therefore are the less liable to jealous and invidious reflections; but they are not the weaker upon that account. In short, our national debt and taxes (besides the inconveniences before-mentioned) have also in their natural consequences thrown such a weight of power into the executive scale of government, as we cannot think was intended by our patriot ancestors; who gloriously struggled for the abolition of the then formidable parts of the prerogative; and by an unaccountable want of foresight established this system in their stead. The entire collection and management of so vast a revenue, being placed in the hands of the crown, have given rise to such a multitude of new officers, created by and removeable at the royal pleasure, that they have extended the influence of government to every corner of the nation. Witness the commissioners, and the multitude of dependents on the customs, in every port of the kingdom; the commissioners of excise, and their numerous subalterns, in every inland district; the postmasters, and their servants, planted in every town, and upon every public road; the commissioners of the stamps, and their distributors, which are full as scattered and full as numerous; the officers of the salt duty, which, though a species of excise and conducted in the same manner, are yet made a distinct corps from the ordinary managers of that revenue; the surveyors of houses and windows; the receivers of the land tax; the managers of lotteries; and the commissioners of hackney coaches; all which are either mediately or immediately appointed by the crown, and removeable at pleasure without any reason assigned: these, it requires but little penetration to see, must give that power, on which they depend for subsistence, an influence most amazingly extensive. To this may be added the frequent opportunities of conferring particular obligations, by preference in loans, subscriptions, tickets, remittances, and other money-transactions, which will greatly encrease this influence; and that over those persons whose attachment, on account of their wealth, is frequently the most desirable. All this is the natural, though perhaps the unforeseen, consequence of erecting our funds of credit, and to support them establishing our present perpetual taxes: the whole of which is entirely new since the restoration in 1660; and by far the greatest part since the revolution in 1688. And the same may be said with regard to the officers in our numerous army, and the places which the army has created. All which put together gives the executive power so persuasive an energy with respect to the persons themselves, and so prevailing an interest with their friends and families, as will amply make amends for the loss of external prerogative.

B U T , though this profusion of offices should have no effect on individuals, there is still another newly acquired branch of power; and that is, not the influence only, but the force of a disciplined army: paid indeed ultimately by the people, but immediately by the crown; raised by the crown, officered by the crown, commanded by the crown. They are kept on foot it is true only from year to year, and that by the power of parliament: but during that year they must, by the nature of our constitution, if raised at all, be at the absolute disposal of the crown. And there need but few words to demonstrate how great a trust is thereby reposed in the prince by his people. A trust, that is more than equivalent to a thousand little troublesome prerogatives. A dd to all this, that, besides the civil list, the immense revenue of seven millions sterling, which is annually paid to the creditors of the publick, or carried to the sinking fund, is first deposited in the royal exchequer, and thence issued out to the respective offices of payment. This revenue the people can never refuse to raise, because it is made perpetual by act of parliament: which also, when well considered, will appear to be a trust of great delicacy and high importance.

U P O N the whole therefore I think it is clear, that, whatever may have become of the *nominal*, the *real* power of the crown has not been too far weakened by any transactions in the last century. Much is indeed given up; but much is also acquired. The stern commands of prerogative have yielded to the milder voice of influence; the slavish and exploded doctrine of non-resistance has given way to a military establishment by law; and to the disuse of parliaments has succeeded a parliamentary trust of an immense perpetual revenue. When, indeed, by the free operation of the sinking fund, our national debts shall be lessened; when the posture of foreign affairs, and the universal introduction of a well planned and national militia, will suffer our formidable army to be thinned and regulated; and when (in consequence of all) our taxes shall be gradually reduced; this adventitious power of the crown will slowly and imperceptibly diminish, as it slowly and imperceptibly rose. But, till that shall happen, it will be our especial duty, as good subjects and good Englishmen, to reverence the crown, and yet guard against corrupt and servile influence from those who are intrusted with it's authority; to be loyal, yet free; obedient, and yet independent: and, above every thing, to hope that we may long, very long, continue to be governed by a sovereign, who, in all those public acts that have personally proceeded from himself, hath manifested the highest veneration for the free constitution of Britain; hath already in more than one instance remarkably strengthened it's outworks; and will therefore never harbour a thought, or adopt a persuasion, in any the remotest degree detrimental to public liberty.

CHAPTER THE NINTH.

OF SUBORDINATE MAGISTRATES.

IN a former chapter of these commentaries we distinguished magistrates into two kinds; supreme, or those in whom the sovereign power of the state resides; and subordinate, or those who act in an inferior secondary sphere. We have hitherto considered the former kind only, namely, the supreme legislative power or parliament, and the supreme executive power, which is the king: and are now to proceed to enquire into the rights and duties of the principal subordinate magistrates.

AND herein we are not to investigate the powers and duties of his majesty's great officers of state, the lord treasurer, lord chamberlain, the principal secretaries, or the like; because I do not know that they are in that capacity in any considerable degree the objects of our laws, or have any very important share of magistracy conferred upon them: except that the secretaries of state are allowed the power of commitment, in order to bring offenders to trial Neither shall I here treat of the office and authority of the lord chancellor, or the other judges of the superior courts of justice; because they will find a more proper place in the third part of these commentaries. Nor shall I enter into any minute disquisitions, with regard to the rights and dignities of mayors and aldermen, or other magistrates of particular corporations; because these are mere private and strictly municipal rights, depending entirely upon the domestic constitution of their respective franchises. But the magistrates and officers, whose rights and duties it will be proper in this chapter to consider, are such as are generally in use and have a jurisdiction and authority dispersedly throughout the kingdom: which are, principally, sheriffs; coroners; justices of the peace; constables; surveyors of highways; and overseers of the poor. In treating of all which I shall enquire into, first, their antiquity and original; next, the manner in which they are appointed and may be removed; and, lastly, their rights and duties. And first of sheriffs.

I. THE sheriff is an officer of very great antiquity in this kingdom, his name being derived from two Saxon words, shire reeve, the bailiff or officer of the shire. He is called in Latin *vice-comes*, as being the deputy of the earl or *comes*; to whom the custody of the shire is said to have been committed at the first division of this kingdom into counties. But the earls in process of time, by reason of their high employments and attendance on the king's person, not being able to transact the business of the county, were delivered of that burden; reserving to themselves the honour, but the labour was laid on the sheriff. So that now the sheriff does all the king's business in the county; and though he be still called *vice-comes*, yet he is entirely independent of, and not subject to the earl; the king by his letters patent committing *custodiam comitatus* to the sheriff, and him alone.

SHERIFFS were formerly chosen by the inhabitants of the several counties. In confirmation of which it was ordained by statute 28 Edw. I. c. 8. that the people should have election of sheriffs in every shire, where the shrievalty is not of inheritance. For antiently in some counties, particularly on the borders, the sheriffs were hereditary; as I apprehend they are in Scotland, and in the county of Westmorland, to this day: and the city of London has also the inheritance of the shrievalty of Middlesex vested in their body by charter. The reason of these popular elections is assigned in the same statute, c. 13. "that the commons might chuse such as would not be a burthen to them." And herein appears plainly a strong trace of the democratical part of our constitution; in which form of government it is an indispensable requisite, that the people should chuse their own magistrates. This election was in all probability not absolutely vested in the commons, but required the royal approbation. For in the Gothic constitution, the judges of their county courts (which office is executed by our sheriff) were elected by the people, but confirmed by the king: and the form of their election was thus managed; the people, or *incolae territorii*, chose *twelve* electors, and they nominated *three* persons, *ex quibus rex unum confirmabat.* But, with us in England, these popular elections, growing tumultuous, were put an end to by the statute 9 Edw. II. st. 2. which enacted, that the sheriffs should from thenceforth be assigned by the lord chancellor, treasurer, and the judges; as being persons in whom the same trust might with confidence be reposed. By statutes 14 Edw. III. c. 7. and 23 Hen. VI. c. 8. the chancellor, treasurer, *chief* justices, and *chief* baron, are to make this election; and that on the morrow of All Souls in the exchequer. But the custom now is (and has been at least ever since the time of Fortescue, who was chief justice and chancellor to Henry the sixth) that *all* the judges, and certain other great officers, meet in the exchequer chamber on the morrow of All Souls yearly, (which day is now altered to the morrow of St. Martin by the act for abbreviating Michaelmas term) and then and there nominate three persons to the king, who afterwards appoints one of them to be sheriff. This custom, of the *twelve* judges nominating *three* persons, seems borrowed from the Gothic constitution beforementioned; with this difference, that among the Goths the twelve nominors were first elected by the people themselves. And this usage of ours at it's first introduction, I am apt to believe, was founded upon some statute, though not now to be found among our printed laws: first, because it is materially different from the directions of all the statutes beforementioned; which it is hard to conceive that the judges would have countenanced by their concurrence, or that Fortescue would have inserted in his book, unless by the authority of some statute: and also, because a statute is expressly referred to in the record, which sir Edward Coke tells us he transcribed from the council book of 3 Mar. 34 Hen. VI. and which is in substance as follows. The king had of his own authority appointed a man sheriff of Lincolnshire, which office he refused to take upon him: whereupon the opinions of the judges were taken, what should be done in this behalf. And the two chief justices, sir John Fortescue and sir John Prisot, delivered the unanimous opinion of them all; "that the king did an error when he made a person sheriff, that was not chosen and presented to him according to the *statute*; that the person refusing was liable to no fine for disobedience, as if he had been one of the *three* persons chosen according to the tenor of the *statute*; that they would advise the king to have recourse to the *three* persons that were chosen according to the *statute*, or that some other thrifty man be intreated to occupy the office for this year; and that, the next year, to eschew such inconveniences, the order of the *statute* in this behalf made be observed." But, notwithstanding this unanimous resolution of all the judges of England, thus entered in the council book, some of our writers have affirmed, that the king, by his prerogative, may name whom he pleases to be sheriff, whether chosen by the judges or no. This is grounded on a very particular case in the fifth year of queen Elizabeth, when, by reason of the plague, there was no Michaelmas term kept at Westminster; so that the judges could not meet there *in crastino Animarum* to nominate the sheriffs: whereupon the queen named them herself, without such previous assembly, appointing for the most part one of the two remaining in the last year's list. And this case, thus circumstanced, is the only precedent in our books for the making these extraordinary sheriffs. It is true, the reporter adds, that it was held that the queen by her prerogative might make a sheriff without the election of the judges, *non obstante aliquo statuto in contrarium*: but the doctrine of *non obstante*'s, which sets the prerogative above the laws, was effectually demolished by the bill of rights at the revolution, and abdicated Westminster-hall when king James abdicated the kingdom. So that sheriffs cannot now be legally appointed, otherwise than according to the known and established law.

S H E R I F F S , by virtue of several old statutes, are to continue in their office no longer than one year; and yet it hath been said that a sheriff may be appointed *durante bene placito*, or during the king's pleasure; and so is the form of the royal writ. Therefore, till a new sheriff be named, his office cannot be determined, unless by his own death, or the demise of the king; in which last case it was usual for the successor to send a new writ to the old sheriff: but now by statute 1 Ann. st. 1. c. 8. all officers appointed by the preceding king may hold their offices for six months after the king's demise, unless sooner displaced by the successor. We may farther observe, that by statute 1 Ric. II. c. 11. no man, that has served the office of sheriff for one year, can be compelled to serve the same again within three years after.

W E shall find it is of the utmost importance to have the sheriff appointed according to law, when we consider his power and duty. These are either as a judge, as the keeper of the king's peace, as a ministerial officer of the superior courts of justice, or as the king's bailiff.

I N his judicial capacity he is to hear and determine all causes of forty shillings value and under, in his county court, of which more in it's proper place: and he has also judicial power in divers other civil cases. He is likewise to decide the elections of knights of the shire, (subject to the control of the house of commons) of coroners, and of verderors; to judge of the qualification of voters, and to return such as he shall determine to be duly elected.

A S the keeper of the king's peace, both by common law and special commission, he is the first man in the county, and superior in rank to any nobleman therein, during his office. He may apprehend, and commit to prison, all persons who break the peace, or attempt to break it: and may bind any one in a recognizance to keep the king's peace. He may, and is bound *ex officio* to, pursue and take all traitors, murderers, felons, and other misdoers, and commit them to gaol for safe custody. He is also to defend his county against any of the king's enemies when they come into the land: and for this purpose, as well as for keeping the peace

125

and pursuing felons, he may command all the people of his county to attend him; which is called the *posse comitatus,* or power of the county: which summons every person above fifteen years old, and under the degree of a peer, is bound to attend upon warning, under pain of fine and imprisonment. But though the sheriff is thus the principal conservator of the peace in his county, yet, by the express directions of the great charter, he, together with the constable, coroner, and certain other officers of the king, are forbidden to hold any pleas of the crown, or, in other words, to try any criminal offence. For it would be highly unbecoming, that the executioners of justice should be also the judges; should impose, as well as levy, fines and amercements; should one day condemn a man to death, and personally execute him the next. Neither may he act as an ordinary justice of the peace during the time of his office: for this would be equally inconsistent; he being in many respects the servant of the justices.

I N his ministerial capacity the sheriff is bound to execute all process issuing from the king's courts of justice. In the commencement of civil causes, he is to serve the writ, to arrest, and to take bail; when the cause comes to trial, he must summon and return the jury; when it is determined, he must see the judgment of the court carried into execution. In criminal matters, he also arrests and imprisons, he returns the jury, he has the custody of the delinquent, and he executes the sentence of the court, though it extend to death itself.

A S the king's bailiff, it is his business to preserve the rights of the king within his bailiwick; for so his county is frequently called in the writs: a word introduced by the princes of the Norman line; in imitation of the French, whose territory is divided into bailiwicks, as that of England into counties. He must seise to the king's use all lands devolved to the crown by attainder or escheat; must levy all fines and forfeitures; must seise and keep all waifs, wrecks, estrays, and the like, unless they be granted to some subject; and must also collect the king's rents within his bailiwick, if commanded by process from the exchequer.

T O execute these various offices, the sheriff has under him many inferior officers; an under-sheriff, bailiffs, and gaolers; who must neither buy, sell, nor farm their offices, on forfeiture of 500*l.*

T H E under-sheriff usually performs all the duties of the office; a very few only excepted, where the personal presence of the high-sheriff is necessary. But no under-sheriff shall abide in his office above one year; and if he does, by statute 23 Hen. VI. c. 8. he forfeits 200*l.*a very large penalty in those early days. And no under-sheriff or sheriff's officer shall practice as an attorney, during the time he continues in such office: for this would be a great inlet to partiality and oppression. But these salutary regulations are shamefully evaded, by practising in the names of other attorneys, and putting in sham deputies by way of nominal under-sheriffs: by reason of which, says Dalton, the under-sheriffs and bailiffs do grow so cunning in their several places, that they are able to deceive, and it may be well feared that many of them do deceive, both the king, the high-sheriff, and the county.

BAILIFFS, or sheriff's officers, are either bailiffs of hundreds, or special bailiffs. Bailiffs of hundreds are officers appointed over those respective districts by the sheriffs, to collect fines therein; to summon juries; to attend the judges and justices at the assises, and quarter sessions; and also to execute writs and process in the several hundreds. But, as these are generally plain men, and not thoroughly skilful in this latter part of their office, that of serving writs, and making arrests and executions, it is now usual to join special bailiffs with them; who are generally mean persons employed by the sheriffs on account only of their adroitness and dexterity in hunting and seising their prey. The sheriff being answerable for the misdemesnors of these bailiffs, they are therefore usually bound in a bond for the due execution of their office, and thence are called bound-bailiffs; which the common people have corrupted into a much more homely appellation.

GAOLERS are also the servants of the sheriff, and he must be responsible for their conduct. Their business is to keep safely all such persons as are committed to them by lawful warrant: and, if they suffer any such to escape, the sheriff shall answer it to the king, if it be a criminal matter; or, in a civil case, to the party injured. And to this end the sheriff must have lands sufficient within the county to answer the king and his people. The abuses of goalers and sheriff's officers toward the unfortunate persons in their custody are well restrained and guarded against by statute 32 Geo. II. c. 28.

THE vast expense, which custom had introduced in serving the office of high-sheriff, was grown such a burthen to the subject, that it was enacted, by statute 13 & 14 Car. II. c. 21. that no sheriff should keep any table at the assises, except for his own family, or give any presents to the judges or their servants, or have more than forty men in livery; yet, for the sake of safety and decency, he may not have less than twenty men in England and twelve in Wales; upon forfeiture, in any of these cases, of 200*l*.

II. THE coroner's is also a very antient office at the common law. He is called coroner, *coronator*, because he hath principally to do with pleas of the crown, or such wherein the king is more immediately concerned. And in this light the lord chief justice of the king's bench is the principal coroner in the kingdom, and may (if he pleases) exercise the jurisdiction of a coroner in any part of the realm. But there are also particular coroners for every county of England; usually four, but sometimes six, and sometimes fewer. This officer is of equal antiquity with the sheriff; and was ordained together with him to keep the peace, when the earls gave up the wardship of the county.

HE is still chosen by all the freeholders in the county court, as by the policy of our antient laws the sheriffs, and conservators of the peace, and all other officers were, who were concerned in matters that affected the liberty of the people; and as verderors of the forests still are, whose business it is to stand between the prerogative and the subject in the execution of the forest laws. For this purpose there is a writ at common law *de coronatore eligendo.* in which it is expressly commanded the sheriff, "*quod talem eligi faciat, qui melius et sciat, et velit, et possit, officio illi intendere.*" And, in order to effect this the more surely, it was enacted by the statute of Westm. I, that none but lawful and discreet knights should be chosen. But it seems it is now sufficient if a man have lands enough to be made a knight, whether he be really knighted or not: and there was an instance in the 5 Edw. III. of a man being removed from this office, because he was only a merchant. The coroner ought also to have estate sufficient to maintain the dignity of his office, and answer any fines that may be set upon him for his misbehaviour: and if he have not enough to answer, his fine shall be levyed on the county, as a punishment for electing an insufficient officer. Now indeed, through the culpable neglect of gentlemen of property, this office has been suffered to fall into disrepute, and get into low and indigent hands: so that, although formerly no coroner would condescend to be paid for serving his country, and they were by the aforesaid statute of Westm. I. expressly forbidden to take a reward, under pain of great forfeiture to the king; yet for many years past they have only desired to be chosen for the sake of their perquisites; being allowed fees for their attendance by the statute 3 Hen. VII. c. 1. which sir Edward Coke complains of heavily; though they have since his time been much enlarged.

T H E coroner is chosen for life: but may be removed, either by being made sheriff, or chosen verderor, which are offices incompatible with the other; or by the king's writ *de coronatore exonerando*, for a cause to be therein assigned, as that he is engaged in other business, is incapacitated by years or sickness, hath not a sufficient estate in the county, or lives in an inconvenient part of it. And by the statute 25 Geo. II. c. 29. extortion, neglect, or misbehaviour, are also made causes of removal.

T H E office and power of a coroner are also, like those of a sheriff, either judicial or ministerial; but principally judicial. This is in great measure ascertained by statute 4 Edw. I. *de officio coronatoris*; and consists, first, in enquiring (when any person is slain or dies suddenly) concerning the manner of his death. And this must be "*super visum corporis*;" for, if the body be not found, the coroner cannot sit. He must also sit at the very place where the death happened; and his enquiry is made by a jury from four, five, or six of the neighbouring towns, over whom he is to preside. If any be found guilty by this inquest of murder, he is to commit to prison for further trial, and is also to enquire concerning their lands, goods and chattels, which are forfeited thereby: but, whether it be murder or not, he must enquire whether any deodand has accrued to the king, or the lord of the franchise, by this death: and must certify the whole of this inquisition to the court of king's bench, or the next assises. Another branch of his office is to enquire concerning shipwrecks; and certify whether wreck or not, and who is in possession of the goods. Concerning treasure trove, he is also to enquire who were the finders, and where it is, and whether any one be suspected of having found and concealed a treasure; "and that may be well perceived (saith the old statute of Edw. I.) where one liveth riotously, haunting taverns, and hath done so of long time:" whereupon he might be attached, and held to bail, upon this suspicion only.

THE ministerial office of the coroner is only as the sheriff's substitute. For when just exception can be taken to the sheriff, for suspicion of partiality, (as that he is interested in the suit, or of kindred to either plaintiff or defendant) the process must then be awarded to the coroner, instead of the sheriff, for execution of the king's writs.

III. THE next species of subordinate magistrates, whom I am to consider, are justices of the peace; the principal of whom is the *custos rotulorum*, or keeper of the records of the county. The common law hath ever had a special care and regard for the conservation of the peace; for peace is the very end and foundation of civil society. And therefore, before the present constitution of justices was invented, there were peculiar officers appointed by the common law for the maintenance of the public peace. Of these some had, and still have, this power annexed to other offices which they hold; others had it merely by itself, and were thence named *custodes* or *conservatores pacis*. Those that were so *virtute officii* still continue; but the latter sort are superseded by the modern justices.

THE kings majesty is, by his office and dignity royal, the principal conservator of the peace within all his dominions; and may give authority to any other to see the peace kept, and to punish such as break it: hence it is usually called the king's peace. The lord chancellor or keeper, the lord treasurer, the lord high steward of England, the lord mareschal, and lord high constable of England (when any such officers are in being) and all the justices of the court of king's bench (by virtue of their offices) and the master of the rolls (by prescription) are general conservators of the peace throughout the whole kingdom, and may commit all breakers of it, or bind them in recognizances to keep it: the other judges are only so in their own courts. The coroner is also a conservator of the peace within his own county; as is also the sheriff; and both of them may take a recognizance or security for the peace. Constables, tythingmen, and the like, are also conservators of the peace within their own jurisdictions; and may apprehend all breakers of the peace, and commit them till they find sureties for their keeping it.

THOSE that were, without any office, simply and merely conservators of the peace, were chosen by the freeholders in full county court before the sheriff; the writ for their election directing them to be chosen "*de probioribus et melioribus in comitatu suo in custodes pacis.*" But when queen Isabel, the wife of Edward II, had contrived to depose her husband by a forced resignation of the crown, and had set up his son Edward III in his place; this, being a thing then without example in England, it was feared would much alarm the people; especially as the old king was living, though hurried about from castle to castle; till at last he met with an untimely death. To prevent therefore any risings, or other disturbance of the peace, the new king sent writs to all the sheriffs in England, the form of which is preserved by Thomas Walsingham, giving a plausible account of the manner of his obtaining the crown; to wit, that it was done *ipsius patris beneplacito*: and withal commanding each sheriff that the peace be kept throughout his bailiwick, on pain and peril of disinheritance and loss of life and limb. And in a few weeks after the date of these writs, it was ordained in parliament, that, for the better maintaining and keeping of the peace in every county, good men and lawful, which were no maintainers of evil, or barretors in the country, should be *assigned* to keep the peace. And in this manner, and upon this occasion, was the election of the conservators of the peace taken from the people, and given to the king; this assignment being construed to be by the king's commission. But still they were called only conservators, wardens, or keepers of the peace, till the statute 34 Edw. III. c. 1. gave them the power of trying felonies; and then they acquired the more honorable appellation of justices.

T H E S E justices are appointed by the king's special commission under the great seal, the form of which was settled by all the judges, *A.D.* 1590. This appoints them all, jointly and severally, to keep the peace, and any two or more of them to enquire of and determine felonies, and other misdemesnors: in which number some particular justices, or one of them, are directed to be always included, and no business to be done without their presence; the words of the commission running thus, "*quorum aliquem vestrum, A. B. C. D. &c. unum esse volumus;*" whence the persons so named are usually called justices of the *quorum.* And formerly it was customary to appoint only a select number of justices, eminent for their skill and discretion, to be of the *quorum;* but now the practice is to advance almost all of them to that dignity, naming them all over again in the *quorum* clause, except perhaps only some one inconsiderable person for the sake of propriety: and no exception is now allowable, for not expressing in the form of warrants, &c., that the justice who issued them is of the *quorum.*

T O U C H I N G the number and qualifications of these justices; it was ordained by statute 18 Edw. III. c. 2. that *two,* or *three,* of the best reputation in each county shall be assigned to be keepers of the peace. But these being found rather too few for that purpose, it was provided by statute 34 Edw. III. c. 1. that one lord, and three, or four, of the most worthy men in the county, with some learned in the law, shall be made justices in every county. But afterwards the number of justices, through the ambition of private persons, became so large, that it was thought necessary by statute 12 Ric. II. c. 10. and 14 Ric II. c. 11. to restrain them at first to six, and afterwards to eight only. But this rule is now disregarded, and the cause seems to be (as Lambard observed long ago) that the growing number of statute laws, committed from time to time to the charge of justices of the peace, have occasioned also (and very reasonably) their encrease to a larger number. And, as to their qualifications, the statutes just cited direct them to be of the best reputation, and most worthy men in the county: and the statute 13 Ric. II. c. 10. orders them to be of the most sufficient knights, esquires, and gentlemen of the law. Also by statute 2 Hen. V. st. 1. c. 4. and st. 2. c. 1. they must be resident in their several counties. And because, contrary to these statutes, men of small substance had crept into the commission, whose poverty made them both covetous and contemptible, it was enacted by statute 18 Hen. VI. c. 11. that no justice should be put in commission, if he had not lands to the value of *20l. per annum.* And, the rate of money being greatly altered since that time, it is now enacted by statute 5 Geo. II. c. 11. that every justice, except as is therein excepted, shall have *100l. per annum* clear of all deductions; and, if he acts without such qualification, he shall forfeit *100l.* which is almost an equivalent to the *20l. per annum* required in Henry the sixth's time: and of this qualification the justice must now make oath. Also it is provided by the act 5

Geo. II. that no practising attorney, solicitor, or proctor, shall be capable of acting as a justice of the peace.

See bishop Fleetwood's calculations in his *chronicon pretiosum.*

A S the office of these justices is conferred by the king, so it subsists only during his pleasure; and is determinable, 1. By the demise of the crown; that is, in six months after. 2. By express writ under the great seal, discharging any particular person, from being any longer justice. 3. By superseding the commission by writ of *supersedeas*, which suspends the power of all the justices, but does not totally destroy it; seeing it may be revived again by another writ, called a *procedendo*. 4. By a new commission, which virtually, though silently, discharges all the former justices that are not included therein; for two commissions cannot subsist at once. 5. By accession of the office of sheriff or coroner. Formerly it was thought, that if a man was named in any commission of the peace, and had afterwards a new dignity conferred upon him, that this determined his office; he no longer answering the description of the commission: but now it is provided, that notwithstanding a new title of dignity, the justice on whom it is conferred shall still continue a justice.

T H E power, office, and duty of a justice of the peace depend on his commission, and on the several statutes, which have created objects of his jurisdiction. His commission, first, empowers him singly to conserve the peace; and thereby gives him all the power of the antient conservators at the common law, in suppressing riots and affrays, in taking securities for the peace, and in apprehending and committing felons and other inferior criminals. It also empowers any two or more of them to hear and determine all felonies and other offences; which is the ground of their jurisdiction at sessions, of which more will be said in it's proper place. And as to the powers given to one, two, or more justices by the several statutes, that from time to time have heaped upon them such an infinite variety of business, that few care to undertake, and fewer understand, the office; they are such and of so great importance to the public, that the country is greatly obliged to any worthy magistrate, that without sinister views of his own will engage in this troublesome service. And therefore, if a well meaning justice makes any undesigned slip in his practice, great lenity and indulgence is shewn to him in the courts of law; and there are many statutes made to protect him in the upright discharge of his office: which, among other privileges, prohibit such justices from being sued for any oversights without notice beforehand; and stop all suits begun, on tender made of sufficient amends. But, on the other hand, any malicious or tyrannical abuse of their office is sure to be severely punished; and all persons who recover a verdict against a justice, for any wilful or malicious injury, are entitled to double costs.

I T is impossible upon our present plan to enter minutely into the particulars of the accumulated authority, thus committed to the charge of these magistrates. I must therefore refer myself at present to such subsequent parts of these commentaries, as will in their turns comprize almost every object of the justices' jurisdiction: and in the mean time recommend to the student the perusal of Mr Lambard's *eirenarcha*, and Dr Burn's *justice of the peace*;

wherein he will find every thing relative to this subject, both in antient and modern practice, collected with great care and accuracy, and disposed in a most clear and judicious method.

I SHALL next consider some officers of lower rank than those which have gone before, and of more confined jurisdiction; but still such as are universally in use through every part of the kingdom.

IV. FOURTHLY, then, of the constable. The word constable is frequently said to be derived from the Saxon, koning-staple, and to signify the support of the king. But, as we borrowed the name as well as the office of constable from the French, I am rather inclined to deduce it, with sir H. Spelman and Dr Cowel, from that language, wherein it is plainly derived from the Latin *comes stabuli*, an officer well known in the empire; so called because, like the great constable of France, as well as the lord high constable of England, he was to regulate all matters of chivalry, tilts, turnaments, and feats of arms, which were performed on horseback. This great office of lord high constable hath been disused in England, except only upon great and solemn occasions, as the king's coronation and the like, ever since the attainder of Stafford duke of Buckingham under king Henry VIII; as in France it was suppressed about a century after by an edict of Louis XIII: but from his office, says Lambard, this lower constableship was at first drawn and fetched, and is as it were a very finger of that hand. For the statute of Winchester, which first appoints them, directs that, for the better keeping of the peace, two constables in every hundred and franchise shall inspect all matters relating to *arms* and *armour*.

CONSTABLES are of two sorts, high constables, and petty constables. The former were first ordained by the statute of Winchester, as before-mentioned; and are appointed at the court leets of the franchise or hundred over which they preside, or, in default of that, by the justices at their quarter sessions; and are removeable by the same authority that appoints them. The petty constables are inferior officers in every town and parish, subordinate to the high constable of the hundred, first instituted about the reign of Edward III. These petty constables have two offices united in them; the one antient, the other modern. Their antient office is that of headborough, tithing-man, or borsholder; of whom we formerly spoke, and who are as antient as the time of king Alfred: their more modern office is that of constable merely; which was appointed (as was observed) so lately as the reign of Edward III, in order to assist the high constable. And in general the antient headboroughs, tithing-men, and borsholders, were made use of to serve as petty constables; though not so generally, but that in many places they still continue distinct officers from the constable. They are all chosen by the jury at the court leet; or, if no court leet be held, are appointed by two justices of the peace.

THE general duty of all constables, both high and petty, as well as of the other officers, is to keep the king's peace in their several districts; and to that purpose they are armed with very large powers, of arresting, and imprisoning, of breaking open houses, and the like: of the extent of which powers, considering what manner of men are for the most part put upon these offices, it is perhaps very well that they are generally kept in ignorance. One of their principal duties, arising from the statute of Winchester, which appoints them, is to keep watch and ward in their respective jurisdictions. Ward, guard, or *custodia*, is chiefly intended of the day time, in order to apprehend rioters, and robbers on the highways; the manner of doing which is left to the discretion of the justices of the peace and the constable, the hundred being however answerable for all robberies committed therein, by day light, for having kept negligent guard. Watch is properly applicable to the night only, (being called among our Teutonic ancestors *wacht* or *wacta*) and it begins at the time when ward ends, and ends when that begins; for, by the statute of Winchester, in walled towns the gates shall be closed from sunsetting to sunrising, and watch shall be kept in every borough and town, especially in the summer season, to apprehend all rogues, vagabonds, and night-walkers, and make them give an account of themselves. The constable may appoint watchmen at his discretion, regulated by the custom of the place; and these, being his deputies, have for the time being the authority of their principal. But, with regard to the infinite number of other minute duties, that are laid upon constables by a diversity of statutes, I must again refer to Mr Lambard and Dr Burn; in whose compilations may be also seen, what duties belong to the constable or tything-man indifferently, and what to the constable only: for the constable may do whatever the tything-man may; but it does not hold *e converso*, for the tithing-man has not an equal power with the constable.

V. W E are next to consider the surveyors of the highways. Every parish is bound of common right to keep the high roads, that go through it, in good and sufficient repair; unless by reason of the tenure of lands, or otherwise, this care is consigned to some particular private person. From this burthen no man was exempt by our antient laws, whatever other immunities he might enjoy: this being part of the *trinoda necessitas*, to which every man's estate was subject; viz. *expeditio contra hostem, arcium constructio, et pontium reparatio*: for, though the reparation of bridges only is expressed, yet that of roads also must be understood; as in the Roman law, *ad instructiones reparationesque itinerum et pontium, nullum genus hominum, nulliusque dignitatis ac venerationis meritis, cessare oportet*. And indeed now, for the most part, the care of the roads only seems to be left to parishes; that of bridges being in great measure devolved upon the county at large, by statute 22 Hen. VIII. c. 5. If the parish neglected these repairs, they might formerly, as they may still, be indicted for such their neglect: but it was not then incumbent on any particular officer to call the parish together, and set them upon this work; for which reason by the statute 2 & 3 Ph. & M. c. 8. surveyors of the highways were ordered to be chosen in every parish.

T H E S E surveyors were originally, according to the statute of Philip and Mary, to be appointed by the constable and churchwardens of the parish; but now they are constituted by two neighbouring justices, out of such substantial inhabitants as have either 10*l. per annum* of their own, or rent 30*l.* a year, or are worth in personal estate 100*l.*

T H E I R office and duty consists in putting in execution a variety of statutes for the repairs of the highways; that is, of ways leading from one town to another: by which it is enacted, 1.

That they may remove all annoyances in the highways, or give notice to the owner to remove them; who is liable to penalties on noncompliance. 2. They are to call together all the inhabitants of the parish, six days in every year, to labour in repairing the highways; all persons keeping draughts, or occupying lands, being obliged to send a team for every draught, and for every 50*l.* a year, which they keep or occupy; and all other persons to work or find a labourer. The work must be completed before harvest; as well for providing a good road for carrying in the corn, as also because all hands are then supposed to be employed in harvest work. And every cartway must be made eight feet wide at the least; and may be increased by the quarter sessions to the breadth of four and twenty feet. 3. The surveyors may lay out their own money in purchasing materials for repairs, where there is not sufficient within the parish, and shall be reimbursed by a rate, to be allowed at a special sessions. 4. In case the personal labour of the parish be not sufficient, the surveyors, with the consent of the quarter sessions, may levy a rate (not exceeding 6*d.* in the pound) on the parish, in aid of the personal duty; for the due application of which they are to account upon oath. As for turnpikes, which are now universally introduced in aid of such rates, and the law relating to them, these depend entirely on the particular powers granted in the several road acts, and therefore have nothing to do with this compendium of general law.

VI. I P R O C E E D therefore, lastly, to consider the overseers of the poor; their original, appointment, and duty.

T H E poor of England, till the time of Henry VIII, subsisted entirely upon private benevolence, and the charity of welldisposed christians. For, though it appears by the mirrour, that by the common law the poor were to be "sustained by parsons, rectors of the church, and the parishioners; so that none of them dye for default of sustenance;" and though by the statutes 12 Ric. II. c. 7. and 19 Hen. VII. c. 12. the poor are directed to be sustained in the cities or towns wherein they were born, or such wherein they had dwelt for three years (which seem to be the first rudiments of parish settlements) yet till the statute 27 Hen. VIII. c. 26. I find no compulsory method chalked out for this purpose: but the poor seem to have been left to such relief as the humanity of their neighbours would afford them. The monasteries were, in particular, their principal resource; and, among other bad effects which attended the monastic institutions, it was not perhaps one of the least (though frequently esteemed quite otherwise) that they supported and fed a very numerous and very idle poor, whose sustenance depended upon what was daily distributed in alms at the gates of the religious houses. But, upon the total dissolution of these, the inconvenience of thus encouraging the poor in habits of indolence and beggary was quickly felt throughout the kingdom: and abundance of statutes were made in the reign of king Henry the eighth, for providing for the poor and impotent; which, the preambles to some of them recite, had of late years *strangely* increased. These poor were principally of two sorts: sick and impotent, and therefore unable to work; idle and sturdy, and therefore able, but not willing, to exercise any honest employment. To provide in some measure for both of these, in and about the metropolis, his son Edward the sixth founded three royal hospitals; Christ's, and St. Thomas's, for the relief of the impotent through infancy or sickness; and Bridewell for the punishment and employment of the vigorous and idle. But these were far from being sufficient for the care of the poor throughout the kingdom at large; and therefore, after many other fruitless experiments, by statute 43 Eliz. c. 2. overseers of the poor were appointed in every parish.

B Y virtue of the statute last mentioned, these overseers are to be nominated yearly in Easter-week, or within one month after, by two justices dwelling near the parish. They must be substantial householders, and so expressed to be in the appointment of the justices.

T H E I R office and duty, according to the same statute, are principally these: first, to raise competent sums for the necessary relief of the poor, impotent, old, blind, and such other, being poor and not able to work: and, secondly, to provide work for such as are able, and cannot otherwise get employment: but this latter part of their duty, which, according to the wise regulations of that salutary statute, should go hand in hand with the other, is now most shamefully neglected. However, for these joint purposes, they are empowered to make and levy rates upon the several inhabitants of the parish, by the same act of parliament; which has been farther explained and enforced by several subsequent statutes.

T H E two great objects of this statute seem to have been, 1. To relieve the impotent poor, and them only. 2. To find employment for such as are able to work: and this principally by providing stocks to be worked up at home, which perhaps might be more beneficial than accumulating all the poor in one common work-house; a practice which tends to destroy all domestic connexions (the only felicity of the honest and industrious labourer) and to put the sober and diligent upon a level, in point of their earnings, with those who are dissolute and idle. Whereas, if none were to be relieved but those who are incapable to get their livings, and that in proportion to their incapacity; if no children were to be removed from their parents, but such as are brought up in rags and idleness; and if every poor man and his family were employed whenever they requested it, and were allowed the whole profits of their labour;—a spirit of chearful industry would soon diffuse itself through every cottage; work would become easy and habitual, when absolutely necessary to their daily subsistence; and the most indigent peasant would go through his task without a murmur, if assured that he and his children (when incapable of work through infancy, age, or infirmity) would then, and then only, be intitled to support from his opulent neighbours.

T H I S appears to have been the plan of the statute of queen Elizabeth; in which the only defect was confining the management of the poor to small, parochial, districts; which are frequently incapable of furnishing proper work, or providing an able director. However, the laborious poor were then at liberty to seek employment wherever it was to be had; none being obliged to reside in the places of their settlement, but such as were unable or unwilling to work; and those places of settlement being only such where they were born, or had made their abode, originally for three years, and afterwards (in the case of vagabonds) for one year only.

AFTER the restoration, a very different plan was adopted, which has rendered the employment of the poor more difficult, by authorizing the subdivision of parishes; has greatly increased their number, by confining them all to their respective districts; has given birth to the intricacy of our poor-laws, by multiplying and rendering more easy the methods of gaining settlements; and, in consequence, has created an infinity of expensive lawsuits between contending neighbourhoods, concerning those settlements and removals. By the statute 13 & 14 Car. II. c. 12. a legal settlement was declared to be gained by birth, inhabitancy, apprenticeship, or service for forty days; within which period all intruders were made removeable from any parish by two justices of the peace, unless they settled in a tenement of the annual value of 10*l.* The frauds, naturally consequent upon this provision, which gave a settlement by so short a residence, produced the statute 1 Jac. II. c. 17. which directed notice in writing to be delivered to the parish officers, before a settlement could be gained by such residence. Subsequent provisions allowed other circumstances of notoriety to be equivalent to such notice given; and those circumstances have from time to time been altered, enlarged, or restrained, whenever the experience of new inconveniences, arising daily from new regulations, suggested the necessity of a remedy. And the doctrine of certificates was invented, by way of counterpoise, to restrain a man and his family from acquiring a new settlement by any length of residence whatever, unless in two particular excepted cases; which makes parishes very cautious of giving such certificates, and of course confines the poor at home, where frequently no adequate employment can be had.

THE law of settlements may be therefore now reduced to the following general heads; or, a settlement in a parish may be acquired, 1. By birth; which is always *prima facie* the place of settlement, until some other can be shewn. This is also always the place of settlement of a bastard child; for a bastard, having in the eye of the law no father, cannot be referred to *his* settlement, as other children may. But, in legitimate children, though the place of birth be *prima facie* the settlement, yet it is not conclusively so; for there are, 2. Settlements by parentage, being the settlement of one's father or mother: all children being really settled in the parish where their parents are settled, until they get a new settlement for themselves. A new settlement may be acquired several ways; as, 3. By marriage. For a woman, marrying a man that is settled in another parish, changes her own: the law not permitting the separation of husband and wife. But if the man be a foreigner, and has no settlement, her's is suspended during his life, if he be able to maintain her; but after his death she may return again to her old settlement. The other methods of acquiring settlements in any parish are all reducible to this one, of forty days residence therein: but this forty days residence (which is construed to be lodging or lying there) must not be by fraud, or stealth, or in any clandestine manner; but accompanied with one or other of the following concomitant circumstances. The next method therefore of gaining a settlement, is, 4. By forty days residence, and notice. For if a stranger comes into a parish, and delivers notice in writing of his place of abode, and number of his family, to one of the overseers (which must be read in the church and registered) and resides there unmolested for forty days after such notice, he is legally settled thereby. For the law presumes that such a one at the time of notice is not likely to become chargeable, else he would not venture to give it; or that, in such case, the parish would take care to remove him. But there are also other circumstances equivalent to such notice: therefore, 5. Renting for a year a tenement of the yearly value of ten pounds, and residing forty days in the parish, gains a settlement without notice; upon the principle of having substance enough to gain credit for such a house. 6. Being charged to and paying the public taxes and levies of the parish; and, 7. Executing any public parochial office for a whole year in the parish, as churchwarden, &c; are both of them equivalent to notice, and gain a settlement, when coupled with a residence of forty days. 8. Being hired for a year, when unmarried, and serving a year in the same service; and 9. Being bound an apprentice for seven years; give the servant and apprentice a settlement, without notice, in that place wherein they serve the last forty days. This is meant to encourage application to trades, and going out to reputable services. 10. Lastly, the having an estate of one's own, and residing thereon forty days, however small the value may be, in case it be acquired by act of law or of a third person, as by descent, gift, devise, &c., is a sufficient settlement: but if a man acquire it by his own act, as by purchase, (in it's popular sense, in consideration of money paid) then unless the consideration advanced, *bona fide*, be 30*l.* it is no settlement for any longer time, than the person shall inhabit thereon. He is in no case removeable from his own property; but he shall not, by any trifling or fraudulent purchase of his own, acquire a permanent and lasting settlement.

A L L persons, not so settled, may be removed to their own parishes, on complaint of the overseers, by two justices of the peace, if they shall adjudge them likely to become chargeable to the parish, into which they have intruded: unless they are in a way of getting a legal settlement, as by having hired a house of 10*l. per annum*, or living in an annual service; for then they are not removeable. And in all other cases, if the parish to which they belong, will grant them a certificate, acknowleging them to be *their* parishioners, they cannot be removed merely because *likely* to become chargeable, but only when they become *actually* chargeable. But such certificated persons can gain no settlement by any of the means above-mentioned; unless by renting a tenement of 10*l. per annum*, or by serving an annual office in the parish, being legally placed therein: neither can an apprentice or servant to such certificated person gain a settlement by such their service.

T H E S E are the general heads of the laws relating to the poor, which, by the resolutions of the courts of justice thereon within a century past, are branched into a great variety. And yet, notwithstanding the pains that has been taken about them, they still remain very imperfect, and inadequate to the purposes they are designed for: a fate, that has generally attended most of our statute laws, where they have not the foundation of the common law to build on. When the shires, the hundreds, and the tithings, were kept in the same admirable order that they were disposed in by the great Alfred, there were no persons idle, consequently none but the impotent that needed relief: and the statute of 43 Eliz. seems entirely founded on the same principle. But when this excellent scheme was neglected and departed from, we cannot but observe with concern, what miserable shifts and lame expedients have from time to time been adopted, in order to patch up the flaws occasioned by this neglect. There is not a more necessary or more certain maxim in the frame and constitution of society, than that every individual must contribute his share, in order to the well-being of the community: and surely they must be very deficient in sound policy, who suffer one half of a parish to continue idle, dissolute, and unemployed; and then form visionary schemes, and at length are amazed to find, that the industry of the other half is not able to maintain the whole.

CHAPTER THE TENTH.

OF THE PEOPLE, WHETHER ALIENS, DENIZENS, OR NATIVES.

HAVING, in the eight preceding chapters, treated of persons as they stand in the public relations of *magistrates*, I now proceed to consider such persons as fall under the denomination of the *people*. And herein all the inferior and subordinate magistrates, treated of in the last chapter, are included.

THE first and most obvious division of the people is into aliens and natural-born subjects. Natural-born subjects are such as are born within the dominions of the crown of England, that is, within the ligeance, or as it is generally called, the allegiance of the king; and aliens, such as are born out of it. Allegiance is the tie, or *ligamen*, which binds the subject to the king, in return for that protection which the king affords the subject. The thing itself, or substantial part of it, is founded in reason and the nature of government; the name and the form are derived to us from our Gothic ancestors. Under the feodal system, every owner of lands held them in subjection to some superior or lord, from whom or whose ancestors the tenant or vasal had received them: and there was a mutual trust or confidence subsisting between the lord and vasal, that the lord should protect the vasal in the enjoyment of the territory he had granted him, and, on the other hand, that the vasal should be faithful to the lord and defend him against all his enemies. This obligation on the part of the vasal was called his *fidelitas* or fealty; and an oath of fealty was required, by the feodal law, to be taken by all tenants to their landlord, which is couched in almost the same terms as our antient oath of allegiance: except that in the usual oath of fealty there was frequently a saving or exception of the faith due to a superior lord by name, under whom the landlord himself was perhaps only a tenant or vasal. But when the acknowlegement was made to the absolute superior himself, who was vasal to no man, it was no longer called the oath of fealty, but the oath of allegiance; and therein the tenant swore to bear faith to his sovereign lord, in opposition to all men, without any saving or exception: "*contra omnes homines fidelitatem fecit.*" Land held by this exalted species of fealty was called *feudum ligium*, a liege fee; the vasals *homines ligii*, or liege men; and the sovereign their *dominus ligius*, or liege lord. And when sovereign princes did homage to each other, for lands held under their respective sovereignties, a distinction was always made between *simple* homage, which was only an acknowlegement of tenure; and *liege* homage, which included the fealty before-mentioned, and the services consequent upon it. Thus when Edward III, in 1329, did homage to Philip VI of France, for his ducal dominions on that continent, it was warmly disputed of what species the homage was to be, whether *liege* or *simple* homage. With us in England, it becoming a settled principle of tenure, that *all* lands in the kingdom are holden of the king as their sovereign and lord paramount, no oath but that of fealty could ever be taken to inferior lords, and the oath of allegiance was necessarily confined to the person of the king alone. By an easy analogy the term of allegiance was soon brought to signify all other engagements, which are due from subjects to their prince, as well as those duties which were simply and merely territorial. And the oath of allegiance, as administred for upwards of six hundred years, contained a promise "to be true and faithful to the king and his heirs, and truth and faith to bear of life and limb and terrene honour, and not to know or hear of any ill or damage intended him, without defending him therefrom." Upon which sir Matthew Halemakes this remark; that it was short and plain, not entangled with long or intricate clauses or declarations, and yet is comprehensive of the whole duty from the subject to his sovereign. But, at the revolution, the terms of this oath being thought perhaps to favour too much the notion of non-resistance, the present form was introduced by the convention parliament, which is more general and indeterminate than the former; the subject only promising "that he will be faithful and bear *true* allegiance to the king," without mentioning "his heirs," or specifying in the least wherein that allegiance consists. The oath of supremacy is principally calculated as a renuntiation of the pope's pretended authority: and the oath of abjuration, introduced in the reign of king William, very amply supplies the loose and general texture of the oath of allegiance; it recognizing the right of his majesty, derived under the act of settlement; engaging to support him to the utmost of the juror's power; promising to disclose all traiterous conspiracies against him; and expressly renouncing any claim of the pretender, by name, in as clear and explicit terms as the English language can furnish. This oath must be taken by all persons in any office, trust, or employment; and may be tendered by two justices of the peace to any person, whom they shall suspect of disaffection. But the oath of allegiance may be tendered to all persons above the age of twelve years, whether natives, denizens, or aliens, either in the court-leet of the manor, or in the sheriff's tourn, which is the court-leet of the county.

B U T , besides these express engagements, the law also holds that there is an implied, original, and virtual allegiance, owing from every subject to his sovereign, antecedently to any express promise; and although the subject never swore any faith or allegiance in form. For as the king, by the very descent of the crown, is fully invested with all the rights and bound to all the duties of sovereignty, before his coronation; so the subject is bound to his prince by an intrinsic allegiance, before the superinduction of those outward bonds of oath, homage, and fealty; which were only instituted to remind the subject of this his previous duty, and for the better securing it's performance. The formal profession therefore, or oath of subjection, is nothing more than a declaration in words of what was before implied in law. Which occasions sir Edward Coke very justly to observe, that "all subjects are equally bounden to their allegiance, as if they had taken the oath; because it is written by the finger of the law in their hearts, and the taking of the corporal oath is but an outward declaration of the same." The sanction of an oath, it is true, in case of violation of duty, makes the guilt still more accumulated, by superadding perjury to treason; but it does not encrease the civil obligation to loyalty; it only strengthens the *social* tie by uniting it with that of *religion*.

ALLEGIANCE, both express and implied, is however distinguished by the law into two sorts or species, the one natural, the other local; the former being also perpetual, the latter temporary. Natural allegiance is such as is due from all men born within the king's dominions immediately upon their birth. For, immediately upon their birth, they are under the king's protection; at a time too, when (during their infancy) they are incapable of protecting themselves. Natural allegiance is therefore a debt of gratitude; which cannot be forfeited, cancelled, or altered, by any change of time, place, or circumstance, nor by any thing but the united concurrence of the legislature. An Englishman who removes to France, or to China, owes the same allegiance to the king of England there as at home, and twenty years hence as well as now. For it is a principle of universal law, that the natural-born subject of one prince cannot by any act of his own, no, not by swearing allegiance to another, put off or discharge his natural allegiance to the former: for this natural allegiance was intrinsic, and primitive, and antecedent to the other; and cannot be devested without the concurrent act of that prince to whom it was first due. Indeed the natural-born subject of one prince, to whom he owes allegiance, may be entangled by subjecting himself absolutely to another; but it is his own act that brings him into these straits and difficulties, of owing service to two masters; and it is unreasonable that, by such voluntary act of his own, he should be able at pleasure to unloose those bands, by which he is connected to his natural prince.

LOCAL allegiance is such as is due from an alien, or stranger born, for so long time as he continues within the king's dominion and protection: and it ceases, the instant such stranger transfers himself from this kingdom to another. Natural allegiance is therefore perpetual, and local temporary only: and that for this reason, evidently founded upon the nature of government; that allegiance is a debt due from the subject, upon an implied contract with the prince, that so long as the one affords protection, so long the other will demean himself faithfully. As therefore the prince is always under a constant tie to protect his natural-born subjects, at all times and in all countries, for this reason their allegiance due to him is equally universal and permanent. But, on the other hand, as the prince affords his protection to an alien, only during his residence in this realm, the allegiance of an alien is confined (in point of time) to the duration of such his residence, and (in point of locality) to the dominions of the British empire. From which considerations sir Matthew Hale deduces this consequence, that, though there be an usurper of the crown, yet it is treason for any subject, while the usurper is in full possession of the sovereignty, to practice any thing against his crown and dignity: wherefore, although the true prince regain the sovereignty, yet such attempts against the usurper (unless in defence or aid of the rightful king) have been afterwards punished with death; because of the breach of that temporary allegiance, which was due to him as king *de facto*. And upon this footing, after Edward IV recovered the crown, which had been long detained from his house by the line of Lancaster, treasons committed against Henry VI were capitally punished, though Henry had been declared an usurper by parliament.

THIS oath of allegiance, or rather the allegiance itself, is held to be applicable not only to the political capacity of the king, or regal office, but to his natural person, and blood-royal: and for the misapplication of their allegiance, viz. to the regal capacity or crown, exclusive of the person of the king, were the Spencers banished in the reign of Edward II. And from hence arose that principle of personal attachment, and affectionate loyalty, which induced our forefathers (and, if occasion required, would doubtless induce their sons) to hazard all that was dear to them, life, fortune, and family, in defence and support of their liege lord and sovereign.

T H I S allegiance then, both express and implied, is the duty of all the king's subjects, under the distinctions here laid down, of local and temporary, or universal and perpetual. Their rights are also distinguishable by the same criterions of time and locality; natural-born subjects having a great variety of rights, which they acquire by being born within the king's ligeance, and can never forfeit by any distance of place or time, but only by their own misbehaviour: the explanation of which rights is the principal subject of the two first books of these commentaries. The same is also in some degree the case of aliens; though their rights are much more circumscribed, being acquired only by residence here, and lost whenever they remove. I shall however here endeavour to chalk out some of the principal lines, whereby they are distinguished from natives, descending to farther particulars when they come in course.

A N alien born may purchase lands, or other estates: but not for his own use; for the king is thereupon entitled to them. If an alien could acquire a permanent property in lands, he must owe an allegiance, equally permanent with that property, to the king of England; which would probably be inconsistent with that, which he owes to his own natural liege lord: besides that thereby the nation might in time be subject to foreign influence, and feel many other inconveniences. Wherefore by the civil law such contracts were also made void: but the prince had no such advantage of escheat thereby, as with us in England. Among other reasons, which might be given for our constitution, it seems to be intended by way of punishment for the alien's presumption, in attempting to acquire any landed property: for the vendor is not affected by it, he having resigned his right, and received an equivalent in exchange. Yet an alien may acquire a property in goods, money, and other personal estate, or may hire a house for his habitation: for personal estate is of a transitory and moveable nature; and, besides, this indulgence to strangers is necessary for the advancement of trade. Aliens also may trade as freely as other people; only they are subject to certain higher duties at the custom-house: and there are also some obsolete statutes of Henry VIII, prohibiting alien artificers to work for themselves in this kingdom; but it is generally held they were virtually repealed by statute 5 Eliz. c. 7. Also an alien may bring an action concerning personal property, and may make a will, and dispose of his personal estate: not as it is in France, where the king at the death of an alien is entitled to all he is worth, by the *droit d'aubaine* or *jus albinatus*, unless he has a peculiar exemption. When I mention these rights of an alien, I must be understood of alien-friends only, or such whose countries are in peace with ours; for alien-enemies have no rights, no privileges, unless by the king's special favour, during the time of war.

WHEN I say, that an alien is one who is born out of the king's dominions, or allegiance, this also must be understood with some restrictions. The common law indeed stood absolutely so; with only a very few exceptions: so that a particular act of parliament became necessary after the restoration, for the naturalization of children of his majesty's English subjects, born in foreign countries during the late troubles. And this maxim of the law proceeded upon a general principle, that every man owes natural allegiance where he is born, and cannot owe two such allegiances, or serve two masters, at once. Yet the children of the king's embassadors born abroad were always held to be natural subjects: for as the father, though in a foreign country, owes not even a local allegiance to the prince to whom he is sent; so, with regard to the son also, he was held (by a kind of *postliminium*) to be born under the king of England's allegiance, represented by his father, the embassador. To encourage also foreign commerce, it was enacted by statute 25 Edw. III. st. 2. that all children born abroad, provided *both* their parents were at the time of the birth in allegiance to the king, and the mother had passed the seas by her husband's consent, might inherit as if born in England: and accordingly it hath been so adjudged in behalf of merchants. But by several more modern statutes these restrictions are still farther taken off: so that all children, born out of the king's ligeance, whose *fathers* were natural-born subjects, are now natural-born subjects themselves, to all intents and purposes, without any exception; unless their said fathers were attainted, or banished beyond sea, for high treason; or were then in the service of a prince at enmity with Great Britain.

THE children of aliens, born here in England, are, generally speaking, natural-born subjects, and entitled to all the privileges of such. In which the constitution of France differs from ours; for there, by their *jus albinatus*, if a child be born of foreign parents, it is an alien.

A DENIZEN is an alien born, but who has obtained *ex donatione regis* letters patent to make him an English subject: a high and incommunicable branch of the royal prerogative. A denizen is in a kind of middle state between an alien, and natural-born subject, and partakes of both of them. He may take lands by purchase or devise, which an alien may not; but cannot take by inheritance: for his parent, through whom he must claim, being an alien had no inheritable blood, and therefore could convey none to the son. And, upon a like defect of hereditary blood, the issue of a denizen, born *before* denization, cannot inherit to him; but his issue born *after*, may. A denizen is not excused from paying the alien's duty, and some other mercantile burthens. And no denizen can be of the privy council, or either house of parliament, or have any office of trust, civil or military, or be capable of any grant from the crown.

NATURALIZATION cannot be performed but by act of parliament: for by this an alien is put in exactly the same state as if he had been born in the king's ligeance; except only that he is incapable, as well as a denizen, of being a member of the privy council, or parliament, &c. No bill for naturalization can be received in either house of parliament, without such disabling clause in it. Neither can any person be naturalized or restored in blood, unless he hath received the sacrament of the Lord's supper within one month before the bringing in of the bill; and unless he also takes the oaths of allegiance and supremacy in the presence of the parliament.

THESE are the principal distinctions between aliens, denizens, and natives: distinctions, which endeavors have been frequently used since the commencement of this century to lay almost totally aside, by one general naturalization-act for all foreign protestants. An attempt which was once carried into execution by the statute 7 Ann. c. 5. but this, after three years experience of it, was repealed by the statute 10 Ann. c. 5. except one clause, which was just now mentioned, for naturalizing the children of English parents born abroad. However, every foreign seaman who in time of war serves two years on board an English ship is *ipso facto* naturalized; and all foreign protestants, and Jews, upon their residing seven years in any of the American colonies, without being absent above two months at a time, are upon taking the oaths naturalized to all intents and purposes, as if they had been born in this kingdom; and therefore are admissible to all such privileges, and no other, as protestants or Jews born in this kingdom are entitled to. What those privileges are, was the subject of very high debates about the time of the famous Jew-bill; which enabled all Jews to prefer bills of naturalization in parliament, without receiving the sacrament, as ordained by statute 7 Jac. I. It is not my intention to revive this controversy again; for the act lived only a few months, and was then repealed: therefore peace be now to it's *manes*.

Chapter the eleventh.
Of the CLERGY.

THE people, whether aliens, denizens, or natural-born subjects, are divisible into two kinds; the clergy and laity: the clergy, comprehending all persons in holy orders, and in ecclesiastical offices, will be the subject of the following chapter.

THIS venerable body of men, being separate and set apart from the rest of the people, in order to attend the more closely to the service of almighty God, have thereupon large privileges allowed them by our municipal laws: and had formerly much greater, which were abridged at the time of the reformation, on account of the ill use which the popish clergy had endeavoured to make of them. For, the laws having exempted them from almost every personal duty, they attempted a total exemption from every secular tie. But it is observed by sir Edward Coke, that, as the overflowing of waters doth many times make the river to lose it's proper chanel, so in times past ecclesiastical persons, seeking to extend their liberties beyond their true bounds, either lost or enjoyed not those which of right belonged to them. The personal exemptions do indeed for the most part continue. A clergyman cannot be compelled to serve on a jury, nor to appear at a court-leet or view of frank pledge; which almost every other person is obliged to do: but, if a layman is summoned on a jury, and before the trial takes orders, he shall notwithstanding appear and be sworn. Neither can he be chosen to any temporal office; as bailiff, reeve, constable, or the like: in regard of his own continual attendance on the sacred function. During his attendance on divine service he is privileged from arrests in civil suits. In cases also of felony, a clerk in orders shall have the benefit of his clergy, without being branded in the hand; and may likewise have it more than once: in both which particulars he is distinguished from a layman. But as they have their privileges, so also they have their disabilities, on account of their spiritual avocations. Clergymen, we have seen, are incapable of sitting in the house of commons; and by statute 21 Hen. VIII. c. 13. are not allowed to take any lands or tenements to farm, upon pain of 10*l. per* month, and total avoidance of the lease; nor shall engage in any manner of trade, nor sell any merchandize, under forfeiture of the treble value. Which prohibition is consonant to the canon law.

IN the frame and constitution of ecclesiastical polity there are divers ranks and degrees: which I shall consider in their respective order, merely as they are taken notice of by the secular laws of England; without intermeddling with the canons and constitutions, by which they have bound themselves. And under each division I shall consider, 1. The method of their appointment; 2. Their rights and duties; and 3. The manner wherein their character or office may cease.

I. AN arch-bishop or bishop is elected by the chapter of his cathedral church, by virtue of a licence from the crown. Election was, in very early times, the usual mode of elevation to the episcopal chair throughout all christendom; and this was promiscuously performed by the laity as well as the clergy: till at length, it becoming tumultuous, the emperors and other sovereigns of the respective kingdoms of Europe took the election in some degree into their own hands; by reserving to themselves the right of confirming these elections, and of granting investiture of the temporalties, which now began almost universally to be annexed to this spiritual dignity; without which confirmation and investiture, the elected bishop could neither be consecrated, nor receive any secular profits. This right was acknowleged in the emperor Charlemagne, *A.D.* 773, by pope Hadrian I, and the council of Lateran, and universally exercised by other christian princes: but the policy of the court of Rome at the same time began by degrees to exclude the laity from any share in these elections, and to confine them wholly to the clergy, which at length was completely effected; the mere form of election appearing to the people to be a thing of little consequence, while the crown was in possession of an absolute negative, which was almost equivalent to a direct right of nomination. Hence the right of appointing to bishopricks is said to have been in the crown of England (as well as other kingdoms in Europe) even in the Saxon times, because the rights of confirmation and investiture were in effect (though not in form) a right of complete donation. But when, by length of time, the custom of making elections by the clergy only was fully established, the popes began to except to the usual method of granting these investitures, which was *per annulum et baculum*, by the prince's delivering to the prelate a ring, and a pastoral staff or crosier; pretending, that this was an encroachment on the church's authority, and an attempt by these symbols to confer a spiritual jurisdiction: and pope Gregory VII, towards the close of the eleventh century, published a bulle of excommunication against all princes who should dare to confer investitures, and all prelates who should venture to receive them. This was a bold step towards effecting the plan then adopted by the Roman see, of rendering the clergy intirely independent of the civil authority: and long and eager were the contests occasioned by this dispute. But at length when the emperor Henry V agreed to remove all suspicion of encroachment on the spiritual character, by conferring investitures for the future *per sceptrum* and not *per annulum et baculum*, and when the kings of England and France consented also to alter the form in their kingdoms, and receive only homage from the bishops for their temporalties, instead of investing them by the ring and crosier; the court of Rome found it prudent to suspend for a while it's other pretensions.

T H I S concession was obtained from king Henry the first in England, by means of that obstinate and arrogant prelate, arch-bishop Anselm: but king John (about a century afterwards) in order to obtain the protection of the pope against his discontented barons, was prevailed upon to give up by a charter, to all the monasteries and cathedrals in the kingdom, the free right of electing their prelates, whether abbots or bishops: reserving only to the crown the custody of the temporalties during the vacancy; the form of granting a licence to elect, (which is the original of our *conge d'eslire*) on refusal whereof the electors might proceed without it; and the right of approbation afterwards, which was not to be denied without a reasonable and lawful cause. This grant was expressly recognized and confirmed in king John's *magna carta*, and was again established by statute 25 Edw. III. st. 6. §. 3.

BUT by statute 25 Hen. VIII. c. 20. the antient right of nomination was, in effect, restored to the crown: it being enacted that, at every future avoidance of a bishoprick, the king may send the dean and chapter his usual licence to proceed to election; which is always to be accompanied with a letter missive from the king, containing the name of the person whom he would have them elect: and, if the dean and chapter delay their election above twelve days, the nomination shall devolve to the king, who may by letters patent appoint such person as he pleases. This election or nomination, if it be of a bishop, must be signified by the king's letters patent to the arch-bishop of the province; if it be of an arch-bishop, to the other arch-bishop and two bishops, or to four bishops; requiring them to confirm, invest, and consecrate the person so elected: which they are bound to perform immediately, without any application to the see of Rome. After which the bishop elect shall sue to the king for his temporalties, shall make oath to the king and none other, and shall take restitution of his secular possessions out of the king's hands only. And if such dean and chapter do not elect in the manner by this act appointed, or if such arch-bishop or bishop do refuse to confirm, invest, and consecrate such bishop elect, they shall incur all the penalties of a *praemunire*.

AN arch-bishop is the chief of the clergy in a whole province; and has the inspection of the bishops of that province, as well as of the inferior clergy, and may deprive them on notorious cause. The arch-bishop has also his own diocese, wherein he exercises episcopal jurisdiction; as in his province he exercises archiepiscopal. As arch-bishop, he, upon receipt of the king's writ, calls the bishops and clergy of his province to meet in convocation: but without the king's writ he cannot assemble them. To him all appeals are made from inferior jurisdictions within his province; and, as an appeal lies from the bishops in person to him in person, so it also lies from the consistory courts of each diocese to his archiepiscopal court. During the vacancy of any see in his province, he is guardian of the spiritualties thereof, as the king is of the temporalties; and he executes all ecclesiastical jurisdiction therein. If an archiepiscopal see be vacant, the dean and chapter are the spiritual guardians, ever since the office of prior of Canterbury was abolished at the reformation. The arch-bishop is entitled to present by lapse to all the ecclesiastical livings in the disposal of his diocesan bishops, if not filled within six months. And the arch-bishop has a customary prerogative, when a bishop is consecrated by him, to name a clerk or chaplain of his own to be provided for by such suffragan bishop; in lieu of which it is now usual for the bishop to make over by deed to the arch-bishop, his executors and assigns, the next presentation of such dignity or benefice in the bishop's disposal within that see, as the arch-bishop himself shall choose; which is therefore called his option: which options are only binding on the bishop himself who grants them, and not his successors. The prerogative itself seems to be derived from the legatine power formerly annexed by the popes to the metropolitan of Canterbury. And we may add, that the papal claim itself (like most others of that encroaching see) was probably set up in imitation of the imperial prerogative called *primae* or *primariae preces*; whereby the emperor exercises, and hath immemorially exercised, a right of naming to the first prebend that becomes vacant after his accession in every church of the empire. A right, that was also exercised by the crown of England in the reign of Edward I; and which probably gave rise to the royal corodies, which were mentioned in a former chapter. It is also the privilege, by custom, of the arch-bishop of Canterbury, to crown the kings and queens of this kingdom. And he hath also by the statute 25 Hen. VIII. c. 21. the power of granting dispensations in any case, not contrary to the holy scriptures and the law of God, where the pope used formerly to grant them: which is the foundation of his granting special licences, to marry at any place or time, to hold two livings, and the like: and on this also is founded the right he exercises of conferring degrees, in prejudice of the two universities.

T H E power and authority of a bishop, besides the administration of certain holy ordinances peculiar to that sacred order, consists principally in inspecting the manners of the people and clergy, and punishing them, in order to reformation, by ecclesiastical censures. To this purpose he has several courts under him, and may visit at pleasure every part of his diocese. His chancellor is appointed to hold his courts for him, and to assist him in matters of ecclesiastical law; who, as well as all other ecclesiastical officers, if lay or married, must be a doctor of the civil law, so created in some university. It is also the business of a bishop to institute and to direct induction to all ecclesiastical livings in his diocese.

A R C H B I S H O P R I C K S and bishopricks may become void by death, deprivation for any very gross and notorious crime, and also by resignation. All resignations must be made to some superior. Therefore a bishop must resign to his metropolitan; but the arch-bishop can resign to none but the king himself.

II. A D E A N and chapter are the council of the bishop, to assist him with their advice in affairs of religion, and also in the temporal concerns of his see. When the rest of the clergy were settled in the several parishes of each diocese (as hath formerly been mentioned) these were reserved for the celebration of divine service in the bishop's own cathedral; and the chief of them, who presided over the rest, obtained the name of *decanus* or dean, being probably at first appointed to superintend *ten* canons or prebendaries.

A L L antient deans are elected by the chapter, by *conge d'eslire* from the king, and letters missive of recommendation; in the same manner as bishops: but in those chapters, that were founded by Henry VIII out of the spoils of the dissolved monasteries, the deanery is donative, and the installation merely by the king's letters patent. The chapter, consisting of canons or prebendaries, are sometimes appointed by the king, sometimes by the bishop, and sometimes elected by each other.

T H E dean and chapter are, as was before observed, the nominal electors of a bishop. The bishop is their ordinary and immediate superior; and has, generally speaking, the power of visiting them, and correcting their excesses and enormities. They had also a check on the bishop at common law: for till the statute 32 Hen. VIII. c. 28. his grant or lease would not have bound his successors, unless confirmed by the dean and chapter.

DEANERIES and prebends may become void, like a bishoprick, by death, by deprivation, or by resignation to either the king or the bishop. Also I may here mention, once for all, that if a dean, prebendary, or other spiritual person be made a bishop, all the preferments he was before possessed of are void; and the king may present to them in right of his prerogative royal. But they are not void by the election, but only by the consecration.

III. AN arch-deacon hath an ecclesiastical jurisdiction, immediately subordinate to the bishop, throughout the whole of his diocese, or in some particular part of it. He is usually appointed by the bishop himself; and hath a kind of episcopal authority, originally derived from the bishop, but now independent and distinct from his. He therefore visits the clergy; and has his separate court for punishment of offenders by spiritual censures, and for hearing all other causes of ecclesiastical cognizance.

IV. THE rural deans are very antient officers of the church, but almost grown out of use; though their deaneries still subsist as an ecclesiastical division of the diocese, or archdeaconry. They seem to have been deputies of the bishop, planted all round his diocese, the better to inspect the conduct of the parochial clergy, and therefore armed with an inferior degree of judicial and coercive authority.

V. THE next, and indeed the most numerous order of men in the system of ecclesiastical polity, are the parsons and vicars of parishes: in treating of whom I shall first mark out the distinction between them; shall next observe the method by which one may become a parson or vicar; shall then briefly touch upon their rights and duties; and shall, lastly, shew how one may cease to be either.

A PARSON, *persona ecclesiae*, is one that hath full possession of all the rights of a parochial church. He is called parson, *persona*, because by his person the church, which is an invisible body, is represented; and he is in himself a body corporate, in order to protect and defend the rights of the church (which he personates) by a perpetual succession. He is sometimes called the rector, or governor, of the church: but the appellation of *parson*, (however it may be depreciated by familiar, clownish, and indiscriminate use) is the most legal, most beneficial, and most honourable title that a parish priest can enjoy; because such a one, (sir Edward Coke observes) and he only, is said *vicem seu personam ecclesiae gerere*. A parson has, during his life, the freehold in himself of the parsonage house, the glebe, the tithes, and other dues. But these are sometimes *appropriated*; that is to say, the benefice is perpetually annexed to some spiritual corporation, either sole or aggregate, being the patron of the living; whom the law esteems equally capable of providing for the service of the church, as any single private clergyman. This contrivance seems to have sprung from the policy of the monastic orders, who have never been deficient in subtle inventions for the increase of their own power and emoluments. At the first establishment of parochial clergy, the tithes of the parish were distributed in a fourfold division; one for the use of the bishop, another for maintaining the fabrick of the church, a third for the poor, and the fourth to provide for the incumbent. When the sees of the bishops became otherwise amply endowed, they were prohibited from demanding their usual share of these tithes, and the division was into three parts only. And hence it was inferred by the monasteries, that a small part was sufficient for the officiating priest, and that the remainder might well be applied to the use of their own fraternities, (the endowment of which was construed to be a work of the most exalted piety) subject to the burthen of repairing the church and providing for it's constant supply. And therefore they begged and bought, for masses and obits, and sometimes even for money, all the advowsons within their reach, and then appropriated the benefices to the use of their own corporation. But, in order to complete such appropriation effectually, the king's licence, and consent of the bishop, must first be obtained; because both the king and the bishop may sometime or other have an interest, by lapse, in the presentation to the benefice; which can never happen if it be appropriated to the use of a corporation, which never dies: and also because the law reposes a confidence in them, that they will not consent to any thing that shall be to the prejudice of the church. The consent of the patron also is necessarily implied, because (as was before observed) the appropriation can be originally made to none, but to such spiritual corporation, as is also the patron of the church; the whole being indeed nothing else, but an allowance for the patrons to retain the tithes and glebe in their own hands, without presenting any clerk, they themselves undertaking to provide for the service of the church. When the appropriation is thus made, the appropriators and their successors are perpetual parsons of the church; and must sue and be sued, in all matters concerning the rights of the church, by the name of parsons.

THIS appropriation may be severed, and the church become disappropriate, two ways: as, first, if the patron or appropriator presents a clerk, who is instituted and inducted to the parsonage: for the incumbent so instituted and inducted is to all intents and purposes complete parson; and the appropriation, being once severed, can never be re-united again, unless by a repetition of the same solemnities. And when the clerk so presented is distinct from the vicar, the rectory thus vested in him becomes what is called a *sine-cure*; because he hath no cure of souls, having a vicar under him to whom that cure is committed. Also, if the corporation which has the appropriation is dissolved, the parsonage becomes disappropriate at common law; because the perpetuity of person is gone, which is necessary to support the appropriation.

IN this manner, and subject to these conditions, may appropriations be made at this day: and thus were most, if not all, of the appropriations at present existing originally made; being annexed to bishopricks, prebends, religious houses, nay, even to nunneries, and certain military orders, all of which were spiritual corporations. At the dissolution of monasteries by statutes 27 Hen. VIII. c. 28. and 31 Hen. VIII. c. 13. the appropriations of the several parsonages, which belonged to those respective religious houses, (amounting to more than one third of all the parishes in England) would have been by the rules of the common law disappropriated; had not a clause in those statutes intervened, to give them to the king in as ample a manner as the abbots, &c., formerly held the same, at the time of their dissolution. This, though perhaps scarcely defensible, was not without example; for the same was done in former reigns, when the alien priories, (that is, such as were filled by foreigners only) were dissolved and given to the crown. And from these two roots have sprung all the lay appropriations or secular parsonages, which we now see in the kingdom; they having been afterwards granted out from time to time by the crown.

T H E S E appropriating corporations, or religious houses, were wont to depute one of their own body to perform divine service, and administer the sacraments, in those parishes of which the society was thus the parson. This officiating minister was in reality no more than a curate, deputy, or vicegerent of the appropriator, and therefore called *vicarius*, or *vicar*. His stipend was at the discretion of the appropriator, who was however bound of common right to find somebody, *qui illi de temporalibus, episcopo de spiritualibus, debeat respondere*. But this was done in so scandalous a manner, and the parishes suffered so much by the neglect of the appropriators, that the legislature was forced to interpose: and accordingly it is enacted by statute 15 Ric. II. c. 6. that in all appropriations of churches, the diocesan bishop shall ordain (in proportion to the value of the church) a competent sum to be distributed among the poor parishioners annually; and that the vicarage shall be *sufficiently* endowed. It seems the parish were frequently sufferers, not only by the want of divine service, but also by withholding those alms, for which, among other purposes, the payment of tithes was originally imposed: and therefore in this act a pension is directed to be distributed among the poor parochians, as well as a sufficient stipend to the vicar. But he, being liable to be removed at the pleasure of the appropriator, was not likely to insist too rigidly on the legal sufficiency of the stipend: and therefore by statute 4 Hen. IV. c. 12. it is ordained, that the vicar shall be a secular person, not a member of any religious house; that he shall be vicar perpetual, not removeable at the caprice of the monastery; and that he shall be canonically instituted and inducted, and be sufficiently endowed, at the discretion of the ordinary, for these three express purposes, to do divine service, to inform the people, and to keep hospitality. The endowments in consequence of these statutes have usually been by a portion of the glebe, or land, belonging to the parsonage, and a particular share of the tithes, which the appropriators found it most troublesome to collect, and which are therefore generally called privy, small, or vicarial, tithes; the greater, or predial, tithes being still referred to their own use. But one and the same rule was not observed in the endowment of all vicarages. Hence some are more liberally, and some more scantily, endowed; and hence many things, as wood in particular, is in some countries a <u>predial</u>, and in some a vicarial tithe.

T H E distinction therefore of a parson and vicar is this; that the parson has for the most part the whole right to all the ecclesiastical dues in his parish; but a vicar has generally an appropriator over him, entitled to the best part of the profits, to whom he is in effect perpetual curate, with a standing salary. Though in some places the vicarage has been considerably augmented by a large share of the great tithes; which augmentations were greatly assisted by the statute 29 Car. II. c. 8. enacted in favour of poor vicars and curates, which rendered such temporary augmentations (when made by the appropriators) perpetual.

T H E method of becoming a parson or vicar is much the same. To both there are four requisites necessary: holy orders; presentation; institution; and induction. The method of conferring the holy orders of deacon and priest, according to the liturgy and canons, is foreign to the purpose of these commentaries; any farther than as they are necessary requisites to make a complete parson or vicar. By common law a deacon, of any age, might be instituted and inducted to a parsonage or vicarage: but it was ordained by statute 13 Eliz. c. 12. that no person under twenty three years of age, and in deacon's orders, should be presented to any benefice with cure; and if he were not ordained priest within one year after his induction, he should be *ipso facto* deprived: and now, by statute 13 & 14 Car. II. c. 4. no person is capable to be admitted to any benefice, unless he hath been first ordained a priest; and then he is, in the language of the law, a clerk in orders. But if he obtains orders, or a licence to preach, by money or corrupt practices (which seems to be the true, though not the common notion of simony) the person giving such orders forfeits 40*l.* and the person receiving 10*l.* and is incapable of any ecclesiastical preferment for seven years afterwards.

A N Y clerk may be presented to a parsonage or vicarage; that is, the patron, to whom the advowson of the church belongs, may offer his clerk to the bishop of the diocese to be instituted. Of advowsons, or the right of presentation, being a species of private property, we shall find a more convenient place to treat in the second part of these commentaries. But when a clerk is presented, the bishop may refuse him upon many accounts. As, 1. If the patron is excommunicated, and remains in contempt forty days. Or, 2. If the clerk be unfit: which unfitness is of several kinds. First, with regard to his person; as if he be a bastard, an outlaw, an excommunicate, an alien, under age, or the like. Next, with regard to his faith or morals; as for any particular heresy, or vice that is *malum in se*: but if the bishop alleges only in generals, as that he is *schismaticus inveteratus*, or objects a fault that is *malum prohibitum* merely, as haunting taverns, playing at unlawful games, or the like; it is not good cause of refusal. Or, lastly, the clerk may be unfit to discharge the pastoral office for want of learning. In any of which cases the bishop may refuse the clerk. In case the refusal is for heresy, schism, inability of learning, or other matter of ecclesiastical cognizance, there the bishop must give notice to the patron of such his cause of refusal, who, being usually a layman, is not supposed to have knowlege of it; else he cannot present by lapse: but if the cause be temporal, there he is not bound to give notice.

I F an action at law be brought by the patron against the bishop, for refusing his clerk, the bishop must assign the cause. If the cause be of a temporal nature and the fact admitted, (as, for instance, outlawry) the judges of the king's courts must determine it's validity, or, whether it be sufficient cause of refusal: but if the fact be denied, it must be determined by a jury. If the cause be of a spiritual nature, (as, heresy, particularly alleged) the fact if denied shall also be determined by a jury; and if the fact be admitted or found, the court upon consultation and advice of learned divines shall decide it's sufficiency. If the cause be want of learning, the bishop need not specify in what points the clerk is deficient, but only allege that he *is* deficient: for the statute 9 Edw. II. st. 1. c. 13. is express, that the examination of the fitness of a person presented to a benefice belongs to the ecclesiastical judge. But because it would be nugatory in this case to demand the reason of refusal from the ordinary, if the patron were bound to abide by his determination, who has already pronounced his clerk unfit; therefore if the bishop returns the clerk to be *minus sufficiens in literatura*, the court shall write to the metropolitan, to reexamine him, and certify his qualifications; which certificate of the arch-bishop is final.

I F the bishop hath no objections, but admits the patron's presentation, the clerk so admitted is next to be instituted by him; which is a kind of investiture of the spiritual part of the benefice: for by institution the care of the souls of the parish is committed to the charge of the clerk. When a vicar is instituted, he (besides the usual forms) takes, if required by the bishop, an oath of perpetual residence; for the maxim of law is, that *vicarius non habet vicarium*: and as the non-residence of the appropriators was the cause of the perpetual establishment of vicarages, the law judges it very improper for them to defeat the end of their constitution, and by absence to create the very mischiefs which they were appointed to remedy: especially as, if any profits are to arise from putting in a curate and living at a distance from the parish, the appropriator, who is the real parson, has undoubtedly the elder title to them. When the ordinary is also the patron, and *confers* the living, the presentation and institution are one and the same act, and are called a collation to a benefice. By institution or collation the church is full, so that there can be no fresh presentation till another vacancy, at least in the case of a common patron; but the church is not full against the king, till induction: nay, even if a clerk is instituted upon the king's presentation, the crown may revoke it before induction, and present another clerk. Upon institution also the clerk may enter on the parsonage house and glebe, and take the tithes; but he cannot grant or let them, or bring any action for them, till induction.

I N D U C T I O N is performed by a mandate from the bishop to the arch-deacon, who usually issues out a precept to other clergymen to perform it for him. It is done by giving the clerk corporal possession of the church, as by holding the ring of the door, tolling a bell, or the like; and is a form required by law, with intent to give all the parishioners due notice, and sufficient certainty of their new minister, to whom their tithes are to be paid. This therefore is the investiture of the temporal part of the benefice, as institution is of the spiritual. And when a clerk is thus presented, instituted, and inducted into a rectory, he is then, and not before, in full and complete possession, and is called in law *persona impersonata*, or parson imparsonee.

T H E rights of a parson or vicar, in his tithes and ecclesiastical dues, fall more properly under the second book of these commentaries: and as to his duties, they are principally of ecclesiastical cognizance; those only excepted which are laid upon him by statute. And those are indeed so numerous that it is impracticable to recite them here with any tolerable conciseness or accuracy. Some of them we may remark, as they arise in the progress of our enquiries, but for the rest I must refer myself to such authors as have compiled treatises expressly upon this subject. I shall only just mention the article of residence, upon the supposition of which the law doth stile every parochial minister an incumbent. By statute 21 Hen. VIII. c. 13. persons wilfully absenting themselves from their benefices, for one month together, or two months in the year, incur a penalty of 5*l.* to the king, and 5*l.* to any person that will sue for the same: except chaplains to the king, or others therein mentioned, during their attendance in the houshold of such as retain them: and also except all heads of houses, magistrates, and professors in the universities, and all students under forty years of age residing there, *bona fide*, for study. Legal residence is not only in the parish, but also in the parsonage house: for it hath been resolved, that the statute intended residence, not only for serving the cure, and for hospitality; but also for maintaining the house, that the successor also may keep hospitality there.

W E have seen that there is but one way, whereby one may become a parson or vicar: there are many ways, by which one may cease to be so. 1. By death. 2. By cession, in taking another benefice. For by statute 21 Hen. VIII. c. 13. if any one having a benefice of 8*l. per annum*, or upwards, in the king's books, (according to the present valuation,) accepts any other, the first shall be adjudged void; unless he obtains a dispensation; which no one is entitled to have, but the chaplains of the king and others therein mentioned, the brethren and sons of lords and knights, and doctors and bachelors of divinity and law, *admitted by the universities* of this realm. And a vacancy thus made, for want of a dispensation, is called cession. 3. By consecration; for, as was mentioned before, when a clerk is promoted to a bishoprick, all his other preferments are void the instant that he is consecrated. But there is a method, by the favour of the crown, of holding such livings *in commendam. Commenda*, or *ecclesia commendata*, is a living commended by the crown to the care of a clerk, to hold till a proper pastor is provided for it. This may be temporary, for one, two, or three years, or perpetual; being a kind of dispensation to avoid the vacancy of the living, and is called a *commenda retinere*. There is also a *commenda recipere*, which is to take a benefice *de novo*, in the bishop's own gift, or the gift of some other patron consenting to the same; and this is the same to him as institution and induction are to another clerk. 4. By resignation. But this is of no avail, till accepted by the ordinary; into whose hands the resignation must be made. 5. By deprivation, either by canonical censures, of which I am not to speak; or in pursuance of divers penal statutes, which declare the benefice void, for some nonfeasance or neglect, or else some malefeasance or crime. As, for simony; for maintaining any doctrine in derogation of the king's supremacy, or of the thirty nine articles, or of the book of common-prayer; for neglecting after institution to read the articles in the church, or make the declarations against popery, or take the abjuration oath; for using any other form of prayer than the liturgy of the church of England; or for absenting himself sixty days in one year from a benefice belonging to a popish patron, to which the clerk was presented by either of the universities; in all which and similar cases the benefice is *ipso facto* void, without any formal sentence of deprivation.

VI. A C U R A T E is the lowest degree in the church; being in the same state that a vicar was formerly, an officiating temporary minister, instead of the real incumbent. Though there are what are called *perpetual* curacies, where all the tithes are appropriated, and no vicarage endowed, (being for some particular reasons exempted from the statute of Hen. IV) but, instead thereof, such perpetual curate is appointed by the appropriator. With regard to the other species of curates, they are the objects of some particular statutes, which ordain, that such as serve a church during it's vacancy shall be paid such stipend as the ordinary thinks reasonable, out of the profits of the vacancy; or, if that be not sufficient, by the successor within fourteen days after he takes possession: and that, if any rector or vicar nominates a curate to the ordinary to be licenced, the ordinary shall settle his stipend under his hand and seal, not exceeding 50*l. per annum*, nor less than 20*l.* and on failure of payment may sequester the profits of the benefice.

THUS much of the clergy, properly so called. There are also certain inferior ecclesiastical officers of whom the common law takes notice; and that, principally, to assist the ecclesiastical jurisdiction, where it is deficient in powers. On which officers I shall make a few cursory remarks.

VII. CHURCHWARDENS are the guardians or keepers of the church, and representatives of the body of the parish. They are sometimes appointed by the minister, sometimes by the parish, sometimes by both together, as custom directs. They are taken, in favour of the church, to be for some purposes a kind of corporation at the common law; that is, they are enabled by that name to have a property in goods and chattels, and to bring actions for them, for the use and profit of the parish. Yet they may not waste the church goods, but may be removed by the parish, and then called to account by action at the common law: but there is no method of calling them to account, but by first removing them; for none can legally do it, but those who are put in their place. As to lands, or other real property, as the church, church-yard, &c., they have no sort of interest therein; but if any damage is done thereto, the parson only or vicar shall have the action. Their office also is to repair the church, and make rates and levies for that purpose: but these are recoverable only in the ecclesiastical court. They are also joined with the overseers in the care and maintenance of the poor. They are to levy a shilling forfeiture on all such as do not repair to church on sundays and holidays, and are empowered to keep all persons orderly while there; to which end it has been held that a churchwarden may justify the pulling off a man's hat, without being guilty of either an assault or trespass. There are also a multitude of other petty parochial powers committed to their charge by divers acts of parliament.

VIII. PARISH clerks and sextons are also regarded by the common law, as persons who have freeholds in their offices; and therefore though they may be punished, yet they cannot be deprived, by ecclesiastical censures. The parish clerk was formerly always in holy orders; and some are so to this day. He is generally appointed by the incumbent, but by custom may be chosen by the inhabitants; and if such custom appears, the court of king's bench will grant a *mandamus* to the arch-deacon to swear him in, for the establishment of the custom turns it into a temporal or civil right.

155

CHAPTER THE TWELFTH.
OF THE CIVIL STATE.

TH E lay part of his majesty's subjects, or such of the people as are not comprehended under the denomination of clergy, may be divided into three distinct states, the civil, the military, and the maritime.

T H A T part of the nation which falls under our first and most comprehensive division, the civil state, includes all orders of men, from the highest nobleman to the meanest peasant; that are not included under either our former division, of clergy, or under one of the two latter, the military and maritime states: and it may sometimes include individuals of the other three orders; since a nobleman, a knight, a gentleman, or a peasant, may become either a divine, a soldier, or a seaman.

T H E civil state consists of the nobility and the commonalty. Of the nobility, the peerage of Great Britain, or lords temporal, as forming (together with the bishops) one of the supreme branches of the legislature, I have before sufficiently spoken: we are here to consider them according to their several degrees, or titles of honour.

A L L degrees of nobility and honour are derived from the king as their fountain: and he may institute what new titles he pleases. Hence it is that all degrees of honour are not of equal antiquity. Those now in use are dukes, marquesses, earls, viscounts, and barons.

1. A *duke*, though it be with us, as a mere title of nobility, inferior in point of antiquity to many others, yet it is superior to all of them in rank; being the first title of dignity after the royal family. Among the Saxons the Latin name of dukes, *duces*, is very frequent, and signified, as among the Romans, the commanders or leaders of their armies, whom in their own language they called ; and in the laws of Henry I (as translated by Lambard) we find them called *heretochii*. But after the Norman conquest, which changed the military polity of the nation, the kings themselves continuing for many generations *dukes* of Normandy, they would not honour any subjects with that title, till the time of Edward III; who, claiming to be king of France, and thereby losing the ducal in the royal dignity, in the eleventh year of his reign created his son, Edward the black prince, duke of Cornwall: and many, of the royal family especially, were afterwards raised to the same honour. However, in the reign of queen Elizabeth, *A.D.* 1572, the whole order became utterly extinct: but it was revived about fifty years afterwards by her successor, who was remarkably prodigal of honours, in the person of George Villiers duke of Buckingham.

3. A N *earl* is a title of nobility so antient, that it's original cannot clearly be traced out. Thus much seems tolerably certain: that among the Saxons they were called *ealdormen, quasi* elder men, signifying the same as *senior* or *senator* among the Romans; and also *schiremen*, because they had each of them the civil government of a several division or shire. On the irruption of the Danes, they changed the name to *eorles*, which, according to Camden, signified the same

in their language. In Latin they are called *comites* (a title first used in the empire) from being the king's attendants; "*a societate nomen sumpserunt, reges enim tales sibi associant.*" After the Norman conquest they were for some time called *counts*, or *countees*, from the French; but they did not long retain that name themselves, though their shires are from thence called counties to this day. It is now become a mere title, they having nothing to do with the government of the county; which, as has been more than once observed, is now entirely devolved on the sheriff, the earl's deputy, or *vice-comes*. In all writs, and commissions, and other formal instruments, the king, when he mentions any peer of the degree of an earl, always stiles him "trusty and well beloved *cousin*:" an appellation as antient as the reign of Henry IV; who being either by his wife, his mother, or his sisters, actually related or allied to every earl in the kingdom, artfully and constantly acknowleged that connexion in all his letters and other public acts; from whence the usage has descended to his successors, though the reason has long ago failed.

4. T H E name of *vice-comes* or *viscount* was afterwards made use of as an arbitrary title of honour, without any shadow of office pertaining to it, by Henry the sixth; when in the eighteenth year of his reign, he created John Beaumont a peer, by the name of viscount Beaumont, which was the first instance of the kind.

2 Inst. 5.

5. A *baron*'s is the most general and universal title of nobility; for originally every one of the peers of superior rank had also a barony annexed to his other titles. But it hath sometimes happened that, when an antient baron hath been raised to a new degree of peerage, in the course of a few generations the two titles have descended differently; one perhaps to the male descendants, the other to the heirs general; whereby the earldom or other superior title hath subsisted without a barony: and there are also modern instances where earls and viscounts have been created without annexing a barony to their other honours: so that now the rule does not hold universally, that all peers are barons. The original and antiquity of baronies has occasioned great enquiries among our English antiquarians. The most probable opinion seems to be, that they were the same with our present lords of manors; to which the name of court baron, (which is the lord's court, and incident to every manor) gives some countenance. It may be collected from king John's *magna carta*, that originally all lords of manors, or barons, that held of the king *in capite*, had seats in the great council or parliament, till about the reign of that prince the conflux of them became so large and troublesome, that the king was obliged to divide them, and summon only the greater barons in person; leaving the small ones to be summoned by the sheriff, and (as it is said) to sit by representation in another house; which gave rise to the separation of the two houses of parliament. By degrees the title came to be confined to the greater barons, or lords of parliament only; and there were no other barons among the peerage but such as were summoned by writ, in respect of the tenure of their lands or baronies, till Richard the second first made it a mere title of honor, by conferring it on divers persons by his letters patent.

H A V I N G made this short enquiry into the original of our several degrees of nobility, I shall next consider the manner in which they may be created. The right of peerage seems to have been originally territorial; that is, annexed to lands, honors, castles, manors, and the like, the proprietors and possessors of which were (in right of those estates) allowed to be peers of the realm, and were summoned to parliament to do suit and service to their sovereign: and, when the land was alienated, the dignity passed with it as appendant. Thus the bishops still sit in the house of lords in right of succession to certain antient baronies annexed, or supposed to be annexed, to their episcopal lands: and thus, in 11 Hen. VI, the possession of the castle of Arundel was adjudged to confer an earldom on it's possessor. But afterwards, when alienations grew to be frequent, the dignity of peerage was confined to the lineage of the party ennobled, and instead of territorial became personal. Actual proof of a tenure by barony became no longer necessary to constitute a lord of parliament; but the record of the writ of summons to them or their ancestors was admitted as a sufficient evidence of the tenure.

P E E R S are now created either by writ, or by patent: for those who claim by prescription must suppose either a writ or patent made to their ancestors; though by length of time it is lost. The creation by writ, or the king's letter, is a summons to attend the house of peers, by the stile and title of that barony, which the king is pleased to confer: that by patent is a royal grant to a subject of any dignity and degree of peerage. The creation by writ is the more antient way; but a man is not ennobled thereby, unless he actually takes his seat in the house of lords: and therefore the most usual, because the surest, way is to grant the dignity by patent, which enures to a man and his heirs according to the limitations thereof, though he never himself makes use of it. Yet it is frequent to call up the eldest son of a peer to the house of lords by writ of summons, in the name of his father's barony: because in that case there is no danger of his children's losing the nobility in case he never takes his seat; for they will succeed to their grand-father. Creation by writ has also one advantage over that by patent: for a person created by writ holds the dignity to him *and his heirs*, without any words to that purport in the writ; but in letters patent there must be words to direct the inheritance, else the dignity enures only to the grantee for life. For a man or woman may be created noble for their own lives, and the dignity not descend to their heirs at all, or descend only to some particular heirs: as where a peerage is limited to a man, and the heirs male of his body by Elizabeth his present lady, and not to such heirs by any former or future wife.

L E T us next take a view of a few of the principal incidents attending the nobility, exclusive of their capacity as members of parliament, and as hereditary counsellors of the crown; both of which we have before considered. And first we must observe, that in criminal cases, a nobleman shall be tried by his peers. The great are always obnoxious to popular envy: were they to be judged by the people, they might be in danger from the prejudice of their judges; and would moreover be deprived of the privilege of the meanest subjects, that of being tried by their equals, which is secured to all the realm by *magna carta*, c. 29. It is said, that this does not extend to bishops; who, though they are lords of parliament, and sit there by virtue of their baronies which they hold *jure ecclesiae*, yet are not ennobled in blood, and consequently not peers with the nobility. As to peeresses, no provision was made for their trial when accused of treason orfelony, till after Eleanor dutchess of Gloucester, wife to the lord protector, had been accused of treason and found guilty of witchcraft, in an ecclesiastical synod, through the intrigues of cardinal Beaufort. This very extraordinary trial gave occasion to a special statute, 20 Hen. VI. c. 9. which enacts that peeresses either in their own right, or by marriage, shall be tried before the same judicature as peers of the realm. If a woman, noble in her own right, marries a commoner, she still remains noble, and shall be tried by her peers: but if she be only noble by marriage, then by a second marriage, with a commoner, she loses her dignity; for as by marriage it is gained, by marriage it is also lost. Yet if a duchess dowager marries a baron, she continues a duchess still; for all the nobility are *pares*, and therefore it is no degradation. A peer, or peeress (either in her own right or by marriage) cannot be arrested in civil cases: and they have also many peculiar privileges annexed to their peerage in the course of judicial proceedings. A peer, sitting in judgment, gives not his verdict upon oath, like an ordinary juryman, but upon his honour: he answers also to bills in chancery upon his honour, and not upon his oath; but, when he is examined as a witness either in civil or criminal cases, he must be sworn: for the respect, which the law shews to the honour of a peer, does not extend so far as to overturn a settled maxim, that *in judicio non creditur nisi juratis*. The honour of peers is however so highly tendered by the law, that it is much more penal to spread false reports of them, and certain other great officers of the realm, than of other men: scandal against them being called by the peculiar name of *scandalum magnatum*; and subjected to peculiar punishment by divers antient statutes.

A PEER cannot lose his nobility, but by death or attainder; hough there was an instance, in the reign of Edward the fourth, of the degradation of George Nevile duke of Bedford by act of parliament, on account of his poverty, which rendered him unable to support his dignity. But this is a singular instance: which serves at the same time, by having happened, to shew the power of parliament; and, by having happened but once, to shew how tender the parliament hath been, in exerting so high a power. It hath been said indeed, that if a baron waste his estate, so that he is not able to support the degree, the *king* may degrade him: but it is expressly held by later authorities, that a peer cannot be degraded but by act of *parliament*.

THE commonalty, like the nobility, are divided into several degrees; and, as the lords, though different in rank, yet all of them are peers in respect of their nobility, so the commoners, though some are greatly superior to others, yet all are in law peers, in respect of their want of nobility.

THE first name of dignity, next beneath a peer, was anciently that of *vidames*, *vice domini*, or *valvasors*: who are mentioned by our antient lawyers as *viri magnae dignitatis*; and sir Edward Coke speaks highly of them. Yet they are now quite out of use; and our legal antiquarians are not so much as agreed upon their original or ancient office.

NOW therefore the first dignity after the nobility, is a *knight* of the order of St. George, or *of the garter*; first instituted by Edward III, *A.D.* 1344. Next follows a *knight banneret*; who indeed by statutes 5 Ric. II. st. 2. c. 4. and 14 Ric. II. c. 11. is ranked next after barons: and that precedence was confirmed to him by order of king James I, in the tenth year of his reign. But, in order to intitle himself to this rank, he must have been created by the king in person, in the field, under the royal banners, in time of open war. Else he ranks after *baronets*, who are the next order: which title is a dignity of inheritance, created by letters patent, and usually descendible to the issue male. It was first instituted by king James the first, *A.D.* 1611. in order to raise a competent sum for the reduction of the province of Ulster in Ireland; for which reason all baronets have the arms of Ulster superadded to their family coat. Next follow *knights of the bath*, an order instituted by king Henry IV, and revived by king George the first. They are so called from the ceremony of bathing, the night before their creation. The last of these inferior nobility are *knights bachelors*, the most antient, though the lowest, order of knighthood amongst us: for we have an instance of king Alfred's conferring this order on his son Athelstan. The custom of the antient Germans was to give their young men a shield and a lance in the great council: this was equivalent to the *toga virilis* of the Romans: before this they were not permitted to bear arms, but were accounted as part of the father's houshold; after it, as part of the public. Hence some derive the usage of knighting, which has prevailed all over the western world, since it's reduction by colonies from those northern heroes. Knights are called in Latin *equites aurati*, *aurati*, from the gilt spurs they wore; and *equites*, because they always served on horseback: for it is observable, that almost all nations call their knights by some appellation derived from an horse. They are also called in our law *milites*, because they formed a part, or indeed the whole of the royal army, in virtue of their feodal tenures; one condition of which was, that every one who held a knights fee (which in Henry the second's time amounted to 20*l. per annum*) was obliged to be knighted, and attend the king in his wars, or fine for his non-compliance. The exertion of this prerogative, as an expedient to raise money in the reign of Charles the first, gave great offence; though warranted by law, and the recent example of queen Elizabeth: but it was, at the restoration, together with all other military branches of the feodal law, abolished; and this kind of knighthood has, since that time, fallen into great disregard.

THESE, sir Edward Coke says, are all the names of *dignity* in this kingdom, esquires and gentlemen being only names of *worship*. But before these last the heralds rank all colonels, serjeants at law, and doctors in the three learned professions.

ESQUIRES and gentlemen are confounded together by sir Edward Coke, who observes, that every esquire is a gentleman, and a gentleman is defined to be one *qui arma gerit*, who bears coat armour, the grant of which adds gentility to a man's family: in like manner as civil nobility, among the Romans, was founded in the *jus imaginum*, or having the image of one ancestor at least, who had borne some curule office. It is indeed a matter somewhat unsettled, what constitutes the distinction, or who is a real *esquire*: for it is not an estate, however large, that confers this rank upon it's owner. Camden, who was himself a herald, distinguishes them the most accurately; and he reckons up four sorts of them: 1. The eldest sons of knights, and their eldest sons, in perpetual succession. 2. The younger sons of peers, and their eldest sons, in like perpetual succession: both which species of esquires sir H. Spelman entitles *armigeri natalitii.* 3. Esquires created by the king's letters patent, or other investiture; and their eldest sons. 4. Esquires by virtue of their offices; as justices of the peace, and others who bear any office of trust under the crown. To these may be added the esquires of knights of the bath, each of whom constitutes three at his installation; and all foreign, nay, Irish peers; and the eldest sons of peers of Great Britain, who, though generally titular lords, are only esquires in the law, and must so be named in all legal proceedings. As for *gentlemen*, says sir Thomas Smith, they be made good cheap in this kingdom: for whosoever studieth the laws of the realm, who studieth in the universities, who professeth liberal sciences, and (to be short) who can live idly, and without manual labour, and will bear the port, charge, and countenance of a gentleman, he shall be called master, and shall be taken for a gentleman. A *yeoman* is he that hath free land of forty shillings by the year; who is thereby qualified to serve on juries, vote for knights of the shire, and do any other act, where the law requires one that is *probus et legalis homo.*

CHAPTER THE THIRTEENTH.

OF THE MILITARY AND MARITIME STATES.

THE military state includes the whole of the soldiery; or, such persons as are peculiarly appointed among the rest of the people, for the safeguard and defence of the realm.

IN a land of liberty it is extremely dangerous to make a distinct order of the profession of arms. In absolute monarchies this is necessary for the safety of the prince, and arises from the main principle of their constitution, which is that of governing by fear: but in free states the profession of a soldier, taken singly and merely as a profession, is justly an object of jealousy. In these no man should take up arms, but with a view to defend his country and it's laws: he puts not off the citizen when he enters the camp; but it is because he is a citizen, and would wish to continue so, that he makes himself for a while a soldier. The laws therefore and constitution of these kingdoms know no such state as that of a perpetual standing soldier, bred up to no other profession than that of war: and it was not till the reign of Henry VII, that the kings of England had so much as a guard about their persons.

IN the time of our Saxon ancestors, as appears from Edward the confessor's laws, the military force of this kingdom was in the hands of the dukes or heretochs, who were constituted through every province and county in the kingdom; being taken out of the principal nobility, and such as were most remarkable for being "*sapientes, fideles, et animosi.*" Their duty was to lead and regulate the English armies, with a very unlimited power; "*prout eis visum fuerit, ad honorem coronae et utilitatem regni.*" And because of this great power they were elected by the people in their full assembly, or folkmote, in the same manner as sheriffs were elected: following still that old fundamental maxim of the Saxon constitution, that where any officer was entrusted with such power, as if abused might tend to the oppression of the people, that power was delegated to him by the vote of the people themselves. So too, among the antient Germans, the ancestors of our Saxon forefathers, they had their dukes, as well as kings, with an independent power over the military, as the kings had over the civil state. The dukes were elective, the kings hereditary: for so only can be consistently understood that passage of Tacitus, "*reges ex nobilitate, duces ex virtute sumunt*;" in constituting their kings, the family, or blood royal, was regarded, in chusing their dukes or leaders, warlike merit: just as Caesar relates of their ancestors in his time, that whenever they went to war, by way either of attack or defence, they *elected* leaders to command them. This large share of power, thus conferred by the people, though intended to preserve the liberty of the subject, was perhaps unreasonably detrimental to the prerogative of the crown: and accordingly we find a very ill use made of it by Edric duke of Mercia, in the reign of king Edmond Ironside; who, by his office of duke or heretoch, was entitled to a large command in the king's army, and by his repeated treacheries at last transferred the crown to Canute the Dane.

IT seems universally agreed by all historians, that king Alfred first settled a national militia in this kingdom, and by his prudent discipline made all the subjects of his dominion soldiers:

but we are unfortunately left in the dark as to the particulars of this his so celebrated regulation; though, from what was last observed, the dukes seem to have been left in possession of too large and independent a power: which enabled duke Harold on the death of Edward the confessor, though a stranger to the royal blood, to mount for a short space the throne of this kingdom, in prejudice of Edgar Atheling, the rightful heir.

U P O N the Norman conquest the feodal law was introduced here in all it's rigor, the whole of which is built on a military plan. I shall not now enter into the particulars of that constitution, which belongs more properly to the next part of our commentaries: but shall only observe, that, in consequence thereof, all the lands in the kingdom were divided into what were called knight's fees, in number above sixty thousand; and for every knight's fee a knight or soldier, *miles*, was bound to attend the king in his wars, for forty days in a year; in which space of time, before war was reduced to a science, the campaign was generally finished, and a kingdom either conquered or victorious. By this means the king had, without any expense, an army of sixty thousand men always ready at his command. And accordingly we find one, among the laws of William the conqueror, which in the king's name commands and firmly enjoins the personal attendance of all knights and others; "*quod habeant et teneant se semper in armis et equis, ut decet et oportet; et quod semper sint prompti et parati ad servitium suum integrum nobis explendum et peragendum, cum opus adfuerit, secundum quod debent de feodis et tenementis suis de jure nobis facere.*" This personal service in process of time degenerated into pecuniary commutations or aids, and at last the military part of the feodal system was abolished at the restoration, by statute 12 Car. II. c. 24.

I N the mean time we are not to imagine that the kingdom was left wholly without defence, in case of domestic insurrections, or the prospect of foreign invasions. Besides those, who by their military tenures were bound to perform forty days service in the field, the statute of Winchester obliged every man, according to his estate and degree, to provide a determinate quantity of such arms as were then in use, in order to keep the peace: and constables were appointed in all hundreds to see that such arms were provided. These weapons were changed, by the statute 4 & 5 Ph. & M. c. 2. into others of more modern service; but both this and the former provision were repealed in the reign of James I. While these continued in force, it was usual from time to time for our princes to to issue commissions of array, and send into every county officers in whom they could confide, to muster and array (or set in military order) the inhabitants of every district: and the form of the commission of array was settled in parliament in the 5 Hen. IV. But at the same time it was provided, that no man should be compelled to go out of the kingdom at any rate, nor out of his shire but in cases of urgent necessity; nor should provide soldiers unless by consent of parliament. About the reign of king Henry the eighth, and his children, lord lieutenants began to be introduced, as standing representatives of the crown, to keep the counties in military order; for we find them mentioned as known officers in the statute 4 & 5 Ph. & M. c. 3. though they had not been then long in use, for Camden speaks of them, in the time of queen Elizabeth, as extraordinary magistrates constituted only in times of difficulty and danger.

IN this state things continued, till the repeal of the statutes of armour in the reign of king James the first: after which, when king Charles the first had, during his northern expeditions, issued commissions of lieutenancy and exerted some military powers which, having been long exercised, were thought to belong to the crown, it became a question in the long parliament, how far the power of the militia did inherently reside in the king; being now unsupported by any statute, and founded only upon immemorial usage. This question, long agitated with great heat and resentment on both sides, became at length the immediate cause of the fatal rupture between the king and his parliament: the two houses not only denying this prerogative of the crown, the legality of which right perhaps might be somewhat doubtful; but also seizing into their own hands the intire power of the militia, the illegality of which step could never be any doubt at all.

SOON after the restoration of king Charles the second, when the military tenures were abolished, it was thought proper to ascertain the power of the militia, to recognize the sole right of the crown to govern and command them, and to put the whole into a more regular method of military subordination: and the order, in which the militia now stands by law, is principally built upon the statutes which were then enacted. It is true the two last of them are apparently repealed; but many of their provisions are re-enacted, with the addition of some new regulations, by the present militia laws: the general scheme of which is to discipline a certain number of the inhabitants of every county, chosen by lot for three years, and officered by the lord lieutenant, the deputy lieutenants, and other principal landholders, under a commission from the crown. They are not compellable to march out of their counties, unless in case of invasion or actual rebellion, nor in any case compellable to march out of the kingdom. They are to be exercised at stated times: and their discipline in general is liberal andeasy; but, when drawn out into actual service, they are subject to the rigours of martial law, as necessary to keep them in order. This is the constitutional security, which our laws have provided for the public peace, and for protecting the realm against foreign or domestic violence; and which the statutes declare is essentially necessary to the safety and prosperity of the kingdom.

WHEN the nation is engaged in a foreign war, more veteran troops and more regular discipline may perhaps be necessary, than can be expected from a mere militia. And therefore at such times particular provisions have been usually made for the raising of armies and the due regulation and discipline of the soldiery: which are to be looked upon only as temporary excrescences bred out of the distemper of the state, and not as any part of the permanent and perpetual laws of the kingdom. For martial law, which is built upon no settled principles, but is entirely arbitrary in it's decisions, is, as sir Matthew Hale observes, in truth and reality no law, but something indulged, rather than allowed as a law: the necessity of order and discipline in an army is the only thing which can give it countenance; and therefore it ought not to be permitted in time of peace, when the king's courts are open for all persons to receive justice according to the laws of the land. Wherefore Edmond earl of Kent being taken at Pontefract, 15 Edw. II. and condemned by martial law, his attainder was reversed 1 Edw. III.

because it was done in time of peace. And it is laid down, that if a lieutenant, or other, that hath commission of martial authority, doth in time of peace hang or otherwise execute any man by colour of martial law, this is murder; for it is against *magna carta*. And the petition of right enacts, that no soldier shall be quartered on the subject without his own consent; and that no commission shall issue to proceed within this land according to martial law. And whereas, after the restoration, king Charles the second kept up about five thousand regular troops, by his own authority, for guards and garrisons; which king James the second by degrees increased to no less than thirty thousand, all paid from his own civil list; it was made one of the articles of the bill of rights, that the raising or keeping a standing army within the kingdom in time of peace, unless it be with consent of parliament, is against law.

B U T , as the fashion of keeping standing armies has universally prevailed over all Europe of late years (though some of it's potentates, being unable themselves to maintain them, are obliged to have recourse to richer powers, and receive subsidiary pensions for that purpose) it has also for many years past been annually judged necessary by our legislature, for the safety of the kingdom, the defence of the possessions of the crown of Great Britain, and the preservation of the balance of power in Europe, to maintain even in time of peace a standing body of troops, under the command of the crown; who are however *ipso facto* disbanded at the expiration of every year, unless continued by parliament.

T O prevent the executive power from being able to oppress, says baron Montesquieu, it is requisite that the armies with which it is entrusted should consist of the people, and have the same spirit with the people; as was the case at Rome, till Marius new-modelled the legions by enlisting the rabble of Italy, and laid the foundation of all the military tyranny that ensued. Nothing then, according to these principles, ought to be more guarded against in a free state, than making the military power, when such a one is necessary to be kept on foot, a body too distinct from the people. Like ours therefore, it should wholly be composed of natural subjects; it ought only to be enlisted for a short and limited time; the soldiers also should live intermixed with the people; no separate camp, no barracks, no inland fortresses should be allowed. And perhaps it might be still better, if, by dismissing a stated number and enlisting others at every renewal of their term, a circulation could be kept up between the army and the people, and the citizen and the soldier be more intimately connected together.

T O keep this body of troops in order, an annual act of parliament likewise passes, "to punish mutiny and desertion, and for the better payment of the army and their quarters." This regulates the manner in which they are to be dispersed among the several inn-keepers and victuallers throughout the kingdom; and establishes a law martial for their government. By this, among other things, it is enacted, that if any officer and soldier shall excite, or join any mutiny, or, knowing of it, shall not give notice to the commanding officer; or shall defect, or list in any other regiment, or sleep upon his post, or leave it before he is relieved, or hold correspondence with a rebel or enemy, or strike or use violence to his superior officer, or shall disobey his lawful commands; such offender shall suffer such punishment as a court martial shall inflict, though it extend to death itself.

H O W E V E R expedient the most strict regulations may be in time of actual war, yet, in times of profound peace, a little relaxation of military rigour would not, one should hope, be productive of much inconvenience. And, upon this principle, though by our standing laws (still remaining in force, though not attended to) desertion in time of war is made felony, without benefit of clergy, and the offence is triable by a jury and before the judges of the common law; yet, by our militia laws beforementioned, a much lighter punishment is inflicted for desertion in time of peace. So, by the Roman law also, desertion in time of war was punished with death, but more mildly in time of tranquillity. But our mutiny act makes no such distinction: for any of the faults therein mentioned are, equally at all times, punishable with death itself, if a court martial shall think proper. This discretionary power of the court martial is indeed to be guided by the directions of the crown; which, with regard to military offences, has almost an absolute legislative power. "His majesty, says the act, may form articles of war, and constitute courts martial, with power to try any crime by such articles, and inflict such penalties as the articles direct." A vast and most important trust! an unlimited power to create crimes, and annex to them any punishments, not extending to life or limb! These are indeed forbidden to be inflicted, except for crimes declared to be so punishable by this act; which crimes we have just enumerated, and, among which, we may observe that any disobedience to lawful commands is one. Perhaps in some future revision of this act, which is in many respects hastily penned, it may be thought worthy the wisdom of parliament to ascertain the limits of military subjection, and to enact express articles of war for the government of the army, as is done for the government of the navy: especially as, by our present constitution, the nobility and gentry of the kingdom, who serve their country as militia officers, are annually subjected to the same arbitrary rule, during their time of exercise.

O N E of the greatest advantages of our English law is, that not only the crimes themselves which it punishes, but also the penalties which it inflicts, are ascertained and notorious: nothing is left to arbitrary discretion: the king by his judges dispenses what the law has previously ordained; but is not himself the legislator. How much therefore is it to be regretted that a set of men, whose bravery has so often preserved the liberties of their country, should be reduced to a state of servitude in the midst of a nation of freemen! for sir Edward Coke will inform us, that it is one of the genuine marks of servitude, to have the law, which is our rule of action, either concealed or precarious: "*misera est servitus, ubi jus est vagum aut incognitum.*" Nor is this state of servitude quite consistent with the maxims of sound policy observed by other free nations. For, the greater the general liberty is which any state enjoys, the more cautious has it usually been of introducing slavery in any particular order or profession. These men, as baron Montesquieu observes, seeing the liberty which others possess, and which they themselves are excluded from, are apt (like eunuchs in the eastern seraglios) to live in a state of perpetual envy and hatred towards the rest of the community; and indulge a malignant pleasure in contributing to destroy those privileges, to which they can never be admitted. Hence have many free states, by departing from this rule, been endangered by the revolt of their slaves: while, in absolute and despotic governments where there no real liberty exists, and consequently no invidious comparisons can be formed, such incidents are extremely rare. Two precautions are therefore advised to be observed in all prudent and free governments; 1. To prevent the introduction of slavery at all: or, 2. If it be already introduced, not to intrust those slaves with arms; who will then find themselves an overmatch for the freemen. Much less ought the soldiery to be an exception to the people in general, and the only state of servitude in the nation.

B U T as soldiers, by this annual act, are thus put in a worse condition than any other subjects, so, by the humanity of our standing laws, they are in some cases put in a much better. By statute 43 Eliz. c. 3. a weekly allowance is to be raised in every county for the relief of soldiers that are sick, hurt, and maimed: not forgetting the royal hospital at Chelsea for such as are worn out in their duty. Officers and soldiers, that have been in the king's service, are by several statutes, enacted at the close of several wars, at liberty to use any trade or occupation they are fit for, in any town in the kingdom (except the two universities) notwithstanding any statute, custom, or charter to the contrary. And soldiers in actual military service may make their wills, and dispose of their goods, wages, and other personal chattels, without those forms, solemnities, and expenses, which the law requires in other cases. Our law does not indeed extend this privilege so far as the civil law; which carried it to an extreme that borders upon the ridiculous. For if a soldier, in the article of death, wrote any thing in bloody letters on his shield, or in the dust of the field with his sword, it was a very good military testament. And thus much for the military state, as acknowleged by the laws of England.

T H E *maritime* state is nearly related to the former; though much more agreeable to the principles of our free constitution. The royal navy of England hath ever been it's greatest defence and ornament: it is it's antient and natural strength; the floating bulwark of the island; an army, from which, however strong and powerful, no danger can ever be apprehended to liberty: and accordingly it has been assiduously cultivated, even from the earliest ages. To so much perfection was our naval reputation arrived in the twelfth century, that the code of maritime laws, which are called the laws of Oleron, and are received by all nations in Europe as the ground and substruction of all their marine constitutions, was confessedly compiled by our king Richard the first, at the isle of Oleron on the coast of France, then part of the possessions of the crown of England. And yet, so vastly inferior were our ancestors in this point to the present age, that even in the maritime reign of queen Elizabeth, sir Edward Coke thinks it matter of boast, that the royal navy of England then consisted of *three and thirty* ships. The present condition of our marine is in great measure owing to the salutary provisions of the statutes, called the navigation-acts; whereby the constant increase of English shipping and seamen was not only encouraged, but rendered unavoidably necessary. By the statute 5 Ric. II. c. 3. in order to augment the navy of England, then greatly diminished, it was ordained, that none of the king's liege people should ship any merchandize out of or into the realm but only in ships of the king's ligeance, on pain of forfeiture. In the next year, by statute 6 Ric. II. c. 8. this wise provision was enervated, by only obliging the merchants to give English ships, (if able and sufficient) the preference. But the most beneficial statute for the trade and commerce of these kingdoms is that navigation-act, the rudiments of which were first framed in 1650, with a narrow partial view: being intended to mortify the sugar islands, which were disaffected to the parliament and still held out for Charles II, by stopping the gainful trade which they then carried on with the Dutch; and at the same time to clip the wings of those our opulent and aspiring neighbours. This prohibited all ships of foreign nations from trading with any English plantations without licence from the council of state. In 1651 the prohibition was extended also to the mother country; and no goods were suffered to be imported into England, or any of it's dependencies, in any other than English bottoms; or in the ships of that European nation of which the merchandize imported was the genuine growth or manufacture. At the restoration, the former provisions were continued, by statute 12 Car. II. c. 18. with this very material improvement, that the master and three fourths of the mariners shall also be English subjects.

M A N Y laws have been made for the supply of the royal navy with seamen; for their regulation when on board; and to confer privileges and rewards on them during and after their service.

I. F I R S T , for their supply. The power of impressing men for the sea service by the king's commission, has been a matter of some dispute, and submitted to with great reluctance; though it hath very clearly and learnedly been shewn, by sir Michael Foster, that the practise of impressing, and granting powers to the admiralty for that purpose, is of very antient date, and hath been uniformly continued by a regular series of precedents to the present time: whence he concludes it to be part of the common law. The difficulty arises from hence, that no statute has expressly declared this power to be in the crown, though many of them very strongly imply it. The statute 2 Ric. II. c. 4. speaks of mariners being arrested and retained for the king's service, as of a thing well known, and practised without dispute; and provides a remedy against their running away. By a later statute, if any waterman, who uses the river Thames, shall hide himself during the execution of any commission of pressing for the king's service, he is liable to heavy penalties. By another, no fisherman shall be taken by the queen's commission to serve as a mariner; but the commission shall be first brought to two justices of the peace, inhabiting near the sea coast where the mariners are to be taken, to the intent that the justices may chuse out and return such a number of ablebodied men, as in the commission are contained, to serve her majesty. And, by others, especial protections are allowed to seamen in particular circumstances, to prevent them from being impressed. All which do most evidently imply a power of impressing to reside somewhere; and, if any where, it must from the spirit of our constitution, as well as from the frequent mention of the king's commission, reside in the crown alone.

B U T , besides this method of impressing, (which is only defensible from public necessity, to which all private considerations must give way) there are other ways that tend to the increase of seamen, and manning the royal navy. Parishes may bind out poor boys apprentices to masters of merchantmen, who shall be protected from impressing for the first three years; and if they are impressed afterwards, the masters shall be allowed their wages: great advantages in point of wages are given to volunteer seamen in order to induce them to enter into his majesty's service: and every foreign seaman, who during a war shall serve two years in any man of war, merchantman, or privateer, is naturalized *ipso facto*. About the middle of king William's reign, a scheme was set on foot for a register of seamen to the number of thirty thousand, for a constant and regular supply of the king's fleet; with great privileges to the registered men, and, on the other hand, heavy penalties in case of their non-appearance when called for: but this registry, being judged to be rather a badge of slavery, was abolished by statute 9 Ann. c. 21.

2. T H E method of ordering seamen in the royal fleet, and keeping up a regular discipline there, is directed by certain express rules, articles and orders, first enacted by the authority of parliament soon after the restoration; but since new-modelled and altered, after the peace of Aix la Chapelle, to remedy some defects which were of fatal consequence in conducting the preceding war. In these articles of the navy almost every possible offence is set down, and the punishment thereof annexed: in which respect the seamen have much the advantage over their brethren in the land service; whose articles of war are not enacted by parliament, but framed from time to time at the pleasure of the crown. Yet from whence this distinction arose, and why the executive power, which is limited so properly with regard to the navy, should be so extensive with regard to the army, it is hard to assign a reason: unless it proceeded from the perpetual establishment of the navy, which rendered a permanent law for their regulation expedient; and the temporary duration of the army, which subsisted only from year to year; and might therefore with less danger be subjected to discretionary government. But, whatever was apprehended at the first formation of the mutiny act, the regular renewal of our standing force at the entrance of every year has made this distinction idle. For, if from experience past we may judge of future events, the army is now lastingly ingrafted into the British constitution; with this singularly fortunate circumstance, that any branch of the legislature may annually put an end to it's legal existence, by refusing to concur in it's continuance.

CHAPTER THE FOURTEENTH.
OF MASTER AND SERVANT.

HAVING thus commented on the rights and duties of persons, as standing in the *public* relations of magistrates and people; the method I have marked out now leads me to consider their rights and duties in *private* oeconomical relations.

THE three great relations in private life are, 1. That of *master and servant*, which is founded in convenience, whereby a man is directed to call in the assistance of others, where his own skill and labour will not be sufficient to answer the cares incumbent upon him. 2. That of *husband and wife*, which is founded in nature, but modified by civil society: the one directing man to continue and multiply his species, the other prescribing the manner in which that natural impulse must be confined and regulated. 3. That of *parent and child*, which is consequential to that of marriage, being it's principal end and design: and it is by virtue of this relation that infants are protected, maintained, and educated. But, since the parents, on whom this care is primarily incumbent, may be snatched away by death or otherwise, before they have completed their duty, the law has therefore provided a fourth relation; 4. That of *guardian and ward*, which is a kind of artificial parentage, in order to supply the deficiency, whenever it happens, of the natural. Of all these relations in their order.

IN discussing the relation of *master and servant*, I shall, first, consider the several sorts of servants, and how this relation is created and destroyed: secondly, the effects of this relation with regard to the parties themselves: and, lastly, it's effect with regard to other persons.

I. AS to the several sorts of servants: I have formerly observed that pure and proper slavery does not, nay cannot, subsist in England; such I mean, whereby an absolute and unlimited power is given to the master over the life and fortune of the slave. And indeed it is repugnant to reason, and the principles of natural law, that such a state should subsist any where. The three origins of the right of slavery assigned by Justinian, are all of them built upon false foundations. As, first, slavery is held to arise "*jure gentium*," from a state of captivity in war; whence slaves are called *mancipia, quasi manu capti*. The conqueror, say the civilians, had a right to the life of his captive; and, having spared that, has a right to deal with him as he pleases. But it is an untrue position, when taken generally, that, by the law of nature or nations, a man may kill his enemy: he has only a right to kill him, in particular cases; in cases of absolute necessity, for self-defence; and it is plain this absolute necessity did not subsist, since the victor did not actually kill him, but made him prisoner. War is itself justifiable only on principles of self-preservation; and therefore it gives no other right over prisoners, but merely to disable them from doing harm to us, by confining their persons: much less can it give a right to kill, torture, abuse, plunder, or even to enslave, an enemy, when the war is over. Since therefore the right of *making* slaves by captivity, depends on a supposed right of slaughter, that foundation failing, the consequence drawn from it must fail likewise. But, secondly, it is said that slavery may begin "*jure civili*," when one man sells himself to another.

This, if only meant of contracts to serve or work for another, is very just: but when applied to strict slavery, in the sense of the laws of old Rome or modern Barbary, is also impossible. Every sale implies a price, a *quid pro quo*, an equivalent given to the seller in lieu of what he transfers to the buyer: but what equivalent can be given for life, and liberty, both of which (in absolute slavery) are held to be in the master's disposal? His property also, the very price he seems to receive, devolves *ipso facto* to his master, the instant he becomes his slave. In this case therefore the buyer gives nothing, and the seller receives nothing: of what validity then can a sale be, which destroys the very principles upon which all sales are founded? Lastly, we are told, that besides these two ways by which slaves "*fiunt*," or are acquired, they may also be hereditary: "*servi nascuntur*," the children of acquired slaves are, *jure naturae*, by a negative kind of birthright, slaves also. But this being built on the two former rights must fall together with them. If neither captivity, nor the sale of oneself, can by the law of nature and reason, reduce the parent to slavery, much less can it reduce the offspring.

U P O N these principles the law of England abhors, and will not endure the existence of, slavery within this nation: so that when an attempt was made to introduce it, by statute 1 Edw. VI. c. 3. which ordained, that all idle vagabonds should be made slaves, and fed upon bread, water, or small drink, and refuse meat; should wear a ring of iron round their necks, arms, or legs; and should be compelled by beating, chaining, or otherwise, to perform the work assigned them, were it never so vile; the spirit of the nation could not brook this condition, even in the most abandoned rogues; and therefore this statute was repealed in two years afterwards. And now it is laid down, that a slave or negro, the instant he lands in England, becomes a freeman; that is, the law will protect him in the enjoyment of his person, his liberty, and his property. Yet, with regard to any right which the master may have acquired, by contract or the like, to the perpetual service of John or Thomas, this will remain exactly in the same state as before: for this is no more than the same state of subjection for life, which every apprentice submits to for the space of seven years, or sometimes for a longer term. Hence too it follows, that the infamous and unchristian practice of withholding baptism from negro servants, lest they should thereby gain their liberty, is totally without foundation, as well as without excuse. The law of England acts upon general and extensive principles: it gives liberty, rightly understood, that is, protection, to a jew, a turk, or a heathen, as well as to those who profess the true religion of Christ; and it will not dissolve a civil contract, either express or implied, between master and servant, on account of the alteration of faith in either of the contracting parties: but the slave is entitled to the same liberty in England before, as after, baptism; and, whatever service the heathen negro owed to his English master, the same is he bound to render when a christian.

1. T H E first sort of servants therefore, acknowleged by the laws of England, are *menial servants*; so called from being *intra moenia*, or domestics. The contract between them and their masters arises upon the hiring. If the hiring be general without any particular time limited, the law construes it to be a hiring for a year; upon a principle of natural equity, that the servant shall serve, and the master maintain him, throughout all the revolutions of the

respective seasons; as well when there is work to be done, as when there is not: but the contract may be made for any larger or smaller term. All single men between twelve years old and sixty, and married ones under thirty years of age, and all single women between twelve and forty, not having any visible livelihood, are compellable by two justices to go out to service, for the promotion of honest industry: and no master can put away his servant, or servant leave his master, either before or at the end of his term, without a quarter's warning; unless upon reasonable cause to be allowed by a justice of the peace: but they may part by consent, or make a special bargain.

2. A N O T H E R species of servants are called *apprentices* (from *apprendre*, to learn) and are usually bound for a term of years, by deed indented or indentures, to serve their masters, and be maintained and instructed by them: for which purpose our statute law has made minors capable of binding themselves. This is usually done to persons of trade, in order to learn their art and mystery; and sometimes very large sums are given with them, as a premium for such their instruction: but it may be done to husbandmen, nay to gentlemen, and others. And children of poor persons may be apprenticed out by the overseers, with consent of two justices, till twenty four years of age, to such persons as are thought fitting; who are also compellable to take them: and it is held, that gentlemen of fortune, and clergymen, are equally liable with others to such compulsion. Apprentices to trades may be discharged on reasonable cause, either at request of themselves or masters, at the quarter sessions, or by one justice, with appeal to the sessions: who may, by the equity of the statute, if they think it reasonable, direct restitution of a ratable share of the money given with the apprentice. And parish apprentices may be discharged in the same manner, by two justices.

3. A T H I R D species of servants are *labourers*, who are only hired by the day or the week, and do not live *intra moenia*, as part of the family; concerning whom the statute so often cited has made many very good regulations; 1. Directing that all persons who have no visible effects may be compelled to work: 2. Defining how long they must continue at work in summer and winter: 3. Punishing such as leave or desert their work: 4. Empowering the justices at sessions, or the sheriff of the county, to settle their wages: and 5. Inflicting penalties on such as either give, or exact, more wages than are so settled.

4. T H E R E is yet a fourth species of servants, if they may be so called, being rather in a superior, a ministerial, capacity; such as *stewards*, *factors*, and *bailiffs*: whom however the law considers as servants *pro tempore*, with regard to such of their acts, as affect their master's or employer's property. Which leads me to consider,

II. T H E manner in which this relation, of service, affects either the master or servant. And, first, by hiring and service for a year, or apprenticeship under indentures, a person gains a settlement in that parish wherein he last served forty days. In the next place persons serving as apprentices to any trade have an exclusive right to exercise that trade in any part of England. This law, with regard to the exclusive part of it, has by turns been looked upon as a hard law, or as a beneficial one, according to the prevailing humour of the times: which has occasioned a great variety of resolutions in the courts of law concerning it; and attempts have been frequently made for it's repeal, though hitherto without success. At common law every man might use what trade he pleased; but this statute restrains that liberty to such as have served as apprentices: the adversaries to which provision say, that all restrictions (which tend to introduce monopolies) are pernicious to trade; the advocates for it alledge, that unskilfulness in trades is equally detrimental to the public, as monopolies. This reason indeed only extends to such trades, in the exercise whereof skill is required: but another of their arguments goes much farther; viz. that apprenticeships are useful to the commonwealth, by employing of youth, and learning them to be early industrious; but that no one would be induced to undergo a seven years servitude, if others, though equally skilful, were allowed the same advantages without having undergone the same discipline: and in this there seems to be much reason. However, the resolutions of the courts have in general rather confined than extended the restriction. No trades are held to be within the statute, but such as were in being at the making of it: for trading in a country village, apprenticeships are not requisite: and following the trade seven years is sufficient without any binding; for the statute only says, the person must serve *as* an apprentice, and does not require an actual apprenticeship to have existed.

A MASTER may by law correct his apprentice or servant for negligence or other misbehaviour, so it be done with moderation: though, if the master's wife beats him, it is good cause of departure. But if any servant, workman, or labourer assaults his master or dame, he shall suffer one year's imprisonment, and other open corporal punishment, not extending to life or limb.

BY service all servants and labourers, except apprentices, become entitled to wages: according to their agreement, if menial servants; or according to the appointment of the sheriff or sessions, if labourers or servants in husbandry: for the statutes for regulation of wages extend to such servants only; it being impossible for any magistrate to be a judge of the employment of menial servants, or of course to assess their wages.

III. LET us, lastly, see how strangers may be affected by this relation of master and servant: or how a master may behave towards others on behalf of his servant; and what a servant may do on behalf of his master.

AND, first, the master may *maintain*, that is, abet and assist his servant in any action at law against a stranger: whereas, in general, it is an offence against public justice to encourage suits and animosities, by helping to bear the expense of them, and is called in law maintenance. A master also may bring an action against any man for beating or maiming his servant; but in such case he must assign, as a special reason for so doing, his own damage by the loss of his service; and this loss must be proved upon the trial. A master likewise may justify an assault in defence of his servant, and a servant in defence of his master: the master, because he has an interest in his servant, not to be deprived of his service; the servant, because it is part of his duty, for which he receives his wages, to stand by and defend his master. Also if any person do hire or retain my servant, being in my service, for which the servant departeth from me and goeth to serve the other, I may have an action for damages against both the new master and the servant, or either of them: but if the new master did not know that he is my servant, no action lies; unless he afterwards refuse to restore him upon information and demand. The reason and foundation upon which all this doctrine is built, seem to be the property that every man has in the service of his domestics; acquired by the contract of hiring, and purchased by giving them wages.

A S for those things which a servant may do on behalf of his master, they seem all to proceed upon this principle, that the master is answerable for the act of his servant, if done by his command, either expressly given, or implied: *nam qui facit per alium, facit per se*. Therefore, if the servant commit a trespass by the command or encouragement of his master, the master shall be guilty of it: not that the servant is excused, for he is only to obey his master in matters that are honest and lawful. If an innkeeper's servants rob his guests, the master is bound to restitution: for as there is a confidence reposed in him, that he will take care to provide honest servants, his negligence is a kind of implied consent to the robbery; *nam, qui non prohibet, cum prohibere possit, jubet*. So likewise if the drawer at a tavern sells a man bad wine, whereby his health is injured, he may bring an action against the master: for, although the master did not expressly order the servant to sell it to that person in particular, yet his permitting him to draw and sell it at all is impliedly a general command.

4 Inst. 109.

Noy's Max. c. 43.

1 Roll. Abr. 95.

I N the same manner, whatever a servant is permitted to do in the usual course of his business, is equivalent to a general command. If I pay money to a banker's servant, the banker is answerable for it: if I pay it to a clergyman's or a physician's servant, whose usual business it is not to receive money for his master, and he imbezzles it, I must pay it over again. If a steward lets a lease of a farm, without the owner's knowlege, the owner must stand to the bargain; for this is the steward's business. A wife, a friend, a relation, that use to transact business for a man, are *quoad hoc* his servants; and the principal must answer for their conduct: for the law implies, that they act under a general command; and, without such a doctrine as this, no mutual intercourse between man and man could subsist with any tolerable convenience. If I usually deal with a tradesman by myself, or constantly pay him ready money, I am not answerable for what my servant takes up upon trust; for here is no implied order to the tradesman to trust my servant: but if I usually send him upon trust, or sometimes on trust, and sometimes with ready money, I am answerable for all he takes up; for the tradesman cannot possibly distinguish when he comes by my order, and when upon his own authority.

Dr & Stud. d. 2. c. 42. Noy's max. c. 44.

IF a servant, lastly, by his negligence does any damage to a stranger, the master shall answer for his neglect: if a smith's servant lames a horse while he is shoing him, an action lies against the master, and not against the servant. But in these cases the damage must be done, while he is actually employed in the master's service; otherwise the servant shall answer for his own misbehaviour. Upon this principle, by the common law, if a servant kept his master's fire negligently, so that his neighbour's house was burned down thereby, an action lay against the master; because this negligence happened in his service: otherwise, if the servant, going along the street with a torch, by negligence sets fire to a house; for there he is not in his master's immediate service, and must himself answer the damage personally. But now the common law is, in the former case, altered by statute 6 Ann. c. 3. which ordains that no action shall be maintained against any, in whose house or chamber any fire shall accidentally begin; for their own loss is sufficient punishment for their own or their servants' carelessness. But if such fire happens through negligence of any servant (whose loss is commonly very little) such servant shall forfeit 100*l*, to be distributed among the sufferers; and, in default of payment, shall be committed to some workhouse and there kept to hard labour for eighteen months. A master is, lastly, chargeable if any of his family layeth or casteth any thing out of his house into the street or common highway, to the damage of any individual, or the common nusance of his majesty's liege people: for the master hath the superintendance and charge of all his houshold. And this also agrees with the civil law; which holds, that the *pater familias*, in this and similar cases, "*ob alterius culpam tenetur, sive servi, sive liberi.*"

WE may observe, that in all the cases here put, the master may be frequently a loser by the trust reposed in his servant, but never can be a gainer: he may frequently be answerable for his servant's misbehaviour, but never can shelter himself from punishment by laying the blame on his agent. The reason of this is still uniform and the same; that the wrong done by the servant is looked upon in law as the wrong of the master himself; and it is a standing maxim, that no man shall be allowed to make any advantage of his own wrong.

CHAPTER THE FIFTEENTH.

OF HUSBAND AND WIFE.

THE second private relation of persons is that of marriage, which includes the reciprocal duties of husband and wife; or, as most of our elder law books call them, of *baron* and *feme*. In the consideration of which I shall in the first place enquire, how marriages may be contracted or made; shall next point out the manner in which they may be dissolved; and shall, lastly, take a view of the legal effects and consequence of marriage.

I. OUR law considers marriage in no other light than as a civil contract. The *holiness* of the matrimonial state is left entirely to the ecclesiastical law: the temporal courts not having jurisdiction to consider unlawful marriages as a sin, but merely as a civil inconvenience. The punishment therefore, or annulling, of incestuous or other unscriptural marriages, is the province of the spiritual courts; which act *pro salute animae*. And, taking it in this civil light, the law treats it as it does all other contracts; allowing it to be good and valid in all cases, where the parties at the time of making it were, in the first place, *willing* to contract; secondly, *able* to contract; and, lastly, actually *did* contract, in the proper forms and solemnities required by law.

FIRST, they must be *willing* to contract. "*Consensus, non concubitus, facit nuptias*," is the maxim of the civil law in this case: and it is adopted by the common lawyers, who indeed have borrowed (especially in antient times) almost all their notions of the legitimacy of marriage from the canon and civil laws.

SECONDLY, they must be *able* to contract. In general, all persons are able to contract themselves in marriage, unless they labour under some particular disabilities, and incapacities. What those are, it will here be our business to enquire.

NOW these disabilities are of two sorts: first, such as are canonical, and therefore sufficient by the ecclesiastical laws to avoid the marriage in the spiritual court; but these in our law only make the marriage voidable, and not *ipso facto* void, until sentence of nullity be obtained. Of this nature are pre-contract; consanguinity, or relation by blood; and affinity, or relation by marriage; and some particular corporal infirmities. And these canonical disabilities are either grounded upon the express words of the divine law, or are consequences plainly deducible from thence: it therefore being sinful in the persons, who labour under them, to attempt to contract matrimony together, they are properly the object of the ecclesiastical magistrate's coercion; in order to separate the offenders, and inflict penance for the offence, *pro salute animarum*. But such marriages not being void *ab initio*, but voidable only by sentence of separation, they are esteemed valid to all civil purposes, unless such separation is actually made during the life of the parties. For, after the death of either of them, the courts of common law will not suffer the spiritual court to declare such marriages to have been void; because such declaration cannot now tend to the reformation of the parties. And therefore when a man had married his first wife's sister, and after her death the bishop's court was proceeding to annul the marriage and bastardize the issue, the court of king's bench granted a prohibition *quoad hoc*; but permitted them to proceed to punish the husband for incest. These canonical disabilities, being entirely the province of the ecclesiastical courts, our books are perfectly silent concerning them. But there are a few statutes, which serve as directories to those courts, of which it will be proper to take notice. By statute 32 Hen. VIII. c. 38. it is declared, that all persons may lawfully marry, but such as are prohibited by God's law; and that all marriages contracted by lawful persons in the face of the church, and consummate with bodily knowlege, and fruit of children, shall be indissoluble. And (because in the times of popery a great variety of degrees of kindred were made impediments to marriage, which impediments might however be bought off for money) it is declared by the same statute, that nothing (God's law except) shall impeach any marriage, but within the Levitical degrees; the farthest of which is that between uncle and niece. By the same statute all impediments, arising from pre-contracts to other persons, were abolished and declared of none effect, unless they had been consummated with bodily knowlege: in which case the canon law holds such contract to be a marriage *de facto*. But this branch of the statute was repealed by statute 2 & 3 Edw. VI. c. 23. How far the act of 26 Geo. II. c. 33. (which prohibits all suits in ecclesiastical courts to compel a marriage, in consequence of any contract) may collaterally extend to revive this clause of Henry VIII's statute, and abolish the impediment of pre-contract, I leave to be considered by T H E other sort of disabilities are those which are created, or at least enforced, by the municipal laws. And, though some of them may be grounded on natural law, yet they are regarded by the laws of the land, not so much in the light of any moral offence, as on account of the civil inconveniences they draw after them. These civil disabilities make the contract void *ab initio*, and not merely voidable: not that they dissolve a contract already formed, but they render the parties incapable of forming any contract at all: they do not put asunder those who are joined together, but they previously hinder the junction. And, if any persons under these legal incapacities come together, it is a meretricious, and not a matrimonial, union.

I. T H E first of these legal disabilities is a prior marriage, or having another husband or wife living; in which case, besides the penalties consequent upon it as a felony, the second marriage is to all intents and purposes void: polygamy being condemned both by the law of the new testament, and the policy of all prudent states, especially in these northern climates. And Justinian, even in the climate of modern Turkey, is express, that "*duas uxores eodem tempore habere non licet.*"

2. T H E next legal disability is want of age. This is sufficient to avoid all other contracts, on account of the imbecillity of judgment in the parties contracting; *a fortiori* therefore it ought to avoid this, the most important contract of any. Therefore if a boy under fourteen, or a girl under twelve years of age, marries, this marriage is only inchoate and imperfect; and, when either of them comes to the age of consent aforesaid, they may disagree and declare the marriage void, without any divorce or sentence in the spiritual court. This is founded on the

civil law. But the canon law pays a greater regard to the constitution, than the age, of the parties: for if they are *habiles ad matrimonium*, it is a good marriage, whatever their age may be. And in our law it is so far a marriage, that, if at the age of consent they agree to continue together, they need not be married again. If the husband be of years of discretion, and the wife under twelve, when she comes to years of discretion he may disagree as well as she may: for in contracts the obligation must be mutual; both must be bound, or neither: and so it is, *vice versa*, when the wife is of years of discretion, and the husband under.

3. A N O T H E R incapacity arises from want of consent of parents or guardians. By the common law, if the parties themselves were of the age of consent, there wanted no other concurrence to make the marriage valid: and this was agreeable to the canon law. But, by several statutes, penalties of 100*l.* are laid on every clergyman who marries a couple either without publication of banns (which may give notice to parents or guardians) or without a licence, to obtain which the consent of parents or guardians must be sworn to. And by the statute 4 & 5 Ph. & M. c. 8. whosoever marries any woman child under the age of sixteen years, without consent of parents or guardians, shall be subject to fine, or five years imprisonment: and her estate during the husband's life shall go to and be enjoyed by the next heir. The civil law indeed required the consent of the parent or tutor at all ages; unless the children were emancipated, or out of the parents power: and, if such consent from the father was wanting, the marriage was null, and the children illegitimate; but the consent of the mother or guardians, if unreasonably withheld, might be redressed and supplied by the judge, or the president of the province: and if the father was *non compos*, a similar remedy was given. These provisions are adopted and imitated by the French and Hollanders, with this difference: that in France the sons cannot marry without consent of parents till thirty years of age, nor the daughters till twenty five; and in Holland, the sons are at their own disposal at twenty five, and the daughters at twenty. Thus hath stood, and thus at present stands, the law in other neighbouring countries. And it has been lately thought proper to introduce somewhat of the same policy into our laws, by statute 26 Geo. II. c. 33. whereby it is enacted, that all marriages celebrated by licence (for banns suppose notice) where either of the parties is under twenty one, (not being a widow or widower, who are supposed emancipated) without the consent of the father, or, if he be not living, of the mother or guardians, shall be absolutely void. A like provision is made as in the civil law, where the mother or guardian is *non compos*, beyond sea, or unreasonably froward, to dispense with such consent at the discretion of the lord chancellor: but no provision is made, in case the father should labour under any mental or other incapacity. Much may be, and much has been, said both for and against this innovation upon our antient laws and constitution. On the one hand, it prevents the clandestine marriages of minors, which are often a terrible inconvenience to those private families wherein they happen. On the other hand, restraints upon marriage, especially among the lower class, are evidently detrimental to the public, by hindering the encrease of people; and to religion and morality, by encouraging licentiousness and debauchery among the single of both sexes; and thereby destroying one end of society and government, which is, *concubitu prohibere vago*. And of this last inconvenience the Roman laws were so sensible, that at the

179

same time that they forbad marriage without the consent of parents or guardians, they were less rigorous upon that very account with regard to other restraints: for, if a parent did not provide a husband for his daughter, by the time she arrived at the age of twenty five, and she afterwards made a slip in her conduct, he was not allowed to disinherit her upon that account; "*quia non sua culpa, sed parentum, id commisisse cognoscitur.*"

4. A F O U R T H incapacity is want of reason; without a competent share of which, as no other, so neither can the matrimonial contract, be valid. Idiots and lunatics, by the old common law, might have married; wherein it was manifestly defective. The civil law judged much more sensibly, when it made such deprivations of reason a previous impediment; though not a cause of divorce, if they happened after marriage. This defect in our laws is however remedied with regard to lunatics, and persons under frenzies, by the express words of the statute 15 Geo. II. c. 30. and idiots, if not within the letter of the statute, are at least within the reason of it.

L A S T L Y , the parties must not only be willing, and able, to contract, but actually must contract themselves in due form of law, to make it a good civil marriage. Any contract made, *per verba de praesenti*, or in words of the present tense, and in case of cohabitation *per verba de futuro* also, between persons able to contract, was before the late act deemed a valid marriage to many purposes; and the parties might be compelled in the spiritual courts to celebrate it *in facie ecclesiae*. But these verbal contracts are now of no force, to compel a future marriage. Neither is any marriage at present valid, that is not celebrated in some parish church or public chapel, unless by dispensation from the arch-bishop of Canterbury. It must also be preceded by publication of banns, or by licence from the spiritual judge. Many other formalities are likewise prescribed by the act; the neglect of which, though penal, does not invalidate the marriage. It is held to be also essential to a marriage, that it be performed by a person in orders; though the intervention of a priest to solemnize this contract is merely *juris positivi*, and not *juris naturalis aut divini*: it being said that pope Innocent the third was the first who ordained the celebration of marriage in the church; before which it was totally a civil contract. And, in the times of the grand rebellion, all marriages were performed by the justices of the peace; and these marriages were declared valid, without any fresh solemnization, by statute 12 Car. II. c. 33. But, as the law now stands, we may upon the whole collect, that no marriage by the temporal law is *ipso facto* void, that is celebrated by a person in orders,—in a parish church or public chapel (or elsewhere, by special dispensation)—in pursuance of banns or a licence,—between single persons,—consenting,—of sound mind,—and of the age of twenty one years;—or of the age of fourteen in males and twelve in females, with consent of parents or guardians, or without it, in case of widowhood. And no marriage is *voidable* by the ecclesiastical law, after the death of either of the parties; nor during their lives, unless for the canonical impediments of pre-contract, if that indeed still exists; of consanguinity; and of affinity, or corporal imbecillity, subsisting previous to the marriage.

II. I AM next to consider the manner in which marriages may be dissolved; and this is either by death, or divorce. There are two kinds of divorce, the one total, the other partial; the one *a vinculo matrimonii*, the other merely *a mensa et thoro*. The total divorce, *a vinculo matrimonii*, must be for some of the canonical causes of impediment before-mentioned; and those, existing *before* the marriage, as is always the case in consanguinity; not supervenient, or arising *afterwards*, as may be the case in affinity or corporal imbecillity. For in cases of total divorce, the marriage is declared null, as having been absolutely unlawful *ab initio*, and the parties are therefore separated *pro salute animarum*: for which reason, as was before observed, no divorce can be obtained, but during the life of the parties. The issue of such marriage, as is thus entirely dissolved, are bastards.

DIVORCE *a mensa et thoro* is when the marriage is just and lawful *ab initio*, and therefore the law is tender of dissolving it; but, for some supervenient cause, it becomes improper or impossible for the parties to live together: as in the case of intolerable ill temper, or adultery, in either of the parties. For the canon law, which the common law follows in this case, deems so highly and with such mysterious reverence of the nuptial tie, that it will not allow it to be unloosed for any cause whatsoever, that arises after the union is made. And this is said to be built on the divine revealed law; though that expressly assigns incontinence as a cause, and indeed the only cause, why a man may put away his wife and marry another. The civil law, which is partly of pagan original, allows many causes of absolute divorce; and some of them pretty severe ones, (as if a wife goes to the theatre or the public games, without the knowlege and consent of the husband) but among them adultery is the principal, and with reason named the first. But with us in England adultery is only a cause of separation from bed and board: for which the best reason that can be given, is, that if divorces were allowed to depend upon a matter within the power of either the parties, they would probably be extremely frequent; as was the case when divorces were allowed for canonical disabilities, on the mere confession of the parties, which is now prohibited by the canons. However, divorces *a vinculo matrimonii*, for adultery, have of late years been frequently granted by act of parliament.

IN case of divorce *a mensa et thoro*, the law allows alimony to the wife; which is that allowance, which is made to a woman for her support out of the husband's estate; being settled at the discretion of the ecclesiastical judge, on consideration of all the circumstances of the case. This is sometimes called her *estovers*; for which, if he refuses payment, there is (besides the ordinary process of excommunication) a writ at common law *de estoveriis habendis*, in order to recover it. It is generally proportioned to the rank and quality of the parties. But in case of elopement, and living with an adulterer, the law allows her no alimony.

III. HAVING thus shewn how marriages may be made, or dissolved, I come now, lastly, to speak of the legal consequences of such making, or dissolution.

BY marriage, the husband and wife are one person in law: that is, the very being or legal existence of the woman is suspended during the marriage, or at least is incorporated and consolidated into that of the husband: under whose wing, protection, and *cover*, she performs every thing; and is therefore called in our law-french a *feme-covert*, is said to be *covert-baron*, or under the protection and influence of her husband, her *baron*, or lord; and her condition during her marriage is called her *coverture*. Upon this principle, of an union of person in husband and wife, depend almost all the legal rights, duties, and disabilities, that either of them acquire by the marriage. I speak not at present of the rights of property, but of such as are merely *personal*. For this reason, a man cannot grant any thing to his wife, or enter into covenant with her: for the grant would be to suppose her separate existence; and to covenant with her, would be only to covenant with himself: and therefore it is also generally true, that all compacts made between husband and wife, when single, are voided by the intermarriage. A woman indeed may be attorney for her husband; for that implies no separation from, but is rather a representation of, her lord. And a husband may also bequeath any thing to his wife by will; for that cannot take effect till the coverture is determined by his death. The husband is bound to provide his wife with necessaries by law, as much as himself; and if she contracts debts for them, he is obliged to pay them: but for any thing besides necessaries, he is not chargeable. Also if a wife elopes, and lives with another man, the husband is not chargeable even for necessaries; at least if the person, who furnishes them, is sufficiently apprized of her elopement. If the wife be indebted before marriage, the husband is bound afterwards to pay the debt; for he has adopted her and her circumstances together. If the wife be injured in her person or her property, she can bring no action for redress without her husband's concurrence, and in his name, as well as her own: neither can she be sued, without making the husband a defendant. There is indeed one case where the wife shall sue and be sued as a feme sole, viz. where the husband has abjured the realm, or is banished: for then he is dead in law; and, the husband being thus disabled to sue for or defend the wife, it would be most unreasonable if she had no remedy, or could make no defence at all. In criminal prosecutions, it is true, the wife may be indicted and punished separately; for the union is only a civil union. But, in trials of any sort, they are not allowed to be evidence for, or against, each other: partly because it is impossible their testimony should be indifferent; but principally because of the union of person: and therefore, if they were admitted to be witnesses *for* each other, they would contradict one maxim of law, "*nemo in propria causa testis esse debet*," and if *against* each other, they would contradict another maxim, "*nemo tenetur seipsum accusare.*" But where the offence is directly against the person of the wife, this rule has been usually dispensed with: and therefore, by statute 3 Hen. VII. c. 2. in case a woman be forcibly taken away, and married, she may be a witness against such her husband, in order to convict him of felony. For in this case she can with no propriety be reckoned his wife; because a main ingredient, her consent, was wanting to the contract: and also there is another maxim of law, that no man shall take advantage of his own wrong; which the ravisher here would do, if by forcibly marrying a woman, he could prevent her from being a witness, who is perhaps the only witness, to that very fact.

BUT, though our law in general considers man and wife as one person, yet there are some instances in which she is separately considered; as inferior to him, and acting by his compulsion. And therefore all deeds executed, and acts done, by her, during her coverture, are void, or at least voidable; except it be a fine, or the like matter of record, in which case she must be solely and secretly examined, to learn if her act be voluntary. She cannot by will devise lands to her husband, unless under special circumstances; for at the time of making it she is supposed to be under his coercion. And in some felonies, and other inferior crimes, committed by her, through constraint of her husband, the law excuses her: but this extends not to treason or murder.

T H E husband also (by the old law) might give his wife moderate correction. For, as he is to answer for her misbehaviour, the law thought it reasonable to intrust him with this power of restraining her, by domestic chastisement, in the same moderation that a man is allowed to correct his servants or children; for whom the master or parent is also liable in some cases to answer. But this power of correction was confined within reasonable bounds; and the husband was prohibited to use any violence to his wife, *aliter quam ad virum, ex causa regiminis et castigationis uxoris suae, licite et rationabiliter pertinet.* The civil law gave the husband the same, or a larger, authority over his wife; allowing him, for some misdemesnors, *flagellis et fustibus acriter verberare uxorem;* for others, only *modicam castigationem adhibere.* But, with us, in the politer reign of Charles the second, this power of correction began to be doubted: and a wife may now have security of the peace against her husband; or, in return, a husband against his wife. Yet the lower rank of people, who were always fond of the old common law, still claim and exert their antient privilege: and the courts of law will still permit a husband to restrain a wife of her liberty, in case of any gross misbehaviour.

Chapter the sixteenth.
Of PARENT and CHILD.

THE next, and the most universal relation in nature, is immediately derived from the preceding, being that between parent and child.

CHILDREN are of two sorts; legitimate, and spurious, or bastards: each of which we shall consider in their order; and first of legitimate children.

I. A LEGITIMATE child is he that is born in lawful wedlock, or within a competent time afterwards. "*Pater est quem nuptiae demonstrant,*" is the rule of the civil law; and this holds with the civilians, whether the nuptials happen before, or after, the birth of the child. With us in England the rule is narrowed, for the nuptials must be precedent to the birth; of which more will be said when we come to consider the case of bastardy. At present let us enquire into, 1. The legal duties of parents to their legitimate children. 2. Their power over them. 3. The duties of such children to their parents.

1. AND, first, the duties of parents to legitimate children: which principally consist in three particulars; their maintenance, their protection, and their education.

THE duty of parents to provide for the *maintenance* of their children is a principle of natural law; an obligation, says Puffendorf, laid on them not only by nature herself, but by their own proper act, in bringing them into the world: for they would be in the highest manner injurious to their issue, if they only gave the children life, that they might afterwards see them perish. By begetting them therefore they have entered into a voluntary obligation, to endeavour, as far as in them lies, that the life which they have bestowed shall be supported and preserved. And thus the children will have a perfect *right* of receiving maintenance from their parents. And the president Montesquieu has a very just observation upon this head: that the establishment of marriage in all civilized states is built on this natural obligation of the father to provide for his children; for that ascertains and makes known the person who is bound to fulfil this obligation: whereas, in promiscuous and illicit conjunctions, the father is unknown; and the mother finds a thousand obstacles in her way;—shame, remorse, the constraint of her sex, and the rigor of laws;—that stifle her inclinations to perform this duty: and besides, she generally wants ability.

THE municipal laws of all well-regulated states have taken care to enforce this duty: though providence has done it more effectually than any laws, by implanting in the breast of every parent that natural or insuperable degree of affection, which not even the deformity of person or mind, not even the wickedness, ingratitude, and rebellion of children, can totally suppress or extinguish.

THE civil law obliges the parent to provide maintenance for his child; and, if he refuses, "*judex de ea re cognoscet.*" Nay, it carries this matter so far, that it will not suffer a parent at his death totally to disinherit his child, without expressly giving his reason for so doing; and there are fourteen such reasons reckoned up, which may justify such disinherison. If the parent alleged no reason, or a bad, or false one, the child might set the will aside, *tanquam testamentum inofficiosum*, a testament contrary to the natural duty of the parent. And it is remarkable under what colour the children were to move for relief in such a case: by suggesting that the parent had lost the use of his reason, when he made the *inofficious* testament. And this, as Puffendorf observes, was not to bring into dispute the testator's power of disinheriting his own offspring; but to examine the motives upon which he did it: and, if they were found defective in reason, then to set them aside. But perhaps this is going rather too far: every man has, or ought to have, by the laws of society, a power over his own property: and, as Grotius very well distinguishes, natural right obliges to give a *necessary* maintenance to children; but what is more than that, they have no other right to, than as it is given them by the favour of their parents, or the positive constitutions of the municipal law.

L E T us next see what provision our own laws have made for this natural duty. It is a principle of law, that there is an obligation on every man to provide for those descended from his loins: and the manner, in which this obligation shall be performed, is thus pointed out. The father, and mother, grandfather, and grandmother of poor impotent persons shall maintain them at their own charges, if of sufficient ability, according as the quarter sessions shall direct: and if a parent runs away, and leaves his children, the churchwardens and overseers of the parish shall seise his rents, goods, and chattels, and dispose of them towards their relief. By the interpretations which the courts of law have made upon these statutes, if a mother or grandmother marries again, and was before such second marriage of sufficient ability to keep the child, the husband shall be charged to maintain it: for this being a debt of hers, when single, shall like others extend to charge the husband. But at her death, the relation being dissolved, the husband is under no farther obligation.

N O person is bound to provide a maintenance for his issue, unless where the children are impotent and unable to work, either through infancy, disease, or accident; and then is only obliged to find them with necessaries, the penalty on refusal being no more than 20*s.* a month. For the policy of our laws, which are ever watchful to promote industry, did not mean to compel a father to maintain his idle and lazy children in ease and indolence: but thought it unjust to oblige the parent, against his will, to provide them with superfluities, and other indulgences of fortune; imagining they might trust to the impulse of nature, if the children were deserving of such favours. Yet, as nothing is so apt to stifle the calls of nature as religious bigotry, it is enacted, that if any popish parent shall refuse to allow his protestant child a fitting maintenance, with a view to compel him to change his religion, the lord chancellor shall by order of court constrain him to do what is just and reasonable. But this did not extend to persons of another religion, of no less bitterness and bigotry than the popish: and therefore in the very next year we find an instance of a Jew of immense riches, whose only daughter having embraced christianity, he turned her out of doors; and on her application for relief, it was held she was intitled to none. But this gave occasion to another statute, which ordains, that if jewish parents refuse to allow their protestant children a fitting maintenance, suitable to the fortune of the parent, the lord chancellor on complaint may make such order therein as he shall see proper.

O U R law has made no provision to prevent the disinheriting of children by will; leaving every man's property in his own disposal, upon a principle of liberty in this, as well as every other, action: though perhaps it had not been amiss, if the parent had been bound to leave them at the least a necessary subsistence. By the custom of London indeed, (which was formerly universal throughout the kingdom) the children of freemen are entitled to one third of their father's effects, to be equally divided among them; of which he cannot deprive them. And, among persons of any rank or fortune, a competence is generally provided for younger children, and the bulk of the estate settled upon the eldest, by the marriage-articles. Heirs also, and children, are favourites of our courts of justice, and cannot be disinherited by any dubious or ambiguous words; there being required the utmost certainty of the testator's intentions to take away the right of an heir.

F R O M the duty of maintenance we may easily pass to that of *protection*; which is also a natural duty, but rather permitted than enjoined by any municipal laws: nature, in this respect, working so strongly as to need rather a check than a spur. A parent may, by our laws, maintain and uphold his children in their lawsuits, without being guilty of the legal crime of maintaining quarrels. A parent may also justify an assault and battery in defence of the persons of his children: nay, where a man's son was beaten by another boy, and the father went near a mile to find him, and there revenged his son's quarrel by beating the other boy, of which beating he afterwards died; it was not held to be murder, but manslaughter merely. Such indulgence does the law shew to the frailty of human nature, and the workings of parental affection.

T H E last duty of parents to their children is that of giving them an *education* suitable to their station in life: a duty pointed out by reason, and of far the greatest importance of any. For, as Puffendorf very well observes, it is not easy to imagine or allow, that a parent has conferred any considerable benefit upon his child, by bringing him into the world; if he afterwards entirely neglects his culture and education, and suffers him to grow up like a mere beast, to lead a life useless to others, and shameful to himself. Yet the municipal laws of most countries seem to be defective in this point, by not constraining the parent to bestow a proper education upon his children. Perhaps they thought it punishment enough to leave the parent, who neglects the instruction of his family, to labour under those griefs and inconveniences, which his family, so uninstructed, will be sure to bring upon him. Our laws, though their defects in this particular cannot be denied, have in one instance made a wise provision for breeding up the rising generation; since the poor and laborious part of the community, when past the age of nurture, are taken out of the hands of their parents, by the statutes for apprenticing poor children; and are placed out by the public in such a manner, as may render their abilities, in their several stations, of the greatest advantage to the commonwealth. The rich indeed are left at their own option, whether they will breed up their children to be ornaments or disgraces to their family. Yet in one case, that of religion, they are under peculiar restrictions: for it is provided, that if any person sends any child under his government beyond the seas, either to prevent it's good education in England, or in order to enter into or reside in any popish college, or to be instructed, persuaded, or strengthened in the popish religion; in such case, besides the disabilities incurred by the child so sent, the parent or person sending shall forfeit 100*l.* which shall go to the sole use and benefit of him that shall discover the offence. And if any parent, or other, shall send or convey any person beyond sea, to enter into, or be resident in, or trained up in, any priory, abbey, nunnery, popish university, college, or school, or house of jesuits, or priests, or in any private popish family, in order to be instructed, persuaded, or confirmed in the popish religion; or shall contribute any thing towards their maintenance when abroad by any pretext whatever, the person both sending and sent shall be disabled to sue in law or equity, or to be executor or administrator to any person, or to enjoy any legacy or deed of gift, or to bear any office in the realm, and shall forfeit all his goods and chattels, and likewise all his real estate for life.

2. T H E *power* of parents over their children is derived from the former consideration, their duty; this authority being given them, partly to enable the parent more effectually to perform his duty, and partly as a recompence for his care and trouble in the faithful discharge of it. And upon this score the municipal laws of some nations have given a much larger authority to the parents, than others. The antient Roman laws gave the father a power of life and death over his children; upon this principle, that he who gave had also the power of taking away. But the rigor of these laws was softened by subsequent constitutions; so that we find a father banished by the emperor Hadrian for killing his son, though he had committed a very heinous crime, upon this maxim, that "*patria potestas in pietate debet, non in atrocitate, consistere.*" But still they maintained to the last a very large and absolute authority: for a son could not acquire any property of his own during the life of his father; but all his acquisitions belonged to the father, or at least the profits of them for his life.

T H E power of a parent by our English laws is much more moderate; but still sufficient to keep the child in order and obedience. He may lawfully correct his child, being under age, in a reasonable manner; for this is for the benefit of his education. The consent or concurrence of the parent to the marriage of his child under age, was also *directed* by our antient law to be obtained: but now it is absolutely *necessary*; for without it the contract is void. And this also is another means, which the law has put into the parent's hands, in order the better to discharge his duty; first, of protecting his children from the snares of artful and designing persons; and, next, of settling them properly in life, by preventing the ill consequences of too early and precipitate marriages. A father has no other power over his sons *estate*, than as his trustee or guardian; for, though he may receive the profits during the child's minority, yet he must account for them when he comes of age. He may indeed have the benefit of his children's labour while they live with him, and are maintained by him: but this is no more than he is entitled to from his apprentices or servants. The legal power of a father (for a mother, as such, is entitled to no power, but only to reverence and respect) the power of a father, I say, over the persons of his children ceases at the age of twenty one: for they are then enfranchised by arriving at years of discretion, or that point which the law has established (as some must necessarily be established) when the empire of the father, or other guardian, gives place to the empire of reason. Yet, till that age arrives, this empire of the father continues even after his death; for he may by his will appoint a guardian to his children. He may also delegate part of his parental authority, during his life, to the tutor or schoolmaster of his child; who is then *in loco parentis*, and has such a portion of the power of the parent committed to his charge, viz. that of restraint and correction, as may be necessary to answer the purposes for which he is employed.

3. T H E *duties* of children to their parents arise from a principle of natural justice and retribution. For to those, who gave us existence, we naturally owe subjection and obedience during our minority, and honour and reverence ever after; they, who protected the weakness of our infancy, are entitled to our protection in the infirmity of their age; they who by sustenance and education have enabled their offspring to prosper, ought in return to be supported by that offspring, in case they stand in need of assistance. Upon this principle proceed all the duties of children to their parents, which are enjoined by positive laws. And the Athenian laws carried this principle into practice with a scrupulous kind of nicety: obliging all children to provide for their father, when fallen into poverty; with an exception to spurious children, to those whose chastity had been prostituted by consent of the father, and to those whom he had not put in any way of gaining a livelyhood. The legislature, says baron Montesquieu, considered, that in the first case the father, being uncertain, had rendered the natural obligation precarious; that, in the second case, he had sullied the life he had given, and done his children the greatest of injuries, in depriving them of their reputation; and that, in the third case, he had rendered their life (so far as in him lay) an insupportable burthen, by furnishing them with no means of subsistence.

O U R laws agree with those of Athens with regard to the first only of these particulars, the case of spurious issue. In the other cases the law does not hold the tie of nature to be dissolved by any misbehaviour of the parent; and therefore a child is equally justifiable in defending the person, or maintaining the cause or suit, of a bad parent, as a good one; and is equally compellable, if of sufficient ability, to maintain and provide for a wicked and unnatural progenitor, as for one who has shewn the greatest tenderness and parental piety.

II. W E are next to consider the case of illegitimate children, or bastards; with regard to whom let us inquire, 1. Who are bastards. 2. The legal duties of the parents towards a bastard child. 3. The rights and incapacities attending such bastard children.

1. W H O are bastards. A bastard, by our English laws, is one that is not only begotten, but born, out of lawful matrimony. The civil and canon laws do not allow a child to remain a bastard, if the parents afterwards intermarry: and herein they differ most materially from our

law; which, though not so strict as to require that the child shall be *begotten*, yet makes it an indispensable condition that it shall be*born*, after lawful wedlock. And the reason of our English law is surely much superior to that of the Roman, if we consider the principal end and design of establishing the contract of marriage, taken in a civil light; abstractedly from any religious view, which has nothing to do with the legitimacy or illegitimacy of the children. The main end and design of marriage therefore being to ascertain and fix upon some certain person, to whom the care, the protection, the maintenance, and the education of the children should belong; this end is undoubtedly better answered by legitimating all issue born after wedlock, than by legitimating all issue of the same parties, even born before wedlock, so as wedlock afterwards ensues: 1. Because of the very great uncertainty there will generally be, in the proof that the issue was really begotten by the same man; whereas, by confining the proof to the birth, and not to the begetting, our law has rendered it perfectly certain, what child is legitimate, and who is to take care of the child. 2. Because by the Roman laws a child may be continued a bastard, or made legitimate, at the option of the father and mother, by a marriage *ex post facto*; thereby opening a door to many frauds and partialities, which by our law are prevented. 3. Because by those laws a man may remain a bastard till forty years of age, and then become legitimate, by the subsequent marriage of his parents; whereby the main end of marriage, the protection of infants, is totally frustrated. 4. Because this rule of the Roman laws admits of no limitations as to the time, or number, of bastards so to be legitimated; but a dozen of them may, twenty years after their birth, by the subsequent marriage of their parents, be admitted to all the privileges of legitimate children. This is plainly a great discouragement to the matrimonial state; to which one main inducement is usually not only the desire of having *children*, but also the desire of procreating lawful *heirs*. Whereas our constitutions guard against this indecency, and at the same time give sufficient allowance to the frailties of human nature. For, if a child be begotten while the parents are single, and they will endeavour to make an early reparation for the offence, by marrying within a few months after, our law is so indulgent as not to bastardize the child, if it be born, though not begotten, in lawful wedlock: for this is an incident that can happen but once; since all future children will be begotten, as well as born, within the rules of honour and civil society. Upon reasons like these we may suppose the peers to have acted at the parliament of Merton, when they refused to enact that children born before marriage should be esteemed legitimate.

F R O M what has been said it appears, that all children born before matrimony are bastards by our law; and so it is of all children born so long after the death of the husband, that, by the usual course of gestation, they could not be begotten by him. But, this being a matter of some uncertainty, the law is not exact as to a few days. And this gives occasion to a proceeding at common law, where a widow is suspected to feign herself with child, in order to produce a supposititious heir to the estate: an attempt which the rigor of the Gothic constitutions esteemed equivalent to the most atrocious theft, and therefore punished with death. In this case with us the heir presumptive may have a writ *de ventre inspiciendo*, to examine whether she be with child, or not; which is entirely conformable to the practice of the civil law: and, if the widow be upon due examination found not pregnant, any issue she may afterwards produce, though within nine months, will be bastard. But if a man dies, and his widow soon after marries again, and a child is born within such a time, as that by the course of nature it might have been the child of either husband; in this case he is said to be more than ordinarily legitimate; for he may, when he arrives to years of discretion, choose which of the fathers he pleases. To prevent this, among other inconveniences, the civil law ordained that no widow should marry *infra annum luctus*; a rule which obtained so early as the reign of Augustus, if not of Romulus: and the same constitution was probably handed down to our early ancestors from the Romans, during their stay in this island; for we find it established under the Saxon and Danish governments.

A S bastards may be born before the coverture, or marriage state, is begun, or after it is determined, so also children born during wedlock may in some circumstances be bastards. As if the husband be out of the kingdom of England (or, as the law somewhat loosely phrases it, *extra quatuor maria*) for above nine months, so that no access to his wife can be presumed, her issue during that period shall be bastard. But, generally, during the coverture access of the husband shall be presumed, unless the contrary can be shewn; which is such a negative as can only be proved by shewing him to be elsewhere: for the general rule is, *praesumitur pro legitimatione*. In a divorce *a mensa et thoro*, if the wife breeds children, they are bastards; for the law will presume the husband and wife conformable to the sentence of separation, unless access be proved: but, in a voluntary separation by agreement, the law will suppose access, unless the negative be shewn. So also if there is an apparent impossibility of procreation on the part of the husband, as if he be only eight years old, or the like, there the issue of the wife shall be bastard. Likewise, in case of divorce in the spiritual court *a vinculo matrimonii*, all the issue born during the coverture are bastards; because such divorce is always upon some cause, that rendered the marriage unlawful and null from the beginning.

2. L E T us next see the duty of parents to their bastard children, by our law; which is principally that of maintenance. For, though bastards are not looked upon as children to any civil purposes, yet the ties of nature, of which maintenance is one, are not so easily dissolved: and they hold indeed as to many other intentions; as, particularly, that a man shall not marry his bastard sister or daughter. The civil law therefore, when it denied maintenance to bastards begotten under certain atrocious circumstances, was neither consonant to nature, nor reason, however profligate and wicked the parents might justly be esteemed.

T H E method in which the English law provides maintenance for them is as follows. When a woman is delivered, or declares herself with child, of a bastard, and will by oath before a justice of peace charge any person having got her with child, the justice shall cause such person to be apprehended, and commit him till he gives security, either to maintain the child, or appear at the next quarter sessions to dispute and try the fact. But if the woman dies, or is married before delivery, or miscarries, or proves not to have been with child, the person shall be discharged: otherwise the sessions, or two justices out of sessions, upon original application to them, may take order for the keeping of the bastard, by charging the mother, or the reputed father with the payment of money or other sustentation for that purpose. And if such putative father, or lewd mother, run away from the parish, the overseers by direction of two justices may seize their rents, goods, and chattels, in order to bring up the said bastard child. Yet such is the humanity of our laws, that no woman can be compulsively questioned concerning the father of her child, till one month after her delivery: which indulgence is however very frequently a hardship upon parishes, by suffering the parents to escape.

3. I PROCEED next to the rights and incapacities which appertain to a bastard. The rights are very few, being only such as he can *acquire*; for he can *inherit* nothing, being looked upon as the son of nobody, and sometimes called *filius nullius*, sometimes *filius populi*. Yet he may gain a sirname by reputation, though he has none by inheritance. All other children have a settlement in their father's parish; but a bastard in the parish where born, for he hath no father. However, in case of fraud, as if a woman be sent either by order of justices, or comes to beg as a vagrant, to a parish which she does not belong to, and drops her bastard there; the bastard shall, in the first case, be settled in the parish from whence she was illegally removed; or, in the latter case, in the mother's own parish, if the mother be apprehended for her vagrancy. The incapacity of a bastard consists principally in this, that he cannot be heir to any one, neither can he have heirs, but of his own body; for, being *nullius filius*, he is therefore of kin to nobody, and has no ancestor from whom any inheritable blood can be derived. A bastard was also, in strictness, incapable of holy orders; and, though that were dispensed with, yet he was utterly disqualified from holding any dignity in the church: but this doctrine seems now obsolete; and in all other respects, there is no distinction between a bastard and another man. And really any other distinction, but that of not inheriting, which civil policy renders necessary, would, with regard to the innocent offspring of his parents' crimes, be odious, unjust, and cruel to the last degree: and yet the civil law, so boasted of for it's equitable decisions, made bastards in some cases incapable even of a gift from their parents. A bastard may, lastly, be made legitimate, and capable of inheriting, by the transcendent power of an act of parliament, and not otherwise: as was done in the case of John of Gant's bastard children, by a statute of Richard the second.

THE only general private relation, now remaining to be discussed, is that of guardian and ward; which bears a very near resemblance to the last, and is plainly derived out of it: the guardian being only a temporary parent; that is, for so long time as the ward is an infant, or under age. In examining this species of relationship, I shall first consider the different kinds of guardians, how they are appointed, and their power and duty: next, the different ages of persons, as defined by the law: and, lastly, the privileges and disabilities of an infant, or one under age and subject to guardianship.

I. THE guardian with us performs the office both of the *tutor* and *curator* of the Roman laws; the former of which had the charge of the maintenance and education of the minor, the latter the care of his fortune; or, according to the language of the court of chancery, the *tutor* was the committee of the person, the *curator* the committee of the estate. But this office was frequently united in the civil law; as it is always in our law with regard to minors, though as to lunatics and idiots it is commonly kept distinct.

Ff. 26. 4. 1.

O F the several species of guardians, the first are guardians *by nature*: viz. the father and (in some cases) the mother of the child. For, if an estate be left to an infant, the father is by common law the guardian, and must account to his child for the profits. And, with regard to daughters, it seems by construction of the statute 4 & 5 Ph. & Mar. c. 8. that the father might by deed or will assign a guardian to any woman-child under the age of sixteen, and if none be so assigned, the mother shall in this case be guardian. There are also guardians *for nurture*, which are, of course, the father or mother, till the infant attains the age of fourteen years: and, in default of father or mother, the ordinary usually assigns some discreet person to take care of the infant's personal estate, and to provide for his maintenance and education. Next are guardians *in socage*, (an appellation which will be fully explained in the second book of these commentaries) who are also called guardians *by the common law*. These take place only when the minor is entitled to some estate in lands, and then by the common law the guardianship devolves upon his next of kin, to whom the inheritance cannot possibly descend; as, where the estate descended from his father, in this case his uncle by the mother's side cannot possibly inherit this estate, and therefore shall be the guardian. For the law judges it improper to trust the person of an infant in his hands, who may by possibility become heir to him; that there may be no temptation, nor even suspicion of temptation, for him to abuse his trust. The Roman laws proceed on a quite contrary principle, committing the care of the minor to him who is the next to succeed to the inheritance, presuming that the next heir would take the best care of an estate, to which he has a prospect of succeeding: and this they boast to be "*summa providentia*." But in the mean time they forget, how much it is the guardian's interest to remove the incumbrance of his pupil's life from that estate, for which he is supposed to have so great a regard. And this affords Fortescue, and sir Edward Coke, an ample opportunity for triumph; they affirming, that to commit the custody of an infant to him that is next in succession, is "*quasi agnum committere lupo, ad devorandum*." These guardians in socage, like those for nurture, continue only till the minor is fourteen years of age; for then, in both cases, he is presumed to have discretion, so far as to choose his own guardian. This he may do, unless one be appointed by father, by virtue of the statute 12 Car. II. c. 24. which, considering the imbecillity of judgment in children of the age of fourteen, and the abolition of guardianship *in chivalry* (which lasted till the age of twenty one, and of which we shall speak hereafter) enacts, that any father, under age or of full age, may by deed or will dispose of the custody of his child, either born or unborn, to any person, except a popish recusant, either in possession or reversion, till such child attains the age of one and twenty years. These are called guardians *by statute*, or *testamentary* guardians. There are also special guardians *by custom* of London, and other places; but they are particular exceptions, and do not fall under the general law.

T H E power and reciprocal duty of a guardian and ward are the same, *pro tempore*, as that of a father and child; and therefore I shall not repeat them: but shall only add, that the guardian, when the ward comes of age, is bound to give him an account of all that he has transacted on his behalf, and must answer for all losses by his wilful default or negligence. In order therefore to prevent disagreeable contests with young gentlemen, it has become a practice for many guardians, of large estates especially, to indemnify themselves by applying to the court of chancery, acting under it's direction, and accounting annually before the officers of that court. For the lord chancellor is, by right derived from the crown, the general and supreme guardian of all infants, as well as idiots and lunatics; that is, of all such persons as have not discretion enough to manage their own concerns. In case therefore any guardian abuses his trust, the court will check and punish him; nay sometimes proceed to the removal of him, and appoint another in his stead.

2. L E T us next consider the ward, or person within age, for whose assistance and support these guardians are constituted by law; or who it is, that is said to be within age. The ages of male and female are different for different purposes. A male at *twelve* years old may take the oath of allegiance; at *fourteen* is at years of discretion, and therefore may consent or disagree to marriage, may choose his guardian, and, if his discretion be actually proved, may make his testament of his personal estate; at *seventeen* may be an executor; and at *twenty one* is at his own disposal, and may aliene his lands, goods, and chattels. A female also at *seven* years of age may be betrothed or given in marriage; at *nine* is entitled to dower; at *twelve* is at years of maturity, and therefore may consent or disagree to marriage, and, if proved to have sufficient discretion, may bequeath her personal estate; at *fourteen* is at years of legal discretion, and may choose a guardian; at *seventeen* may be executrix; and at *twenty one* may dispose of herself and her lands. So that full age in male or female, is twenty one years, which age is completed on the day preceding the anniversary of a person's birth; who till that time is an infant, and so stiled in law. Among the antient Greeks and Romans *women* were never of age, but subject to perpetual guardianship, unless when married, "*nisi convenissent in manum viri.*" and, when that perpetual tutelage wore away in process of time, we find that, in females as well as males, full age was not till twenty five years. Thus, by the constitutions of different kingdoms, this period, which is merely arbitrary, and *juris positivi*, is fixed at different times. Scotland agrees with England in this point; (both probably copying from the old Saxon constitutions on the continent, which extended the age of minority "*ad annum vigesimum primum, et eo usque juvenes sub tutelam reponunt*") but in Naples they are of full age at *eighteen*; in France, with regard to marriage, not till *thirty*; and in Holland at *twenty five*.

3. I N F A N T S have various privileges, and various disabilities: but their very disabilities are privileges; in order to secure them from hurting themselves by their own improvident acts. An infant cannot be sued but under the protection, and joining the name, of his guardian; for he is to defend him against all attacks as well by law as otherwise: but he may sue either by his guardian, or *prochein amy*, his next friend who is not his guardian. This *prochein amy* may be any person who will undertake the infant's cause; and it frequently happens, that an infant, by

his *prochein amy*, institutes a suit in equity against a fraudulent guardian. In criminal cases, an infant of the age of *fourteen* years may be capitally punished for any capital offence: but under the age of *seven* he cannot. The period between *seven* and *fourteen* is subject to much incertainty: for the infant shall, generally speaking, be judged *prima facie* innocent; yet if he was *doli capax*, and could discern between good and evil at the time of the offence committed, he may be convicted and undergo judgment and execution of death, though he hath not attained to years of puberty or discretion. And sir Matthew Hale gives us two instances, one of a girl of thirteen, who was burned for killing her mistress; another of a boy still younger, that had killed his companion, and hid himself, who was hanged; for it appeared by his hiding that he knew he had done wrong, and could discern between good and evil; and in such cases the maxim of law is, that *malitia supplet aetatem*.

W I T H regard to estates and civil property, an infant hath many privileges, which will be better understood when we come to treat more particularly of those matters: but this may be said in general, that an infant shall lose nothing by non-claim, or neglect of demanding his right; nor shall any other *laches* or negligence be imputed to an infant, except in some very particular cases.

I T is generally true, that an infant can neither aliene his lands, nor do any legal act, nor make a deed, nor indeed any manner of contract, that will bind him. But still to all these rules there are some exceptions; part of which were just now mentioned in reckoning up the different capacities which they assume at different ages: and there are others, a few of which it may not be improper to recite, as a general specimen of the whole. And, first, it is true, that infants cannot aliene their estates: but infant trustees, or mortgagees, are enabled to convey, under the direction of the court of chancery or exchequer, the estates they hold in trust or mortgage, to such person as the court shall appoint. Also it is generally true, that an infant can do no legal act: yet an infant who has an advowson, may present to the benefice when it becomes void. For the law in this case dispenses with one rule, in order to maintain others of far greater consequence: it permits an infant to present a clerk (who, if unfit, may be rejected by the bishop) rather than either suffer the church to be unserved till he comes of age, or permit the infant to be debarred of his right by lapse to the bishop. An infant may also purchase lands, but his purchase is incomplete: for, when he comes to age, he may either agree or disagree to it, as he thinks prudent or proper, without alleging any reason; and so may his heirs after him, if he dies without having completed his agreement. It is, farther, generally true, that an infant, under twenty one, can make no deed that is of any force or effect: yet he may bind himself apprentice by deed indented, or indentures, for seven years; and he may by deed or will appoint a guardian to his children, if he has any. Lastly, it is generally true, that an infant can make no other contract that will bind him: yet he may bind himself to pay for his necessary meat, drink, apparel, physic, and such other necessaries; and likewise for his good teaching and instruction, whereby he may profit himself afterwards. And thus much, at present, for the privileges and disabilities of infants.

Chapter the eighteenth.

Of CORPORATIONS.

WE have hitherto considered persons in their natural capacities, and have treated of their rights and duties. But, as all personal rights die with the person; and, as the necessary forms of investing a series of individuals, one after another, with the same identical rights, would be very inconvenient, if not impracticable; it has been found necessary, when it is for the advantage of the public to have any particular rights kept on foot and continued, to constitute artificial persons, who may maintain a perpetual succession, and enjoy a kind of legal immortality.

THESE artificial persons are called bodies politic, bodies corporate, (*corpora corporata*) or corporations: of which there is a great variety subsisting, for the advancement of religion, of learning, and of commerce; in order to preserve entire and for ever those rights and immunities, which, if they were granted only to those individuals of which the body corporate is composed, would upon their death be utterly lost and extinct. To shew the advantages of these incorporations, let us consider the case of a college in either of our universities, founded *ad studendum et orandum*, for the encouragement and support of religion and learning. If this was a mere voluntary assembly, the individuals which compose it might indeed read, pray, study, and perform scholastic exercises together, so long as they could agree to do so: but they could neither frame, nor receive, any laws or rules of their conduct; none at least, which would have any binding force, for want of a coercive power to create a sufficient obligation. Neither could they be capable of retaining any privileges or immunities: for, if such privileges be attacked, which of all this unconnected assembly has the right, or ability, to defend them? And, when they are dispersed by death or otherwise, how shall they transfer these advantages to another set of students, equally unconnected as themselves? So also, with regard to holding estates or other property, if land be granted for the purposes of religion or learning to twenty individuals not incorporated, there is no legal way of continuing the property to any other persons for the same purposes, but by endless conveyances from one to the other, as often as the hands are changed. But, when they are consolidated and united into a corporation, they and their successors are then considered as one person in law: as one person, they have one will, which is collected from the sense of the majority of the individuals: this one will may establish rules and orders for the regulation of the whole, which are a sort of municipal laws of this little republic; or rules and statutes may be prescribed to it at it's creation, which are then in the place of natural laws: the privileges and immunities, the estates and possessions, of the corporation, when once vested in them, will be for ever vested, without any new conveyance to new successions; for all the individual members that have existed from the foundation to the present time, or that shall ever hereafter exist, are but one person in law, a person that never dies: in like manner as the river Thames is still the same river, though the parts which compose it are changing every instant.

T H E honour of originally inventing these political constitutions entirely belongs to the Romans. They were introduced, as Plutarch says, by Numa; who finding, upon his accession, the city torn to pieces by the two rival factions of Sabines, and Romans, thought it a prudent and politic measure, to subdivide these two into many smaller ones, by instituting separate societies of every manual trade and profession. They were afterwards much considered by the civil law, in which they were called *universitates*, as forming one whole out of many individuals; or *collegia*, from being gathered together: they were adopted also by the canon law, for the maintenance of ecclesiastical discipline; and from them our spiritual corporations are derived. But our laws have considerably refined and improved upon the invention, according to the usual genius of the English nation: particularly with regard to sole corporations, consisting of one person only, of which the Roman lawyers had no notion; their maxim being that "*tres faciunt collegium.*" Though they held, that if a corporation, originally consisting of three persons, be reduced to one, "*si universitas ad unum redit,*" it may still subsist as a corporation, "*et stet nomen universitatis.*"

B E F O R E we proceed to treat of the several incidents of corporations, as regarded by the laws of England, let us first take a view of the several sorts of them; and then we shall be better enabled to apprehend their respective qualities.

T H E first division of corporations is into *aggregate* and *sole*. Corporations aggregate consist of many persons united together into one society, and are kept up by a perpetual succession of members, so as to continue for ever: of which kind are the mayor and commonalty of a city, the head and fellows of a college, the dean and chapter of a cathedral church. Corporations sole consist of one person only and his successors, in some particular station, who are incorporated by law, in order to give them some legal capacities and advantages, particularly that of perpetuity, which in their natural persons they could not have had. In this sense the king is a sole corporation: so is a bishop: so are some deans, and prebendaries, distinct from their several chapters: and so is every parson and vicar. And the necessity, or at least use, of this institution will be very apparent, if we consider the case of a parson of a church. At the original endowment of parish churches, the freehold of the church, the church-yard, the parsonage house, the glebe, and the tithes of the parish, were vested in the then parson by the bounty of the donor, as a temporal recompence to him for his spiritual care of the inhabitants, and with intent that the same emoluments should ever afterwards continue as a recompense for the same care. But how was this to be effected? The freehold was vested in the parson; and, if we suppose it vested in his natural capacity, on his death it might descend to his heir, and would be liable to his debts and incumbrances: or, at best, the heir might be compellable, at some trouble and expense, to convey these rights to the succeeding incumbent. The law therefore has wisely ordained, that the parson, *quatenus* parson, shall never die, any more than the king; by making him and his successors a corporation. By which means all the original rights of the parsonage are preserved entire to the successor: for the present incumbent, and his predecessor who lived seven centuries ago, are in law one and the same person; and what was given to the one was given to the other also.

ANOTHER division of corporations, either sole or aggregate, is into *ecclesiastical* and *lay*. Ecclesiastical corporations are where the members that compose it are entirely spiritual persons; such as bishops; certain deans, and prebendaries; all archdeacons, parsons, and vicars; which are sole corporations: deans and chapters at present, and formerly prior and convent, abbot and monks, and the like, bodies aggregate. These are erected for the furtherance of religion, and the perpetuating the rights of the church. Lay corporations are of two sorts, *civil* and *eleemosynary*. The civil are such as are erected for a variety of temporal purposes. The king, for instance, is made a corporation to prevent in general the possibility of an *interregnum* or vacancy of the throne, and to preserve the possessions of the crown entire; for, immediately upon the demise of one king, his successor is, as we have formerly seen, in full possession of the regal rights and dignity. Other lay corporations are erected for the good government of a town or particular district, as a mayor and commonalty, bailiff and burgesses, or the like: some for the advancement and regulation of manufactures and commerce; as the trading companies of London, and other towns: and some for the better carrying on of divers special purposes; as churchwardens, for conservation of the goods of the parish; the college of physicians and company of surgeons in London, for the improvement of the medical science; the royal society, for the advancement of natural knowlege; and the society of antiquarians, for promoting the study of antiquities. And among these I am inclined to think the general corporate bodies of the universities of Oxford and Cambridge must be ranked: for it is clear they are not spiritual or ecclesiastical corporations, being composed of more laymen than clergy: neither are they eleemosynary foundations, though stipends are annexed to particular magistrates and professors, any more than other corporations where the acting officers have standing salaries; for these are rewards *pro opera et labore*, not charitable donations only, since every stipend is preceded by service and duty: they seem therefore to be merely civil corporations. The eleemosynary sort are such as are constituted for the perpetual distribution of the free alms, or bounty, of the founder of them to such persons as he has directed. Of this kind are all hospitals for the maintenance of the poor, sick, and impotent; and all colleges, both *in* our universities and *out* of them: which colleges are founded for two purposes; 1. For the promotion of piety and learning by proper regulations and ordinances. 2. For imparting assistance to the members of those bodies, in order to enable them to prosecute their devotion and studies with greater ease and assiduity. And all these eleemosynary corporations are, strictly speaking, lay and not ecclesiastical, even though composed of ecclesiastical persons, and although they in some things partake of the nature, privileges, and restrictions of ecclesiastical bodies.

HAVING thus marshalled the several species of corporations, let us next proceed to consider, 1. How corporations, in general, may be created. 2. What are their powers, capacities, and incapacities. 3. How corporations are visited. And 4. How they may be dissolved.

I. CORPORATIONS, by the civil law, seem to have been created by the mere act, and voluntary association of their members; provided such convention was not contrary to law, for then it was *illicitum collegium*. It does not appear that the prince's consent was necessary to be actually given to the foundation of them; but merely that the original founders of these voluntary and friendly societies (for they were little more than such) should not establish any meetings in opposition to the laws of the state.

B U T, with us in England, the king's consent is absolutely necessary to the erection of any corporation, either impliedly or expressly given. The king's implied consent is to be found in corporations which exist by force of the *common law*, to which our former kings are supposed to have given their concurrence; common law being nothing else but custom, arising from the universal agreement of the whole community. Of this sort are the king himself, all bishops, parsons, vicars, churchwardens, and some others; who by common law have ever been held (as far as our books can shew us) to have been corporations, *virtute officii*: and this incorporation is so inseparably annexed to their offices, that we cannot frame a complete legal idea of any of these persons, but we must also have an idea of a corporation, capable to transmit his rights to his successors, at the same time. Another method of implication, whereby the king's consent is presumed, is as to all corporations by *prescription*, such as the city of London, and many others, which have existed as corporations, time whereof the memory of man runneth not to the contrary; and therefore are looked upon in law to be well created. For though the members thereof can shew no legal charter of incorporation, yet in cases of such high antiquity the law presumes there once was one; and that by the variety of accidents, which a length of time may produce, the charter is lost or destroyed. The methods, by which the king's consent is expressly given, are either by act of parliament or charter. By act of parliament, of which the royal assent is a necessary ingredient, corporations may undoubtedly be created: but it is observable, that most of those statutes, which are usually cited as having created corporations, do either confirm such as have been before created by the king; as in the case of the college of physicians, erected by charter 10 Hen. VIII, which charter was afterwards confirmed in parliament; or, they permit the king to erect a corporation *in futuro* with such and such powers; as is the case of the bank of England, and the society of the British fishery. So that the immediate creative act is usually performed by the king alone, in virtue of his royal prerogative.

A L L the other methods therefore whereby corporations exist, by common law, by prescription, and by act of parliament, are for the most part reducible to this of the king's letters patent, or charter of incorporation. The king's creation may be performed by the words "*creamus, erigimus, fundamus, incorporamus*," or the like. Nay it is held, that if the king grants to a set of men to have *gildam mercatoriam*, a mercantile meeting or assembly, this is alone sufficient to incorporate and establish them for ever.

T H E parliament, we observed, by it's absolute and transcendent authority, may perform this, or any other act whatsoever: and actually did perform it to a great extent, by statute 39 Eliz. c. 5. which incorporated all hospitals and houses of correction founded by charitable persons, without farther trouble: and the same has been done in other cases of charitable foundations. But otherwise it is not usual thus to intrench upon the prerogative of the crown, and the king may prevent it when he pleases. And, in the particular instance before-mentioned, it was done, as sir Edward Coke observes, to avoid the charges of incorporation and licences of mortmain in small benefactions; which in his days were grown so great, that it discouraged many men to undertake these pious and charitable works.

T H E king may grant to a subject the power of erecting corporations, though the contrary was formerly held: that is, he may permit the subject to name the persons and powers of the corporation at his pleasure; but it is really the king that erects, and the subject is but the instrument: for though none but the king can make a corporation, yet *qui facit per alium, facit per se*. In this manner the chancellor of the university of Oxford has power by charter to erect corporations; and has actually often exerted it, in the erection of several matriculated companies, now subsisting, of tradesmen subservient to the students.

W H E N a corporation is erected, a name must be given it; and by that name alone it must sue, and be sued, and do all legal acts; though a very minute variation therein is not material. Such name is the very being of it's constitution; and, though it is the will of the king that erects the corporation, yet the name is the knot of it's combination, without which it could not perform it's corporate functions. The name of incorporation, says sir Edward Coke, is as a proper name, or name of baptism; and therefore when a private founder gives his college or hospital a name, he does it only as godfather; and by that same name the king baptizes the incorporation.

II. A F T E R a corporation is so formed and named, it acquires many powers, rights, capacities, and incapacities, which we are next to consider. Some of these are necessarily and inseparably incident to every corporation; which incidents, as soon as a corporation is duly erected, are tacitly annexed of course. As, 1. To have perpetual succession. This is the very end of it's incorporation: for there cannot be a succession for ever without an incorporation; and therefore all aggregate corporations have a power necessarily implied of electing members in the room of such as go off. 2. To sue or be sued, implead or be impleaded, grant or receive, by it's corporate name, and do all other acts as natural persons may. 3. To purchase lands, and hold them, for the benefit of themselves and their successors: which two are consequential to the former. 4. To have a common seal. For a corporation, being an invisible body, cannot manifest it's intentions by any personal act or oral discourse: it therefore acts and speaks only by it's common seal. For, though the particular members may express their private consents to any act, by words, or signing their names, yet this does not bind the corporation: it is the fixing of the seal, and that only, which unites the several assents of the individuals, who compose the community, and makes one joint assent of the whole. 5. To make by-laws or private statutes for the better government of the corporation; which are binding upon themselves, unless contrary to the laws of the land, and then they are void. This is also included by law in the very act of incorporation: for, as natural reason is given to the natural body for the governing it, so by-laws or statutes are a sort of political reason to govern the body politic. And this right of making by-laws for their own government, not contrary to the law of the land, was allowed by the law of the twelve tables at Rome. But no trading company is, with us, allowed to make by-laws, which may affect the king's prerogative, or the common profit of the people, unless they be approved by the chancellor, treasurer, and chief justices, or the judges of assise in their circuits. These five powers are inseparably incident to every corporation, at least to every corporation *aggregate*: for two of them, though they may be practised, yet are very unnecessary to a corporation *sole*; viz. to have a corporate seal to testify his sole assent, and to make statutes for the regulation of his own conduct.

T H E R E are also certain privileges and disabilities that attend an aggregate corporation, and are not applicable to such as are sole; the reason of them ceasing, and of course the law. It must always appear by attorney; for it cannot appear in person, being, as sir Edward Coke says, invisible, and existing only in intendment and consideration of law. It can neither maintain, or be made defendant to, an action of battery or such like personal injuries; for a corporation can neither beat, nor be beaten, in it's body politic. A corporation cannot commit treason, or felony, or other crime, in it's corporate capacity: though it's members may, in their distinct individual capacities. Neither is it capable of suffering a traitor's, or felon's punishment, for it is not liable to corporal penalties, nor to attainder, forfeiture, or corruption of blood. It cannot be executor or administrator, or perform any personal duties; for it cannot take an oath for the due execution of the office. It cannot be a trustee; for such kind of confidence is foreign to the ends of it's institution: neither can it be compelled to perform such trust, because it cannot be committed to prison; for it's existence being ideal, no man can apprehend or arrest it. And therefore also it cannot be outlawed; for outlawry always supposes a precedent right of arresting, which has been defeated by the parties absconding, and that also a corporation cannot do: for which reasons the proceedings to compel a corporation to appear to any suit by attorney are always by distress on their lands and goods. Neither can a corporation be excommunicated; for it has no soul, as is gravely observed by sir Edward Coke: and therefore also it is not liable to be summoned into the ecclesiastical courts upon any account; for those courts act only *pro salute animae*, and their sentences can only be inforced by spiritual censures: a consideration, which, carried to it's full extent, would alone demonstrate the impropriety of these courts interfering in any temporal rights whatsoever.

T H E R E are also other incidents and powers, which belong to some sort of corporations, and not to others. An aggregate corporation may take goods and chattels for the benefit of themselves and their successors, but a sole corporation cannot: for such moveable property is liable to be lost or imbezzled, and would raise a multitude of disputes between the successor and executor; which the law is careful to avoid. In ecclesiastical and eleemosynary foundations, the king or the founder may give them rules, laws, statutes, and ordinances, which they are bound to observe: but corporations merely lay, constituted for civil purposes, are subject to no particular statutes; but to the common law, and to their own by-laws, not contrary to the laws of the realm. Aggregate corporations also, that have by their constitution a head, as a dean, warden, master, or the like, cannot do any acts during the vacancy of the headship, except only appointing another: neither are they then capable of receiving a grant; for such corporation is incomplete without a head. But there may be a corporation aggregate constituted without a head: as the collegiate church of Southwell in Nottinghamshire, which consists only of prebendaries; and the governors of the Charter-house, London, who have no president or superior, but are all of equal authority. In aggregate corporations also, the act of the major part is esteemed the act of the whole. By the civil law this major part must have consisted of two thirds of the whole; else no act could be performed: which perhaps may be one reason why they required three at least to make a corporation. But, with us, *any* majority is sufficient to determine the act of the whole body. And whereas, notwithstanding the law stood thus, some founders of corporations had made statutes in derogation of the common law, making very frequently the unanimous assent of the society to be necessary to any corporate act; (which king Henry VIII found to be a great obstruction to his projected scheme of obtaining a surrender of the lands of ecclesiastical corporations) it was therefore enacted by statute 33 Hen. VIII. c. 27. that all private statutes shall be utterly void, whereby any grant or election, made by the head, with the concurrence of the major part of the body, is liable to be obstructed by any one or more, being the minority: but this statute extends not to any negative or necessary voice, given by the founder to the head of any such society.

W E before observed that it was incident to every corporation, to have a capacity to purchase lands for themselves and successors: and this is regularly true at the common law. But they are excepted out of the statute of wills; so that no devise of lands to a corporation by will is good: except for charitable uses, by statute 43 Eliz. c. 4. And also, by a great variety of statutes, their privilege even of purchasing from any living grantor is greatly abridged; so that now a corporation, either ecclesiastical or lay, must have a licence from the king to purchase, before they can exert that capacity which is vested in them by the common law: nor is even this in all cases sufficient. These statutes are generally called the statutes of *mortmain*; all purchases made by corporate bodies being said to be purchases in mortmain, *in mortua manu*: for the reason of which appellation sir Edward Coke offers many conjectures; but there is one which seems more probable than any that he has given us: viz. that these purchases being usually made by ecclesiastical bodies, the members of which (being professed) were reckoned dead persons in law, land therefore, holden by them, might with great propriety be said to be held *in mortua manu*.

I SHALL defer the more particular exposition of these statutes of mortmain, till the next book of these commentaries, when we shall consider the nature and tenures of estates; and also the exposition of those disabling statutes of queen Elizabeth, which restrain spiritual and eleemosynary corporations from aliening such lands as they are present in legal possession of: only mentioning them in this place, for the sake of regularity, as statutable incapacities incident and relative to corporations.

T H E general *duties* of all bodies politic, considered in their corporate capacity, may, like those of natural persons, be reduced to this single one; that of acting up to the end or design, whatever it be, for which they were created by their founder.

III. I P R O C E E D therefore next to enquire, how these corporations may be *visited.* For corporations being composed of individuals, subject to human frailties, are liable, as well as private persons, to deviate from the end of their institution. And for that reason the law has provided proper persons to visit, enquire into, and correct all irregularities that arise in such corporations, either sole or aggregate, and whether ecclesiastical, civil, or eleemosynary. With regard to all ecclesiastical corporations, the ordinary is their visitor, so constituted by the canon law, and from thence derived to us. The pope formerly, and now the king, as supreme ordinary, is the visitor of the arch-bishop or metropolitan; the metropolitan has the charge and coercion of all his suffragan bishops; and the bishops in their several dioceses are the visitors of all deans and chapters, of all parsons and vicars, and of all other spiritual corporations. With respect to all lay corporations, the founder, his heirs, or assigns, are the visitors, whether the foundation be civil or eleemosynary; for in a lay incorporation the ordinary neither can nor ought to visit.

I K N O W it is generally said, that civil corporations are subject to no visitation, but merely to the common law of the land; and this shall be presently explained. But first, as I have laid it down as a rule that the founder, his heirs, or assigns, are the visitors of all lay-corporations, let us enquire what is meant by the *founder*. The founder of all corporations in the strictest and original sense is the king alone, for he only can incorporate a society: and in civil incorporations, such as mayor and commonalty, &c., where there are no possessions or endowments given to the body, there is no other founder but the king: but in eleemosynary foundations, such as colleges and hospitals, where there is an endowment of lands, the law distinguishes, and makes two species of foundation; the one *fundatio incipiens*, or the incorporation, in which sense the king is the general founder of all colleges and hospitals; the other *fundatio perficiens*, or the dotation of it, in which sense the first gift of the revenues is the foundation, and he who gives them is in law the founder: and it is in this last sense that we generally call a man the founder of a college or hospital. But here the king has his prerogative: for, if the king and a private man join in endowing an eleemosynary foundation, the king alone shall be the founder of it. And, in general, the king being the sole founder of all civil corporations, and the endower the perficient founder of all eleemosynary ones, the right of visitation of the former results, according to the rule laid down, to the king; and of the latter, to the patron or endower.

T H E king being thus constituted by law the visitor of all civil corporations, the law has also appointed the place, wherein he shall exercise this jurisdiction: which is the court of king's bench; where, and where only, all misbehaviours of this kind of corporations are enquired into and redressed, and all their controversies decided. And this is what I understand to be the meaning of our lawyers, when they say that these civil corporations are liable to no visitation;

that is, that the law having by immemorial usage appointed them to be visited and inspected by the king their founder, in his majesty's court of king's bench, according to the rules of the common law, they ought not to be visited elsewhere, or by any other authority. And this is so strictly true, that though the king by his letters patent had subjected the college of physicians to the visitation of four very respectable persons, the lord chancellor, the two chief justices, and the chief baron; though the college had accepted this charter with all possible marks of acquiescence, and had acted under it for near a century; yet, in 1753, the authority of this provision coming in dispute, on an appeal preferred to these supposed visitors, they directed the legality of their own appointment to be argued: and, as this college was a mere civil, and not an eleemosynary foundation, they at length determined, upon several days solemn debate, that they had no jurisdiction as visitors; and remitted the appellant (if aggrieved) to his regular remedy in his majesty's court of king's bench.

AS to eleemosynary corporations, by the dotation the founder and his heirs are of common right the legal visitors, to see that that property is rightly employed, which would otherwise have descended to the visitor himself: but, if the founder has appointed and assigned any other person to be visitor, then his assignee so appointed is invested with all the founder's power, in exclusion of his heir. Eleemosynary corporations are chiefly hospitals, or colleges in the university. These were all of them considered by the popish clergy, as of mere ecclesiastical jurisdiction: however, the law of the land judged otherwise; and, with regard to hospitals, it has long been held, that if the hospital be spiritual, the bishop shall visit; but if lay, the patron. This right of lay patrons was indeed abridged by statute 2 Hen. V. c. 1. which ordained, that the ordinary should visit *all* hospitals founded by subjects; though the king's right was reserved, to visit by his commissioners such as were of royal foundation. But the subject's right was in part restored by statute 14 Eliz. c. 5. which directs the bishop to visit such hospitals only, where no visitor is appointed by the founders thereof: and all the hospitals founded by virtue of the statute 39 Eliz. c. 5. are to be visited by such persons as shall be nominated by the respective founders. But still, if the founder appoints nobody, the bishop of the diocese must visit.

COLLEGES in the universities (whatever the common law may now, or might formerly, judge) were certainly considered by the popish clergy, under whose direction they were, as *ecclesiastical*, or at least as *clerical*, corporations; and therefore the right of visitation was claimed by the ordinary of the diocese. This is evident, because in many of our most ancient colleges, where the founder had a mind to subject them to a visitor of his own nomination, he obtained for that purpose a papal bulle to exempt them from the jurisdiction of the ordinary; several of which are still preserved in the archives of the respective societies. And I have reason to believe, that in one of our colleges, (wherein the bishop of that diocese, in which Oxford was formerly comprized, has immemorially exercised visitatorial authority) there is no special visitor appointed by the college statutes: so that the bishop's interposition can be ascribed to nothing else, but his supposed title as ordinary to visit this, among other ecclesiastical foundations. And it is not impossible, that the number of colleges in Cambridge, which are visited by the bishop of Ely, may in part be derived from the same original.

B U T, whatever might be formerly the opinion of the clergy, it is now held as established common law, that colleges are lay-corporations, though sometimes totally composed of ecclesiastical persons; and that the right of visitation does not arise from any principles of the canon law, but of necessity was created by the common law. And yet the power and jurisdiction of visitors in colleges was left so much in the dark at common law, that the whole doctrine was very unsettled till king William's time; in the sixth year of whose reign, the famous case of *Philips and Bury* happened. In this the main question was, whether the sentence of the bishop of Exeter, who (as visitor) had deprived doctor Bury the rector of Exeter college, could be examined and redressed by the court of king's bench. And the three puisne judges were of opinion, that it might be reviewed, for that the visitor's jurisdiction could not exclude the common law; and accordingly judgment was given in that court. But the lord chief justice, Holt, was of a contrary opinion; and held, that by the common law the office of visitor is to judge according to the statutes of the college, and to expel and deprive upon just occasions, and to hear all appeals of course; and that from him, and him only, the party grieved ought to have redress; the founder having reposed in him so entire a confidence, that he will administer justice impartially, that his determinations are final, and examinable in no other court whatsoever. And, upon this, a writ of error being brought in the house of lords, they reversed the judgment of the court of king's bench, and concurred in sir John Holt's opinion. And to this leading case all subsequent determinations have been conformable. But, where the visitor is under a temporary disability, there the court of king's bench will interpose, to prevent a defect of justice. Thus the bishop of Chester is visitor of Manchester college: but, happening also to be warden, the court held that his power was suspended during the union of those offices; and therefore issued a peremptory *mandamus* to him, as warden, to admit a person intitled to a chaplainship. Also it is said, that if a founder of an eleemosynary foundation appoints a visitor, and limits his jurisdiction by rules and statutes, if the visitor in his sentence exceeds those rules, an action lies against him; but it is otherwise, where he mistakes in a thing within his power.

IV. W E come now, in the last place, to consider how corporations may be dissolved. Any particular member may be disfranchised, or lose his place in the corporation, by acting contrary to the laws of the society, or the laws of the land; or he may resign it by his own voluntary act. But the body politic may also itself be dissolved in several ways; which dissolution is the civil death of the corporation: and in this case their lands and tenements shall revert to the person, or his heirs, who granted them to the corporation; for the law doth annex a condition to every such grant, that if the corporation be dissolved, the grantor shall have the lands again, because the cause of the grant faileth. The grant is indeed only during the life of the corporation; which *may* endure for ever: but, when that life is determined by the dissolution of the body politic, the grantor takes it back by reversion, as in the case of every other grant for life. And hence it appears how injurious, as well to private as public rights, those statutes were, which vested in king Henry VIII, instead of the heirs of the founder, the lands of the dissolved monasteries. The debts of a corporation, either to or from it, are totally extinguished by it's dissolution; so that the members thereof cannot recover, or be charged with them, in their natural capacities: agreeable to that maxim of the civil law, "*si quid universitati debetur, singulis non debetur; nec, quod debet universitas, singuli debent.*"

A CORPORATION may be dissolved, 1. By act of parliament, which is boundless in it's operations; 2. By the natural death of all it's members, in case of an aggregate corporation; 3. By surrender of it's franchises into the hands of the king, which is a kind of suicide; 4. By forfeiture of it's charter, through negligence or abuse of it's franchises; in which case the law judges that the body politic has broken the condition upon which it was incorporated, and thereupon the incorporation is void. And the regular course is to bring a writ of *quo warranto*, to enquire by what warrant the members now exercise their corporate power, having forfeited it by such and such proceedings. The exertion of this act of law, for the purposes of the state, in the reigns of king Charles and king James the second, particularly by seising the charter of the city of London, gave great and just offence; though perhaps, in strictness of law, the proceedings were sufficiently regular: but now it is enacted, that the charter of the city of London shall never more be forfeited for any cause whatsoever. And, because by the common law corporations were dissolved, in case the mayor or head officer was not duly elected on the day appointed in the charter or established by prescription, it is now provided, that for the future no corporation shall be dissolved upon that account; and ample directions are given for appointing a new officer, in case there be no election, or a void one, made upon the charter or prescriptive day.

Made in the USA
Lexington, KY
27 September 2014